The Sand Bar

Titles by Owen Keehnen

The Sand Bar
Jim Flint: The Boy From Peoria (with Tracy Baim)
We're Here, We're Queer: The Gay 90s and Beyond
Leatherman: The Legend of Chuck Renslow (with Tracy Baim)
Doorway Unto Darkness
I May Not Be Much But I'm All I Think About
Nothing Personal: Chronicles of Chicago's LGBTQ Community 1977-1997—
    The Writings of Jon-Henri Damski. co-editor (with John Vore and
    Albert Williams).
Rising Starz
Ultimate Starz
More Starz
Starz

The Sand Bar

Owen Keehnen

Lethe Press, Maple Shade, New Jersey

The Sand Bar

Published in 2012 by Lethe Press, Inc.
118 Heritage Avenue • Maple Shade, NJ 08052-3018
www.lethepressbooks.com • lethepress@aol.com
ISBN: 1-59021-018-2
ISBN-13: 978-159021-018-5

This book is a work of fiction. Names, characters, places, and incidents are products of the author's imagination or are used fictitiously.

Set in Hoefler Text, Destroy, and FFF Tusj.
Interior design: Alex Jeffers.
Cover design: Niki Smith.

LIBRARY OF CONGRESS CATALOGING-IN-PUBLICATION DATA

Keehnen, Owen.
  The sand bar / Owen Keehnen.
    p. cm.
  ISBN 978-1-59021-018-5 (pbk. : alk. paper) -- ISBN 1-59021-018-2 (print)
  1. Bars (Drinking establishments)--Fiction. 2. Gay men--Fiction. 3. Southern States--Fiction. I. Title.
  PS3611.E334S26 2012
  813'.6--dc23
                                        2012008642

To Carl,
Without Home There is Nothing.

To my parents
For their support,
their love,
and for everything I never said.

Acknowledgements:

Thanks to Steve and Craig
and Lethe Press for their ongoing
encouragement and support.

The Sand Bar

The Frear was a flat red mix of clay and current when Leo Dunsten rambled into Bayetteville behind the wheel of his rusted Ford. Crossing the bordering marshland he was relieved the trip was finally coming to an end.

He came to town for his uncle's funeral. As the sole living relative he felt an obligation, especially after learning he was a beneficiary. Leo had hinted and fished and eventually asked straight out about the sum, but the lawyer wasn't willing to go into particulars over the phone.

Turn out for the funeral was sparse, very sparse. The white spring sunlight seemed to mock the solemn nature of the occasion. Birds and squirrels chirped and chattered non-stop in the cemetery, forcing Father Owen to shout portions of the chosen Bible passage. As the casket was lowered he spoke of Uncle Hector in such a general way that Leo figured the priest was either reciting a formula eulogy or he didn't know Hector too well—probably both. Leo reckoned Hector got religion when nothing else would have him.

When the priest finished speaking Leo tossed a shovel of dirt onto the domed lid and everyone awkwardly shook hands. The entire burial was a no nonsense affair and quick as a breakfast special. Father Owen had back-to-back weddings afterwards so he didn't have time for any leisurely launch into the afterlife.

Leo accompanied the attorney and an old gent with hanging jowls and a nose like a turnip back to the law office. Fifteen minutes later Leo was stunned to hear he'd inherited just under twenty-five thousand dollars. His impulse was to leap from his seat, but he managed to limit his excitement to a tight grin and some restless leg jiggling. Over the years he could only recall seeing his uncle twice, and both times Hector had been crotchety. Leo recalled his purse strings scowl and bleached walnut face. Who'd have guessed that wet hen would lay a golden egg? The old man with the turnip nose was the other beneficiary. He was a war buddy of Uncle Hector's by the name of Marvin. He got the house.

Since he wasn't due back at work until the following Monday, Leo decided to stay on at the Friendship Inn another night. Now he was worth too much to drive home without a decent night's sleep. He looked to the sky and pinched himself again—twenty-five grand. Those three little words meant a whole new start. He needed to give some serious thought as to what he was going to do with the money. This sort of chance wasn't likely to come again. As worries go it was a welcome quandary. Leo could hardly believe it was his life.

The money couldn't have come at a better time. His mill job in the Quad Cities was a nightmare he'd awakened to five days a week for five long years. It paid a decent wage, but other than payday the sole thrill of being there was hearing the shift siren scream at the end of the day. The rest of his time Leo spent trying to obliterate the fact that he had to return there in the morning. Living to escape was no way to live.

After an hour in his motel room Leo got bored with the TV selection and irritated by the reception. He punched a spot in the pillow and dozed. Muffled shouts from the next room roused him. The exact words couldn't be heard, but Leo figured it was about sex. Arguments in motel rooms always seemed to concern someone getting it or not getting it or getting it where they shouldn't be getting it. He'd been in his share of those disagreements half the time in places just like the Friendship Inn. The shouting persisted upwards of an hour. He lay listening with his head hung over the foot of the bed. He stared into the carpet and thought about upgrading his room, but rightfully assumed the Friendship Inn wasn't likely to have a luxury suite. Swinging his feet off the mattress he wandered into the yellow tinged bathroom. Flipping the light he spied a couple of roaches scurry beneath a rolling rift in the linoleum. This was no place to be. He brushed his teeth, washed his face, and slipped a clean t-shirt over his head before wandering down to the corner bar.

The Angler Tap was a dark wood and lone drinkers sort of establishment. He took a stool, ordered a boilermaker, and toasted his departed uncle; "Here's to new beginnings...for both of us, gracias Uncle Hector." Leo decided to tie one on in homage. Not that he ever needed much of a reason, but twenty-five grand was the finest excuse he'd had for a hangover since he started drinking twenty-five years ago. Tilting his glass for another he noticed a slender fellow in faded jeans and flannel straddling a seat two to his right. The man finger combed his beige hair, lit a cigarette, and cupped his chin in his hand. In a moment he turned and stared at Leo with eyes as brown and glassy as his beer bottle. "Evening," he said, lifting his longneck.

Leo smiled. He could tell the man was queer for guys too. The stranger wasn't his type, not that he really had himself one. After a longer second look Leo decided he wasn't that drunk, not yet anyways. He was still a good eight brews from that set of beer goggles. It was best to just put his balls on hold for now, but a little companionship would be welcome. He raised his glass to the man and took a drink. "Evening."

The man tilted his head in reply.

"So what do you do around here for fun?"

The man fingered his jaw, scooted his bony ass two stools down until he was right beside Leo and leaned closer. "Truth be told, mostly we do each other."

Leo looked at him for a moment before he busted out laughing. "God Almighty!" He'd needed a good laugh. "Is that so?"

The man nodded. "Bayetteville is about the same as anywhere, only in this town there's just a handful of dim places to go if you know what I mean. The rest stop up at Devil's Point is probably the most popular spot."

Leo's chin was crowding his collar. This fellow sure had his number. He laughed again at the stranger's frankness and didn't know just how to take the fact that this fellow's presumptions were so accurate. Leo didn't have many illusions about himself, but he liked to think his private doings were only privy to consenting strangers. "Is that how I look to you?"

"No, but I'd wager that's how you are."

"And what makes you so flat out sure."

The man gave a warm look and just shrugged. He didn't seem like much of a stranger anymore. "Just a feeling."

"You been spying on me through a glory hole?"

The man laughed and hissed out a column of smoke towards the stuffed moose head. "Honey, I never worship with my eyes open or spy with my mouth full."

Leo slapped a hand to his thigh and bought him a shot for that snappy retort. He wasn't usually so free with a dollar, but now he could afford to be generous. They clinked shot glasses and downed them in unison.

The man eyed Leo. It wasn't a sex look, but it wasn't altogether empty either. Leo couldn't put a word to what it meant. Maybe it was just the liquor.

"Yep, in Bayetteville it is all tearooms and chance encounters, but I've got a feeling you're going to change all that?"

"Oh really?"

"Really."

"Well, that's where you are wrong." Leo shook his head and straightened the soggy napkin beneath his beer. "I'm only in town for tonight."

"A lot can happen in one night."

Leo about spit out a mouthful of beer. What was that supposed to mean? Bumping pussies with this skinny so-and-so wasn't on his mind at all.

The man sensed his perplexion and laughed before polishing off his longneck backwash. "Sorry, I'm just getting carried away on all this liquor." He extended a hand. "My name is Christian."

"I'm a pagan myself."

With an extravagant roll of his red-threaded eyes Christian straightened his back and clicked his tongue. The queen was not amused. "Wish I had me a dime for ever time I heard that."

"Sorry, the name is Leo, Leo Dunsten. Let me buy you another as payback for speaking the obvious."

"Well... I'm not one for holding a grudge, especially where free liquor is concerned." The bartender set another Hamms before Christian. Taking a gulp he offered up an extended "Aaaahhhh." In a moment he smiled, "Truth be told, it isn't the most common response, but it's in the top three."

Leo caught the bartender's eye and signaled for two more shooters. No telling where this night was headed, but he was sure he'd be headed there with a zigzagging stagger. "This one's for honesty."

After a couple more drinks and a hazardous game of darts they blustered out of the Angler and laughed the half block to Marie's. They did more shots and sang along with a jukebox that Christian swore had the finest selection in town. Given the circumstances that wasn't necessarily a good thing. Christian's singing voice was one of the worst Leo had ever heard. "...Like a horse pissing steady on a flat rock," was how he thought of it.

"There's everything on here, everything," said Christian with a hazardous gesture to the jukebox.

Every so often Leo fretted their flamboyant behavior might not be welcome, but folks gave it no never mind. They were tossing around too much money for anyone to give a rat's ass or a good goddamn. Most weeknight bartenders couldn't afford to discriminate about where their tips came from so long as they kept on coming. After another couple drinks the part of Leo's brain that worried what other people thought was too marshy to function. It felt good being himself or at least a looser version of it. Things looked bleary but a hell of a lot better than they had in a long time. Twenty-five grand and a good buzz go an long way in turning an attitude around.

Leo told Christian the highlights of his inheritance story as they stumbled out of Marie's. Hearing the overhead squeak of a swinging Budweiser sign, Christian asked, "What has two mouths and is thirsty as hell..."

Leo gave him a blank look.

"...Us!" Grabbing Leo by the arm he pulled him inside the Riddle Room for a nightcap. They ended up staying much longer.

During one of the four games on the bowling machine Christian slid his puck to Leo and confessed that the first time he saw him he felt he was meeting a best friend. "It hit me right in the chest plain as anything, like one of them electric heart paddles that make you flop like a fish, that's how it was when I saw you on that barstool." He thumped himself squarely for emphasis. "Sitting there it was BOOM—and the next thing I knew I was like a fish having a cardigan arrest."

Leo gave him a holding stare. He liked to consider himself nobody's fool. "Uh huh."

"I'm serious as a heart attack."

"And I'm sure our relationship was tied up with ribbons and bows once I got to talking about the inheritance.

Sister shooed the comment aside with a spray of spittle. "I swear on the Bible, and I'm a religious man. Every Sunday at nine, come hell, high water, hemorrhoids, or hangover, I'm at St. Elizabeth's."

"You spend a lot of time on your knees don't you?"

Sister grinned. "That I cannot, will not, and shall not deny."

"Well you are a holy one... Our Lady of the Sacred Libations, Sister of the Seven and Sevens..."

Christian blew a tight stream of smoke his direction. "Don't go feeling a need to continue on my account."

Leo was too drunk to listen. He could be awful single-minded when he thought he was being clever. "That's going to be my name for you." Leo gave a slack laugh and dipped his fingers in the moisture ring around his glass. Flicking them in Christian's general direction he proclaimed, "I baptize thee Sister."

Both turned when the bartender hollered closing.

Sister smiled, "One last shot Bernie?"

Bernie nodded. It was easier agreeing than arguing. Nothing galled him more than haggling with a drunk over a final drink. Good God Almighty! Most nights he just didn't have the energy for it. He poured them two whiskeys and cracked a smile when Sister tipped two dollars.

"Here's to the future buddy," toasted Sister.

"It's been one hell of a night, one I'll wish I remembered."

They laughed and threw back the shots. "Whew," Sister grimaced with a smack of his lips, "That one kicked like a country mule!"

Both shrieked when the houselights came on. Leaping off their stools they yanked open the tavern door. Outside the streets were wet and silvery beneath the streetlights. "When did it rain?" They said simultaneously before looking at each other and bursting into laughter.

For no reason they began running down the street. Elm was deserted at that time of night, especially on a Tuesday. Sister hooked a rail thin arm on a parking meter, swung around, and threw his hands against a boarded storefront. A "For Sale" sign was nailed to the plywood. "You got nothing but that shit job up in the Quad Cities; why not take your money and open a bar here," said Sister, slapping the plywood again.

The quiet of the night made his voice and the slap seem louder than they actually were.

"Because my mama didn't raise no fool."

"...Lord knows we need a tavern. There's a gaggle of us around, and half of us are drunks."

Leo was saying "Oh no, oh no" and shaking his head as Sister wiggled a pen from the back of his Levis.

"Bend over...and don't fret, I'm just going to take your temperature... I'm kidding. Get over here." He pushed Leo over. Sister wobbled, widened his eyes, and tried to focus. He wrote the realtor's number on the back of Leo's t-shirt and slapped his behind to let him know he was done. "I'm serious, you should think about opening a place. I'm not just saying so because I'm drunk. Fact is, many times I think better with a lightly pickled brain."

"Yeah?"

"Yeah."

"Well..." Leo broke off in a yawn.

They staggered the three blocks to the Friendship Inn and laughed over this and that and nothing at all until they both passed out around five. Early the next afternoon they ran out of cigarettes and mustered the energy and courage to venture out for breakfast. They sat across from one another at the Pancake Palace, silent and hung over and mostly staring at the table or into the saggy eyed reflections in their coffees. They smoked and were quietly grateful for the bottomless cup. They recoiled from the patch of sunlight as it moved across the surface of their table. Sister finally reached up and yanked down the yellowed blind. The cashier gave him a look like she thought he was taking liberties, but he just raised his cup to her.

After a couple hours Leo and Sister felt jittery and a little queasy but otherwise fine...or at least sound enough to resume their carousing. The second night began at the Angler and got out of hand in much the same manner as the night before.

Over the next couple days Leo tore up the town with Sister. As his fondness for the town and Sister's company grew, the idea of opening a bar there started seeming less like a wild hair and more like a plan. He was already sure about leaving the mill. "Sure as I'm shitting here," he said with a slur and a laugh that second night. To drive home the point he grabbed the undersides of his barstool so tight he nearly tipped himself. That was one decision he could make without a lick of remorse. He wasn't put on this earth for a life that mundane. That said, he was still confused. Leo was sure of what he didn't want, but wasn't certain moving to Bayetteville was the solution.

After a third night of bar crawls they plodded back to the Friendship Inn before passing out. Around dawn, Leo's eyes opened wide. He bolted upright in bed. Sister was slumped in a chair before the rolling TV screen and shifted, snorted, and resumed snoring almost immediately. Looking around in the blue broadcast glow, Leo was suddenly sure about opening the bar. He flipped off the TV and shook Sister awake. All Leo said was "Yes." Sister lifted his head from the headrest. He looked half dead, and that was the better half. With that one word Sister knew just what Leo meant. He smiled, gave a lazy whoop, and deflated back into sleep.

The next morning they ate again at the Pancake Palace. Over BLT platters and coffee they compared aches and formed a vague plan of action. The thrill of the bar enterprise and bottomless cups eventually lifted the pall of their hangovers. When they returned to the room, Leo pulled his dirty t-shirt from the clothes pile in the corner. After a few moments of squinting and guessing, Sister called the realtor. The price was less than Leo expected.

"This ain't exactly the Hamptons," offered Sister by way of an explanation.

Two months later the Sand Bar opened for business. Sister had aided him every step of the way so Leo gave him a wage, a finder's fee, and the promise of free drinks until the end of time. "...Or until you give up drinking; whichever comes first."

Sister laughed that husky laugh. "Might as well sign this place over to me now."

"Well, free drinks—but no call brands."

Truth was there wasn't much left to sign over. Leo was justifiably anxious. The Sand Bar had to succeed. Renovations and stock and licenses and all the et-ceteras had exhausted almost the entirety of his inheritance, along with what little savings he had.

The building overhaul began with bricking in the glass storefront and painting the outside black. The official entrance was off the rippled alley in back. A wide gravel lot lay to one side for parking. Both Sister and Leo agreed that discretion would boost business better than advertising. Sister assured him he would spread the word. "I am better than any flashing sign." As witness to Sister's gift of gab and knack for spreading things in general, Leo had little reason to doubt him.

The bar itself was shaped like a shoebox with a long main room dominated by a curved wooden bar. It was a handsome place with a floor of inlaid planks and a ceiling of etched tin. Mirror tiles were arranged in a checkerboard fashion along the opposite wall with black wall exposed in between. The cute little stud at the building supply store said it would make the room look wider and since Leo was being flirty, he bought a case. Mostly the mirrors just made people feel drunker than they actually were, especially since Leo and Sister had a few before putting them up and some of the rows weren't what you'd call even.

At the far end of the bar was a dance floor flanked by a few cocktail tables they had acquired for practically nothing at a restaurant auction. Saving money there left extra for the rose and gold jukebox they placed just off the dance floor. One afternoon, Leo and Sister almost went into self-soiling hysterics selecting the songs and sampling some liquor. Upon finishing, Sister proclaimed in a slurred and grandiose manner that the Sand Bar now had the finest jukebox in town. "Nothing can hold a goddamn candle to it, not even Marie's."

Finding it necessary to budget himself whenever possible, Leo opted to live in the tiny apartment upstairs. Staying there would make coming to work convenient and staggering home even easier. He knew the bar would consume a good amount of the next couple years. Bars had been doing that since he was sipping beer out of jelly jars, so the thought didn't bother him. At least now he'd have something to show for the time invested besides a hangover and a pocket of quarters. He rented a U-haul and carted all his old furniture down from Davenport. It was mostly broken down and junky, but Leo figured he'd only be upstairs to sleep anyways.

Miraculously everything was set to go with the bar right on schedule. "That's on account of us doing the Lord's work," said Sister.

Leo laughed, recalling the comment as he propped open the back door that first day of business. He sure hoped Sister had been lighting candles and counting his beads. This was a matter of sink or swim and Leo didn't relish the thought of sinking back into factory work. He knew where that conveyor belt led. He fanned the air and made a note to pickup a ceiling fan. The place still smelled of paint, plywood, and creosote. With Sister around it would smell like cigarettes soon enough.

Leo stood at the bar sipping vodka and lemonade. He jumped and spilled a bit when he felt something between his legs. Looking down he saw a black kitten weaving around his feet. He picked it up at the belly and brought it close to his face. "So ma'am...I mean sir, I didn't expect no pussy as my first customer." Leo jumped again when he saw the kitten had a single eye.

"It's open!" Sister burst through the back door with his hands waving overhead like treetops in a thunderstorm. The startled kitten leapt from Leo's arms and scamper-slid across the polished dance floor. Sister shrieked and splayed a hand over his chest. "What in the hell was that?"

Leo shook his head and put down his drink. "A kitten wandered in here not two minutes ago."

Sister cocked a brow. "That's a sign my dear, it means good fortune."

"I thought a black cat was bad luck?"

"That's only if it crosses your path, when it crosses your threshold it means abundance up the butthole and knowing your butthole you've got room enough to be a millionaire in nickels several times over."

"I could use some of that."

"Butthole pleasure?"

"No, well that too—but some abundance."

"Then go and get a hold of that damn thing before it gets behind the jukebox and lectrocutes itself."

Leo's boot falls clicked across the floorboards. Sister poured himself a glass of amber joy juice and shook his head. He couldn't suppress a grin. When he saw that poor one-eyed thing at the shelter he knew it was the one. If he just gave the cat to Leo he might refuse, but rightfully assumed that wouldn't be the case if it wandered in as if by fate.

Sister sniffed Leo's glass. "What the hell are you drinking?" He looked up to laugh as Leo returned to the bar with the kitten twisting this way and that in his hands. Suddenly the kitten ceased its squirming and began to idly paw a button on Leo's shirt. "He's a wild one, but it looks like he's adopted you. Now you have family here."

Leo looked up at Sister and then down at the cat. "Yep."

"Never refuse an omen."

Leo smiled.

Sister went over to the jukebox and slipped in a couple quarters. While making his selections he yelled over his shoulder. "What are you going to call him?"

"I don't know."

"He's not yours until you name him."

"Any suggestions?"

"Something that shows he takes after his uncle."

Leo mixed himself another. Over the clink of ice cubes he said, "How about Tramp? Or Cocksucker?"

Sister turned and gave a leveling look that made Leo laugh and spill a bit of vodka. Sister sauntered back and leaned on his dry ruddy elbows. "Something campy but regal."

Leo laughed and gassed his cocktail through the straw. Sometimes Sister had a way of saying the last thing he expected. "Regal? I think your tiara is a little tight and a little tarnished Queenie."

Sister waved his comment aside and stirred the ice in his glass. "How about Fabian or Constantine or Sebastian or..."

"I like Sebastian."

"It's got a good ring to it." Sister grabbed one of the kitten's back paws. "Hey, what do you think of that?"

The kitten meowed.

"That sounds like a yes. Sebastian it is." Sister scratched it behind an ear.

Sister and Leo turned at the sound of footsteps on the three cement steps outside. "Hello sweet cheeks!" Sister ran open armed to the crumpled man sloughing down the back hall and led him over. Sister introduced him as Jack-O. "Don't make me tell you how he got that name."

"I can only guess." Leo poured Jack-O a complimentary shot as his first customer. Jack-O reciprocated with a quick appreciative smile that deepened the rut between his brows and radial wrinkles longside his mouth. He was the sort with enough slack skin for a second face. He tossed back a shot of whiskey. It settled his jitters and seemed to inflate his hollows. He dug in his wallet and gave Leo a single for the draft.

"That goes here." Sister pulled an appropriately sized picture frame from a shopping bag. "Ten cents at the Salvation Army, but I sure do favor the cut of this wood."

Leo had to thank fate or God or the devil himself for bringing such a friend into his life. Sister was already more of a mate than any friend he'd ever had. "You never miss a trick do you?"

"It's the tricks who miss me."

Leo grabbed a hammer and nail and hung the framed bill above the register. From that night on Jack-O proudly pointed to the dollar whenever he was conversing with someone he thought didn't know about it, or whenever he wished to emphasize his loyalty to the tavern. It made the Sand Bar feel that much more like home.

Jack-O was the quiet introverted type until you put a few drinks in him, then most anything could happen. He did clerical work for the coroner and was forever teetering on the brink of quitting or dismissal. That hate-my-job-but-terrified-to-lose-it state was the sort of thing that spelled bar regular. Coming in when he did and being there so much he almost seemed a final piece of bar furniture. The next week Leo hired Jack-O's boyfriend as the full-time bartender.

Leo didn't think much of Ben. He was okay at making drinks and easy on the eyes, especially in a dim bar, but Ben wasn't the agreeable type unless he stood to benefit from whatever he was doing. It was clear from the get go Ben was playing Jack-O. The relationship was one-sided and all about feeding Ben's ego and buying Ben toys. To Ben, Jack-O's best quality was his blatant adoration and Ben sure loved putting it to the test. Sister mostly shook his head when Ben came up in conversation. Leo said that one figured he was God's gift.

The following week Leo took on a second bartender. No one could pronounce or remember his name so they ended up just calling him Finn. He was a wiry queen from Finland, so pale most every branch and tributary of his vascular system was apparent in the sunlight. Finn was a Cher fanatic. His room at the transient hotel, the Roosevelt, was a shrine to her—wallpapered with pictures and clippings and a supposedly original Bob Mackie costume from the variety series. Finn knew only a smidgen of English, but he knew every lyric to Half Breed and Dark Lady. Leo saved a bundle by hiring him. Finn didn't have a green card so Leo could pay him dirt cheap under the table. No one knew exactly how Finn ended up in Bayetteville and he didn't seem to know enough English to explain.

The second customer that first night was Lulu. She arrived with a cloud of gravel dust trailing her bike and a date wrapped around her waist. Seeing her come through the door Sister leaned close to Leo, "Lulu is all woman and more man than you could ever hope to find." She was wearing her trademark black with her hair slicked back. Sister called her a living homage to Elvis. Lulu's conversation consisted primarily of laughter and nods or curses and grimaces depending on the topic and her mood. If she found something extremely funny or aggravating she slapped the bar, startling those around her. When she had a point to make it she made by tapping out each word and then repeating it tap for tap before sitting back to let her listener fully absorb her comment.

Lulu was a pool shark and over the next few weeks she convinced Leo to get a table. Actually she strong-armed him into doing it and drove the notion home with three full rounds of bar poking. The investment paid off. Once Leo got the table, Lulu's pals from across the river came over almost every weekend. Soon Leo acquired a second table and the tri-state lesbians began having informal tournaments there on Saturdays. Lulu was the undisputed champ, though sometimes a black girl from the next county over by the name of Hester proved a formidable opponent.

Bruschetta appeared opening night as well. She teetered in on spiked heels oozing sophistication, femininity, and attitude. "Adore me, but don't fuck with me" was the message she broadcast loud and clear. Bruschetta's breasts were gigantic and her hips quite rounded. She dressed in outfits that emphasized both, making her frequently look like a sequined peanut. She lived in an abandoned building further down on Elm. The owner let her stay there. Bruschetta never said exactly why. She was always very discreet about her gentlemen friends. Her past was a mystery and strictly anecdotal. There were lots of episodes but no cohesive story. No one knew who she was, who she'd been, or where she came from. Bruschetta just suddenly surfaced, a spontaneous creation like the Sand Bar itself.

Most Saturday mornings that first year, when Leo mopped the floor and cleaned the toilets; he listened for the heavyset kid who rummaged through the garbage. The little urchin was always rooting around for something. Leo was never sure what. He thought he might be retarded or at least slow. The soft set of the kid's wide blue eyes told Leo he was also a little pansy waiting to flower. It made Leo a bit misty-eyed to watch over his morning coffee and chores. Leo would sigh and recall his own youth, though by that age he was already giving blow-jobs to truckers and sneaking out to honky-tonks.

One Saturday night Leo mentioned the trash gnome in passing. Bruschetta turned from the dance floor and patted her upswept do with a manicured hand. "He goes through my garbage all the time." She said a couple weeks prior she caught him messing around in her building with another kid. Bruschetta said she didn't say a word, just sauntered down the hall to let them know someone was living there and to take that carrying on elsewhere. It wasn't that she was prudish. "It's a matter of respecting what's yours and what isn't," she said to Leo. She added that when they saw her the one boy ran, but the garbage kid hid. "If you call crouching in a room full of flat cardboard boxes hiding!" Bruschetta said he'd high-tailed it by the time she got back from buying cigarettes.

Leo shrugged and poured her another gin and tonic. "Suppose I'll be pouring him cocktails soon enough."

Not too long after that the trash kid stopped frequenting the dumpster on Saturday mornings. In a few weeks Leo stopped listening for him and for the most part he was too busy to give it much thought. It wasn't until years later that he saw him again.

Street Urchin

Fred collected bottle caps and like most of his interests, it was an obsession. It soon determined a large part of his behavior. Given the energy he invested as well as a decided lack of competition, it wasn't surprising that he soon had the finest collection in all Bayetteville.

Every Saturday he took the bus downtown. The #10 always reeked of perfume, booze, and peanut butter. The kids lined the backseats, laughing and cracking gum all the way to the movie house. They made Fred nervous. Drunks rode the bus to sleep one off, escape the elements, or escape to the cheapest bars in town. Some of the elderly were scattered about the seats as well. A few were heading for doctor visits and various appointments, but most went to browse the thinning bins at the three run-down department stores. They went more out of habit than anything. No one shopped downtown anymore. To Fred that unthinking return to the familiar made them ghosts in training. The only step left was death. They'd already become invisible to most everyone and their cries were only heard by a select few.

Fred took the bus for the sake of his collection. The alleys dissecting the downtown area had the finest dumpsters in town. Trash there was inspiring. A tavern crowned every corner and a heaping dumpster was behind every one—Marie's, the Tempest Tavern, the Angler, the Riddle Room, the Sand Bar... No downtown bars served beer in cans. Bottle caps made garbage a big part of Fred's life and Saturday morning trash was an unparalleled thrill, especially after a bustling Friday night of paycheck guzzlers. Bayetteville had more than its fair share of those.

Rooting in the rubbish Fred was often harassed by bartenders and patrons alike. Seeing him rifle through the bins made folks treat him like a cockroach, a rodent, or one of their own kids. He was a magnet for pent frustrations, for all the crap of the week, and for the past in general. More than a few angry drunks called Bayetteville home and Saturdays found most of them hung over and ornery.

Mostly he got cussed out. A couple of times he was grabbed. Once he was hit square on the head with a longneck flung by a halo-haired brute on a binge. The bottle skittered into a patch of crusted snow. Blood stippled the ice. Fred ran round the corner, ducked behind a rusted ash drum, and touched his head. He could feel a knot rising. Pain made something out of what was nothing. The area was tender and felt mushy beneath his thick brown hair. He licked the blood from his fingers and watched his breath lift in little clouds.

"Fucking cretin," shouted the red-faced ogre. Fred bowed lower. Was that what he was? When the man finished pissing he staggered down the street.

More than once Fred was chased through those back ways and over the trash and pigeon shit with his heart pounding in his ears. Panic carried him more than reason, beyond worrying where he should or shouldn't go. Sometimes he darted like a lunatic into traffic and got blasted by horns and squealing tires and a few raised fists. Other times he ran into strange buildings and down derelict hallways.

Once a burly teen Fred had seen around town chased him through the boarded back of a building and into a room filled with flattened cardboard. Broken down boxes were thick upon the floor and gave beneath his feet like a soggy pair of sneakers. The room had only one door. The windows were barred. His pursuer blew a glob of snot out his nose and leaned longside the doorframe. His laugh could've meant anything. A sudden noise sent the kid running. Fred poked his head from the door a moment later and saw the gyrating rear of a platinum blonde round a corner at the end of the hall. He figured he'd caught a brief glimpse of his guardian angel.

On several occasions Fred was stopped by the police who suspected he was a petty thief, a sad looking street urchin, or just up to no good. They seemed to get a twisted delight questioning him. Fred was too secretive to be truthful so mostly he just stood open-mouthed, blinked slow, and scratched the side of his head. By the time they finished their interrogation the downtown patrol figured him for a halfwit and told him to move along. There was little pleasure derived from harassing an oaf. "We're keeping an eye on you boy," or something comparable was what they usually said as the squad car pulled away.

Sometimes Fred happened upon death in the alleys. It shocked more than frightened him. The carcasses were never human. It was so simple for animals to die. It was just the end of life and the start of decay. There were no questions or charges...even when they were killed.

Every spring a festering flock of poisoned pigeons hardened into shells along the alley floors courtesy of City Hall. Maggots churned in eye sockets and chest cavities and looked like magnified television snow. Sometimes Fred came upon cats gnawing the remains. It never seemed to hurt them. He assumed the city crew used some unique sort of special pigeon-only killing blend.

Once Fred rounded a crook at the end of a favorite alley and stumbled over a flattened cat. She had been birthing. The pressure from a tire burst her like a ripe July melon. Fred scraped his shoe and crouched over the strange mess of dead kittens. They looked like plum petals or a litter of purple space aliens no bigger than a quarter. He poked at them with a stick and eventually tried flipping them like flapjacks.

Another time he flipped the metal lid of a dumpster behind the Vienna Beef and found a dead speckled hound caked in cooking grease. "Jesus," he cried, backing up. The lid slammed and echoed with a deafening din causing him to jump a second time. In a moment he raised it again. A slab of yellow lard halved the dog. The discolored tongue hung limp and disappeared into the hard cream of the grease. The caking divided an open eye. Below the crust was a mystery. For all Fred knew he could have been looking at half a dog. Last week his folks' friends, the Grunwalds, had rhapsodized about the onion rings at that diner while playing cards. A smile curled at the corners of his mouth. His folks said the Grunwalds could be "awful uppity".

"And what with her being born and raised down by the river," his mother had added.

The seasons turned his alley world into something altogether different. Winter made the back ways pale blue from the gray sky and threw faint shadows across the crusted snow. Ice burst from overrun gutters and hung in shimmering toothed rows overhead. They glistened in the sun, dripping and dropping in tinkling explosions, sometimes falling to stab the white belly of winter. The soothing coo of pigeons rolled from the eaves, soft and heavy as fog. Those frantic purrs made Fred feel more isolated than ever.

Sometimes a storm sewer froze or grates clogged and an entire alley became unfamiliar terrain. Yellow overlapping bubble ice congealed to capture bottles, boxes, and even bottle caps. All sorts of things were held beneath and within that clouded surface. It was spilled glue in Fred's desk at school, a faded wasteland on a Jupiter moon, or a glimpse at the end of the world. Maybe it was an open eye on the other side of a hardened lard land. His imagination could stretch it any old way.

The ice made it difficult for Fred to keep his footing, but he didn't mind. Bruises made his paradise more real. It was a dark purple eye onto his alien world. It linked here to there. Sometimes he would run and spin over the uneven surface or surf the slick folds. The ridges were sharp. He ruined more than one pair of trousers that way.

In winter, the Frear River crashed its frozen face into the three pylons of the Broadway Bridge. Fred stared as the floes rammed the pillars, pulled by the current and pushed by ice from behind. Looking down, the cement supports seemed to be moving forward and advancing like the bow of a ship. He watched the ice crunch up in shards or buckle and submerge. It boomed in deep wails from beneath the arches of the bridge. The sound and the sight seemed the river's rage against the concrete.

If he stared long enough, Fred felt the bridge begin to sway and lean as if on the verge of collapse. If he looked longer he felt himself flip over the railing and onto the floe. He imagined ice crashing and collapsing underfoot—edging him closer to the bone cold water. He imagined falling in, heavy in his ratty coat and breathless with the cold. He'd sink and in the silent chill look up to see a mosaic ceiling of floes with sunlight setting off every edge. It'd be lovely. He could imagine taking that fantasy all the way to the grave.

Once he gave the vision too free a rein and fainted right there on the bridge. He came to almost at once and was thankful there were no witnesses. Behaving that way would concern his parents. He'd be lost if his folks forbade his trips downtown, but they rarely did that sort of thing. The Walshes weren't that way. Denying Fred would mean admitting they knew that side of his life. Forbidding meant seeing something was wrong and that was nothing they cared to do. Only an outside source, like a gossipy neighbor or a police call, could cause them to acknowledge it.

When winter moved on into spring and finally summer, Fred's parents became even more lenient. In summer the alleys grew lush and wild, all but threatening to burst their confines and consume the town. Everything battled for sunlight. Weeds clawed through the cement cracks in clumps, making the pavement seem like a forest lid with the weedy greens as high leaves of trees pushing through the sky to this level.

Fred wondered if the world below the pavement was where he belonged. Most times he didn't feel he belonged above. Asphalt seemed the only thing keeping the worlds apart. He wondered if going below was simple as flipping up a hunk of concrete and shimmying down a tree. Maybe it was as easy as being swept through a sewer grate during the next heavy rain. Maybe it was nothing more than deciding it was where he was meant to be.

In summer the alley stench grew oppressive. The sweet stink of rot blended with piss and stale beer. Fred willed himself to adjust. To him there wasn't a choice. It was a simple matter of priorities. He was committed to his bottle cap collection.

Swarms of biting flies hovered above most every dumpster and the scuffling of rats could be heard above the traffic and wind. Whenever Fred spied them the rats stared with flat mica eyes. Some grew as big as dogs but Fred was never afraid. Mostly he felt kinship. Bar trash was an integral part of their lives too.

Women sometimes took men, and vice versa, into the back ways and doorways. A loose laugh or the scrape of a heel usually warned him.

Fred never grew accustomed to hearing a couple squish and moan. Twice he'd hidden and watched. It wasn't sexy or enticing. Strange was what it was.

One Saturday in May an exhausted looking redhead took a bald man into the alley. She slipped down the straps of her tank top as Fred crouched behind a whirring industrial fan. Her breasts hung like two bags of veiny flour. Good Lord, Fred thought, bending lower until he felt like a rat peeking from its hole. He understood the strange things seen behind flat mica eyes. The woman said something Fred couldn't hear and then laughed again. Her lemon scented perfume was an accent to the fermenting trash. She propped her body against the brick building with arms spread and palms flat, as though she was holding the whole thing up. The bald man was frantically going at it. His balls were slapping her like a pair of sugar beets. Gravel ground beneath her heels. Afterwards she laughed and stumbled while hauling up her panties. Everything she said was followed by a laugh. She fingered her dime store beads and crossed her arms over the shelf of her stomach while the man hiked up his britches. He slipped her a couple bills without a word while looking the other way. She nodded as she took the cash. No laugh. They left the alley and headed opposite directions.

The boldness of the alley world intrigued Fred. Regular rules didn't apply. It was like the underside where the forest erupted through the asphalt, ice floes moved like clouds overhead, and a dog's eye hung like the moon in a pale milky sky. In the alleys everything seemed more than what it was because it's exactly what it was. The harsh honesty of it amazed him. It was the polar opposite of Fred's home life.

Much of Fred's understanding of adults came from his alley education. Adults loved to indulge while preaching restraint. His parents and teachers certainly did. Those dos and don'ts were all part of the show. Fred knew different. The truth of adult lives was heaped behind every downtown bar and that truth was much more appealing than any of the nonsense they tried to teach about life. Swizzle sticks oozed sophistication. Glamour was stamped on every lipstick smeared cigarette butt. Cracked cocktail glasses and crumpled napkins spoke of illicit thrills.

Bottle caps were his symbols of that raunchy world. They were the metallic scales of the Serpent. It was no demon. It didn't live in the underworld, but right there in Bayetteville. Fred had the proof. He kept thousands of bottlecaps in a Coca-Cola cooler he'd found behind a ransacked diner one day after school. He had dragged it home and then down to the basement. He played with his caps most every night. He liked the stale beer and cigarette smell that lingered even after a washing. He was so partial to the stink that eventually he stopped cleaning his newly acquired caps at all.

The sound pleased Fred as well. It was a tinny grating folded upon itself into a league of tambourines. He loved stirring his hand around in the cooler as fast as he could until he was consumed by the sound or cut bloody or heard hollering from upstairs that they couldn't hear the TV.

Much as he loved his bottle caps, at around this time Fred found a new interest. It began one overcast Saturday. In an uncharacteristic show of parental authority, his folks forbade him to go outside. They'd be gone the entire day attending his great uncle's funeral. Uncle Virgil had keeled over in the Mercantile onto a table of sale socks which then buckled to fold him into a sort of sock and old man taco. Fred wondered what Aunt Mae could have meant by saying, "Virgil would have wanted it that way."

Unable to roam the downtown alleys that Saturday, Fred grew bored playing with his bottle caps. Seeing the old TV on a low shelf longside the rinse tubs, he carried it up to his room with the cord bouncing on the steps behind him. The set was troublesome and required a matchbook to hold the tuner in place. That afternoon he watched a double feature, then a made-for-TV thriller in the evening. His folks returned during the closing credits. They were a bit drunk from Cousin Enid's open house following the burial. They spoke of there being a great number of toasts—to this, to that, to him and not me. Fred heard his mother exclaim that the undertaker sure put a strange look on Virgil's face, "like he was out of sorts being dead and not at all pleased about being in a discount casket."

Fred heard his father's loose laugh and the sound of him unscrewing a cap and the gurgle of another drink being poured. "Lord Lila, you think everyone who's passed on is out of sorts."

"Well, didn't it look that way?"

They would both maintain the same sides of the same conversation until bedtime. They never seemed to tire of saying the same thing like a chant and response. Fred supposed there was comfort in the redundancy. The habit saved them the trouble of coming up with anything new.

Fred upped the volume on the TV. He liked listening to different dialogue for a change.

The following Saturday he slept in after Friday night *Creature Features* and didn't go downtown. The Saturday after that he dragged the his cooler of caps down to Magnolia Creek and one by one, and eventually in bunches floated his bottle tops downstream. He was setting them free, releasing the Serpent. It took all morning and most of the afternoon. They sank quick in the gurgling current and skittered over the base pebbles. Fred wondered how long it would take for them to be dragged and fed into the Frear. The notion of littering didn't occur to him. He wouldn't have cared if it had. Garbage was as much a part of the landscape as anything.

The TV screen became his new world. Movies made him feel things he didn't in real life. They taught him a bit about everything. It was the fantasy side never found in the alleys and what most of those paycheck guzzlers were hoping to find or forget. The Zenith was a porthole on the psyche of the world. It showed him the icons of that temple and all it held sacred. It also showed him how far he was from that ideal. He'd never be a big-toothed bit of confidence, but he hoped with a bit of practice he could imitate something similar. Movies showed that it wasn't who you were but how you played it that was important. Maybe life was nothing more than what occurred between the opening and closing credits.

Fred imagined living in rooms without ceilings and walls that weren't really walls. Rooms without a world outside sounded ideal. He liked the idea of everything being purposeful, arranged just so, and set secure on a mark. He dreamt of a world without the plot-less doings of the everyday where characters mostly merited their fates.

Within a month most parts of his life flattened into two dimensions and his folks were just too thick to realize it. After another couple weeks they recognized a problem, but by then it was a chore for Fred to function outside a formula plot. By then his mind was a sinkhole of scenes and dialogue blocs and reaction shots. His eyes had become a camera and his mouth a microphone.

His folks worried separately and silently, as they did about most everything. His father's drinking and his mother's hypochondria complicated all Walsh dramas. Nothing was real. Reality was just that stretch where everybody's own world overlapped. The all of it made everyone real aware of what they said and how and when they said it. So much was happening beneath the surface that it was easy to keep busy with windows to wash, a split hose to tape, and a lily-of-the-valley garden to tend. When Fred's movie viewing started to cause problems, his parents kept mum and puttered to exhaustion. They prayed it was just another one of his phases. He'd already had so many.

After a while it seemed inappropriate to challenge his newest pastime. He wasn't hurting anything. Pity was easier than confrontation. His mother shed tears over his father's drinking, the household budget, and her every ache and sniffle. She cried to think of the Kennedy widows and secretly craved the attention they got from those two assassinations. Sometimes she even cried to hear the muted Late Show theme and see the TV glow play across the floorboards neath Fred's door. She knew how Fred could be. There was nothing she could do. Telling him no more TV would cause a scene and her nerves couldn't handle that. "If only he was watching sports," she thought.

At the time Lila Walsh was heard speaking of the situation at the Shop-N-Go. Feeling lightheaded from a combination of medications she approached the dead-eyed pharmacist, Herbert Cole, and patted down her sausage curls with a fluttering hand. She sighed once and again and then just started talking. "My boy is frittering his youth away with television, ruining his eyes, and soaking up radiation like a sponge. If he isn't a prime candidate for corrective eyewear and radiation poisoning I don't know who is. There's been a good amount of hair on his pillow of late, and his gums have been looking funny." Lila put a second bottle of zinc in her convenience basket and wondered just where she'd erred to have such trials brought to her doorstep. Those Kennedy women weren't the only ones with troubles.

When Mr. Cole finally looked up and said "What?" Lila shook her head and felt foolish. Now she'd gone and made a spectacle! She apologized for talking to herself and ran a hand across her forehead. "It must be the heat." Herman cocked a brow and thought otherwise. People were accustomed to Lila's peculiar ways and routine dramas so they didn't pay her much mind. Some ribbed that she'd complain to an ear of corn if she had the urge.

Rog Walsh worried Fred was a loner, but not his own person at all. He shook his head, sure his unusual boy would grow into an unusual man and just as certain that he must take after Lila's relations. Rog dealt with Fred's movie watching and secretiveness the same way he did most everything. He liked to think about things over a drink or two. After a couple Manhattans, most tribulations disappeared, at least for the time being. The urge to solve all problems got lost in the fortifying. Relief was the simplest solution.

His folks couldn't understand the time they saw Fred wasting, but he never saw it that way. "It was just time in low gear." That phrase was from an old Mickey Rooney movie about stock car racing. Rote responses were one result of his new obsession. Too many fine lines had settled in his brain to know which were his own words or thoughts. Phrases came to him automatically and sometimes didn't make much sense. Context took backseat to delivery. Most folks thought him bizarre to begin with, but since all this began talking to him was either confusing or brought an uneasy sense of the familiar. Most avoided him altogether.

Seeing all those idealized worlds and stories unfold spoiled reality for Fred. Patience was never a particular strength of his, but movies had a way of making him expect resolution in ninety minutes or two hours tops, with commercials. Though he did nothing to speak of, and certainly nothing noteworthy, he was also impatient for fame.

Attention and the love of strangers are what most seem to be looking for when it comes to fame. It was adoration at a distance. Fred wanted those things but that wasn't the main thing. Mostly he wanted to be held on film. That was immortality to him more surely than the fluffy kingdom of God stuff in all those Bible passages. Movie folk could never die or age or have bad hair. It was worship all right, reverence plain and simple. He'd finally found a higher power. More than anything he wanted to be flat and immortal. To his way of thinking nothing seemed more real.

That Damn Clock

Del heard the bells ring like slaps and slamming doors, shaking his place to its foundation and rattling the world to bits. That's what it was like, but not what it was. In real life it was mostly in his head. Out there it mostly ticked as simple as anything so no one understood. Living was near impossible with it around, building like a sneeze and Del feeling like snot set to be blasted end over end and stuck to wall or balled in a Kleenex. Nobody knew how it was. It was just in his place.

"Tick Tock" was how he heard a clock talked about in a book he read. A dead drunk guy named Poe wrote a story called "The Tell Tale Heart." The words even sound like a clock—tell tale, tick tock. His little sister Molly scribbled across the book. She made waxy green loops and Del bitched to his ma, but Molly didn't get slapped. She was too young to be anything but an idiot. How could he get mad at someone who ran around in underpants with jelly on her face? His ma just said, "Oh Delbert" or "life isn't fair" when Molly and him fought.

After he told his ma about Molly coloring in his book she slammed down her coffee and said the story was too scary anyways. Del thought, "Christ Almighty!" She acted sometimes like he was a toddler set to piss his pants. The story was bad but her damn bomb clock was okay. Del figured that'd be the end of it, but the next day his ma wrote a note for him to take to school warning Miss Oberlin not to assign any more of that crap. She said it was giving Del nightmares! Del about had a fit when he saw that. Nightmares! That was a lie. He stuffed the note deep in his pocket. He was eleven and he'd die before taking a pansy ass note like that to school. Halfway to St. Elizabeth's he crumpled up that bit of nonsense and tossed it into Magnolia Creek where it feeds into the Frear. He hoped it'd get carried as far as the ocean and even farther so some foreigner way over in Paris or China could see how crazy Ma was.

She'd been acting weird more and more. The slightest thing was liable to set her into action. Del saw her as wound up, just waiting for something to trip her spring. The damn bomb clock was making her worse every day. She looked like a mole moving about that dark apartment with circles neath her eyes, hands all shaky and red, fiddling with the busted blinds so no light got in. She was starting to stink too.

Most nights Del wished the next tick wouldn't come or that the whole works would just explode and be done with instead of all that hissing on the mantle like a riled badger. They never used it anyways. The kitchen clock worked for making sure they didn't miss any good TV. He and Molly turned the volume knob so high they plugged their ears when guys hawked stuff on commercials, so loud they could hear the fuzzing of snow and Mrs. Korbert, the crabby bag of very close veins downstairs, banged on her pipes. No matter how loud it went Del still heard the ticking. The sound was but the half of it. The hands glowed when the lights went out so even at night it splashed every corner of that place in a creepy shade of green.

Del's dad had got it for Del's ma the anniversary before he passed. It looked like some celebration—the anniversary, not his dying. The two got all dressed up and painted the town five shades of red. Over a perch dinner at Staley's his ma got the clock and his dad got a camera. She told the story so many times it was like Del was there in the booth between them. Most times when she told it Del looked at the six pictures they took that night. Actually, beings that the two of them are in every picture it must have been someone else taking photos. Looking through those snapshots was weird on account of Del's dad setting the clock when he gave it to his wife. They carried it around the whole night because leaving it in the car would've been asinine what with that busted door lock. So seeing the clock meant seeing precisely how much time had passed between pictures and how loopy they started looking once they headed to the Angler Inn after dinner. Five months after he giving her that clock, Del's dad was dead. Two months after Molly was born.

Sometimes Del caught his ma crying at the clock, crying real, and not just faking so they'd clean their rooms or take out the trash. She was weepy that way most afternoons when Del got home from school. Since there was nothing he could do to help, Del started hanging out other places and taking his sweet time coming home. No one could blame him for not wanting to come home to that. Whenever Del saw his ma crying at the clock she always said something was in her eye but Del knew she was crying because both eyes were red because of that damn clock.

The fall before last she planned on giving it to his cousin Nadine as a wedding present. The box and the tissue paper for wrapping it were spread across her bed and Del's ma was passed out on the lot of it one day when he got home from school. Soon she was snoring even louder than the TV with both the clock and the bottle cradled in her arms. That nonsense didn't last but a day, but at least lying there she had a smile on her face.

Nadine knew what she was getting from them and knew it was sec-ondhand, but she always liked that clock. "My that is a handsome timepiece," was what she used to say. Del's ma thought things would be easier if the clock wasn't around ticking every second and gonging every half hour to remind her she was a widow. Most considered it the sanest thought she'd had in years.

Del never understood the ways of adult folks. His ma was crazy and so was his cousin Nadine but the craziest of all had to be the guy Nadine was marrying. To Del's way of thinking it was lunacy. Nadine wasn't pretty or smart or funny or rich. She didn't have big titties or blonde hair or any of the stuff Del expected guys to go for in a girl. On top of all that she smelled of bologna half the time and salami the other half. Ma always said, "Hush" when Del would say that. Del wasn't being mean, it was the truth. His ma knew it too. She was al-ways trying to douse Nadine in perfume or toilet water.

Tyson, Nadine's intended, was no prize either with his lazy ways and a strawberry birthmark that made him look like he'd just been slapped, and slapped real hard! Del's ma said it colored his attitude on things. Building a life with Tyson would take hard work. It was something else his ma always said. She was always full of advice when it came to other folks. Del wondered why she didn't turn her mouth around and talk sense to herself.

The week before the wedding, Tyson loaded his pickup and left town. He never even called Nadine before taking off. Making things worse, it was when that song "Delta Dawn" was so popular. When-ever it came on the radio, Del thought of Nadine. He supposed a lot of people did. She never lost her mind or walked downtown with a suitcase in her hand looking for a mysterious dark-haired man, mostly because she couldn't afford to. Still, there was no debating the fact that her story was one sad ballad.

Del's ma heard through Tyson's people that he'd found work in Ra-leigh and was marrying his boss' daughter. She said that was a wise move for that lazy so-and-so. Tyson got himself set up in a track home out there. He and his bride had twins on Nadine's birthday. The babies were a bigger kick in the gut than his up and leaving town. Nadine was mostly marrying Tyson on account of wanting kids. Ever since she was a child herself, that's all she wanted. That's what Del heard her telling his ma over coffee at the kitchen table. She was all teary eyed about it, too. "All I ever wanted was babies." Del's ma agreed with a sigh, add-ing that Nadine always was a fiend for doll collecting.

Del's ma told her some lucky fellow would come along, but so far none of the lucky ones have come within spitting distance. Nadine was still working as a cashier out at the Piggly Wiggly and living over the drug store on Main. Del and his ma and Molly lived catty-corner to her with that damn bomb clock still ticking on their mantle.

The Father/Son Banquet

Each year without fail the Bayetteville phone company had a father/son banquet. Fred attended the banquet twice. The first year, snow and ice covered Bayetteville and by early evening all the warnings and talk of it being the storm of the century were routine. Everywhere folks were giving worried looks out windows and talking about accumulation, wind chill, drifting, cancellations and the like. The father/son event was not cancelled, but it was seriously curtailed. The educational tour as well as the banquet had an air of dread. It was in the snow talk, the watch checking, and the snow watching. Flurries fell like ash outside the windows of the phone company. Seeing it come down Fred wondered if heaven itself was afire.

Touring the central activity pod call load approached the very limits of capacity. The guide reported the fact while standing with her back to the operators. Panels of light flashed behind her, giving her an unnatural glow as she went on about severe weather upping caller volume. It all excited her. Hairs rose on one side of her bob, swaying to and fro with her every move.

The way she was carrying on over things, Fred started seeing her as some sort of alien. Fred imagined the real guide getting sucked through each strand of hair and some alien creature settling inside her. He'd seen a Late Show along similar lines. He let loose with a gasp and saw the strands of her bob as deadly antennae. A moment of contact was coming. Fred saw it a moment before it came to pass. A spark flashed green when she touched the Customer Service Supervisor on the shoulder. Both jumped at the jolt. Fred laughed to see his fantasy suddenly real. Both supervisor and guide turned his direction. Fred drifted behind some taller sons. By this point in life he'd grown skilled at getting himself invisible.

That year the banquet was so rushed some fathers and sons ate with their coats on and zipped. A couple even kept a scarf round their neck. That year Mr. Connors choked on a mouthful of biscuit and chicken. No one knew what was happening until he turned red as a beet and rose from his chair flailing his arms like he was a marsh crane set to take off. His loud green sports coat was going one way and his paisley tie another. With a heavy back slap he hunched over the table and yakked up the globule like a cat with a hairball. He quick covered it with his napkin. The shrouded lump was near-about impossible to ignore, being just aside the centerpiece and all.

The following year there was no snow or weather warning whatsoever. Looking to the sky Fred adjusted his cap. Far as the eye could see was blue. Way too clear for even a faint hope of doom. A pale afternoon moon hung like a dog's eye in a lard white sky. Fred prayed for clouds to gather and shut his eyes tight. Nothing. The only sound was the steady December wind soughing round naked branches and the ruins of corn. His prayers didn't bring a blessed thing. Looking down from the unchanging sky he kicked a stone halfway to Hadley. Lack of divine intervention was so typical. He pulled his coat tighter and wondered if God was as powerless as he was.

Getting home from St. Elizabeth's his shirt, trousers, socks, underpants, and belt were draped over the back of different dining room chairs. His shoes were on the seat of the sixth. The disguise for the night had been chosen for him, but if he'd had the chance he'd have picked something similar. Not fitting in taught him awful quick that how something looks goes a long ways in how folks see it.

He grabbed the three dollars on the table. Attached was a note explaining where to go, when to be there, and instructions on getting downtown. Fred went to the kitchen and ate a handful of cereal out of the box. He shook his head at how little his parents knew or what they denied knowing. They never questioned him about the bottle caps, his Saturday morning doings, or anything really. He was free as a breeze to come and go. He wondered if it was on account of his being clever or their being trusting. Maybe it was because it didn't matter or maybe *he* didn't matter. Seeing the note irked him and made him feel grateful and sad all at once.

Fifteen minutes later he was dressed and seated halfway back on the #10 bus. Different folks rode the bus on weekdays. It was more respectable. The bushy-browed driver eyed him in the rearview mirror as Fred two-lined a cross on the filthy window. "Sacrifice," he thought before clearing it away with a swipe. All that he was being asked to do was endure. If he could thicken his shell and turn himself to stone it'd end eventually. He'd done it enough before. Martyrs were nothing but stone statues with pudding for souls. He would do or be whatever he had to. When he looked up the driver was punching a transfer and negotiating afternoon traffic.

Moving through the revolving door into the main lobby, Fred read four-fifteen on the oversized wall clock. The tour wasn't scheduled until five. He should've walked around a little, but knew if he did he'd end up in the alleys. That couldn't happen. He had to remain presentable. Bottle caps were out of his blood but those garbage-strewn back ways were still a bonafide sanctuary. He understood that world a lot more than this one. They were known, and Fred was desperate for something to make him feel secure.

Fred stood in the foyer and stared through the glass at his father's desk. A ghost of himself was reflected back in the pane. Rog looked up in a moment; his bifocals magnified the blankness of his expression. Seeing Fred he slapped on a salesman smile and came through the door adjusting his belt. He asked how school went and looked uneasy when Fred mumbled fine.

Rog eyed his watch, then his desk, and rocked once or twice on the balls of his feet. Fred heard the ticking of the wall clock. His skin grew hot and prickly and he finally said he'd like to explore the building. The creases along his father's forehead shallowed to mere lines. The Bayetteville Bell Building was a full ten stories, not including the radio antennae. Fred's excuse was believable enough. What boy didn't like tall buildings? He had to get away. Standing there made them both uneasy.

They agreed to meet in the same spot at five.

Fred rode the elevator to the top floor and roamed the halls. He dreamed of where he was going and why and remembered movies with similar hallways of elbows and straight-aways lined with offices and whatnot. Fred eased his steps and imagined psychos roaming the halls with candy bars and scalpels. It was an ideal crime scene. There'd be no witnesses. Only muffled voices were heard behind the frosted glass doors with stenciled names and titles and credentials of every letter and sort.

He looked out the north window. Psychos were down there too. From here people were no more than specks of color, moving like flies over a dumpster, crawling and buzzing, sucking for food, and hot to lay eggs in the rot. He looked to the river. It wound through town before disappearing round a bend near the railroad tracks. The surface was starting to crust. It shimmered like a curled strip of tin in the late afternoon sun. Fred had been staring for a half hour when the click of a closing office door snapped him back to where and who he was.

He took the elevator down to the lobby. The door whooshed open. Voices rushed in like flames with more chatter and heels and laughter revolving in from the sidewalk. He caught his father's eye. They drifted towards one another like sidling bits of debris. After a silent moment Rog asked Fred how school went—for the second time. This time he looked uneasy even before asking the question.

As the fathers and sons were herded into the conference room for *The History of Communication* film short, Rog asked Tom Dickens if Fred could tag along with him and his boy. Rog said he had to make sure things were okay at the restaurant. Tom nodded and straightened his glasses before giving Fred a quick look. Tom Dickens didn't think much of Fred. He thought him soft, not a boy's boy at all. Tyler, his son, was one of Fred's primary tormentors at school. Fred never told his father that sort of thing—or much of anything really. Half Fred's silence was due to embarrassment and the other half from not wanting to shatter any son fantasies Rog might still harbor.

Fred looked at Tyler. He was a lanky tough with a hawk nose and a pronounced Adam's apple. With his dark leadership qualities, Tyler was anything but soft. He had a cocky way about him, a bold entitlement to more than his fair share of things. He was a predator. Fred sensed Tyler planning something and saw him rub his hands like an insect's forelegs. Fred wasn't dumb. He drifted to the fringes of the group.

The tour group had the same guide as the year previous. She had a new hairdo and no static. Her sticker badge said Helene Green. Fred was thankful she didn't seem to remember him. When she smiled to greet the group he could see red on her teeth. He figured it best to seer clear of the fantasy. He didn't want any of his dark wishes coming true.

Fred stood and willed the world to pass through him, yet his biggest fears remained—too large to filter. There was the turn of Tyler's throat. Fred felt a prickling long the nape of his neck from those flat reptilian eyes. He went chicken-skinned a second before hearing his name whispered, then the word "faggot." He heard it move from son to son and the not-quite stifled laughter. Fred tried pretending he wasn't there. He tried becoming invisible. He tried turning to stone but his jellied insides were sliding to the carpet. He tried breathing deep and then he wished their heads would explode. He willed silverfish to burrow into their eyes and leeches to spill from those filthy mouths. He had a headache. Maybe it'd got turned around. Maybe the bugs were breeding in his head. He couldn't make it not matter because no matter how often it happened it still humiliated him. There was no getting used to it. He still heard the whispers. Fred pinched his eyes shut and swore to heaven and hell and on the sacred heart of Jesus he'd never be a martyr for his father again.

Mr. Dickens was oblivious to Tyler's behavior. He was rocking on his heels with his arms crossed. He was wearing a grin and making eyes at Miss Helene Green over the top of his glasses. She was no beauty queen, but the new hairdo was much more flattering.

At the tour's end Fred high-tailed it out the exit. He wanted to disappear down a side street and rush home but he couldn't. He headed towards the Golden Calf. He heard the snickering pack behind him. He heard someone say, "You belong at the Sand Bar along with the other pansies."

Taunts and kissing sounds rose from behind. Those fathers weren't about to censure their sons. They just kept smiling good old boy smiles and thanked God the outcast was someone else's kid. Fred wasn't sure who he hated more. He tried to burrow into the sound of his footfalls. One day he wouldn't run away. One day he would turn right around. He loped Elm on the yellow light and they were stuck behind. *Let them rot there, let them rot like the vile lot they are.* He broke into a full run and kept going until he was through the door of the Golden Calf.

His father leaned on his elbows at the bar. A fresh Manhattan and the end of another sweated before him. Rog only drank Manhattans. In his mind alcoholics drank anything. His father had. If he only drank Manhattans the worst he could be called was a New Yorker. That line was always good for a laugh and for putting to rest any unspoken accusations.

Barry, the bartender, opened two bottles of Old Style for a couple old timers. Fred recalled the blue dumpster behind the restaurant between a bent phone pole and a sawed-off sapling. Golden Calf garbage was supreme. A variety of international bottled beers made rummaging for caps in their trash especially exciting.

His father's broad guffaw pulled Fred back. He was sharing in-jokes with Barry and Vi, the hefty cocktail waitress. The pack of sons and fathers entered. Rog turned from the bar, then back. "So long Barry, so long Vi. Barry, let me know what you intend on using that damn thing for." The comment brought bawdy laughs from all three, causing more than a few of the tour group to pause while hanging their coats and look towards the bar.

The fathers and sons were led to some white-draped tables set up in a "U" and laid out with red bubble candles and sports-themed centerpieces. On each plate was a tented navy-blue napkin, crisp as a new bill. The Walshes were on an arm of the giant vowel.

"This one's on Vi," said a hooped and bobbed waitress named Dana. She set an amber glass before Rog with a flash of cleavage that caused several sons to nudge and snicker. Dana nodded towards the waitress station. Rog raised his drink to her and Vi replied with a swipe of a hand. She wore a black cocktail dress, black hose, and black pumps with an unflattering red vinyl belt about her ample waist. Watching her move through the dark bar area was like seeing a neon hoop floating about of its own accord. Vi grabbed a pen from one side of her beehive and swung her hips towards three businessmen at a four top. In seconds she was a flirtatious band of red hovering aside their table.

Rog took a gulp of his Manhattan and clanked his glass against his plate setting it back down. The noise roused Fred's headache. The room began to throb. Shards of sound poked at the pain behind his eyes. It was getting hot. He wanted water. He wanted to drink so much water that he'd wash himself away or drown himself and wake up on the other side of things. The night was already too long.

In a minute Penny and Dana took the drink orders and soon after the food emerged atop huge platters. Identical plates of roast beef, scalloped potatoes, string bean casserole, peas, and cornbread moved in clouds of steam down the arms of the "U." The Golden Calf was known throughout the tri-states for its plentiful servings of down-home food.

After dinner came the traditional father-introducing-son part of the evening. Fred felt the stabbing sharpen. He wondered why the folks in charge couldn't just let things be. Introductions began. The first and second fathers and sons stood with wide smiles. There was some banter, some laughter, and mutual backslaps. They passed. The first two were typical, or at least seemed to be, and were therefore tough to follow. The Walshes were third.

Rog was passable at first. When he stood his sloppiness went away, but as he started to speak his intoxication started to become more and more clear. He laughed too loosely and sawed his nose with a coat sleeve. There was some muttering. "I'm Rog Walsh and this is..." Rog looked at Fred and went silent. His head lifted as if on the scent of the right words. The buzz thickened like flies over trash. A good-natured laugh failed to cover the gap. The crowd stared. Fred reddened, though the rose bubble candles somewhat hid his coloring.

He whispered his name to his father who looked at him blankly. Fred could feel those eyes, the faces, the judgement. It was all crowding him. He caught sight of a red hoop was poised beyond the railing.

Fred rose too quick, meekly introduced himself, and bumped the table sitting down. His empty water glass tipped and his move to right it caused the table to shake again. The next father stood and pressure moved down the line. Tyler tilted back in his chair, crossed his insect arms, and smirked across the "U."

Fred felt himself fall further inside. He could see the outline of his body like chalk marks around a homicide. He was shrinking into his skin. His insides were seeping through a hole in the floor, dripping down to rain on the underside or seeping into the sewers.

After the introductions came the gift raffle. The prizes were a slingshot, a baseball, a football, and hockey tickets. Fred kept his eyes on his hands and his plate. His head pounded. He concentrated on not winning and won the football. He knew he'd won a split second before his name was called. With a weak bit of clapping he scurried to the podium. He dropped the football when it was handed to him, picked it up, and hurried on back to his seat with his eyes set to the carpet. It was too quick for him to think outside his panic. Sitting down he realized he should have said something or introduced himself or thanked someone. All the other winners at least said thanks. Even after he returned to his seat his father kept on clapping and said, "How about that." He slapped Fred on the back, and said it a second time. Fred stared at the linen, a chain of interlocked rings from his father's cock-tail looped across the cloth.

Next was a jovial speaker with a flattop and no neck to speak of who spoke too long about not much at all. His every pause was punctuated with a deep chuckle that rose like a bullfrog's croak. Fred wished he'd just shut up, but the speaker kept prattling on and looking about with a jack-o-lantern smile. Fred picked at the side of his thumb until it bled and pressed it to the tail of the white table spread. Now there was a mark of him.

Rog was in the men's room when he was thanked for setting things up for the night. It was the toastmaster's first levity-free comment. Applause was light. When people looked to the empty chair Fred's jaw tightened. The speaker thanked the Golden Calf, the cooks, and servers Dana and Penny. The thunderous applause and whistles for the staff caused some to turn and eye Rog's chair a second time. Finally the speaker wished everyone a goodnight. With a beaming "Drive careful" the father/son banquet was concluded. His final chuckle co-incided with Rog's lead-footed return.

There were quick farewells and a mundane mix-up involving identical powder blue ski vests. With a lipstick-smeared smile Vi adjusted the black velvet bow in her hair and told Fred he reminded her of his dad. Each Walsh looked at the other in confusion. The comment was followed with goodbyes.

Rog and Fred opened the heavy door of the Golden Calf. The street glistened. It was snowing. Fred shook his head. God had been too late to spare him this time. The Almighty was always offering too little too late and to top if off was asking an awful lot in return. They took a taxi home. Rog closed his eyes and smiled. He began to lightly hum. He figured his son had a great time on account of winning the football.

Born from Below

Fred liked the thought of starting life
anew and one spring day his imagining came true. Presumably it was by
accident, but it's hard being certain when a body's desire is so strong.

The new Fred began in the cool and wet, sudden as a bolt of lightning or the splitting of a cell. Drowning was the first he knew of life.
Sunshine rolled through the water, slithering down like a roused nest
of rattlers, reaching like arms to lift him into the land of the living. He
was the snake and the boy and the motion.

He saw himself from the outside a second before slipping into his
skin. Then he was inside, a scarecrow slowly falling—toes then thighs
grazing the mud bottom. The current was nothing more than the wet
heavy wind of the underside rushing by. All assaults on his flesh felt
as if he was wearing a thick coat. Once he realized it was his hide
the scrapes and scratches roused him, from exactly what he wasn't
certain.

Maybe he'd been perfectly dead or no more than a hollow-eyed bit
of debris looking up through the haze. Maybe he'd rolled along the
bottom like a rotten log from twenty miles upstream. Or maybe he'd
slid through the whiskered mouth of some great catfish lying down by
the dam. There were rumors of giant bottom feeders that settled in a
single spot and spent their entire lives letting the river flow through
them. Everything they needed to fatten and survive came with the
current. Some people were that way too.

Two fishermen rowing towards an outcropping of rocks near the
Kavanaugh Bridge saw him. Abe and Rolf stuck an oar beneath his
butt and heave-hoed till the paddle cracked and Fred broke the surface sputtering and coughing. He breathed. Maybe in that instant
his gills swelled and hollowed into lungs. Newborns are supposed to
do something similar. Rough hands grabbed his arms and raised him
from the water, limp as Jesus down from the cross. All he could see
was the blood.

Abe took a pack of Salems from his shirt pocket and tapped one
free. With his first exhalation he said, "What in tarnashun were you
doing riding your bike down that incline like a bronco buster?"

Fred remained silent and stared at Abe's squared fingers. His filthy nails were worn to shape.

Abe and Rolf looked down into the Frear and agreed his three-speed was lost. "Too bad," they added with a syncopated shake of heads. Abe said it looked downright comical when he hit that upright slab of limestone, flipped in the air, and landed in the river with his bike on top of him. "You couldn't do that again if you tried. Course it wouldn't have been so funny if you'd a drowned."

"No, that would've been no laughing matter," agreed Rolf who appeared little more than a sagging collection of spots and creases.

Fred stared at their raw-boned faces. They smelled of bait, tobacco, and gum disease. Nothing they said made sense. It was idle chatter in a foreign tongue.

Abe lifted the catch line from the water. "Ain't but two fish on the string."

"I could have sworn we got more."

"Well, ain't but two on there."

"Doesn't that beat all? I could have sworn we got more."

"Must've been yesterday."

"Must've been."

The flat blare of a lumber barge paused their ambling back and forth chatter. All three turned to watch it glide downstream.

Abe and Rolf didn't squawk about the blood running into their boat. The rivulets had already collected in a small pool on the bottom. Each time Fred looked down the drips from his nose came faster, so he put his head back and eyed the sky. It was a brilliant blue with a series of small stippled clouds. It looked like an ocean of fish floating belly-up...or the same school of fish alive from below.

Fred insisted he was fine as best he could around the blood trickling down his gullet. Abe flicked his cigarette into the waves, slapped a fly on the back of his neck, and tossed it into the blood on the bottom of the boat. "Don't want them fish getting filled up on free food," he laughed and knitted his knobby fingers over his belly.

Rolf nodded. "Sure don't want that."

Rowing to shore, Rolf lifted an oar and laughed about Fred's butt cracking it. Fred couldn't quite understand why it didn't make them angry, though Abe and Rolf did seem a difficult pair to upset. They had a life long fishermen sense of calm that came from always waiting for something bigger. Abe was picking something out of his yellowed teeth with a matchbook and staring off at nothing when the prow cut the bank behind Winslow's Appliances. After sitting a second Fred repeated that he was fine. Abe and Rolf shared a look and shrugged. Fred didn't think they'd actually believe him. When they did there was little more to say. Fred hopped from the boat and sank to his ankles in muck. He thanked them for saving his life and all.

Abe said, "It weren't nothing" and added that they would be much obliged if Fred would give them a shove. With a grunt and some dizziness Fred pushed them into the current. Abe and Rolf's good deed for the day was done. Maybe now their fishing luck would change. Abe and Rolf were superstitious that way.

A moment later Fred realized he was nowhere near fine and began to wander in dithering loops round the rutted gravel lot. He stumbled and righted himself and looked around for someplace to be. The flat sunlight made every surface rise in bold relief. The clarity confused him more. His eyes began to cloud. His vision narrowed. He heard himself begin to mumble that he'd been wounded. A radio was blaring from above the drugstore on the far side of the lot. Nothing made sense, but he recognized the song "Jolene." He stood below the window and lifted his head like a chick awaiting a worm. A moment later a redhead with uneven bangs stuck her head out the window and shook a rug. Balls of cat hair filled the air and floated down around him. Some went in his mouth and some in his eyes. Fred was back in the murk again. As soon as she saw him she stopped and leaned out the sill over ruddy elbows. "Hey, you okay?"

Still standing with his mouth open Fred said something more about being lost or maybe he was just thinking it. The woman cocked her head and Fred kept staring. He could tell she didn't hear him but assumed his appearance said more than he could explain.

She disappeared for a moment and the radio clicked off. When she returned she said to come up the back. A white cat jumped on the windowsill and did a pacing love-rub against her as she spoke. She tossed down a metallic rainbow of keys. It was the green one. The jingling bomb nearly cracked him on the skull.

Fred opened a dented screen door at the rear of the building. Inside the stink was overpowering. A fat and matted cocker spaniel lay snarling in a far corner of the cluttered porch. Nadine yelled from the top of the steps that Peanut had chronic diarrhea and apologized for the smell. Peanut seemed protective of her illness. Looking down Fred noticed his blood freckling the shit-streaked linoleum.

Nadine was husky with red puffy hands and eyes. Her bare feet were dainty and dirty. She wore a loose blue blouse. Denim cut-offs dug into her white dimpled thighs. Hearty seemed an apt description and was probably much kinder than how she was usually described.

Fred removed his muddy sneakers and banged them on the back stoop before climbing the stairs to her kitchen. It was cluttered with dirty dishes, hanging plants, and tabloids. It looked like she had either just moved in or had lived there a very long time. She raised her arms to the mess and said she was in the midst of cleaning. When her hands dropped they slapped her hips and left phantom prints that lingered before fading.

Her living room was piled high with science fiction paperbacks, magazines, empty cans, more plants, shoes, and pet toys. A chipped red toy box overflowing with dolls was wedged into one corner.

"I used to collect them," she said noticing Fred's gaze. "Now I just have them."

Heads and arms peeked over the rim as if the plastic and porcelain mob was froze in a pose of escape. Two walls were lined with cluttered shelves of souvenirs—bells, spoons, charms—the same shiny things that'd attract a crow.

Nadine pulled aside a striped sheet that doubled as the bathroom door, handed him a towel, and said he could wash up in there. With a muddled expression Fred ducked round the draping. Inside was padded and frilly and feminine. Most surfaces were covered with a canary yellow fur that matched the area rug. It was like stepping inside a tennis ball.

Fred looked into the bathroom mirror. It was worse than he figured. His face was a grotesque portrait from a gallery wall. A tooth felt loose. His nose hooked to one side and two ribbons of blood ran from his nostrils to a split lip. His eyes were red and unfocused and it seemed impossible that he was seeing the world through them. Red rivulets ran down his legs into the yellow towel splayed at his feet. Nadine must have realized it would be ruined, but having a dog with chronic diarrhea probably made her awful tolerant when it came to stains. Several faded brown marks scarred the rug.

Fred found it odd that Nadine hadn't been more unnerved by his appearance. Abe and Rolf didn't think much of it either. His wounds brought little concern. Didn't anyone see how beaten he was? He looked back into the mirror. He was a monster. How could they be blind to the horror there? A gouge had removed much of one cheek. If he moved his tongue just so he could see the tip right through the webbed pink tissue. Scrapes and lacerations lined what remained. Looking down at his bleeding legs, he lost himself in the current. Following the flow made it feel like he was rising, coming from the carnage like a bird straightening to soar. Nadine startled him when she rapped on the doorframe and asked if he was doing okay.

When he said "Yeah" she pulled aside the sheet and handed him a pair of jeans and a Cardinals t-shirt. She wanted to throw his things in her compact washer/dryer. Stripping quickly he handed her the bundle along with the bloody towel. She said hot water would be best, otherwise the river stench would linger on the fabric.

Sunlight streamed through the frosted glass of the bathroom window. Standing naked and bloody in the diffused glow he looked like a called-upon saint. He'd suffered it all for some unknown God. He wasn't sure why the sight made him cry, but there was something there. His tears mixed with the blood. In a moment he wiped them away with an arm. When he turned back to the mirror his injuries had disappeared except for a trickle of blood coming from his mouth. He was nothing he'd thought he was. He wondered if he'd been shown mercy or if he'd been shown the truth. The carnage had been reduced to a bitten lip. He wiped it away with a bit of toilet paper before taking a shower.

When he eventually emerged from the bathroom Nadine was darting about trying to make the place presentable, but with so much clutter there wasn't much she could do beyond rearranging and cramming things into closets and drawers. Though she was doing an admirable job, Fred offered half-hearted assistance. He was relieved when she said everything was under control. He pushed aside some old magazines and sat down in an overstuffed armchair. Comet, her cat, began rubbing against the side of his hand. Nadine smiled and said Comet didn't get along with just anyone, unless she was in heat.

It was Nadine's free day and she was getting things ready for a guy named Stash. He was coming over later. She said they had already been on two dates in a way that made Fred think she was trying to justify the fuss rather than fill him in on details. "He won't be another Tyson, I can tell you that much." She paused for a moment and looked at Fred, half expecting a comment. He was still in a daze. She'd already made the meatloaf. It only needed to go in the oven. The potatoes and carrots had been washed and peeled. An orange Jell-O seashell with suspended mini-marshmallows was setting in the refrigerator. She shot a falling fog of air freshener about the kitchen and cursed Peanut's diarrhea. She handed Fred a root beer and began to vacuum.

A photo on her mantle was familiar. Fred rose from the chair for a closer look. From the depths of his haze something finally took form. It was a picture of a boy in his class. He recognized the jutting chin, the narrowed eyes, and the scowl. The photo went a long way in capturing the boy's contempt for the world.

Nadine nodded towards the picture and shouted over the Hoover. "You should meet my cousin Delbert; he's about your age. Lives just catty-corner from here."

Fred nodded and sipped his soda.

By the time she finished piling paperbacks and magazines in the closet Fred's clothes were dry. Soon after changing he said he'd better get going. Nadine looked relieved. She still had a lot to do before Stash arrived. She paused at the hall mirror. Lifting her hair up and the letting it down she asked Fred how she should wear it. Seeing his blank expression she shook her head and said never mind. "Guys never care." She scribbled her phone number on a Three Musketeers wrapper and told him to give her a ring and let her know he got home all right. She handed him two garbage bags to take down to the dumpster on his way out.

His feet carried him home, leading him down side streets and through a vacant lot until he reached Polk. His shadow stretched before him like a ghost he was trailing. He was doing nothing more than flowing with the current. Once the house came into view he recognized it and everything about its design. No room or door, step or cranny was a mystery. It was as though the sets had been used for a previous life. The only mystery was the life he'd lived there and that changed soon enough. Once there the part came to him naturally. He was playing a role. Whatever person or part of himself was here before must have been lost along with his bike.

Movies remained as his primary memories. At least he thought it was movies that flashed like lightning in his mind, sometimes clear and sometimes flecked with broadcast snow. Fred wondered if the fall had flattened him or thrown him from his depth or from a film. There was no way of telling. It wasn't the sort of thing he could ask. Even if he had someone to confide in he had no idea who that person might be.

Assuming Fred's identity was simple as wearing the costume and filling his skin. It was slipping on his hands like gloves and wearing his head like a hood. It was easier to act like Fred than be him. He imagined tackling Fred's everyday life as anything but a role would be unpleasant and mundane. A victim who merited no sympathy was a thankless part.

Fitting into his new universe was essential. Discovery was his biggest fear, accompanied by thoughts of his head beneath a surgeon's tent. A thin line traced the scalpel across the stalks of his brain. He wondered if he could be removed by slicing off a tiny piece and fretted that he was nothing more than a thorn or shard of glass stuck in just the right spot. The thought of losing this chance at life was nothing he wanted to consider. He didn't want to return to that black pool of possibility. He had to keep reminding himself that the old Fred was dead and gone. It was his turn now. He was born of the river, filled his lungs, and walked on land. Now he would survive. It was that simple.

In time he began to realize Fred was more dormant than deceased. Memories of the past began to return in bits and chunks. He'd be eating and suddenly a birthday party would be recalled. The clink of ice in a glass brought to mind his father's favorite bar. The medicine chest brought him eye to eye with his mother's medical woes. Opening a soda pop, the metal top bounced upon the counter and he remembered his cap collection floating one by one down the creek. He knew that it'd all happened to him but at the same time knew he was someone different now. *I am him but I am more me.* The past seemed part of some half-forgotten dream.

After the first week his fear of being discovered was all but gone. No one suspected a thing, though truth be told they weren't paying much attention. An alien ate dinner, sat on the toilet, climbed the stairs, watched endless TV, and masturbated under the same roof and no one knew. A stranger pulsed in this flesh and no one suspected. No one. He found it difficult to understand until he realized that everyone was busy trying to blend in themselves, especially the parents.

The father was small and wiry and the mother was a brickish square. Both were nervous types with graying brown hair and brownish gray skin. Each was weakened by work in a hardened way. They sat watching television with drinks in hand and eyes that grew heavier as the news approached. That was last call for alcohol. The weather forecast was the typical end of the day. Knowing a bit of what tomorrow would bring gave their skittish minds something to latch onto.

Fred said nothing about the fishermen or Nadine. He didn't want to arouse suspicion by being too forthcoming or honest. In a few days he told them his bicycle had been stolen. It explained the loss. His mother sighed and closely eyed a mole in the crook of her arm. The TV seemed unnaturally loud in the drawn-out pause. Fred was secretly comforted by his father's exasperated comment of "That is so like you."

That night he dreamt his bike was buried deep in river silt and that he was still pinned beneath it. It was cold below the sand and grit. Bottle caps lodged in his eyes. Crawfish climbed in his mouth and curled in his ears. For a frightening moment, he was unable to breathe and rose to the light. He awoke gasping and chilled and stared out his bedroom window until dawn. He didn't want to go back there. Not ever.

School seemed a strange magic of another sort. Passing under the carved stone arch of St. Elizabeth's something awoke inside that enabled him to perform the required work. It wasn't necessarily familiar, but it was known. It was as though all he needed was held in his hand or in the pencil rather than his mind. It started as a sort of magic, but he caught on quick.

When it came time for his semester evaluation Sister Carlotta, his pulpy-faced homeroom teacher, said she was pleased with his academic progress. She tugged at the reddened ridge where the wimple dug into her chin. "You're a new boy," she said with a vaguely inspiring but mostly dismissive curl of her lips. Since any change in Fred was considered an improvement the new Fred was never questioned. Puberty was an easy time to become someone different. Change was expected. Old selves were dying right and left in those hallways.

Schoolwork wasn't any sort of real challenge aside from keeping his mind on the lessons. Delbert was in his freshman class. Fred used to sit and stare and think about Nadine's cluttered living room. He recalled how Del's face had surfaced from that sea of framed photos on the mantle. That was his first connection from the old world to the new.

Del frequently caught him staring, but that wasn't hard to do. He only had to turn around. He was visibly hostile. He sneered in Fred's direction. Del was an outsider too, a unique discipline problem since even the other students disliked him. There was no debating his no account status. He was always getting into brawls even though he wasn't much of a fighter. The world was his enemy but he brought most of it on himself. Even relaxed his hands were balled into fists. Fred wondered if he slept that way too and if he scowled in his dreams all the while.

The bony curve of Del's back made Fred imagine him with his shirt off. Del was his first crush, but Fred saw it as more. The moment he saw Del's picture at Nadine's, Fred felt their lives were destined to intertwine. Seeing Del in the flesh, Fred was certain. He was born or reborn or emerged for this. He knew it as sure as he'd recognized the sky. Del's outside was Fred's inside and vice versa. They were the same person in a different world, outsiders on opposite banks of the mainstream, flip sides of the earth, the underside to Del's above. To Fred's way of thinking each was what the other needed to balance and survive.

The taunts and snickers of others didn't bother Fred so much anymore. What they thought didn't amount to a hill of beans. Those idiots only knew the half of things. Del was his sole measure of acceptance. All else was background noise.

Each day Fred sat at his desk and waited for the antics to begin. Whenever Del sassed or tossed paper wads or made barnyard noises behind the Sisters' back it seemed he was performing just for him. Fred always approved. When it came to Del, he was a rapt fan and devotee.

When Del was absent or unusually quiet Fred, cut class. Instead of returning after lunchtime, he tailed his shadow across the dandelion-splattered green to the cathedral. St. Elizabeth's Church rose like a bleached stone fist raised to heaven. It sent a sharp and booming message that God was enduring, intimidating, and a whole lot bigger. "Majesty amidst mediocrity" was how he overhead a couple of tittering priests refer to it in the vestibule one afternoon. The clergy and nuns who were aware of his skipping class cast a blind eye on his behavior. The Lord was a higher priority.

But Fred's fascination wasn't with God or Jesus or anything rooted in scripture. To him St. Elizabeth's was the womb to another world. It was neutral territory. Candles glowed like sunlight through the Frear and made him remember those first moments of life. Inside those walls everyday sounds rumbled. Stained glass Stations of the Cross windows depicted a brutal scenario. Painted statues with exposed hearts and open wounds looked on with liquid eyes of agony and bliss. He understood the connection. The cathedral freed up his mind. He imagined phantoms circling the vaulted ceiling and lurking in the shadowy recesses with the rot and stink of the grave draped upon them. This was more his world than anything out there.

The blessed perversity of it all and the fine line betwixt the grotesque and the divine came to him as a deeper truth. All that death and suffering carried his thoughts to strange new places. If he knelt too long or allowed his mind to float too far he feared he might not be able to return. Maybe the current would carry him away. Perhaps the old Fred was one of those circling phantoms waiting on a chance to swoop down and reclaim his flesh and his life. Fred worried that if he wasn't careful he'd be ousted and relegated to watching from the wings again. That was no way to be.

Fear was no longer an issue involving what anyone else might do to him. Fear was now a dread of returning to nothing, fading like radio reception beyond range of the broadcast tower...or too near a stronger signal. Whenever Fred felt his borders begin to blur he remembered the framed photo of Delbert and it reset that clear sense of himself. He'd won. He'd proven the stronger and more deserving. The other Fred would have never survived. Del gave him the focus to remain a resident of this flesh. And that was worth any cost or hardship.

Depot Grazing

CODY FINE WAS WALKING bOW-legged
when he hopped off the Greyhound bus in Bayetteville. He mopped
his forehead and rolled his neck one way and then the other. His legs
were stiff from being cramped, his back was stiff from being curled
towards the window, and his crotch was just plain stiff. The ride had
lasted ten hours already and it was but halfway over. It was a thrill to
see such a big part of the country, even though much of it didn't seem
all that noteworthy. From the tinted bus window this great nation appeared to be in most ways a hodge-podge of highways, cornfields, and
peeling billboards.

At twenty-one, Cody was ready for some serious living. He'd spent
his entire life in Cane Springs and had been out of the county on only
four occasions. This was the first time his wristwatch had ever needed
adjusting. He got a charge out of that.

Nothing important was left for him back home and his past seemed
like something it would be awful easy to forget. Cody was from a large
family that was neither rich nor close. The Fines resided in a good-
sized farmhouse that was still never quite big enough. Privacy was an
unfamiliar concept. Leaving home was something he could do for the
common good as well as his own. Besides, twenty-one was a little old
to still be living under his daddy's roof and rule.

When he left, he didn't mention he was leaving for good. He'd do
that later by phone. It wasn't a hard decision. He could see the whole
of his future if he remained and it was nothing he wanted his life to be.
He hungered for something more, something different. Staying where
he was just because it was what he knew and where he happened to
come onto this earth was a sorry excuse that too many took for truth.
Life was too important for that brand of passive compromise.

Living there hadn't always been so mundane. When Frank was
around, living there had brought him everything he wanted. Cane
Springs had been paradise. It was odd to even imagine it as the same
place. Then Frank's dad lost his municipal job and harbored a grudge
against the entire state. He decided to head north and the next month
found a job at a plastics plant outside of Minneapolis. When the Lend-

ers packed their belongings and moved last summer Frank swore he'd write, but that promise was too few letters ago. Cody feared life with his best pal was fading into nothing more than some fond memories and a few photos. Then Frank called and invited him for a visit. The excitement it ignited made Cody aware of how numb and hollow he'd been feeling. His life had become eating, sleeping, working, and picayune doings. He excitedly told Frank he'd be there soon as he took care of a few things. That didn't amount to much. Instead of taking vacation time at the creamery he gave notice, and then only stayed for one of his two weeks. It wasn't like he owed them anything.

Cody smiled. Now he was en route to see Frank again. In a few hours they'd be tipping back longnecks and remembering those crazy days at Taft...and their days were triflings compared to the nights. Those were the times Cody found himself missing most of all.

He and Frank had been sex buddies, diddling and exploring since just prior to Cody's thirteenth birthday. At first they manipulated one another with soap and water, but that stung like mad. Hand lotion was better but it had such a distinct smell that he felt marked afterwards. He still didn't think the feeling could be beat so it was a genuine revelation when they discovered blow-jobs. In no time they'd become adept at it. At the time of Frank's departure they'd just been getting mighty good at butt fucking. Most every night they would steal away to the outskirts of town and park near a bottle-green backwater before going at it in the cab of Frank's pick-up. The smells and sensations came back to him. Cody sighed with the memory. It was something worth missing.

He was anxious for them to get together like that again. It blanketed all his thoughts and memories of Frank. He hoped Frank felt the same and that was why he'd called. He hadn't come right out and said so over the phone, but Frank wasn't the sort who would. They never really talked about doing it even when it was almost all they were doing.

If things went smooth with Frank, Cody resolved to settle there. He'd already yanked up his roots for the most part. Maybe he and Frank could find a place together. Things could be like they were, only better. He wanted it real bad, but Cody was hesitant to seriously think it might come to pass. Hope could sting like a scorpion. It was best kept at a safe distance.

His connecting bus to St. Paul was still a good four hours away. He walked up to the ticket booth to double-check the departure time. The lemur-eyed fellow at the counter told him it was running late. Cody looked at the clock and back at the man. He looked like a bow-tied housefly with one eye cocked for the swatter. Fingerprints riddled his bifocals and obsidian hair fanned from either nostril.

Cody sighed in frustration and looked round the dingy box of a room. Silver and faded green vending machines lined one wall, pinball machines and a bank of telephones were spread along another. He sat down in an orange plastic chair and fed a quarter into the attached television. He'd never seen such a contrivance, not clamped onto a chair anyway. He watched some cartoons before moving to an end seat where he had the added luxury of stretching his legs. The chairs and benches stood in rows like pews only facing a clock instead of a cross. Cody grinned to think that what you worship all depends on where you are.

He opened his Ludlum novel and closed it again after a couple of pages. His eyes ached. His Uncle Luke, a farm machinery salesman, always said traveling was hell on the eyes. Of course Lucas Fine said a lot of things, plenty of them bordering on lunacy. He maintained that after driving through Utah in the early fifties his vision worsened something considerable. He would tell anyone within earshot it was on account of top secret government testing in the area and that he was starting a sizeable lawsuit just as soon as "the plentitude of evidence was collected." Uncle Lucas loved talking conspiracy and sure loved his Ludlum. Cody raked his hair back and thought about Uncle Lucas' recent stroke. Now Lucas wore diapers and didn't even recognize himself when he looked in the mirror. Any conspiracy or cover-up aimed at keeping him quiet couldn't have done a better job.

Cody shifted on the bench and eyed the clock. Thirty-five minutes had passed. Anticipation had a way of making time move like molasses. Standing with an exhausted yawn, he curled his fists behind his head causing his t-shirt to hike up his belly. A stitch of dark brown hair ran from his navel to the lip of his jeans. He rubbed along the line with an uncurling fist and walked towards the lavatory.

Directly inside was a sunburned man longside a silver standing ashtray. He had acne scars, bloodshot eyes, and a graying mustache shaped like a down-turned staple. His lips were as fleshy and red. Tugging the pouch of his faded jeans he offered a holding stare and watched Cody pass. He let out a low whistle and uttered "Mmm-mmm" in a tacky fashion. The comment was justified. Cody's ass was a high, tight, and round bit of blue-jeaned perfection. That kind of behind inspired grinding fantasies.

Cody looked back over his shoulder with gathered brows. The man hooked a thumb in his hip pocket and splayed his fingers in a web towards his crotch. Rounding the corner of the L-shaped room, Cody was hit by a crude combination of urine, cigarettes, and mildew. The stench was so potent it seemed a blast of heat. It wasn't enough to deter him. Any pisser had to be an improvement over that bouncing broom closet on-board the bus.

He rolled his shoulders and lolled his neck and tried to relax. The faded white tile was splattered with green blotches and the rusted partitions were riddled with graffiti. Cody stared at the huge detailed rendering of a spurting cock gouged in the metal. He imagined the sound at its creation and cringed. Below the drawing was a hole with irregular edges like a sort of primitive window or doorway. He squinted. There was movement inside.

Cody moved his wallet to a front pocket and stepped before the second urinal. He heard the raspy flare of a match—then the smell of sulphur. The man from the hallway had moved. He was now leaning against the far wall by the towel dispenser. He was studying him. He took a drag off his cigarette and slowly rubbed the legs of his mustache. Smoke bowled from his nostrils as he raised a boot back against the tile. Cody turned back to the dingy squares above the hanging trough. A finger was hooked in the stall hole.

Despite the tension held in that dank air Cody felt his dick begin to stir when he looped the elastic band of his underpants below his balls. The odor of his cramped crotch rose and blended with the men's room stench. At eye-level "Show It Hard" was scrawled this way and that across the tile grout like a random and repeated hieroglyph or whispered command.

"Hey kid, let me suck your cock."

Cody felt the hair on his arms rise. He turned towards the hole. Now two fingers were hooked there. Through the opening he could see the faint outline of moving lips. A window. A doorway into another world. "Come on, stick it through. Let me suck it. Stick it through and let me have my way with that sweet thing. Nobody'll be the wiser."

A scrape broke the spell of that coaxing voice. The man beside the towel dispenser slid a boot down the wall and snubbed his cigarette on his boot sole. His heels clicked as he crossed the room. He unzipped along the way, exposing himself even before reaching the pisser to Cody's right. Cody kept his eyes averted but could feel the man staring. His breathing grew shallow, and even shallower until it seemed the tension was preventing him from breathing at all. After a silent moment or so the stranger reached down and wrapped a hand around Cody's rising cock and began stroking it base to tip.

"Nice nuts kid," he muttered into Cody's ear while holding his balls in a cluster. When he paused in his manipulations Cody's cock was lurching skyward like a rocket at ten seconds and counting. The man then began to milk his own uncircumcised dick.

The raspy-edged voice through the hole maintained a steady stream of filth. "Come on, look how your cock is crying for it. Let me work that thing. Look how it's ready. Stick it through and it'll feel better than you could imagine. There's another side to things. Come on..."

Blood throbbed in Cody's head and his cock. His heart pounded, feeling two sizes larger than his sizeable chest. Sporadic muscles in his body began to twitch. The guy beside him wheezed and moaned as he rolled the thin moistened hood over the head of his dick. Cody heard nothing but whispering, heavy breathing, and the steady beating of meat. All sound was thickened and enhanced in that cavernous room.

A timed flush put all activity on hold until the gurgling whistle rose and faded.

The man at the urinal nodded towards Cody. "Looks as if you could use some relief. He's real good. Stick it on through. I'll keep an eye to the door for you. The layout of this place makes it near-about impossible to get caught with someone watching."

Cody looked back towards the hole before looking down at himself.

"Let me make you feel fine."

"Go on," urged the man beside him, lifting his chin towards the stall.

Cody thought he shouldn't be doing this. It wasn't smart and it wasn't right and he didn't know these folks from Adam, but thinking didn't have a lot to do with it. He turned from the urinal and followed his bobbing cock to the partition. A doorway. A window. He eased the head of it on through and into some moist and magical place. He felt a bit of bristle around the base, a kissing along the underside, a fluttering of lips, and then a tongue smooth as silk lapping the length of him. In seconds his pecker was dripping spit. It felt so fine Cody had trouble controlling himself. He slammed into that sweet suction again and again. Hitting the metal stall with his hips made the sensations on his dick feel even more electric. A hand ran the length of his business, bobbing in rhythm with his mouth. Cody could all but see the pearly gates…a doorway into another world.

The man watching the door moved towards him with those clicking boots. "Feels good, don't it?" Cody flinched to hear his whispers so near. He'd been distracted. The mustached man bent close. The lips were touching his ear now. "That's it boy, be a saint and feed the hungry—give it to the needy." Cody could smell beer and cigarettes on the man's breath.

Calloused fingers reached up and under Cody's t-shirt and commenced to tugging on his nipples. The combined sensations caused him to thrash. Twisting from the fingers he slammed harder into the partition, driving himself further into that heaven-sent mouth.

"Oh yeah, come on. I can tell you're getting set, those balls are lifting in their sac." The man ran a hand across Cody's ass as it clenched with every thrust.

Cody batted his hand away. "Leave my ass alone."

The man spit on his fingertips, reached between Cody's thighs, and caught his nuts in his fingers. He pulled them with a sure grip and rubbed with the rough caress of a workingman's palm.

Cody hooked his hands over the partition top and set his legs wide, looking like an X of flesh pegged into a hole. He fit there. He'd become part and piece of the place. If anyone were to come through that door right now there'd be nothing he could do. Nothing. The risk added to the moment. He couldn't stop, not now. He was stuck for the long haul which wouldn't be long at all. It felt so good, and still the sucking and the whispers and the hungry hands continued.

With one hand holding his nuts, another on his abdomen, and his torso flat to the stall, Cody's body might've been pinioned, but his mind was flying. He imagined a wild creature that fed off sperm living in that world through the hole. It wouldn't stop one drop shy of its life-nourishment. He was trapped into giving up his seed. His dick was the only possible point of release. He rose on his toes, brought his legs together, clenched his thighs, and about snapped the wrist between them.

His back arched like a cobra and his ass quivered. He threw his head back and then forward hitting it against the partition. His cock expanded. He felt the ridge between crown and shaft widen as that tongue lapped again and again. The head was everything. Cold metal pressed against his chest, flattening his nipples to the scratched steel. A moan wiggled from deep inside along with a choice string of cuss words. His legs twitched and rolled and spasmed. He fought to hush his yelling but heard the moans rise from his throat as he felt himself exploding and bucking the metal partition...freedom, freedom, freedom.

Layover

It was the first time Leo ever heard
Sister gag which was saying something since his throat was as big
around as a sewer pipe and he was mighty seasoned at relaxing those
particular muscles.

Sister was the first born, sissified, and hell-raising son of a back-
woods preacher. Christian Sr. spoke in tongues, drank poison, handled
serpents, and about every other part of the whole carnival of God
shebang. The name Sister Christian, or just Sister, was a damn perfect
fit. That scrawny tramp never missed a Sunday of churchgoing. No
matter what, who, or just how down and dirty he let himself be on
Saturday night he'd stagger on into nine a.m. services, stinking up the
place with yesterday's sins. Heaven protect St. Elizabeth's! Leo always
ribbed him that one day he was apt to forget himself and whittle a
glory hole into the confessional wall or call for a cocktail at the communion rail. Sister always laughed to think what his daddy would say
if he got wind his son turned Catholic. A papist in the fold! Sister suspected Christian Sr. would sooner find out he was a cocksucker.

The morning Cody came to town Sister and Leo were at the depot
doing flips. That's what they liked to call it. Since they knew every
cop in the county, one of them planted hisself inside the men's room
door and was ready to fake a sneeze if the sheriff or one of his depu-
ties came nosing about. Meanwhile the other one squatted in wait for
some action to stroll in from Nashville or St. Louis or Little Rock.
They weren't particular as to where. It was the what that they were
after.

After the one on the shitter got some they'd switch. It went back
and forth...back and forth...and back and forth. Some days they'd be
holed up in there for hours on end. It was busier than the rest stop up
at Devil's Point and offered a greater variety of meat on the menu. By
day's end they always were pleasured to have some ribald tales to tell.

Sister had done the fretting queen at the ticket counter a few weeks
back, so now the poor thing stood with his eyes the size of coffee
saucers whenever they were about. Little Nell of the Time Tables was
afraid to let on that he knew what was happening. He was petrified

47

Sister and Leo were going to announce to the world that he fancied weenie so he pretended not to notice that they stayed in there for hours on end and never took a bus. Sister said Nell was a nasty little number once he cut loose. To Leo that seemed hard to imagine and even harder to stomach. That's what made a glory hole such a great equalizer. Sex wasn't about the who but rather the what. It was dick worship plain and simple! It made sex with most anyone possible.

The tearoom was a hopping place. Lots of men are horny after a lengthy bus ride. All that vibrating was a likely cause. It's the same as trucker balls. A layover and a needy pecker is a promising combo for any aspiring dick smoker. "Time to kill and jism to spill," was how Sister referred to it. Leo had to agree. They were a traveler's convenience, just like the automatic shoe buffers, only their spit shine was a courtesy service. It wasn't coins that went in the slot and the deposit wasn't monetary.

Cody came strutting in that day with half a hard-on tucked against a thigh and a four-hour layover. Leo was doing the door when he bounced on through, a strapping strawberry blond with a jiggling basket—so hot, so cute, so *mmm*. He was fuzzy-eyed and of haphazard appearance that looked to be the result of a long bus ride. Even all knotty-headed he was the sort to pull Leo's crank and line up all the cherries. Watching that denimed high-water booty round the corner Leo was drooling so much his cigarette filter got soggy.

Though he took great pride in it, Leo's word had its limits, and Cody was pushing it right on up to the line. Leo was tempted to break the sacred flipping pact, smuggle him back to his place over the bar, and do him two ways to Sunday. Truth speaking, his word wasn't stopping him so much as that gold toothed semen pump hunkered down in the first stall. Sister wasn't too Christian when it came to forgiveness, especially when that had to do with sex. Cody may have been prime stock, but he still wasn't worth the likely aftermath. Our Lady of Perpetual Grudges sometimes took an incarnation or two to get over things. Taking off with Cody would be construed as an underhanded act of tearoom betrayal and an out and out declaration of war.

One thing was for damn sure; if Leo wasn't going to do this stud he sure as hell intended on watching him get done. After a minute or so he tailed him into the main bathroom. Half the lights were either out or flickering. Mildew made the place appear even darker. The scummy walls were never cleaned and the floor probably got mopped once every new moon. No sound was coming from the lobby, not even the crackle of overhead speakers. Leo lit a cigarette and leaned against the wall.

Cody stood in front of the urinal and made like he was cracking his neck, but it was clear he was turning his head to sly eye the graffiti and that glory hole. He stared at the pecker etching by Dick the Clapper.

That big-veined monster Dick drew was a beaut, complete with a full pair of low-hangers. Carved jism was fanned across the stall wall. That drawing alone was enough to stir many a man's juices, even jaded bits of goods like Leo and Sister. It was working wonders on Cody. Dick left quite a few raunchy masterpieces at tearoom galleries in the area.

The atmosphere was seducing the kid and they knew how he felt. Leo tugged at his crotch and watched as that urge swelled right up and over any bit of upbringing, religion, resolve, or sense of right and wrong. Once those primal fires commence to burning a tearoom becomes a temple. It's as pure and as filthy as one place can be. That was Sister's philosophy. Leo never would've thought to put it that way.

At first Cody fought the yearning, but once it gets a grip on you, there's only one way to shake a spell of horniness. It demands a sacrifice. Following that brief bit of resistance, Cody let go of his hesitation and shoved it on through the hole. And that pecker was a mighty special delivery!

In no time Cody was cussing a blue streak. You could've painted Leo red and called him a wagon! Cody didn't seem the blue language type, but men are full of surprises once they get going. Sex can turn a man into something else altogether. All men have another side and sex is a real common doorway to getting there. More than a cock starts to rising when that all takes over.

In three minutes Cody was flat to the stall and Sister was taking holy communion. Sister was a snake handler of a different kind. Leo was leaning into Cody from behind, tugging his nuts and just taking in that glorious backside—the kind of butt you could crack an egg on. All in all Leo didn't do much, but he still considered it the hottest three-way he'd had at the bus station in months.

When Sister stopped gagging Leo all but dragged his greedy ass on off that stool. Seconds are better than nothing, and with the right stud sometimes it's better. It isn't quite so frantic as the first. Leo licked what spunk Sister hadn't swallowed from around Cody's crotch and tongued the length of his dick. By the time he'd done that Cody's piece was spit slick he was set to go again. Youthful stamina is a blessed thing. It's even better in pretty packages and God Almighty that boy was one savory piece of eye candy. Leo wrapped my fist around the base of his cock and deep-throated him before moving his hand with his mouth. Cody let out a yelp and slammed his body against the stall, all but knocking bolts from the wall.

Leo gave him his best, which was guaranteed to have you tiptoed and howling *hallelujah* in seconds. When Leo spoke of it in those terms he wasn't bragging, but just relaying on a fact. Once he had their cock in his mouth Leo could get most anyone off in three minutes. Speed is a handy skill for the tearoom connoisseur. Most want to get in, get off, and get going. It's safest that way.

Cody's second load took but two minutes. He let loose with a good dose of tangy juice in the same swearing and bucking frenzy as before. When the big moment passed Leo milked him until his breathing evened and he took a step back from the hole.

He said, "Whew... Shit..." and shook his head before bending over the sink to splash some water on his face. Sister and Leo just stood there watching and waiting for heaven knows what. They were still in awe. Then something happened which almost never does in those situations. Neither Leo nor Sister or even Cody quite recalled the particulars, but the three of them began talking. Normal speaking voices sounded so odd in there.

Cody bummed a cigarette—that surprised Leo and Sister. He didn't seem the smoking type. That boy was a bundle of surprises. They all stood around the ashtray sharing a smoke and getting on like respectable folks at afternoon tea.

Sister asked where he was going and some other things that were none of his business. Sister wasn't being tacky about it. Not that one. He could charm a field mouse out of a snake's belly if a situation called for it. Cody said he was waiting for an eleven o'clock connection to the Quad Cities, then on to Minneapolis. He was coming all the way from Cane Springs.

"I'm a Georgia boy too! I thought that accent sounded like home," laughed Leo. They shook hands, which seemed strangely formal what with his jism still sloshing around in Leo's belly. But this was a social thing and the social side and elemental side were as different as night and day.

Sister rolled his eyes and suggested they all head out for a drink. "The bus station bathroom isn't the best place for socializing," he said all la-de-dah. Cody pillowed out his sweaty t-shirt and said it was only eight in the morning. Sister said it was a decent hour in Rome. "The Pope is probably having himself a goblet of Boone's Farm right now!"

It took some added coaxing, but they finally cajoled Cody into joining them for a few.

The Sand Bar didn't open until four, so Leo unlocked the door and they all went in for a private cocktail. By that time they knew Cody was twenty-one, happy to be away from home, and eager to see some guy in Minneapolis. From what he said and the way he said it they gathered this Frank fellow was his lover, his ex, or a full-bodied crush. He didn't say and Leo didn't pry, mostly because he figured Sister would do the asking. Not that any explanation was really necessary. When Cody began talking about that Frank fellow he alternately blushed or got misty-eyed. He was in love all right, whether he was wise to the fact or not.

"Make him treat you right honey," was Sister's sole comment. It was unusually terse coming from him. Sister was known for tossing more than a few pennies when it came to giving his two cents worth.

Who's to say? Maybe the flush in Cody's cheeks was from the margaritas. He sure loved those Sand Bar specials. He sucked down the first two like a lush in training and then asked how to make them. He was a bit tipsy, but caught on quick and sure looked great concocting a cocktail. Sister caught Leo's eye and cocked a brow when Cody said his last name was Fine. It was just so all out fitting.

With a giggle, Cody poured three more. "Holy Toledo, this is a blast."

The whole thing struck Leo and Sister as downright comical, to be hearing those homespun sayings from the same mouth that was cussing a blue streak not an hour before. "Holy Toledo?"

Sister fanned a hand across his chest like Theda Bara. "There's nothing holy there, or in all of Ohio as far as I know." Leo just shook his head. Sister had a sassy comeback for most everything.

Cody staggered down the hall to take a piss before they all had the first official taste of his margaritas. As the men's room door creaked closed Sister took a drag off his smoke and told Leo to hire him. He said it just like that! He croaked it like an order, and then blew three ideal smoke rings each inside the other.

"What?"

"I said hire him."

"I heard you...that wasn't the meaning of my 'What?'"

"Leo, he'll be gangbusters for business and you know it."

"But I..."

"Dammit, Leo, don't be an oaf. He's charming, he seems honest, and he's gorgeous. Which of those three qualities does Ben-Hur have? Not a one! Ben has nothing going for him except the fact that he's Jack-O's boyfriend, and that's sure nothing to puff out your chest about. You've been waiting for someone to replace his lazy ass anyway. Ask the kid."

"A beanbag chair could replace Ben-Wah."

"So hire a brick shithouse."

Leo laughed and said okay he'd ask and swiveled a bit on his stool. In truth Leo was a mite irked. This was his place after all. Sometimes Sister just crossed the line with being so bossy but there was no talking to him about it. That was just Sister's way.

"Besides, with you both being from Georgia you could do Scarlett drag together."

"Shut up already, I said I'd say something...besides, Mr. Burt Reynolds also happens to be from the state of Georgia."

Sister rolled his eyes. "Lordy, you and those down home boys."

Offering Cody a bartending job was a great idea. Sister was always wisest after his second drink. If anyone was thinking about seeking his advice or counsel on any matter that was typically the best time for asking.

When Cody returned from the pisser Leo asked point blank if he'd be interested in a position. He didn't catch his meaning at first so Leo repeated myself using the word job. Cody thanked him, blushed, and said he was real anxious to get out of Cane Springs, but that he needed to see his friend up in Minneapolis first. Leo said the offer was open and to let him know if he changed his mind.

Sister shrugged and lifted his glass in a toast. "To friendships old and new. I think you'll be back. It may take a while, but you'll be back."

Sister was known to have premonitions. They usually came after the second drink as well, at least anymore. When he was a boy, Christian Sr. had peddled his ass all across the southwest as a child prophet. Sister said they drove every back road of Texas and Oklahoma in a baby-blue station wagon with "The Second Coming" hand-painted in gold on the hood. Eventually the pressure of preaching every day through a megaphone, guessing baby due dates, and giving crop and livestock advice clogged his pipeline of visions and gift of prophecy. It wasn't meant to be used that way. His daddy took his visions drying up as personal and with the sole intent of maligning his good name. The result wasn't pretty. Sister always said Christian Sr. had an ego on him.

These days, a couple drinks were the only things that opened up Sister's third eye. A couple more drinks and a whole lot more than that got loose. "I see a big old pecker in my future," he'd joke, squirming on his barstool.

All three lifted their drinks and clinked glasses. Cody's margaritas were exquisite. Sister smacked his lips. "I want these served in my heaven by a buck naked Jack Wrangler."

When Cody said "Who?" Sister crossed himself and told him to never mind.

Leo flipped on the jukebox. They sang along with "Don't Leave Me This Way." Sister lit a joint and they passed it around while dancing to "Got to Give it Up." They ate two bags of ripple chips and a tin of Chex Mix. After all that salt you could have struck a match on their tongues, so they switched to beer and proceeded to get all the more drunk. Then Sister remembered the bus.

They raced to the station and cut off the eleven o'clock northbound just as it was pulling from the lot at twenty minutes past. They jumped out of Sister's green Bonneville and left the doors wide open. They drunkenly ran around the Greyhound, flailing arms and yelling, "Wait! Wait! Wait!" Stumbling on board they wove down the aisle, losing their balance more than once. Sister and Leo poured the kid into a window seat in back, pulled the shade, and turned to face some of the most vicious stares either had ever received, and those two had gotten their fair share of glares.

"Now he's really going to need that kidney," cackled Sister, vamping down the grooved stairs, tripping, and falling flat on his ass upon the asphalt. The driver honked and told them to get the hell out of the way.

Leo lifted Sister's butt off the pavement, ran to the Bonneville, and screeched that beater back into a space. "Wherever we go from here, let's walk." They didn't recall which of them said it, but it was a wise idea. The cops in this town had only so much tolerance and it was likely they'd used up their supply a few years back.

Waving so long to the row of sour faces on the departing bus Leo was thankful to be standing on solid ground though even the pavement was a mite shaky at that point. Poor Cody must have been puking after two minutes in that rattling stale-aired oven. Sister and Leo looked at each other. Sister's eyes were so glassy they reflected the clouds. Leo dabbed his eyes like he was crying and Sister batted his lashes back.

"Tea time," he laughed, shouldering his way through the depot door. "I've got your ticket right here Nell!" Sister shouted, grabbing his crotch and waving to the information desk clerk who frozen in place before struggling to focus on straightening a stack of papers.

Leo dragged Sister through the waiting area and into the john. They burst through the door going "Shhh" "Shhh" "Shhh" back and forth to one another. They were the only two inside so they ended up in front of the dingy mirror giggling at how wasted they looked.

"But I feel fine," said Sister, which got them to laughing all the more. Then he opened his arms, looked heavenward, and said, "Listen my brothers and sisters, vanity must be cast from thy..." His sermonizing was silenced by the whoosh of the lavatory door. Leo and Sister caught each other's eye in the mirror before jostling for the first stall. When they saw it was Information Nell they stopped fighting and laughed until each threatened to cough up a lung. Sister actually doubled over and fell onto that scummy tile in a fit of sissy squealing. Nell went white as parchment and turned so quick on his heel Leo was half-surprised he didn't corkscrew right into the floor.

Leo yanked Sister to his feet and got their drunken asses out of there. They ran all ten blocks back to the Sand Bar hugging half the phone poles and street signs along the way. When they got to the alley Leo could see the back door to the bar was ajar. They'd been drunker than he thought if they left it open...and he figured them for knee-walking drunk. All of a sudden the door flew wide and a kid high-tailed it out with a bottle of Southern Comfort cradled to his chest. It scared the hell out of Leo and Sister who jumped into each other's arms. At least there was no cash inside. The kid didn't look to be carrying anything else. He jumped the back three stairs and hit the ground running. A scattering of pigeons sailed into the air.

The kid saw Leo and Sister and froze for a second. They were too drunk to chase him so they just laughed some more. Judging from the confused look on his face their reaction must've surely shocked him. He took another look over his shoulder and at the same time slipped on some gravel at the end of the alley. He landed smack on his butt which made them laugh all the harder. The bottle survived the fall and the kid was up in a flash and round the corner quick as a scalded dog. His footsteps blended with other sounds almost immediately. Sister and Leo looked at each other.

"Youth," he laughed.

Leo just shook his head. That kid's ballsy behavior reminded him of himself at that age. Nothing was too stupid to try and liquor was worth supreme risks. Leo could tell right then that kid was full of the devil. Damned if he wasn't right.

Map on the Wall

Slowing to round the corner at the end
of the alley, Del skidded and slipped but was back on his feet fast as
he fell. He checked the bottle and looked over his shoulder. Getting
busted was not an option. The way he saw it once the cops in town
had you pegged they never forgot. You became a piece they liked to fit
into whatever bit of lowdown doings they were working on. He knew
how cops were. He breathed heavy through his mouth and wiped away
a bit of spit with a shirtsleeve.

Those two queers were swaying like sea plants out behind the bar,
watching him with liquor-swelled eyes. Del knew who they were, everyone in Bayetteville had seen those two butt bandits about. Luckily
they were too juiced to follow. Every ounce of their concentration
was required just to remain upright. Laughter made them jitter like
sawdust puppets.

Del shook his head. There was nothing funny about the situation.
Nothing at all. Crazy drunk bastards. Both had seen him come kicking out the back door of the bar. It'd been no mystery he was stealing. Del tightened his grip round the neck of the Southern Comfort
bottle. Fucking loonies was what they were.

Cutting through the alley earlier he'd heard a banging. The back
door of the Sand Bar was opening and slamming in the river breeze. It
was the sound of opportunity knocking. Hearing that invitation, Del
knew it was his lucky day and he was long overdue for one. Looking
both directions he crept up the steps and slipped on inside. The bar
was dark and reeked of weed. There was no answer when he called
out "Hello". Remembering it all he cursed himself for not snatching
a second bottle, but at the time he was all about getting some and
getting gone. It was downright spooky in there what with the sweaty
bottles, glasses still cold on the bar, and a cigarette still burning. The
only sound was the lopsided whirl of the ceiling fan.

He grabbed the first bottle he saw. Not a bad grab. Southern Comfort had been Janis Joplin's drink of choice. His ma used to play her
records all the time before they hocked the hi-fi and before his ma

became someone else entirely. Now he and Molly had to make do with the radio.

Del checked over his shoulder again and slapped the crud from his pants without stopping. He rounded a pecker-riddled phone pole halfway down an adjoining alley. Sweeping aside the waterfall hang of willow and morning glory, he lifted the pullout door of his grandma's garage. It had rusted free of its track and the struggle of raising it tended to annoy him. Not this time. Today he was grinning. A full bottle meant party time.

Since March he'd been frequenting the garage. He'd sit for hours at a stretch—drinking whatever he could pilfer, getting high, cursing his sad situation, and devising plans for getting the hell out. For Del it was about escaping to a different world, a different planet, or a different life. The garage was a ramshackle sanctuary. He could get hold of his thoughts there. No one used it anymore, so it stayed just the way he left it. Del looked out the four-paned window. Branches waved beyond the filth-streaked glass and broke whatever sunlight managed to eke through. A rib-thin mutt nosed and pissed on a neighbor's garage, then stood stock still as the woodpeckers started tapping again. Del craned his neck either way. Not a soul had trailed him. He was home-free.

Del let out a self-satisfied sigh, sat on a milk can, and raised his feet to the lowest rung on the ladder. The dog got bored with the birds and moved further down the alley towards a patch of half-dead hedges. Moving longside an old gas can, Del leaned back against the window ledge. He broke the seal on the bottle and took a swig. He shuddered and went three shades of red as it burned a trail to his stomach. Janis sure liked some nasty shit, no wonder she sounded that way.

Del eyed a cobweb blanketing an old mower. He reached down, snagged a trespassing cricket, and tossed it into the web. Its struggle roused the spider from its whorled den. The spider paused a second as if doubting its good fortune. "Got to pass the luck around," laughed Del, lifting the bottle. The spider stung and wound the cricket before skittering back to its hole. Now the cricket was nothing but a white-pouched blip in the fine lined pattern of the web.

Willow branches threw shadows across the floor and wall. He watched the waves of motion a moment before letting his eyes roam over the garage miscellanies of wooden planks, outdated appliances, a croquet set, plastic lawn cranes, bargain vases, rat poison, and things so thick with dust and age they seemed nothing more than gray fuzzy shapes. An ancient oil stain marked the cement floor.

The garage was dark and filthy, but still a welcome reprieve from his home life. The apartment seemed considerably smaller since his mother's beau began hanging around, winking as he slipped his skivvies on her bedroom doorknob. Del knew what that meant. Who did

Lester think he was, behaving that way? That was his mom, for Christ sakes! Loathsome brain-dead bastard!

Lester was a lean mean son-of-a-bitch and handsome in a fierce sort of way. It didn't take much to rouse his ugly side; usually all it took was a couple drinks. Once that side of him came to light most anything could happen.

He worked nights at the filtration plant just this side of Edgartown. Most nights after work he and some shift buddies went and had a few cocktails. Sometimes after staggering back to the apartment he would let Del have it, accusing him of acting like he was better. Thinking about it, Del had to laugh. Damn straight he was better. That didn't take much. Del figured his tiniest turd had more smarts than was in Lester's entire brain.

Del could always tell what was coming by the sound of Lester's keys hitting the kitchen table. Sometimes Lester slammed the front door so hard it shook pictures off the wall. At first Del tried hiding, but the apartment was small and hiding only made it worse. "You're playing with the big boys now," was what Lester usually said to Del before undoing his belt to crack him one or two or a few times.

His ma always pretended it wasn't happening at all, like she was either unaware or didn't care to offend the bum. She just hummed to herself. Maybe she just didn't want to get belted. Del had to wonder what that decidedly blonde head of hers was thinking. She sat down with him and Molly and said they didn't have to call him dad. No shit! Now she was always saying she didn't know what she would do if Lester ever left her. She even got rid of the clock for him. Del found it hard to do anything but stare at her whenever she started mewling on about Lester.

He didn't want to think what his daddy would do if he knew the state of things.

Del curled his mouth around the lip of the bottle and took another swig before lighting a cigarette. Anymore Lester's vile presence permeated every inch of home, and he showed no signs of improving with familiarity or mellowing with time. Assholes that big only get bigger until one day you find yourself all sucked up in their shit. Del couldn't tolerate the state of things and Lester seemed intent on putting down stakes. If Del gave his ma the Him or Me ultimatum he knew what her decision would be. That's what killed him. It hurt more than anything Lester could do.

Over the past couple months Del grew set on not giving her that choice. He was making plans on moving out soon as possible. He doubted his decision would be met with anything more than an obligatory plea and a forced tear or two. It wasn't expensive to rent a place downtown. Not at all. He could even live in the goddamned garage if need be or sleep beneath the steel ribbed rise of the bridge. He could live in a goddamn cardboard box or dig himself a hole for that matter. Nothing could be worse than the way things were.

There was plenty he could do to earn money. He could get a job in a factory or restaurant or anyplace. The thought didn't bother him. He could be real clever once his belly started talking. He'd always been that way. If life had taught him anything it was pointers on survival.

Thoughts of freedom and adventure along with a liquor buzz sent a spasm clear to his toes. "Hell if I'm not getting out," he thought, blowing a column of smoke up towards a hanging lantern. For now he was just biding his time, keeping his head above water until it came time to swim.

He felt for Molly. She was too young to get away and Del couldn't take her along. Lester never hit her, at least not to Del's knowledge. That better not be the case. He would kill that lowdown son-of-a-bitch if he so much as thought about doing something like that. Molly had still changed since Lester's arrival. She was never a carefree child, but lately she'd taken to twisting her hair into knots and pulling out her eyebrows quicker than they could grow. Beneath her freckles she was already sporting eye bags. She was looking borderline freakish. Del always got knotted and sad at the thought of her, but he was in no position for saving anyone but himself, at least for now. Maybe he'd send for her later.

Lester was ruining what little the three of them had salvaged since his daddy passed. The cancer had been an ugly thing. Del still had nightmares of the hacking and wheezing and gasping for breath and the sound of that damn ticking clock as his suffering went on and on. The sound of his slow suffocation was even worse than witnessing his withering. The entire thing had been especially rough on Ma. Del wanted her to be happy again, but not like this. They were surviving before Lester. It wasn't great but it wasn't awful either, not this awful anyways. They'd had each other, but that must not have been enough. Ma needed a man to shoulder her way from day to day.

Now they were being ripped apart. One night Del tried explaining it to her, but the words came out all jumbled up and wrong. By his second breath he knew he wasn't making sense, at least not the sense he'd intended to. "Why bother," he finally thought.

"You're upset because you think I'm replacing your dad...that's natural." She dismissed him and all he'd said with a ruffle of his hair, tossed a dishrag over her shoulder, and walked out of the room. She didn't care to hear another word. She was getting laid regular so nothing he had to say amounted to much. He swore he wouldn't be that selfish if he were in her shoes.

Del crushed out his smoke. Ma would be blind to the devil himself for a chance to be in love again. That big eraser could wipe the slate clean, almost. Sometimes it felt like she considered him and Molly an unwanted inheritance instead of her own kids. He could see how she looked at them. She'd go to her grave denying it, but Del knew it was there behind every smile. If that's what she thought of them, she could hop a greased pole straight to hell! She never behaved that way before Lester came along with his pointed boots, squared sideburns, and low-slung jeans. Del leaned his head back and let out a sigh.

He took another drink and balanced the bottle on his bony hip. School was almost as bad. They weren't teaching him anything useful. He couldn't wait to get out of there. He wasn't dumb, but he was sure treated like it. Those nuns thought being a bride of Christ was like being queen or something. They treated him like a fool or a criminal or an infectious disease. "A corrupt and disruptive element" was how they referred to him. He'd been suspended more times than he could count, but they never expelled him. They considered themselves too forgiving and compassionate for that. He was too pitiable a social case for dismissal. The greatest hope they placed on him was that he'd settle into lower class docility, live inoffensively, and not breed. Above all they didn't want him to be an embarrassment. But Del didn't plan on living his life as some well-behaved farm animal.

He ran his tongue over his numbing teeth and smiled to think about how it'd be and how he'd show them. He wasn't going to sit back and take anything, not from them, not from anyone. "Think again," he thought, tipping back another swallow. He shook his head, eyed the level of the bottle and grinned. Now that was what he called progress.

Del lit another cigarette. The sole thing at St. Elizabeth's that buoyed his esteem was crazy Fred Walsh. He was the weirdest kid in school, but it still pleased Del to have him so infatuated. He laughed at how pathetic it sounded. He wouldn't have even admitted it to himself if he wasn't drunk. The past couple years that fat pansy had been all but drooling over his ass. Del liked turning around in class to catch him staring. Fred never said a word, but anyone with a glass eye and half a dozen brain cells could see how it was.

Eating corn on the cob one night, Del's ma said she was talking to cousin Nadine at the Piggly Wiggly the other day and Nadine said Fred Walsh had been stopping by her place on Saturdays. The disclosure about caused Del to choke on a fish stick. What was he doing hanging round across the street? Del imagined it as some brand of crazy tactic for getting to him, but figured Fred was too dense to be that calculating. It stood to reason that he and Nadine would be friends. Those two losers belonged together.

Nadine said she and Fred watched movies whenever he came over and that she considered Fred to be the little brother she never had.

...*Or another doll or another dog with the chronic shits,* thought Del, consciously lowering the sides of his mouth so as not to laugh.

Del's ma saw his smirk and slurped her lemonade. "Be nice." She said it was good for Nadine to befriend folks. "But to my mind Nadine needs to meet men her own age." His ma had grown so superior acting since Lester came sniffing around, like she was romance expert for the whole county. "Poor Nadine," was what she said.

Poor you, was what Del thought. *Poor you and poor me and poor cousin Nadine. The poor lot of us.* Del thought she shouldn't be so charitable with her pity. Save some for yourself. Still, he had to agree that cousin Nadine was one sorry case. Nadine looked hungry for a husband. That alone sent most single men with half a brain running.

"Not even the tide would take her out." It was one of the few funny things Del could recall Lester saying.

"Now Les," was what his ma had said, but Lester leveled his eyes towards her and she didn't dare say another word until she asked if he wanted dessert. Del suspected he'd smacked her too.

Del imagined Nadine and Fred with their barn door asses parked in front of her TV. He saw them gorging on Oreos, Fritos, frozen egg rolls, pizza pops, and every other assorted snack they could lay their hands on, and guzzling it all down with Piggly Wiggly bargain soda pop. Del imagined empty wrappers strewn across Nadine's coffee table and the stench of her dog. He let loose with a laugh that echoed into the mostly empty bottle of Southern Comfort. The frump and the fruitcake.

He shook his head. None of that mattered. Six months from now it would all be ancient history. Once he turned sixteen, things were going to change. That was the time frame he was working with. He dreamt of a new life, starting with a new name. He hated Delbert. What the hell had they been thinking? Someday he was going to march down to the courthouse and have it changed. He wasn't familiar with the legalities, but had heard the process wasn't too complicated. The thought of bounding down those stone steps as someone else made him grin ear to ear. A new name and none of this would matter.

He not only had plans of who he wanted to be, but where he wanted to be it. New York was where things were happening so that's where he dreamt of going. He'd be there by his seventeenth birthday. Last week he swiped a New York City map from the school library and nailed it inside the door of his grandma's garage. Just seeing the city spread out like that made it seem closer and his current home seem further away.

Del lit another cigarette and rose from the milk can. He bounced a palm across the low ceiling beams. He was feeling the liquor. He sank to the floor and rummaged through a haphazard stack of wooden cigar boxes. Inside a box of nails and washers and screws he found a medal that had belonged to his granddad. He wiped it clean, slipped the rotting ribbon over his head, and lifted the gold shield for closer inspection. He never knew the man. He'd died a full two decades before Del was born. Granddad had seen action during WWI and lived in Europe for two years after, first in Paris and then in Barcelona. That always impressed Del as about the most exciting thing anyone in his family had ever done. It was about the only twist on the working shit jobs and dying young theme. Grandpa had died young too, but at least when his heart exploded he went with a story to tell.

It was getting dark outside or maybe a storm was coming. It was hard to tell inside the garage. The rough-edged clouds were purple and blue and laced with gold, the hues of bruises. Del bent his elbow and eyed a welt on the inside of his arm. He imagined a bolt of lightning cutting through the sky like the lashing tail of some gigantic beast to turn Lester into a pile of ash. Maybe that would bring Ma to her senses. Maybe that would break the spell.

The wind tumbled trash down the alley. He imagined a twister dropping from a black cloud and zigzagging across the fields towards the convent. He took another swig and smiled when his mind's eye saw all those nuns sucked into the funnel like so many whirligigs before being spit out across the land. He saw them hurled over barbwire fences and landing in crumpled heaps atop cars. He wondered if their final words would be curses or prayers. Maybe then they'd understand. Maybe then they'd wonder what they'd done to deserve their fates as well.

Del curled up on a car mat spread out on the cement floor. He pressed granddad's medal to his chest. It was going to be his reminder of all the dreams that he had. Raindrops started splattering the roof, getting louder and denser until it sounded like TV snow or a cheering crowd. Rain beaded along the timbers and gathered and ran until the drops fell here and there onto the floor. Thunder rumbled. He got up and vomited in an old ice chest. When the spasms subsided he flipped down the lid and crawled back to the car mat. He'd deal with that later. Del rolled onto his side and passed out staring at the map and dreaming of his wide-open future. He'd show them all, each and every one of them. He was going to make something of himself. It was only a matter of time.

Townfolk on Tap

It was the first blistering day of the
summer. Two weeks earlier Leo and Sister had tried making stars on
the ceiling with glow-in-the-dark paint. Since they were drunk the
paint ended up dripping all over everything. Spots were on the bar,
the floor, and practically everywhere else. Drops on the ceiling fan
circled above like shooting stars.

Ben absently toweled a beer mug while eyeing himself in the bar
mirror. He liked cruising himself. He was mighty proud of the fact
that he always prompted a double take. Today was no exception. His
white baseball jersey showed his tan and physique to prime advantage.
He smiled at his reflection. He'd do himself in a New York minute.
There was no shame in saying so. It wasn't vanity. He was just being
honest.

Jack-O lit a cigarette and blew a stream of smoke up to the spinning stars. "You still out of Southern Comfort? It's been going on a
month."

Ben turned from the glass. It didn't take a leap in the mercury to
make his blood commence to boiling. "I know we're out and I'm well
aware of just how long it has been. Not a day has gone by that you
haven't pestered me about it."

Despite the tone in Ben's voice, Jack-O continued. He thought by
persevering he might make amends or undo whatever it was that he'd
done. Maybe with a few more words he'd say the right thing in the
right way. "When you think you'll be getting more?"

Ben put down the mug and thinned his lips. "Don't you monopolize
me."

"I wasn't."

"You were and you are."

Jack-O shifted on his stool and looked side to side. Now he'd gone
and done it. "Well if I was I didn't meant to."

"That's the problem, you don't mean to, you never mean to do nothing, you always just do."

"Well now that I know..."

Ben exhaled. "You don't know Adam from adenoids." Beads of sweat dewed his forehead and his words were laced with verbal italics. "We've had this conversation before and it hasn't changed a blessed thing. You sit there all night every goddamn shift I work and ask things you don't give a rat's ass about. Every fucking shift! You don't even drink Southern Comfort for Christ sakes!"

"I care." Jack-O looked down into his beer and felt himself quake with palpitations. He was partly pained and partly shamed by the diatribe. Ben had already resumed washing glasses. Jack-O could kick himself for making all the same blunders. He couldn't help it. All those questions came out his mouth because he never knew quite what to say to Ben. He felt obliged to say something, after all they were boyfriends. Jack-O took another swallow and tried not letting it weigh on him. He looked around. It was this place more than anything. Ben wasn't cut out for this life and the Sand Bar just had a way of making him irritable.

At the far end of the bar Sister leaned closer to Bob the Blob. "At it again...or rather, still. Just take it to divorce court."

Bob sniggered in a way that shook his entire frame. He might as well have added "Ho Ho Ho." Bob was born premature and from the look of things he'd been hoarding food ever since. He weighed upwards of four hundred pounds and folks swore he was growing wider by the week. He already had to sidle his way through normal sized doorways. Seeing him waddling down the street some whispered that he was crazy fat, but he wasn't that way. He still got out and socialized. His weight had to do with his thyroid. Supposedly his parents suffered from glandular problems as well.

"It's all about having an audience."

Bob grinned and wiped a hand over his balding black-freckled head. The whole thing was nothing new. Jack-O and Ben had near-about the same exchange most every day. "I thought drama queens were at least supposed to be interesting."

Sister shook his head. "Maybe for about two seconds! The drama might change but it's the same old scenario..."

"...Over and over and over again," they said in unison before busting out laughing and falling into each other.

Bob lit a cigarette.

"Thought you quit smoking."

"I quit and then I start."

The back door opened with a spate of daylight and Lulu sauntered in wiping sweat from her brow. Despite the summer's heat she wore her trademark black from head to toe. She was wind-blown from the ride and still looked to be fighting a head wind. Wings of hair curled from either side of her face. Once her eyes adjusted she saw Bob and Sister and walked on over. Hooking her sunglasses on the collar of her t-shirt she gave each a hearty slap on the back. "Hey boys. Hot as hell out there, ain't it? Lordy, I am dry as dirt!"

"It's so damn close," agreed Bob, signaling Ben to grab Lulu a beer. "What brings you out on a school night?"

"A woman, what else?" Lulu laughed and pinched the end of her nose. "I met a real nice lady the other day at the antique mall out on Highway J. Real nice. Her name's Stephanie. She's got herself a booth out there." Lulu arched her brows and offered an easy smile. The combined effect made it clear she was a bit moony over this new lady friend.

"Cute eh?"

Lulu waffled her hand. "Not the word I would use, she's more on the refined side. Looks about ready to pull needlepoint out of her purse every time I see her."

"How many times is that?"

"Just the once."

The response made Bob and Sister laugh.

"She's meeting me here at seven..."

Sister rubbed his hands "Ooooo, a show."

"...So don't you bitches be going on or I'll pulverize your butts. If either of you do a thing to embarrass me, you'll be sorry."

Bob checked his watch. His wrists were surprisingly petite for being attached to such flabby arms. "You've got some time then, pull up a seat and plunk your bohukus down."

Lulu took a pack of smokes from her t-shirt pocket and tapped one clear as she straddled the stool. "Don't mind if I do."

The intro beat of "Take Me Home" was on the jukebox.

Lulu grinned around the filter of her cigarette and lifted her chin to the speaker. "Finn here?"

Sister laughed. "Surprise, surprise. That record is so worn it's a miracle there's any groove left."

"You should talk."

It took Sister a beat or two to catch the innuendo and when he did he drew back snakelike and gave Bob a look. "Don't you be going there, bitch."

Bob raised his hands in a gesture of helplessness. When he grinned, his eyes sank like two raisins in a tin of baking dough. "Sorry, I just couldn't resist."

"Well next time fight the urge."

Lulu leaned back on her stool and crossed her arms before craning her neck either direction. "Leo here?"

"He'll be in later."

"You think he'd be interested in donating cash for a pool trophy?"

Sister's eyes widened along with his grin. "I don't know, he can be a little tight with a nickel."

"A little!" laughed Bob

They all turned when they heard a clap. It was Finn returning from the john with his hands waving in the air, singing along with Cher.

Sister giggled, "I wish that snow queen would just slip on one of those Bob Mackie jobs and some antlers and get all that out of his system."

Bob sipped his beer. "You don't understand him."

Sister gave him a wink. "Oh. I understand plenty."

"He doesn't want to be Cher as much as worship her."

Sister lit a fresh smoke. "As I see it, that comes down to damn near the same thing."

"The hell it does. You go to church but that doesn't mean you want to be God."

"Don't you be so sure about that, after all—you're talking to a child prophet."

Lulu laughed, "Who the hell wants to be God? Too much responsibility if you ask me."

"Or none at all, depending on how you see things. There'd be no one to answer to."

Lulu shook her head. "You're all talking too deep for my blood, so I'll just keep still and drink your beer."

"Hey Finn," called Bob. The Blob was sweet on Finn but wasn't about to act on it. Sister and Leo were the only ones he'd confided his longing to and that was only after getting sloshed one night and waxing sentimental on the subject. Both assured him he wasn't telling them anything they didn't already know, but they'd have said that no matter what he'd disclosed.

Romance was Bob's fondest desire. It occupied his fantasies more than purely carnal thoughts. He could have sex with himself. He wanted his heart to soar. That's how he wrote of it in his journal. The words embarrassed him. Despite his dwelling on it, romance didn't seem worth the risk. Things were fine from a distance and he intended on keeping it that way. Blubber insulated him and stopped that fantasy from being anything more.

"My man." Finn sounded ludicrous whenever he used American jargon, mostly because everything he said came out his mouth with the tail end lifted like a scorpion.

Sister finished his beer in a slow swallow and circled with his finger for another round. Ben gave a low grumble and acted like it was some sort of petty demand rather than the reason he was standing behind the bar. When he handed Lulu her longneck he asked if she was waiting for her fish.

Lulu's jaw went stiff as a horseshoe. Comments of that sort roiled her. She did not joke or tease with Ben. She leaned across the bar on her elbows and got up in his face. "Ben, I've slept with more women that you'll ever know and none of them has ever smelled like fish—raw or cooked!"

Ben pulled back. He would've gone red if it weren't for his tan. As it was he went from mud to clay. "Just a joke, shit." He rutted his brow like Lulu was half-mad. Once he managed to muster his nonchalance, he moved back down to the other end of the bar.

Sister bit a lip. Actually Esther, one of Lulu's old flames, *did* smell an awful lot like fish, but then she worked the gutting line at the catfish farm so that was to be expected. Besides, that wasn't what Ben meant at all. Sister leaned over to Lulu. "Don't mind Ben, he's like dandruff, always leaves you just scratching your head."

"He's soft in the head is what he is! And if he don't watch it that surly son-of-a-bitch is liable to get his head more than scratched." Lulu made sure every word was clear enough for Ben to hear even with the jukebox and the ceiling fan and the air conditioner all running.

Grace Jones came on the jukebox.

Finn began jittering and clapping. "Who wants to dance?"

"It's too damn hot! When is this place going to get some decent air-conditioning?"

Sister shrugged, "Don't ask me, I'm just a fixture."

Finn looked at Bob, "Go for it Bob, you never dance with me."

Bob shook his head. "I don't dance, I shake." As Bob saw it, there were certain things fat people shouldn't do—and dancing was at the top of the list. He had no intention of making a fool of himself. That was about the worst thing a person could do. He even quit chewing gum after he overheard a comment that he looked like a cow chewing its cud. Bob nodded towards Dick, who was at the far end of the bar talking to Bruschetta. "Dick will."

Lulu nodded. "That's a fact. Dick is always up for dancing."

"Hey, Dick," hollered Finn, pointing towards the dance floor.

Dick put down his drink and mouthed, "Let's go."

Sister reached over and squeezed the side of Bob's neck.

Lulu didn't notice a thing. Her eyes were occupied. She leaned towards Sister. "Who's that sitting with Bruschetta?"

"A divorcée."

"Oh?" The coiffure-dominated redhead visibly intrigued Lulu. That woman clearly owned a curling iron and from the looks of it one of those with all the special attachments.

Bruschetta called for another margarita and one for Kitra as well.

"...So I said, 'Screw you, I'm ready to do some living.'"

Bruschetta nodded slightly. "He was holding you back?"

"Damn right! An anchor, a fricking anchor, that's what Merlin was."

"Well then it's best you're rid of him, you're too vital to go taking on ballast."

Kitra blushed at the compliment, though not so deeply as if she hadn't been drinking. She ran her fingers through her hair and fancied the felicitation as gospel. Merlin was never one for compliments, so they were nice to hear for a change. "Once I get up from this barstool you'll see I'm taking on plenty of ballast on my own. I don't need any extra."

Bruschetta laughed in her husky way.

Kitra worked hard at being as attractive as possible and the effort showed. She was primped and perfumed and crossed her legs just so. She was a list of "dos" from all the current women's magazines. She was a few years past her prime, but only a few and in favorable lighting she didn't look to be much past it at all. Kitra worked as a sales representative out at the Chrysler dealership in Omro. Her divorce was finalized only the week before. "...I don't know, the way I've been wronged, I just don't want any more hassles from men."

Bruschetta sucked on the end of her straw. She knew it accentuated her cheekbones. "Try sleeping with a couple women and see what you think."

"Me? Are you kidding?"

"It's not such a wild notion. After all, honey, you are in a gay bar."

"I just need to learn to trust men again."

Bruschetta was growing bored. Kitra had said almost all the same things when they started talking on Saturday night. The first time it had been interesting, or at least a unique spin on things for the Sand Bar. Now listening was mostly a courtesy. *Just what this bar needs, another broken record,* thought Bruschetta with a long sip of her margarita.

"...I don't know."

Bruschetta shrugged and tried to refrain from making her glazed attention too apparent.

Kitra looked down. Her voice went a little softer. "Did you always know what you wanted?"

Bruschetta wasn't really paying attention so it took a moment for the question to register. "Hell no."

"I mean—did you always know you wanted to be a woman?"

Bruschetta splayed a hand across her chest. "I don't want to be a woman, or a man for that matter. I just always wanted to be me and that's somewhere in between. I knew I was a third-world girl after doing it as a dare. It was like recognizing myself in a mirror. It all made sense after that."

Kitra fashioned a triangle with her straw and placed it longside her glass. It was followed by an extended pause. "Can I ask you something personal?"

Bruschetta cocked a penciled brow. "You can ask, but whether I answer or not depends."

Picking the triangle back up, Kitra began to fidget and turn it about between her fingers. "You still got your manhood right?"

"Yeah, but I've tucked so long it's about growing up my butt."

Kitra laughed, more out of prim embarrassment than anything. She pulled her fresh drink near and took a sip. Sand Bar margaritas had a way of bolstering courage and lubricating conversation. "Well, how come you never went all the way?"

"I'm attached to it and it's attached to me." Bruschetta rolled the ember of her cigarette one way and then the other along the ashtray groove. "I've only added to me. I enhance. That's my rule and I've only made exceptions for liposuction and the smidgen of cartilage Dr. Carl took from my nose."

Ben emptied their ashtray. "What are you two so thick about?"

"My manhood."

Ben backed up and wrinkled his brow just as the back door opened. Every head turned like so many weather vanes in a shifting wind. A befuddled looking woman stood just inside. She pushed back her hair with the palm of her hand and dabbed at the perspiring sides of her neck with a hankie. It was clear she was still day-blind. She didn't seem accustomed to being disoriented and lifted her chin slightly as if to rise above any discomfort the feeling might cause.

Lulu straightened the points of her collar and polished off her beer. "There's my lady love. Well boys, it's been a pleasure, but destiny calls."

Sister gave her a beer heavy buss on the cheek. "I don't think that's what's calling you darling, but good luck anyway."

She grinned. "At this point it's a skill, and I've sure been doing my homework."

"Boning up huh?"

"Speak for yourself." Lulu popped a mint and rose from the stool. She dug a hand in her front jean pocket and ambled over to Stephanie.

Sister leaned close to Bob. "I bet you that Stephanie is a wild thing between the sheets."

Bob asked why on earth he'd say such a thing.

"Those librarian types always are. Just look at her! Lordy, if that bun was one bit tighter she couldn't close her mouth."

They turned back and watched Lulu steer Stephanie over to the bar and call for a couple of drinks. Stephanie stood straight as a rake while Lulu leaned on an elbow and looked every inch the smooth operator. Sparks were already starting to fly.

Bob turned to Sister with a grin. "Aren't they the odd couple?"

"Lulu likes them refined."

"Well I..."

"Hey Jack-O, get your butt on over here," yelled Sister. Jack-O was a pitiable sight sitting alone at the end of the bar and spinning his draft between his thumbs. Sister couldn't tell if Jack-O was drunk or depressed. Most likely it was a combination. It almost always was with him.

Bob snubbed out a cigarette. "Ben has no call to be so all out mean to him."

"Jack-O takes it. Besides, Ben is a shit to everyone, especially now that his birthday has come and gone and there's no reason for him to be anything but his ornery old self."

"Must not have got what he wanted huh?"

"That kind never does, they only want twice of what they got and all of what they don't. No gratitude for nothing. Take a look, that right there is the real makings of a bitter old queen."

Jack-O sidled up, a beer in one hand and jingling his pocket change with the other. That habit had most everybody climbing the speckled Sand Bar walls. "Hey fellas, how goes it?"

"Hey Jack-O."

"Hey Jack." Bob couldn't bring himself to address Jack-O that way and his greeting always drew more attention for what it lacked.

"Trouble with Ben?"

"Don't pay him no never mind," advised Bob.

Jack-O shrugged and slipped onto a stool. "He's just high strung."

Bob and Sister exchanged looks. "Yeah, well sometimes I think he ought to be strung high."

"He's frustrated."

"He's a turd!" Sister never minced words when it came to Ben, but that didn't ruffle Jack-O. The way others felt only made Ben seem more Jack-O's own. Jack-O was shamed by the noxious way Ben treated him, but pleased it made others see him with added consideration. Being a victim was at least being something. Sympathy was a good sight better than indifference.

"Boy am I worn!" Finn came back from the dance floor with his pale skin glistening. A limp lock of colorless hair curled across his damp forehead. In the bar light he looked like a melting icicle. "There is nothing like dancing. It turns me into a bird."

"You and Dick looked good out there. Where did he go anyways?"

"Bathroom."

Sister laughed, "We'll probably have more graffiti and another glory hole by the time he comes out."

Bob nudged him. "Then you'd feel even more at home here."

"Isn't possible, I couldn't feel more at home in this place than I do now. By the way, that's two snide comments out of you. You're treading on thin ice." Sister didn't mean the thin ice comment in a fat way, but Bob probably took it as such. He was real sensitive that way. Bob needed to loose weight or thicken his hide.

Finn ordered a beer and looked back and forth. It was clear by his wide eyes and half smile he was in a cow daze and didn't understand what was going on. Sometimes talk just moved too fast.

"Sister turned to Jack-O, "So what's new at the coroners?"

"Not a thing but death, and that's nothing new."

Bob slapped the edge of the bar with his hand. "Hey, speaking of, I about saw someone off themselves today."

"Where at?"

"Down around Kavanaugh Bridge, a jumper."

Sister nodded. "I saw the cops down there fishing him out on my way back from the grocery. Word was he was okay but they carted him off by ambulance. He was just sixteen years old."

Bob shook his head as if to indicate the sad state of the world. "What can be so god awful at that age?"

Sister looked at him. "Think back on it, everything can be bad at sixteen."

Bob lit another Salem. He had to agree. "That's Bayetteville for you, biggest ratio of suicides and churches in the state."

"Highest alcoholism rate too."

Sister straightened up on his stool. "Is that comment directed at anyone in particular?"

Bob laughed. "Lord no, I'd hate to have to choose favorites. Besides, I'm too drunk to touch my own nose much less go pointing fingers."

Filling the Shadow

It was never Fred's intent to do what they said. He'd meant to jump, but nothing more. He wasn't sure how he expected his leap to change things. All he knew was that it worked before. It'd happened so quick. He'd get a clear head about it once all the agitated details settled.

The water moved in rushes and eddies below the Kavanaugh Bridge. The river was still swollen from an early summer flood. It was heavy with debris. Branches and bits of wood, paper parts, quavering swatches of cloth, and other samplings floated by. Fred looked down into it. The river was a frothy mirror of the sky, reflecting the overhang of trees and the underbelly of the bridge. Fred was a shadow rolling over it all, an empty space below the clouds. He was the darkness. He looked through his reflection. He remembered his loosening grip and letting go and wanting so badly to fill those hollow borders. He wanted to make that nothing into something.

Kavanaugh Bridge was where trains crossed the Frear at dusk and dawn en route to the station and factories. Cables fanned in a staid pattern from the primary anchorage poles like the strands of an elongated web. It was low to the river. The flood clearance was shy of six feet.

If he'd been set on offing himself he'd have leapt from a higher bridge or done something else altogether. He could've stayed in his own backyard and driven a garden dribble into his belly or gone into the garage and idled the car into oblivion. He could do that now that he was a licensed driver, not that killing himself required approval from the Secretary of State. There were any number of ways he could've undone himself. Jumping wasn't about that. It was another attempt to shake the demons that had got beneath his skin and sucked out his insides.

The rescue squad was too busy saving and strapping and prodding and testing to listen. They heard the babble and blather of his explanation but none of the words. Attention was on him, but being talked about like he wasn't there made him feel beyond rescue. It'd turned him into a thing. Eventually Fred went still and stared stone-faced into the azure sky where birds were turning wheels. A flood always meant a feast for the fowl.

He didn't want to be seen as a fool or a freak, but that's all he'd succeeded in doing. People of this town had a way of spreading misinformation and their memories routinely reached back decades for an anecdote. Fred knew the way of Bayetteville minds and mouths. He figured he'd be associated with that incident on the bridge for twenty years to come. He'd made quite a splash, especially beings that he'd never made much of one before.

He awoke with hazy memories of the scent and dazzle of an angel, but there was no evidence of her anymore. He was in a stark white room in a green hospital gown laced up the back and green slip-ons. It smelled there. The scent of masked odors had a scent all its own.

At St. Xavier's he was treated with an unsettling mix of scorn and concern. As an attempted suicide, he was a mental patient. He was a criminal in the eyes of the state and a heathen in the eyes of the Lord. He was low any way you cut it. He lay in his bed and watched the nuns move up and down the hall like frocked feather dusters, muttering constant prayers neath their wimples and fingering the beads about their waists.

Though not nearly so heaven directed, the dog-tired doctors were far from attentive. Most were walking around blank-eyed. Fred was just more work for the overtaxed. At the start he kept real tight lipped as to all but the particulars of the day. It was atypical for him to be so contrary.

Eventually Fred changed his tune and hoped against hope they might help him. Maybe it'd be his chance. He'd felt different for so long, he just assumed that was how he was. Maybe he'd been wrong. Maybe they could put an end to it and make him just like everybody else. He supposed talking about it was the first step, but he supposed wrong. The doctors had set ideas about what had happened and why he'd done what he'd done. They weren't hearing one word to the contrary. He'd be cured as soon as he confirmed their convictions. They weren't wrong, Fred was simply in denial. If he'd only acknowledge their theories, he'd be free to go after a mandatory observation period.

It didn't matter. Basically all Fred wanted was to leave anyways. The next time the doctor stopped by, he complied and tried answering the questions correctly rather than honestly. It wasn't difficult to say the right things. The doctor did most of the talking and Fred mostly followed his lead and nodded.

The real story wasn't quite so clear. He recalled walking and thinking of nothing really. His feet carried him more than his brain. His attention was aimed to the ground like a hound on a scent. He spent upwards of an hour wending all about the downtown he'd known so well. Suicide never entered his mind. In truth, he already felt dead.

Wandering was just another way of haunting. It wasn't a bad feeling. It wasn't really a feeling at all. It was the opposite. It was just another degree of detachment.

At the grocers, he turned the corner from Front onto Kavanaugh. When he saw the bridge, he knew it was where he had to be. A sour breeze rolled from the river and curled about in the heat. Frogs were singing long the banks and the grass was waving silver in the sun. The bugs got thicker as he moved through a flourish of weeds to the macadam approach of the bridge. It was still pasty with silt from the flood's crest two days prior. The Frear was receding now, settling with a rolling sigh back into the heat of summer.

Fred wondered if Del had a lazy summer planned. Del had left school three weeks before the year's end. One May day, he just wasn't there. Then it was two days, three, and then a week. In two weeks his name was no longer on of the attendance sheet. He'd vanished. There was whispering, but nobody knew diddly. Just the sight of that empty desk took Fred to the brink of panic. With Del gone, there was nothing to ground him and that old fear of floating away and back into the blackness returned stronger than ever.

The anxiety over Del up and disappearing got to be so much that it could no longer be contained. When Nadine mentioned his name in passing during a midday matinee, Fred grew red as a radish and blurted, "Where could he be?" With a ragged sob he grabbed a windmill cookie from the lazy Susan. "I have half a mind to go knock on their door."

Nadine tried calming him, but Fred was not to be consoled. She could see he was in love. Nadine didn't give the implications of it much thought. It was something she'd pretty much known. To her the important thing was sorting it all out. She confessed she hadn't heard beans about Del but planned to talk to her cousin. "And I mean now." She grabbed her shoulder bag and slipped on her beaded moccasins. "I'll be back before the end of the movie." She lifted her limp puss from the rocker and handed her to Fred. "Comet, you keep Fred company."

Del's ma had no idea. "I suppose he's getting along or else I would have heard...no news is good news," she added with a quick smile, as though there was no earthly sense in debating a cliché. She shook her blonde curls and scraped some frosting from a Pop-Tart with her fingernail. She said Del had been impertinent lately and his backtalk was giving her migraines. "That boy was just getting to be too much to handle and all that sass was a bad influence on Molly." She listed a couple more offenses as if gathering evidence for a plea of indifference. She wasn't sorry to see him go, at least not as sorry as she would have liked. That much was clear.

Nadine sipped her coffee and tried not to show her shock. Things weren't hers to judge. She understood what Pearl Louise was saying, but found it hard to imagine her views. Nadine let out a sigh. Sometimes the way of the world was so unfair. She wanted to give so much but didn't have kids; Pearl had two yet didn't seem to care. As Pearl Louise went on about her new beau, Nadine was mustering the courage to ask if she could take Del in when he returned. It pained her to realize that her cousin wouldn't give her much of an argument. Nadine stopped just shy of inquiring and decided to sleep on it. She had to be sure taking Del in was something she was capable of doing.

When she looked up Molly was hovering in the doorway like a shadow. Nadine smiled her way and they shared hellos before Molly rolled back down the wall to her room.

Pearl Louise followed Molly with her eyes and fingered the beads about her neck. She said Del's running off came as no surprise. Not really. "The friction between him and Lester could have put a set of false teeth on edge...and it was worsening by the week. It'll do everybody a world of good not to be around that powder keg." They talked a few minutes more before Nadine left holding a cookie recipe and shaking her head. That Lester sure must be something. Pearl Louise had become a regular hothouse flower.

Del's disappearance caused Fred to pine all the more. He loved Del with the innocence of youth. He loved him fully and to a dangerous degree. Time had only added to those feelings. Del was his life and his life was suddenly gone. Fred couldn't imagine things different.

Fred began crossing the bridge. As he stepped from tie to tie he got dizzy seeing the Frear flowing below. Halfway across he stopped a moment and grabbed one of the support cables. The wind was blowing and the sun was blazing and some men were hollering from a barge upstream. It let out a blast and a covey of birds rose from the shore. Struggling to keep a breath, Fred closed his eyes. Opening them slowly, he looked down into the water. Through the shadow of himself, he imagined Del smirking up from just below the surface. He was down there. For a moment it was all so clear. His shadow was a window to the underside and getting there was just a matter of going through it.

His fingers uncurled from the suspension cable. Letting go was putting his trust in a union with Del. He trusted that with all his heart. It was an act of faith rather than desperation. He had to fall to ground himself. The momentum carried him forward. His reflection cleared as he neared the water. His features connected. He saw his eyes and mouth open wide as he hit the surface. Was he screaming?

Half the town turned out to watch him dragged to shore, strapped on a stretcher, and shuttled off to St. Xavier's. In Bayetteville, crowds had a way of forming out of thin air whenever something was astir. Folks there had to find excitement where they could. It seemed that since about the cradle they started developing a crafty way of sniffing out talk. They seemed to have a sixth sense about it. The legitimate thrill of saying they were there when such and such happened caused them to gather like moths to a porch light.

Fred looked upward. He imagined he'd always remember that summer sky and the faces above him and how it all felt. He didn't, of course. What he recalled was the silence. When the water rolled out of his ears the first thing he heard was the wind, then the rustle of heads shaking in disapproval. Feeling superior was another favorite Bayetteville pastime. Whispers and clucks began to pepper the silence and grew and grew, until by the time he was finally slid into the ambulance, the riverbank sounded like a chicken coop. There'd be talk in bars and barbershops, beauty salons, and right on the sidewalk. It'd all been such a big mistake. As he was raced to St. Xavier's, Fred swore that screaming siren had to be coming from inside his head.

Dr. Wilcox allowed parental visitation on the second day. Rog and Lila looked concerned and uncomfortable. They were wearing church clothes. For unknown reasons, the nuns made a fuss over them and bounced their hooded heads about like a coy patch of tulips. Lila said "Oh my" and was clearly embarrassed. She didn't fancy attention, not here. This was a place of discretion and she preferred being left to her shame and pain. She was tender but foggy and seemed to move at a reduced speed. Fred wondered if she was sedated too. She brought a tin of oatmeal cookies and held them white-knuckled throughout the visit. She almost forgot to leave them when it came time to go.

Rog smelled of Old Spice and was animated by three Manhattans. His response was to counterbalance circumstances by being up, up, up! Even in a psychiatric ward, his false buoyancy seemed disturbing behavior. Rog told Fred he had a surprise for him when he was released on Monday. Lila shot him a look and squeezed the tin so tight it buckled. "We weren't supposed to tell." It was the first Fred had heard about getting out. It came as a huge relief. He briefly wondered why he wasn't supposed to know before putting on a wide smile. He pretended it was because of the surprise.

The next few days came and went in a looping cycle of loose routine. There were therapist visits, priest visits, and nuns popping in and out. They would stare at him while boldly scooping a cookie or two into their wide sleeves and then scurry away. They ate the whole tin of cookies without once asking.

By Monday Fred was desperate for privacy, freedom, and the chance to masturbate. Rog and Lila arrived right on time and signed some papers. Releasing him was easier than renting a fishing rod. Fred looked around, suddenly unsure whether it'd all been a dream or some fancified scene from *The Late Late Show*.

On the drive home there was small talk galore—Lila and the garden, Rog and the neighbors, Lila and the neighbor's gardens... They'd been actively storing chitchat to fill those awkward first moments. By the time the car pulled from the hospital lot Fred had stopped listening. Fortunately experience had made him a pro at the carefully placed "Mmm-hmm".

His daydreaming came to an end when Rog parked on Maple in front of the Vienna Beef and turned around in the driver's seat. From his creased expression it was clear this was important. "Son, a crony of mine is the proprietor of this place. He needed some help so I gave him your name. It's not the best job and I don't mean to be pushing you, but me and your mother think steady work will do you more good than all that head probing will."

"You just need to keep busy, honey."

"That's right, too much idle time."

Fred sat back. After everything that had happened, he was in no position to put up a fuss. It was prudent to be agreeable. Even if they didn't hold St. Xavier's in high regard, his parents could still send him back. He could be locked away until he was old and gray and never see Del again. He had to keep his sights on the big picture. He'd given up a lot of rights with that fall. He mustered some enthusiasm and nodded back to his father.

"And if you hold the job for a solid year your mother and I will add two hundred dollars to your bank account."

Lila was beaming and nodding after every word.

"Great, this'll be great." Fred wasn't faking, not entirely. Maybe they were right. Maybe all he needed was to keep busy. In any case he'd be satisfying his folks, putting this humiliating episode somewhat behind him, making money, and taking another step towards independence. Truth be told Fred wasn't quite so clear in his thinking, but he rightly surmised that there were abundant plusses.

Lila fished something out of the glove compartment and handed him a white paper bag. "I don't mean to embarrass you, honey, but here. I picked up some acne goop at the Woolworth. It was on sale with the coupon." She turned back around in her seat but kept talking over her shoulder at a right angle. "What with all that worrying you've really started sprouting some blemishes and I'd hate to think of my baby growing up with visible scars."

Vienna Beef Booth 3

When Kevin told Stacie they were in- compatible and hadn't exactly been getting along lately she seethed, "That's bullcrap, and no one gets along exactly."

Kevin looked down at his burger. This wasn't going to be easy.

Stacie lit a Newport.

Fred was slouched on his elbows at the counter watching the television from six inches away with the volume turned low. Kevin caught his eye, yelled for onion rings, and yanked half a dozen napkins from the dispenser in the next booth.

Fred shook an order of frozen rings from the foil bag into the fryer basket. They hissed as he lowered the cage. He enjoyed working the deep fryer.

Stacie grabbed Kevin's arm, "You settle your ass down because you're going to listen to what I have to say." She wanted to know where all this incompatible talk was coming from and where his head had been lately. Stacie said he'd never find another woman who loved him as much and that she'd had it up to her goddamn tits with his funks and moods. "The last straw is coming, Kevin, and when it does my sweet ass is out the door, and I don't turn around for nobody, including you."

Kevin raked his rust-colored hair. He couldn't provide an adequate explanation. Lately he'd been behaving like a real butthole and instigating fights just this side of warfare. They'd been bickering steady for weeks. It used to add spice but now it added nothing, and even when the fights subsided the oppressive feelings that started it all remained. Kevin wondered if he was set on sabotaging things. Sometimes that seemed the only explanation. The past few months he couldn't make sense of half the things he'd been thinking, much less doing. He still loved Stacie, but he'd had other longings.

Keeping quiet about it seemed his sole alternative. It was the first time he'd kept something from her other than what he'd bought her for Christmas or her birthday, surprises along those lines. It was the only secret he'd harbored out of shame and as a result he was compiling quite a list of lies and deceptions.

Shortly after they moved into a small place over on Hudson last fall, Kevin had begun diddling with men. Guys! He couldn't tell Stacie something like that, not in a million years. And he was terrified she'd find out.

The first time was after a softball league game at Devil's Point. He waved so long to Mac and Moses as they hopped in Mac's Trans Am and fishtailed out of the lot in a spray of gravel. Kevin was in good spirits. A baseball victory always made him happy. They'd clobbered those jokers from Lupinski's. "Eighteen to three, shit." He stuck his head under the outside spigot and splashed the grime from his face and the back of his neck. He shook the water from his hair and ruffled it damp before heading to the john for a piss.

The men's room was wide and muddy and reeked of stale piss. The high ceiling and naked bulbs created a lot of overlapping shadows. Someone was inside at the urinal. In a puddle's reflection Kevin glimpsed the man's erection. The fellow knew he saw it and gave a self-satisfied grin before giving it a shake. Kevin stared a moment and then looked up into a pair of dark deep-set eyes, the kind that could mesmerize and even hypnotize. The intensity hit him like a punch to the gut. It was raw enough to rouse something inside and pull it right to the surface. The moment, the man, and that all-consuming lust eclipsed all of life as Kevin knew it.

When the guy shook his dick a second time Kevin moved to the adjoining urinal. The stranger was lanky and mostly attractive. He smelled of sweat and grease. Dried white spittle flecked the corners of his mouth. With trembling hands Kevin popped the buttons of his jeans.

They stood side-by-side playing with themselves, neither touching the other nor saying a word. Kevin felt the strangest thing wasn't that it was happening, but that it hadn't happened before. He felt like he'd been waiting for something like this all his life...something to show him who and what he really was. Their groans grew. In a moment Kevin rose on the toes of his sneakers and ejaculated into the porcelain trough. The reality of it rushed in soon after. Ten seconds later he was buckled up and halfway across the lot.

Since then he'd returned several times. Each visit was another go with another man. His desire wasn't something to be satisfied, it was something to be purged until it gathered again. Anticipation drew him there. Who'd be there? What'd they look like? What'd they have down there? Their hungry eyes gave Kevin a moment when he was but something to be lusted after. Once he'd tasted that, his need for that moment was impossible to ignore. Afterwards, guilt rushed over him just as completely. He tensed to recall his doings in that deserted men's room. Each time he drove that winding stretch of blacktop to

Devil's Point he swore it'd be his last. *This is it!* He meant it every time.

A month ago, Kevin took the next step. He mustered courage enough to go to the Sand Bar. Coming through the back door, he looked around. The inside resembled a Wild West bordello, red and mirrored and aglow with speckles. Every inch of that place was new and different and strange. He couldn't believe they still played disco. Meeting other men without a urinal in the room was a thrilling concept, but it didn't happen. Kevin was terrified of being recognized and even more afraid of feeling he belonged.

He bought a beer from Ben. He was cuter than most of the Devil's Point bunch. Ben could sense desire as sure as radar. He lived for those moments. With a wink he handed Kevin his change and a phone number along with it. "Here you go, handsome."

Kevin blushed, overtipped, and moved to a table on the fringes of the dance floor where he sat sweating near-about as much as his beer. Sister referred to that far table as Siberia. People always noticed who was sitting in that "don't notice me" spot.

Sister recognized Kevin. He'd seen him round town and at Devil's Point once or twice. He'd never had the pleasure of doing him, but sure wanted to. He nudged Leo when Kevin took a seat. There was no need. Leo had been eyeing him from the second he stepped inside. It was evident Kevin was green to things and nervous as a Mormon bride. Leo decided to wait until next time before making his move. It wasn't as compassionate as it sounded. Leo had other things in mind. That night he already had his eye on Del. Leo laughed. That shaggy-haired punk had been coming around trying to pass for nineteen.

Kevin left after one longneck and drove up to Devil's Point. The bar wasn't as bold or as sleazy as he'd hoped. He wanted sex, not small talk. For his purposes, it was easier if it was all just about getting off.

When he got home, Stacie was rocking on the creaking front porch swing with an overflowing ashtray in her lap. She knew something was going on and it made her mad as a bee in a beer bottle not to know what that something was. He slammed the car door, straightened himself, and said he'd been out with friends.

"What friends?"

"New friends, guys from work."

She went red and hurled the ashtray into the yard before storming inside. She gave the bedroom door a kick that sent the knob deep into the plaster. Stacie thought he was screwing around with her bulimic nursing school "friend" Connie. *That cunt!*

Sitting at the Vienna Beef, Kevin tried to remove all that from his mind. It seemed part of a dream, though he knew it was true. So much unbelievable stuff had been happening. Over the past few months he'd had his wanger sucked and had done some sucking. He was guilty of doing every blessed thing he used to razz his buddies about. He wondered how it all could have changed and if it ever would've if he hadn't gone for a pee following that game.

He couldn't tell Stacie. Just the thought of doing that made him thick-tongued and dopey. Maybe one day the timing would be right, but he found that difficult to imagine. She probably wouldn't believe him. "Bullshit," she'd say. Convincing her otherwise would be tough. Pride had a way of blinding her to the truth. If he did persuade Stacie he was being honest, Kevin was sure she'd pitch a fit and be teary, disgusted and eventually vengeful. She'd get ten of her brother's yahoo buddies to pulverize his ass. The whole thing was a no-win situation, but the longer he did nothing the worse it was bound to be. All of it was burning a hole in his belly.

Stacie slammed her back against the orange vinyl booth and brushed a blonde streak from her face. She twirled the salt dispenser, clenched her jaw, and kicked her foot against the metal table leg. Stacie always did four or five things at once, which made her an excellent lover. Their still active sex life confused Kevin all the more. It made him worry as well. What if he brought something home to her? His worries and concerns made it nearly impossible to lose himself in lovemaking. Sex with her had become consumed by caution and too much about convincing to be fulfilling.

Stacie lit a Newport from the butt of the one she was smoking and wiped away a lip-gloss smudge with her finger. She was about to speak when Fred yelled that the rings were ready. Stacie and Kevin held eyes a moment before Kevin went and paid. He eyed a ripe zit on the tip of Fred's nose and another on his chin. He didn't want to think about that kid bent over his food. Fred took his money with a flat "Thanks" and turned back to the TV. By the time Kevin got the rings back to the booth the wax envelope was translucent with grease.

Stacie was sitting bolt upright and staring ahead with a set mouth that spelled trouble. Kevin gave her a dodgy look. Her eyes were flat and hard. He scratched a bit of chin stubble and stared at the Formica tabletop. He hadn't touched his cheeseburger. He wasn't up for another fight and that's where this was headed. He was sorry he'd brought the whole thing up. All he wanted to do was eat. He felt trapped, defensive, and frustrated as fuck.

He lifted his hands and waved them palms out. "This is twisted. You're turning this into what you want it to be and that's not helping matters." He didn't want to fight or hurt her, but he wasn't eager to be picked to pieces neither. "I'm sorry, I'm tired."

"We only got up a couple hours ago."

"I'm still tired."

"You're always tired."

"I'm tired of this, this shit." That was what he wanted to say. He wanted to shout that he had to leave, not just this place, but her as well. He saw no other solution. The Hudson Street apartment had been a big mistake. Living together seemed the right thing at the time, but that was a lifetime ago. He needed to live another life someplace else.

Fred turned from the TV and yawned. With a stupid grin he looked at the Mountain Dew wall clock and refilled his soda cup. Kevin looked over to him. His zits were barely apparent from booth three.

"Stacie, I…"

Stacie was chewing on an onion ring and bouncing her foot on the booth. "Go on, this should be good."

"Stacie this isn't about you. I just need to back off for a while."

"I'd say that's about me! We're a team, Kevin. I'll tell you what it's about…" She took a pickle from his cheeseburger, shook her hair, and fingered it behind one ear and then the other. "We go through some sort of crisis every time your old lady plans a visit. If you could get that through your fucking thick skull maybe I could help you, but don't take all your little boy bullshit out on me. I'm Stacie, not your Jesus freak old lady." She jiggled an ice cube from his cola and bit it.

Kevin squeezed the bridge of his nose. "Stacie, this isn't…"

An ambulance screamed down Maple. Both looked out the frost-ferned window. It was too fogged to catch more than the red flashing blur and muted headlights. Fred turned from the television. Kevin caught his eye and quickly looked down. The yellowed tiles along the inside sill were peppered with dead flies and beetles. He lifted the bun from his burger and stared at the charred meat. It was tasty, but seeing a bunch of dead bugs so near took away a good share of his appetite.

"Kevin, you know I'm right. We've been through too much to let outside crap break us up. She's not a part of us. Living together ain't a sin just because her God says so. Her God isn't ours. He don't rule us."

Kevin looked into her eyes. Stacie's face was red and pleated with intensity. Now was not the time. He agreed about his mother and bit open a couple ketchup packages. He spit a bit of foil onto the table. He hated fancy ketchup. "You got any regular ketchup?"

Fred turned from the TV with a look that made it clear he'd no idea what Kevin was talking about. He shook his head "No" anyway.

"Where do they get these people," he said, turning back to Stacie.

Stacie lit a Newport and stretched out her legs. She snatched another onion ring from Kevin's plate. Taking a drag off her cigarette she let out a narrow column of smoke. The diameter of her exhalations was always an clear gauge of her moods. Stacie was completely unaware of it. It was one of the little things Kevin loved about her. He smiled to recall the rolling fog of her after sex cigarette.

"What?" she said, responding to his smile.

"What?"

"What was that look for?"

"I don't know."

"I'm trying to explain myself and air a grievance and you sit smirking. Well, I for one do not find this so all out funny. I don't know why I bother?"

"Sorry." Kevin swallowed a lump of cheeseburger and tried untangling the thoughts in his head. Maybe now was the time. Maybe it was time to admit he was mixed-up and tell her everything. He reached for her hand. "That's why I think we should step back."

Her lips thinned and she snatched her hand away. "Fuck you! You're not willing to work at nothing!" She narrowed her eyes. "If you think you can waltz right out of this relationship simple as that you've got another thing coming. We are committed." She sat up quickly, which made a fart sound on the vinyl. Fred looked over from the TV. There was a long pause. Stacie blushed. Kevin gave a gap-toothed grin and made a fart sound on his forearm. Stacie covered her face with her hands and laughed. Even Fred laughed when he turned back to the TV. If they were being cruel or poking fun he didn't want to know.

Kevin grabbed Stacie's hand again. He was being a fool earlier. A complete jackass. He didn't want to leave her or the life they had together. It was worth the sacrifice. Being with Stacie was what he wanted and being her old man was who he was meant to be. He wasn't hiding, he was choosing. Even when things were at their worst, Stacie still made him feel something no one else could.

Kevin was determined to make this guy phase a thing of the past. He swore nevermore to drive the Dodge up to Devil's Point. Sitting in booth three, his love for Stacie suddenly felt strong as ever. There was hardly a flicker of doubt in his mind.

He admitted being a fuckup but said he still loved her. The moment he said it, he worried those words would only muddy things in the long run. He worried it was a lie, only it wasn't. He did love her, it was just... He looked down at his hands and wiped the mustard from his fingers.

Stacie called him callous. "Sometimes just loving me is just not enough."

Kevin threw an onion ring down in the ketchup. What did she want? She was eating up this drama and begging for dessert. "Don't you turn all that shit loose on me. This is something you concocted with them bitch friends of yours. The argument was over and now you want to ruck it back up so you can recount a big show to them. This is the sort of something I just can't take anymore. I hate crap like this. If you love drama so much you should have stuck with Mac."

A forked vein sprouted on Stacie's forehead. She slammed her hand on the table, causing a considerable jump from both Kevin and the condiment carousel. Fred turned from the TV and looked over with a lazy stare. This sort of thing happened all the time there. After six months, the goings on that unfolded in these booths didn't throw him in the least.

Kevin tapped a cigarette from the pack. Neither he nor Stacie said a word for a minute. Finally Kevin spoke, "Sorry, I've got a lot on my mind."

"No shit, so either tell me about it or get rid of it. I'm warning you, if it's another broad, you're both dead meat." She rolled up the sleeve of his sweatshirt and fingered the tattoo of her name on his forearm. "This means something, you know."

Kevin said it wasn't another woman and held her eye so she knew he was telling the truth. Looking at her, Kevin wondered how he could've doubted he loved Stacie and women. Maybe he was the one creating the drama. He picked up an onion ring and slowly licked around the edges. He said the long strong tongue alone was worth the bother.

After a couple seconds, Stacie blew a snot glob out her nose so Kevin knew she really thought it was funny. She wiped it away with a napkin and threw it at him. He ducked and they laughed as it rolled over the tabletop behind them. She called him a crazy shithead, leaned over, and kissed him. She could open a beer can with her tongue, maybe even a longneck. Their tongues were compatible.

Kevin closed his eyes. They belonged. The guy stuff didn't fit. He reached beneath the table and fingered the inseam of her black fashion jeans. Stacie still did it for him. He was set for action. She made a face and gave her lips a nasty lick. Kevin said he had just the thing for her frustration. "Doctor says repeated insertion should lower your fever." He grabbed his crotch. Standing would take some adjustment.

Another ambulance flashed past but this time neither turned. The shadow of falling snow crossed the window. Fred flipped the station to the swelling score of another movie. He looked up and their eyes met. Kevin could tell the counter kid was queer too. He felt a tingle race boots to scalp at seeing they were alike. Maybe before, but that was over. Things would be different from now on. He would see to that. He bumped the edge of the table getting up.

Stacie crushed out her cigarette in his ketchup and grabbed her denim purse. She gave him a playful punch on the shoulder. "And don't you ever fucking try breaking up with me again. Incompatibility my ass!" She slipped on her coat and slung the purse strap over a shoulder.

Kevin grabbed a napkin and wiped some ketchup from his jaw. They left the orange tray on the table and pushed through the jingling door with a hand in each other's ass pocket.

Fred hated it when folks left a mess. He walked over to clear the table and saw them standing outside in the falling snow. Kevin rubbed Stacie's shoulder for a moment before leaning over to lick a melting flake from her ear. She whispered something before bunching up his coat sleeve and feather touching that tattoo on his forearm.

Glazed Chicken

First time Del stepped inside, he was hit up for an ID. He figured it was the way he looked or was trying to look, what with his long hair and dagger earring. He figured the sleaze owner doing the asking didn't give a shit about any law. Confronted head-on with the legal drinking age; Del slapped his front and back pockets and said "Fuck" and "Piss" a few times. That was getting him nowhere fast so he inched his fingers crotch-ward and gave Leo a look that said he could be his bad boy fantasy in more ways than he could count. Leo's eyes zeroed in on Del's hand. *Bingo,* thought Del, and he was right.

Leo had a Fu Manchu mustache, ice blue eyes, a slender fag frame, and a leathery hide that he looked to have shrunk inside. He was from somewhere in Georgia and it saved Del's underage butt that he fancied the look of rebel youth. Del didn't even think the rebel part had much to do with it. Leo just liked them young.

He gave Del a lopsided grin and a slow toe to head look and back down again before suggesting they discuss that misplaced ID upstairs. There was no mistaking the proposition. Del shifted his weight like there was a some ethical debate taking place in his head. That wasn't likely. When it came to ethics, Del travelled awful light. His mind was already set, but looking eager wasn't the way to play that sort of situation. Hesitating made them want it more. After a bit Del eyed Leo's basket and said "Sounds good."

Leo yelled to Sister he'd be back in a few.

"Have a nice lunch," Sister hollered back.

Del couldn't believe that damn loud-mouthed drunk. Everybody in the place who wasn't already looking turned to gawk after that.

"Don't worry none about me, Sister," Leo yelled back.

All the while, Del was just standing there getting more and more steamed until he was about set to put his fist through a wall or grind his teeth to grit. Just as he was about to say, "Fuck this" and storm out Leo turned. "Let's go."

About fucking time, was all Del could think.

A minute later, he was tailing Leo's pancake ass up some hard wood stairs that felt about to buckle with every step. A gouged and peeling green door stood at the top. Leo fumbled with the lock and half looked over his shoulder to make sure Del was still there. Del didn't know where else he expected him to be.

Once the door sputtered open they stepped inside. Leo unbuttoned his shirt, dropped to his knees, and began lapping at Del's crotch right through his dungarees. His was the only flat in the building, but Del still reached back and slammed the door. He wasn't doing nothing he was too proud of.

Leo unzipped Del so quick it threw him off balance, but he settled down to business soon enough. And Leo knew his business. He was good, real good. Good as Del had gotten at that point. Del started tugging Leo's greasy hair, letting loose with little moans, and finally giving him a good old face fucking. Leo might not have been much in the looks department, but he sure knew the wherewithal's of pleasuring a pecker.

Leo's flat was just as seedy looking as he was. Del found it hard believing anyone lived there and that was coming from somebody who spent half his time living in a garage. It was a complete shit hole! Leo's aptly named squat reeked of cat piss and cigarettes and unsavory bodily smells. If the window wouldn't have been open Del would have lost it right there. As it was, that stench near-about gave him a doubled-over dose of dry heaves.

Del figured old Leo must have put his cash in a savings account, up his nose, up his butt, into craps, somewhere and anywhere but there. Anyone who lived in a place like that didn't seem likely to have much more. There was a ratty green couch, two three-legged chairs, and a throw rug matted with cat hair. It was the sort of place drunks came to die.

Sitting in the far corner, atop a surplus frame and box springs, was a cum and piss stained mattress. Leo was inching forward on his knees and backing Del up against it without taking the cock from his mouth. Del was damned if he was going to sit, much less lie, on that filthy thing. No way! Even the floor was sticky; Del was sure it was tacky from jism and cat yak. He looked to the window and hoped for a stiff breeze to bring in some fresh air. A pair of squirrels chased one another across the phone lines. It was hard telling if their little dance was about sex or aggression. Del figured it was a bit of both. The same could be said of Leo.

The squirrels put Del in a bit of a panic. He worried one would jump through that torn screen and take a bite out of him. Rabies was not his idea of a good time. One hand went to his neck and fingered his granddad's medallion. He could always use that as a weapon if need be. Thinking on all that must have got him to shaking because Leo figured he was about to bust a nut and was saying shit like, "Come on, and blow for me." When nothing happened Del just shrugged. Leo's one-eyed tom seemed used to the goings on. Sebastian sat indifferent on the ledge with paws tucked underneath him like a sill hen with his hollow socket turned towards the outdoors.

Leo unzipped and started beating his thing while he sucked. He didn't want Del touching him. Del didn't mind. One look at that nasty pecker with nearly fifteen thousand miles on it and Del thanked the powers that be Leo opted for the self-service pump. Del was trying to focus on the pleasure and not let his eyes go to the window or to Leo or have his nose get a whiff of the cat piss. It didn't matter. Truth was he wasn't much involved. This was between Leo and his pecker. It wasn't two minutes later that Del clenched his fists and blasted with shakes and growls and a stomping of his foot.

Head from Leo was damn near a right of passage for Del's entering the Sand Bar. It didn't take long for Del to put two and two together and figure out Leo was into numbers, and some mighty high ones by the time he waltzed in there. Maybe for him salvation would come with a million.

Getting in the Sand Bar was no problem for Del following that, since Leo didn't have sex with underage guys. Sometimes the shit people told themselves dumbfounded Del. Whenever he came in the bar after that Leo would nod "Hello" and give him some looks, but mostly he was scoping about for his next conquest. Having Leo swing on his thing was a career move. He was using what he had to get what he needed, simple as that. Given the way things were for Del, he wasn't sleeping his way to the top so much as fucking up from the bottom.

When Del first started hanging out at the Sand Bar he went there early afternoons. Ben was usually there watching TV or something. Mostly he'd be alone, but sometimes Jack-O would be hovering around, usually knee walking drunk despite the time of day. Ben usually let Del drink for free if he'd give him a spliff or a hit of speed or something to keep him happy. That was no problem. They provided for each other that way. The friendship was what they call sympatico.

Leo wasn't so easy to win over. Once he noticed Del was using his place to make some coin, he gave him an ultimatum. Looking Del dead in the eye, he stroked his mustache and said, "No drug dealing on the premises." He also suggested that if Del wanted to keep coming there that he rent his place for ten bucks a trick. Leo smelled pimp profits. If Del didn't agree to a cut he could just stay out. Leo implied that he might drop a dime on him as well, though it was hard to imagine the owner of a queer bar going and calling the police. Still, he had Del bare-assed over a barrel. Del shook his head and thought, *What do you know?* Leo wasn't ruled by his dick alone.

Forking over ten bucks every time was a royal pain in Del's ass and one hell of a healthy cut. He didn't know who Leo thought patronized the Sand Bar but it sure wasn't a monied crowd. Leo did have a good amount of connections. He always seemed to know someone looking for some and willing to pay for it. A few times he paired Del up, brought the twosome upstairs, and flogged his beaten looking meat while watching them get it on. Whenever that happened he let Del pocket the ten and then expected him to be all grateful. "Hope you liked the free show," was more what Del wanted to say.

Overall, Del supposed striking that deal was a good stroke of luck. He needed a place to bring guys. Grandma's garage was a place to crash, but nothing more. It wouldn't be cool for every trick in the tri-states to come sniffing round every time he threw a bone. By then, Del was spending most nights at the Roosevelt anyways. That pasty bartender Finn told him about the place. He'd lived there going on two years.

Staying there meant a single room to live in, but since Del could only be in one room at a time he figured it didn't matter. Having a bathroom at the end of the hall took some adjustment but he kept a pickle jar in the room for convenience sake. There was no bringing men to your room. The Roosevelt was a respectable establishment. They actually said that to his face. The prissy proprietors wouldn't tolerate that sort of thing. They may have been green at one time, but no more. They kept a close eye on the three or four working boys who stayed there, as if the Roosevelt had some snooty reputation to uphold rather than being a half step up from the gutter.

It may not have been the best, but Del liked the freedom. Before he'd had it at home and gotten together the money to get out, midnight had been his curfew. He could do anything except get on nerves or get arrested, but if his tail wasn't in the door by twelve he could count on having the living shit kicked out of him. Lester got his jollies that way and lived for Del's being late. Sometimes he'd give Del a belt-bollocking even if he was on time. With Lester, there was always some excuse. Beatings had more to do with what was going on with him than anything Del ever said or did.

Del only took that crap for a couple months after he started doing guys. Once he had some cash saved, he knew the next time Lester raised a hand to him, he could say, "Fuck you, fuck Ma, fuck this," and be gone. That's what he did too. Del said it right to his face more or less, ducked a punch and bolted out the back before another attack. He took nothing but the clothes he was wearing.

The next day, he hid in a hedge across the street and waited until they were all gone before crawling in the bathroom window to get his stash of cash and tapes and such. Molly came home just as he was climbing out. Del gave her such a start the hairs about stood straight off her scalp. He hugged her hard when he left. It was sad saying good-bye to her. She was too young to know what was going on and there wasn't time or the words to explain. Del made her promise not to mention seeing him.

Leaving there was the smartest thing he ever did. Del had some plans, and not no rinky-dink ones. He was London-bound with no plans of coming back. He was going to make a name for myself on the underground music scene. He'd already started writing songs—good songs, songs with balls and guts and about the truth. Even if his songs needed work, he had the look and the attitude down. That was most of it.

The day after leaving home, he stopped going to school. He didn't want Ma or Lester being able to find him on the off chance they'd give a shit. He wasn't learning anything there that was going to do him any good anyways. Del knew something better was out there. Those holy rollers had been on him since he got there. Lately they'd been harping on him to cut his hair because his appearance was disruptive. Del got slapped when he said that Jesus had longer hair than he did. It didn't matter. Del didn't give a shit what they thought about his being disruptive. That's what he was all about. Del left there with no regrets save for the fact of not having done it sooner.

After dropping out Del met up with Slagger. His real name was Santiago and his folks lived down by the river. Del had seen him around school that first year, but Santiago left that semester. Del couldn't blame him for hating it there. All those assholes had called him Santa's Taco. Next time Del saw him was during Bayetteville Dayz, the annual carnival at the fairgrounds that most of the town went to because Bayetteville was so damn boring. It was small time thrills—booths, strings of colored lights, piddly-ass rides—the whole ring toss, pick-a-duck, cotton candy, and shooting gallery ball of wax.

Santiago was selling spliffs by the cyclone fence behind the Tilt-A-Whirl. He looked like Billy Idol's ugly ass kid brother. He was a Mexican with bleached blonde hair. The look was pretty severe. Del liked it. Santiago was the first guy he ever knew who wore eyeliner. He was red-eyed when Del saw him, wearing a grin like he'd just toked up his profits. When Del approached, the two guys Santiago was hanging out with took off. Del said, "Hey," and asked Santiago if he was holding.

"I'm always holding, and call me Slagger."

"Slagger it is." They split a doobie and Del told him that he'd left St. Elizabeth's. Slagger nodded like he'd lived that story.

They ended up hanging out all weekend. Slagger was a good side-kick. He pushed Del to be more of a punk than he already was. They ran wild in the streets, lit trash bins afire, nicked wine, nabbed dash-board smokes, clipped carnival tickets, and basically terrorized the shit out of the carnival goers. It was a good time. Despite differences, those two got to be real tight over the next few weeks, even though Del had plans of leaving someday soon.

He was keeping his clothes, music, and whatnot stored at Slagger's squat on Maple. Del didn't want a lease tying him down or telling him where he had to be tomorrow. In that respect, the Roosevelt suited him just fine. Del didn't plan on being in Bayetteville one day longer than he had to, but it took funds to get to London.

His whoring cash was his ticket out, so he tried cheating Leo every chance he got. The way he saw things, it wasn't cheating so much as planning for his future. If he'd have saved the money it would've been an investment. He figured it all as preparation and even thought about learning as much about the UK as he could, but never got around to doing it.

Given the shape he was in and the things he was doing, Del wasn't inclined to learn much of anything. He got a bit crazed with the partying. Those days were a haze blurred by anything and everything he could take or do. The all of it spun around and around like the world or a record or a toilet. If Del's eyes followed that whirl for too long all he could do was puke, so he ended up closing his eyes tight, laughing his ass off, and hanging on like a kid at the playground.

A Mighty Fine Turn

over a year after Sister and Leo
poured his pert butt into that Minneapolis-bound bus, Leo was at the
back door of the bar hanging a No-Pest Strip when who should stroll
in and drop a duffel bag at the foot of the stepladder but Cody.

He was leaner but didn't look to have lost an ounce of muscle. The
cowlick was gone and something else was different as well, something
Leo couldn't put a finger on. He was still sexy, maybe even more so,
but in a knowing way. Instead of being just a part of him, now his good
looks seemed to be something he'd gotten wise about using. Similar
things had happened to most good-looking men Leo had known.

"Leo." He reached and gave his hand a shake and flashed his dimples
all at once. Yowsah! Leo about got blown backwards off the ladder
by all the charm. He gave a smile right back and jumped down. Cody
slapped Leo's shoulder and without blushing a bit asked if the job offer was still open. He'd gotten bolder, not cocky, just sure of himself
and how he came across.

His question took Leo by surprise, but he just laughed. "Hell yes!"
The words to turn that one down were not in his vocabulary.

"Good, then I'm back for a spell."

"Well, welcome back. How long you plan on staying?"

Cody shifted his weight. "Not sure, as long as it feels right, I suppose."

Leo couldn't argue with that, only he was hoping that meant a good
stretch of time. "Shit, you look good boy!"

"You, too." He said it like he meant it and despite Leo being a jaded
bit of baggage he still felt a clear case of the all overs.

Just then Sister came out of the john, stopped dead in his tracks,
and let out such a sissy squeal that hounds two counties over commenced to howling. Everybody who wasn't already watching turned.
Bruschetta spun so quick she about lost her wig.

"Well, I'll be damned!" Sister gave Cody a hug and a couple slaps on
the back. Leo and Sister wrapped arms around that boy's waist and
led him back into the bar proper. "Now set yourself down and tell us
everything." Leo gestured for Ben to line up some shooters.

Cody shrugged. "Ain't much to tell. I'm back, that's all."

"That's plenty!" Sister lifted one up and toasted his return.

After a few more drinks and a lot more laughs, Sister leaned over and with a liquor-heavy shake of his head said he could've told Leo that Cody would be back. "I still got the gift." Sister leaned back on his stool and sighed. He always claimed "the sight" was a burden. "It's problem enough coping with the present; I don't welcome having to contend with the future as well."

Two minutes after their butts hit the vinyl, Kitra started laughing and flipping her hair, crossing and uncrossing her legs, and thrusting out her blouse until reality clicked under that big Barbie doll hair of hers: she finally surmised that Cody was gay too. Even then, she didn't entirely abandon her flirting. It must have been frustrating as hell to frequent a place where she could never get man-laid.

More than a few folks got to scratching their heads to consider that girl. At first, Kitra claimed she didn't care to be around straight men. They all took that to mean she was itching for a woman but bashful about coming right out and saying so. Lulu had been interested for a while. "I'll be glad to show her all she's been missing," she confided to the Blob and Sister one night. Sister was daring Lulu to tell her there was an open seat on her face.

"I ain't crude like you boys."

Lulu was known for being a real operator when a woman struck her fancy, but Kitra froze up whenever she was about and Lulu didn't have the patience to wait for the thaw. It was all for the best anyway. A couple weeks later, Lulu met Anna at Midtown Pool... And like that Kitra was out of the picture.

Then Hester had asked her out. Kitra turned her down cold, saying she wasn't *that way*.

As it was, Kitra had been a semi-regular for months and far as anyone knew, she was still as chaste as an Osmond. Boring! Whenever Kitra came through the door, Sister whispered that she was visiting the mission. Seeing her straight-woman moves on Cody that night was a clear sign of her desperation, as well as his across-the-board appeal.

Leo redid the schedule right then and there, though he was feeling a bit too good to make the lines straight. Seniority didn't mean shit. Ben's jaw tightened as soon as he saw what was going on. He could taste the food scraps and see the hand-me-downs in his future.

The following Sunday was Cody's Sand Bar debut. He ribbed Leo that he was shocked the bar was open on the Sabbath.

"Hell, yes, we're open, and serving everything but God."

Sister was dead on about Cody's effect on business. From day one the ring was up during his shifts. That could've been attributed to the fact that Ben had been stealing, but even without that sticky-fingered factor business was up. When word about the new bartender spread, business rose quicker than a lumberjack's pecker. It was even a bigger boom than after the pool tables arrived. In under two weeks time Cody had the stools lined with admirers sighing like schoolgirls, giving coy glances, and fanning themselves whilst he moved about behind the bar in tight t-shirts and jeans snug as sausage skins. Cody knew just what to wear and how to move to make it seem he wasn't flaunting what he had so much as stating the fact of his having it. The fact came across loud and clear! Cody had a decent ego, but was sly over letting that be known. He had a dread of being fingered as vain.

Cody had a way of making everyone feel special and giving them the hope that maybe, just maybe, they could end up between the sheets with him. That was one sweet carrot to be a dangling. The potential of future sex when he talked and listened and laughed was his secret. His charm and looks wormed the cash from some of the tightest pockets in the tri-states. That brand of talent wasn't entirely unscripted, so Leo and Sister figured he must have gotten wise in Minneapolis. He told Sister he'd tended bar there, but that's about all he'd say of the year he'd been away.

Sister and Leo wondered just what had transpired and why he'd returned. Leo waved the air with a cigarette, "Don't get me wrong, I'm happy as a pig in shit over his being back, but I'm still curious as to the particulars." Cody never mentioned one word about that Frank character he was so all fired up to see. All signs pointed towards true love gone sour. Whenever he was asked, Cody would just shrug and say it was time for a change. After a bit, Leo and Sister figured it best not to pry, especially when he wasn't saying anything anyways.

For a while after his return, a buddy of his from up there by the name of Ricardo was coming around. They'd moved to town together but it didn't seem romantic. Ricardo was a hot little tamale who worked the door at the Onyx. Leo liked to say that Ricardo had one of those butts that looked able to pickup a dime and give you change.

Cody must have said something to Ricardo about keeping quiet over doings in Minneapolis, because he was just as tight lipped about it as Cody. After coming in weekly for a couple of months, Ricardo up and left town. He was just there getting some money together. Cody didn't seem too shook up to see him go. To Leo, it appeared that Cody took comfort in knowing the last of his Minneapolis connections was gone.

With Cody hungry for hours, Ben-Gay and Finn dwindled down to part time. Ben worked so little, he decided it wasn't worth it. He acted like he didn't care, but truth was Ben couldn't stomach not being the most desired, the most butch, the most handsome, and *the most* in general. Most was being conservative. By most estimates, he wanted it all. He wasn't one to share when he was a kid and he hadn't grown into the habit. With Cody around, Ben was one sorry-ass second. Of course, Ben claimed to have had his fill with the bar and the patrons and the town and every other thing he could name. the feeling certainly seemed mutual. There was no big or even small movement to try and keep him in Bayetteville.

Ben commenced to making other plans. Ben thought that maybe when Leo saw him doing that, he'd break down and ask him to stay. The next month, Leo did everything but pack his bags and drive him to the bus station. As it was, Leo gave him a send-off that cost a week's worth of profits; to Leo's way of thinking, Ben leaving town was cause enough for everyone to tie one on.

One afternoon, not long after his departure Slagger and Del came stumbling in the bar laughing and carrying on. Slags was waving an envelope and raking that white hair which made him look two weeks dead and more Santa's Taco than ever. All it did was bring out the bags beneath his eyes and the pimpling of his skin. "It's a letter from Ben. I haven't even opened it yet."

"Well, open it!" said Sister, lighting a smoke.

Bruschetta swiveled on her stool and crossed her legs. "Go on now and read it to us."

Slagger looked around and tore open the letter. He cleared his throat and drew back before slowly moving forward. Santiago had the money for every sort of drug but not a cent for a proper pair of reading glasses. Ben wrote that he got a job at some swank downtown department store and went on some about the rich clientele but also made a big to-do of saying that was all temporary. "Can you see me doing this the rest of my life? Hell no! I am set to break into the country music business." When Slagger read the last part Sister snubbed out his cigarette and rolled his eyes.

"Country music?" said Hester.

Bruschetta chuckled, "Get on. It doesn't say that."

"It does so!"

Del took a swallow of his beer. The line of his brow grew serious. "Ben got that idea from me, only I'm sure as shit not interested in that redneck crap. Punk is the way to go. One day, you can all say you knew me when..."

Sister rolled his eyes a second time. Leo chuckled to think that Sister was likely to give himself a headache if he didn't watch his reactions.

Slagger turned the letter over and stared a moment at the blank page. "That's about all it says."

Bruschetta unclasped her clutch and pulled out some stationery. She looked over at Sister. "I am always prepared." Handing the paper to Slagger she tapped a nail on the bar. "Now write Ben back and tell him to get his butt on over to Nashville if songwriting is what he has a mind to do." Sometimes Slagger took offense to that sort of thing, but not that afternoon. He just offered a slack-jawed look before writing down just exactly what she said.

Del slapped the side of the bar. "And tell him Reese got busted for possession. He'd want to know about that."

"Tell him we're all commencing to say we knew Del when..." laughed Hester.

Del glared in her direction.

"Hold on, hold on, I can only write so fast."

Truth was it surprised most that Slagger could write at all. When he did he parted his lips and leaned close like he was about seven years old.

After a minute he looked up. "You want me to say anything from you Leo?"

Leo didn't know quite how to respond to that. "No, just tell him to take care of himself."

Sister looked at Leo with a smirk. Leo shrugged and mouthed, "Fuck You," right back. He couldn't think of a word to say to Ben. Actually, he could think of plenty, only nothing he saw as proper to be putting in a letter.

Slagger sent the note off the following day. The coming week Ben replied and said he met a Roger something or other in Memphis and they had been working on some songs. He said Brenda Lee was thinking about recording one. Nothing ever came of it, or at least nothing anybody ever heard a word more about. *Sweet Nothin's* was right! The folks at the Sand Bar all figured it was just more of Ben's big talk and always needing to brag. Truth was everyone knew his ego was fragile as bone china.

Slagger sniffed the letter and gave a chipped tooth smile. He said it sounded like the songwriter was Ben's new lover.

Del nodded.

The rest of the folks there looked around to see if Jack-O was lurking about before agreeing.

Bruschetta took a cigarette from her tortoise-shell case and paused for Slagger to give her a light. "Thanks darling... Now to my way of thinking Ben has only one lover, and that's Ben."

"That can't be too satisfying."

"And it's got to be real high maintenance."

"Maybe he's getting sick of himself."

"I know I got sick of him."

Bruschetta tsked. "Now hush—don't you all be so catty."

"It's not being catty, it's preaching gospel. And to me it sounds like Ben is using this man as a stepping stone."

Sister nodded. "That's Ben all right."

No matter how Christian folks tried to be, nobody could really imagine Ben behaving any different. It was all a means to an end to him; only Ben didn't have any real end in sight. This country music thing was just another passing fancy. Even Slagger and Del agreed about his using folks and they were Ben's tightest pals. Those three had been busy misbehaving and carousing since last summer.

Leo looked over at Del in his ripped jeans and licked his lips to recall their afternoon upstairs. They'd sort of had themselves a repeat performance a couple weeks back. Del was a wild thing—half bird, half colt, and mostly cock. By then he was making regular money selling that attitude and pecker of his, but with all his bad habits, he never had ten cents to his name. Guys liked him because he was the sort they couldn't get for free. You can only work that act for so long. Sister couldn't stomach him and said there were too many reasons to say exactly why. He understood Leo's attraction but it was one they never shared.

The last time Ben wrote, he said Memphis was a bust. He was planning on moving to Branson soon as he took care of some things. "Branson is the spot for making my mark, a town lined with nothing but clubs and honky-tonks and all sorts of entertainment types clamoring for fresh material." He predicted success within a year.

Leo turned to Sister. "What's your gift say about that?"

Sister gave a long pause. "I don't need no gift to see the future there. That's a future without a future. The only mystery is if he's delusional or an out and out liar."

"He's followed this dream longer than I expected."

"And further..." added Hester.

Slagger scratched his head and let loose a choppy laugh. He never knew half of what was going on. Del nudged him and mumbled something. Two minutes later they were off their stools and out the back.

Sister shook his head. "Ten to one they're even more fucked up by the time they stumble back in."

"That's another sure thing."

The next note sent to Ben was returned, address unknown.

Jack-O was downcast and pouty that Ben kept in touch with Slagger but not him. His booze-fuelled lamentation of the snub became a nightly routine. He couldn't see that Ben didn't give a hoot as to him. Or anybody. Most folks felt for him, but there are few things on the good earth more pathetic than a sucker who gets taken but won't get wise to the fact.

As time went by, Jack-O rhapsodized about Ben in such a favorable light you would've thought Ben was a saint—instead of the vain little con-artist everybody knew him to be. Jack-O could talk himself hoarse on the subject. And after a while, most everybody stopped listening or considered it a kind of white noise.

Seeing his sloppy public airing night after night got Leo to sometimes feeling low over redoing the schedule, but the feeling passed.

He liked Jack-O. The guy probably dropped more cash at his place than most anybody. For the most part Jack-O was an okay guy, if you could sidestep all his problems and shut off his chatter. Leo didn't want to hurt him and it pained him that Jack-O held him responsible for Ben's leaving, but Leo knew he'd do it again in a heartbeat. Business was business and Jack-O wasn't part of his decision. He had every right to cut Ben's hours on the schedule. He'd put up with his bull crap for too long as it was. With that bad attitude, he was nobody Leo wanted in his employ. He told Jack-O as much, but there was no telling him one word he didn't want to hear. Drunks had a record playing in their head; they said the same things, thought the same things, and heard the same things. Whenever Leo tried talking to Jack-O about it, he'd just get too drunk to listen and then get all pissy over something else. At some point Leo stopped trying to explain.

The way Leo saw it, cutting Ben's time looked to be a lot less messy than confronting him about missing money and bottles. If that happened Leo figured he could count on fireworks, and some big ones. Ben was awful theatrical. He loved a scene and Leo avoided that sort of thing at all costs, at least in business. There was usually enough drama happening on the other side of the bar without his adding more to it.

Finn stayed on. He tended bar Tuesdays and worked at Staley's on weekends. Between the two, he made enough to scrape by living at the Roosevelt. With no green card, he didn't have many options and with his looks and charm those choices were even less. He had a good heart, but unless you talked about Cher he was bland as a barrel of egg whites.

Finn didn't say much and when he did it was mostly a rewording of what was already told to him...only decidedly s-l-o-w-e-r. That used to drive folks batty. When Lulu was courting Anna and they were in that giddy phase, Finn used to always give them the giggles. They called him the Statue, on account of his being so pale and standing stock-still and staring off into space until someone asked for a drink.

"Like he's in another world," said Sister.

Lulu nudged Sister a minute later. "All that's missing is the pigeon crap on his shoulders." Sister got a good laugh out of that.

"Nord" was a word that got bantered back and forth for a while. Folks used it whenever anybody got vacant-eyed or repeated something someone else had just said. Nordic was what it stood for. Folks weren't being mean so much as finding cause to cut up. It was all in fun. Bob used to bristle when he heard that, but he was too sensitive about his weight to say anything. Every one who did it was a pal, but he knew bar folks could turn vicious awful quick and the Blob lived in mortal fear of being a target. Stepping in the middle of things would make him fair game, and should somebody be looking, there was a whole lot of him to aim for.

Sister and Leo never understood why the Blob was all moony for Finn anyways. "I suppose it takes all kinds," said Sister. Be that as it may, Finn didn't seem to be anyone's type—except maybe one of them necrophiliacs. Leo told Bob more than once that since he wasn't going to act on it anyways, he should at least pick a fantasy man with a readable pulse. He only said that when his brain was mostly pickled. Bob never took offense. That sort of talk embarrassed him. He'd get all flustered and say "Oh well" or some such.

With Finn on Tuesdays and Leo on Mondays, Cody took over the rest of the week. Leo knew he was doing speed. The signs were big as the snow caps of Everest. Since he worked upwards of sixty hours a week, Leo figured he had a right. Sister maintained that Leo should say something, but when it came to things of that sort, Leo was all for keeping to his own side of the fence. "It's my place, but that is none of my business." Besides, Leo couldn't help but feel hypocritical giving a lecture to someone on the rights and wrongs of overindulgence. Leo finally said to Sister that there were worse things than a hyped-up worker in a place where a lot needed getting done. Cody was always wiping and Windexing, straightening bottles, mopping, and selling a good amount of booze too. Sister always gave Leo a look when Cody ducked in the can for his evening boost. Cody never caught on that they knew.

Whenever Leo didn't agree with Sister or went against his wishes, Sister would pull his drink close and get all tight-lipped. Leo would think, "Oh there he goes again, sitting there with small mouth." Sister only stayed mad long enough for Leo to see he was mad and to get his point across. That was never long. Two minutes later, they'd be laughing their fool heads off over one thing or another. Buddies couldn't be mad for long, especially when shots were involved.

The Ed Smock

Fred would never forget the summer of his first sexual experience. It happened the summer disco died. He was reminded of the fact with every Disco Sucks t-shirt he saw on the streets and at the Vienna Beef. Despite a booming start, Bayetteville's big dance club, the Onyx, celebrated its second anniversary by closing its doors. The sinking popularity and hatred for disco didn't mean much to Fred. Its dying only made him love it more.

Everything seemed to be changing. Earlier that year, the near impossible happened and Nadine found herself a beau. She'd been dating Walter Winchell since January—not THE Walter Winchell—though when he wrote a check at Nadine's register out at the Piggly Wiggly, it was his name which sparked their conversing, that and his conspicuous lack of a wedding band. It wasn't long after that Walter began coming by her place on Saturdays. There was some whispering over the fact that most Sunday mornings his Rambler was still parked in the gravel lot longside her building.

Every other weekend, Walter had visitation rights with his two preteen daughters. Nadine began joining the three of them on outings. Pammy and Charlene adored her. More than once, Nadine invited Fred to tag along, but Fred had declined. Tagging along wasn't his way. He didn't enjoy being an afterthought. The fact of Nadine being occupied didn't bother him. Besides, he was getting a little old for going over there anyways. Nadine's falling in love was a nice way of putting some space in their friendship. To compensate for what she considered a slight, Nadine invited Fred to lunch every so often. It was thoughtful, but the things they shared were all a part of Fred's past. He'd commenced to thinking ahead.

Fred decided he needed a change in his life and went walking down along the railroad tracks. The heat always did things to his head and that day was a scorcher. The dry grass whistled in the wind and the tree leaves flashed silver undersides. Fred looked down at his feet. If he followed the ties, he'd reach the river at the spot of his jump. That wouldn't happen again. He wouldn't follow the same path, and even if he did, he wouldn't look down into the flow or be hypnotized by the waves. He tried focusing on the ties, the gravel sides, and the odd bits of metal and glass scattered across the rubble ballast. He seemed on the verge of finding something extraordinary and that promise kept him going. The river was just around the bend. Once he rounded the turn there'd be a parting of weeds, and then the bridge. It would not happen again. He couldn't risk it. He'd never go back to St. Xavier's.

When the wind died down, he heard music and pounding. Across the overgrown lot up ahead, he saw the cement block rear of Frear Park Auto. The doors were open and autos filled all five bays at varying levels of elevation.

Deciding he could do with a soda, Fred crossed the vacant lot to the garage. He went inside and got change for the pop machine. A Help Wanted sign caught his eye. He didn't really think much about what he was doing when he filled out the application. He'd been flipping burgers and dropping fry baskets for over a year. This place paid more than the Vienna Beef. He probably couldn't watch TV all day, but that was growing old too. He'd already cashed his two-hundred-dollar year-on-the-job check and won back a tolerable amount of his folks' trust.

The scraggly blond attendant wiped a greasy finger across his nose and ran a pen down the length of his application. He lifted the hair from the nape of his neck and held it atop his head in a surprisingly feminine, but heat justifiable, pose. His shirt said *Joshua*. Fred couldn't tell if he was eighteen or thirty-five. Veins slithered beneath his filthy, sweaty skin. Joshua sat down and tilted his chair back against the wall. The gesture made Fred figure him closer to eighteen.

Joshua asked a question or two but didn't seem interested in the answers. He really didn't even look at Fred. "Sounds okay" was his sole comment. Tossing the application back onto the desk, he told Fred to be there Monday at eight sharp. Fred nodded and shook his greasy hand. When he picked up his Grape Nehi a minute later the bottle slipped from his grip and landed upside down in the garbage bin. Joshua just laughed, "See you Monday Slick."

Fred wiped his hands on his pants and bought another soda. Leaving the garage, he felt anxious and proud but confused. It'd all happened so quickly. He'd been sure of it at the time, now second thoughts were starting to sprout. He nearly jumped out of his skin when a semi-tractor blew its exhaust stack and air horn. The driver waved "So long" to a couple mechanics and right-angled his rig from the lot.

Fred shook his head and walked back down the tracks towards downtown with his shoes crunching on the side gravel. At a switch stand, he veered off along a closure trail. He looked inside an abandoned Plymouth with a cluster of wild grass sprouting from the engine. He walked further and scaled some terraced limestone slabs along a dry filler stream. It was the perfect place to toss some rocks and do some thinking.

His parents would be pleased. He'd made a wise career move, and it was a manly job. Anything with the potential to butch him up would please them. They'd never come right out and call him girly. Saying so would mean recognizing something was amiss. That wasn't their way. They were more likely just to show a sort of sad embarrassment.

He called Mr. Nadir that night and said Sunday had to be his last day at the Vienna Beef. Mr. Nadir exhaled loudly. Fred imagined his nostrils flaring and that nose hair of his tickling the receiver like fan flags. He seemed to get it all out of his system in a single breath. After that, he made a big to-do over Fred's leaving being no big deal. "Do what you want. It's a free country. Leave your smock by the register. Those are harder to replace than most of you workers." After that, it was pretty much over.

That weekend, he was understandably anxious about his new job. It was a step up, but he wasn't sure that up was the direction he wanted to go. There'd been safety in his old routine. Now all this change was rousing him from his rut. He worried his co-workers would tease him and that it'd be nothing but a fresh spin on his outsider life. That was something he swore he'd do different. This time, he'd do whatever it took to fit in.

On Monday, Fred arrived at his new job a half hour early. He cursed his over soon habit, and sat in the lot fingering his rabbit's foot key chain. It was balding, yellowing, and freckled with ink stains. Fred inherited it years ago from a boy down the block who was hit by a truck. Fred had no memory of Ricky, but had heard his mother talk herself hoarse with the Story often enough.

It happened during a solar eclipse. Supposedly Fred was sitting on the back stoop watching the sky reflected in a dish tub of water while his mother made lunch. Lila wasn't about to step outdoors with all the talk of how dangerous the sun's rays could be at a time like that. To her it was no different than hopping right inside one of those microwave ovens.

Ricky dashed out into traffic after a plastic ball. There was no scream, only a screeching of brakes. A semi of Georgia peaches dragged him half a block down Pine before locking to a hissing halt. The flashers of police cars, a fire truck, and an ambulance cut the golden dusk of the blocked sun. The driver claimed the eclipse had momentarily blinded him.

Lila saw the all of it from the kitchen window. The sight was so upsetting she dropped a mayonnaise jar right onto her foot. A second ambulance had to come for her. She hobbled about on crutches the rest of that spring.

Lila felt obligated to go to the funeral after witnessing the accident and breaking two toes and all. At the gravesite Ricky's mother slipped the key chain into Lila's hand. She said it would please her for Fred to have it, which was odd since the families had never socialized. Ricky's father thought Rog was a lush and Rog thought Ricky's father "never hurt for nothing." Besides, Fred didn't really play with other children. He was always off by himself. Lila took the good luck charm anyway, rightly assuming Ricky's mother had a mind to be rid of it.

Fred couldn't recall much good luck it had brought him, but then again he'd never been maimed or undone by catastrophe. He wondered if the best breaks a person had were in what had been avoided, and what never occurred.. After all, Ricky hadn't been carrying the key chain the day he got squashed.

Cars began to cluster in the lot. Fred waited a few minutes, then walked up to the front door. Entering, he realized he should've stayed in the car a while longer. It was still a full ten minutes to the hour and someone was just trying to ready things for opening. Fred stood near the desk and tried looking as inconspicuous as possible. He heard the bay doors roll open and the voices of the mechanics pour into the garage. A flash of heat rushed toe to head when Fred realized he was leaning against the time clock. He ducked around the doorway and sat down quick in an orange plastic chair. A huge clock hung on one wall. The Poker Playing Dogs were on another. It was the waiting room. A beat up coffee machine gurgled longside three peaks of white Styrofoam cups.

"You Fred?"

Fred jumped at the booming voice and turned to the man in the doorway. He wore a white shirt with a Roy patch. A deflated belly hung over his belt like an old bitch's teat. He was so bow-legged, word was he couldn't cross his legs if he tried. He was middle-aged with a lazy eye and a weather-worn face. The combined effects made Fred think of a shriveled potato. His pointed purplish ears even resembled a couple of side roots.

Fred nodded.

"What the hell are you doing hiding in here? Come on." Roy shook Fred's hand and led him to the service desk. The lenses of Roy's glasses darkened as they entered the garage. Over revving, clanging engines, and a blaring tape deck, he explained the job. Roy was invoice clerk at Frear Park's sister establishment, Hot City Oil and Lube. He appeared sometimes slender and sometimes hefty, depending on the angle. Though missing two fingers and the tip of a thumb, he still managed to juggle a telephone, pen, and cigarette while training Fred. His remaining six fingers were thick as sausages and his one full thumb was huge.

Tilting up his feed hat, Roy said he was sick and planned to move back home soon as he could afford it. He looked down at his feet when he talked about the cancer as though it was a source of shame. His bringing it up made Fred uncomfortable, too. He didn't know what to say, so he remained silent. By noon, Roy had explained everything. He left after lunch.

According to the bold print on his Xeroxed employee sheet, Fred's primary duty as invoice clerk was writing bills by itemizing parts and labor, calculating tax, totaling cost, and collecting payment. When a car came in for service, Fred wrote up a work description and hung the invoice on a bungee cord with a clothespin magic-markered with the service pin number. He looked up parts in catalogues and matched the right muffler, alternator, or spark plugs to the right make and model car. It wasn't difficult, but it got more respect than flipping burgers.

As invoice clerk, he was also in charge of answering the telephone, an act of some courage, since Fred had always been self-conscious of his voice. Mostly he mumbled. Hearing phone voices in that noisy garage was tougher than being heard. It caused him to hold the handset so tight his cheeks got smudged with grease. That macho rouge filled him with guy pride and balanced his having to do less masculine tasks like tidying up the waiting room.

Lounge upkeep meant sweeping the linoleum, emptying ashtrays, straightening magazines, and dusting the plastic plants. However, the real chore was maintaining the coffee supply and gathering up discarded cups. Roy had whispered to try and reuse the cups unless they had discernible tooth marks or fingernail etches or excessive lipstick along the rim.

Keeping his promise to fit in, Fred saw he had to make some changes. At Frear Park Auto. life centered on Molly Hatchet and AC/DC, Confederate flags, and super jams at the speedway. His co-workers were mostly bony-chested boys with homemade tattoos and teenage brides in tube tops and high heels. Everyone chained smoked and spontaneous air-guitar licks were a way of life. "Party" was the most common noun, verb, and exclamation. Fitting in there meant taking on a new self altogether.

Fred's sense of being someone else began his first day when Roy handed him a navy blue smock with the name patch Rhonda. He felt a flickering in his belly but calmed himself. They weren't poking fun at him, but something like this could sure give them ideas. A spare Fred smock would've been too much to hope for. Roy shifted his weight, put his big thumb aside his nose, and explained that in a couple weeks time he'd have a personalized smock. But until then the Rhonda smock would have to do.

The mechanics razzed him about it and predictably called him Rhonda a couple times. It bothered Fred less than he would have supposed. In some ways, the Rhonda smock was a good decoy to divert those barbs from digging deeper. Still, it annoyed him enough to want a change. After making coffee the next morning, he rooted through the linen closet in the mechanic's john and found an old oversized smock with an Ed name patch.

Wearing the Ed smock didn't bother Fred, since he didn't feel like himself working there. It was a part of the bigger disguise. Slipping in the arms of that smock was like slipping into another man's hide. Ed lived a life Fred would never have. Ed was no pansy. He cranked the radio for Judas Priest, Motley Crue, Def Leppard, and Iron Maiden. He knew things guys always knew and talked cars, sports, and boobs. Ed had a hot fox of a girlfriend who lived in Edgartown. Fred said her name was Denise and she was a nursing student with a mole on her left ass cheek. His words and lies rolled upon themselves and he couldn't see his lies revealed much more than the truth. The scripted falseness was plain to everyone, even slow Emmet, who rarely caught the obvious. The mechanics exchanged grins whenever Fred ran off at the mouth about cars or women or music.

Fred's Ed identity was modeled on Mac. Fred longed for him almost as much as he had for Del, but in a different way. This wasn't a soul connection. This yearning was more the carnal sort. From the moment Fred saw him bent over a 383 engine, looking sexy and intense, Mac became the shining star of his sex fantasies. He was equal parts brash, scary, and passionate. Fred got silly over the entire situation and imagined that Mac was the reason he'd chanced upon the job. Fate or some raunchy angel had brought him here. He was always partial for having a bigger reason for things.

Mac was a hell-raising mechanic and the yoke of the crew. He played bass for a garage band named Acid Rain. Mac looked like a sleazier Frampton with soft brown eyes and wild brown hair. A tuft of the stuff sprouted from the unbuttoned collar of his uniform. That hook of hair always snagged Fred's attention and dragged him lower into some sort of sort of nasty fantasy. Mac's endless talk of pussy quests, told in a guttural bass voice, always left Fred near-about breathless.

Fred stammered whenever Mac was about and blushed just to see him ruffle his mane or blow snot out a nostril. A whiff of Mac's sweat could get him high. There was nothing finer than seeing Mac stretched out on a dolly beneath the bumper of a car. Fred wanted to kneel down and do his own brand of servicing. His eyes roamed to that wondrous crotch countless times a day and he hadn't yet learned discretion with such things.

For some reason, Mac took a liking to Fred. Sometimes they talked during breaks. Mac talked mostly about himself. Fred found it easier to listen anyways. Mac told Fred he was going to make something of himself and planned to do it through music. "It don't get no better than rock and roll for pay." Mac shared his dreams for Acid Rain and said he knew one day some manager or producer would come along and sign him to a better band. That sort of thing was common in the music business. He was biding his time and reading psychology books about focus. Fred gave him encouragement from recycled movie-dialogue. Mac sucked it up until he was full as a deer tick.

One Thursday, while totaling exhaust repairs on a Mustang, Mac invited Fred to an Acid Rain rehearsal. Fred looked up open-mouthed and nodded. Mac wrote the directions down on a strip of adding machine tape. Fred stared at the curling piece of paper and worried he'd accepted the invite too quickly. He fretted the rest of the afternoon over what to wear and how to act.

Following Mac's directions, he wound up in an alley that was a branch of one of his main garbage-picking thoroughfares. He recognized some of the older dumpsters. Acid Rain was tuning up in a flip-door garage just ahead. At first he felt awkward, but quickly noticed that the group was too stoned for hostility. Sitting on that cooler and handing out beers as the need arose, Fred felt like a groupie and with good reason.

Mac growled when he sang and his upper lip assumed an "M" shape. He backed away from the microphone when it was guitar time, and it always seemed guitar time. Acid Rain featured a loud guitarist named Kevin, a louder one named Morey, and Mac, the loudest decibel defier of them all. The group also included Elf, a dazed drummer with bad teeth and worse breath. It was his granny's garage. Old Mrs. Waverhoffen actually sat on her back porch steps for the better part of an hour tapping her fat ankled foot until *Truth or Consequences* started.

At best, the music was bad. They were spirited amateurs in need of practice. They weren't making rock, they were aping it. Volume was top priority and there was a serious problem with feedback, but despite any lack of talent, Fred was never hotter for Mac. The music took backseat to the worship of the ass-kicker archetype and Mac was a snug fit in that pagan prince of rock and roll mold.

Fred coyly covered his crotch. "That was great," Fred said after the multi guitar lick close of their final song.

Though partially deaf and a little drunk, Fred was sure he'd heard someone shout "Thank fucking God" from somewheres down the alley. It sounded like Del. Craning his neck Fred couldn't see a thing. His ears were ringing so he figured he must've imagined it.

When Mac asked if he wanted to go get high, Fred said, "Sure." His heart was racing. Mac said so long to the guys and nabbed a six pack from the cooler. They cruised town in Mac's Trans Am. Passing a fat joint between them, Mac mused about nymphomaniacal groupies and his plans to van it westward doing gigs, partying, getting established, and getting laid. Mac pressed the gas and cruised eighty until they got to a pier on the Frear just north of town. It was a balmy August night. Heat lightning shorted in the western sky. They watched the flashes and listened to the lapping waves. Gnats skittered over the surface and circled in shadowy clouds. It was just like paradise lying on those planks and talking with Mac.

Fred watched Mac take a drag off his Salem and realized he wanted to *be* Mac more than bed him. Mac enjoyed the adoration, but he could never understand the things Fred felt deep inside and Fred could never express those things as Ed. A smile crossed his lips. So much suddenly made sense. It was never necessary to express himself to Del. He'd always just known.

Mac kept talking about Acid Rain. Looking down into the waves Fred's mind continued to wander. Mac's life was so different and Fred knew that despite his efforts he could never make their two worlds mesh. He was a closeted homo and discophile in love with a straight rock and roller. There was no future in that.

The hopelessness of things with Mac wasn't what had changed. Fred was used to impossible dreams and relying on absurd long shots. The change came when he saw Del again. It was then that he realized there could never be another.

Lately, Fred had been spending most evenings hanging out and dancing at the Sand Bar. Just hearing the music and seeing the lights was a big thrill. Everything felt so alive there, pulsing to the music beneath a drapery of pale smoke. At Frear Park Auto, dancing with another guy to disco music would be seen as the most perverse of all perversions.

Two nights prior at the Sand Bar, right in the middle of "If My Friends Could See Me Now," Fred saw Del reflected in the mirror behind the dance floor. Fred about choked on an ice cube! Del was dancing with two other guys. His hair had gotten long. Silver skulls swung from his ears. His weight loss was clear in his tight black jeans and British flag t-shirt. Fred never expected to see him there, but seeing him there made perfect sense. It was another slice of destiny. He must've burned a hole with his staring since Del paused halfway through a spin to offer a sloppy grin that looked part contempt, part recognition, and part the old pleasure of having an audience.

Fred remembered the framed photo on Nadine's bureau and the feelings that had filled him ever since. That level of magic and attraction was still deeper than anything life had shown him. Mac was a fantasy. Del was the real thing and even beyond that. Del was everything. He and Del shared the same source.

Last week when he and Nadine met for lunch at Staley's, Nadine took one bite from her hot beef special and said Del turned up during her Tuesday shift at Piggly Wiggly. "He looked like I don't know what and asked flat out to borrow cash. He was thin as a rail and seemed bordering on starvation." Nadine wanted Del to come stay with her, but Del was adamant about his independence. When the manager gave Nadine a look she slipped Del thirty dollars and asked him to stick around a half hour until her break. "Del just shook his head and said he had to be someplace. He was out the door so quick I didn't get a chance to find out just where he was living." After some careful consideration Nadine decided not to mention seeing him to Pearl Louise. "That boy needs to feel somebody is on his side."

Fred had only seen Del once since he'd stopped coming to school. One night driving home late from work, Fred caught sight of him hanging out in front of an empty storefront downtown. When Fred honked, Del spun around and flipped him off. Fred wasn't hurt or offended. For Del, that was a reflex response. Besides, Del could've never seen who was cruising Elm at that time of evening.

Standing beside Del that night was the same snow-capped character that he was dancing with at the Sand Bar. Fred figured it was his boyfriend. There was another guy on the floor longside them, strutting around with his chest out and his ass tucked like the definition of cocky. Later Fred found out it was Santiago and Ben. Sweat smudged Santiago's eyeliner and dripped onto his lean shirtless chest. He wore nothing but jeans and suspenders. Ben had on a faded baseball jersey. It was clear all three were having a party and that most of it was taking place in their heads...or their bloodstreams.

"They're all pals and all trouble," semi-shouted a buxom blonde into Fred's ear. Fred fought the urge to stare and failed. She didn't sound like she looked. The woman was familiar, but he couldn't tell from where. He assumed it was because she looked like a movie star with her blonde mane and the black spaghetti strap cocktail dress that was practically painted onto her curves. She fished a cigarette from the pack and paused for him to light it. Exhaling she extended a manicured hand. "I'm Bruschetta." Fred wasn't sure if he should shake it or kiss it but he opted for the former. He couldn't help but stare at her sizable boobs.

"Don't eye my pink-nosed puppies like you're a bill collector. They're bought and paid for."

Fred blushed and glanced down before stumbling over a mumbled introduction.

"Don't fret, I won't have you kicked off the playground."

It took Fred a moment to realize she was teasing him. When he figured it out, he laughed.

"There. You're much more handsome when you smile." Fred's mother always said the same thing.

"Now, as I was saying about those three..."

"Hello, gorgeous." A man bent to kiss Bruschetta's cheek. He introduced himself as Dick and grinned in Fred's direction. Clearly Dick took considerable pride in the precise trim of his mustache. In seconds, Dick and Bruschetta began a hushed discussion about Lulu and Anna moving in together. With syncopated nods, both said they saw it coming from a mile away.

Fred looked around. His heart and head throbbed to the beat. A mirror ball spritzed light across the dance floor. He eyed Del in the mirror and knew in his bones that he could get used to this. The people were friendly and the glitz was bliss. It was everything movies had been but in three dimensions, and he was a part of it. Fred took another guzzle of his drink. It was years coming, but he finally felt like he belonged. Not as Ed or as anyone else, but as himself.

The hope of seeing Del, the Sand Bar brand of glamour, and that feeling of belonging lured Fred back the two following nights. Del was there both times, and both times he was wasted.

The next Saturday when Fred arrived, Ben was celebrating his final bartending shift and giving out free shots fast as he could pour them. He was cross-eyed from the rum and missing the glass half the time he poured.

Hester laughed and said that at this rate they could mop the floor and have another party tomorrow.

"You bet your black ass we can have another party tomorrow. Yes!" whooped Ben before settling down and talking in meandering loops about moving to Memphis the following week. He slurred that it would be the start of some real living for him. "I am full up with this cow town. You know? Nothing but a goddamned cow town."

Bruschetta whispered to Fred that this cow town had had about enough of him as well. "So moooo-ve." She added that the truth behind Ben's leaving was on account of Cody getting all the tips and attention. "His high-tailing it is nothing more than that green-eyed monster known as jealousy."

Leo confirmed her opinion with a single nod and said it was time he stepped behind the bar. "So much for having a night off. It's plain as a pig on a sofa Ben is too drunk to work."

Not everyone was there to wish Ben luck. Slouched on a stool beside Fred was Ben's boyfriend, Jack-O. He was drunk and distraught, lower than whale shit and not a bit shy about letting the world know it. Ben was moving to Memphis alone even though Jack-O offered to accompany him. He turned to Fred. "What does he want from me?"

"Sounds like he wants you to stay here," said Fred without thinking. Bruschetta and Hester giggled at his bluntness and Leo poured them all a shot. They clinked glasses, threw them back, and slammed the empties on the bar.

Jack-O rambled on. Dancing was about the only mannerly means of escape, so Fred excused himself and fled to the dance floor. He'd never danced before. Fueled by booze, he swallowed his fear and started spinning and chasing the light, but to the beat. It felt good and like everything else there, it felt right. Once the floor began to fill, he found a partner. After almost an hour of continuous discoing, Fred left the dance floor hand in hand with Dick. The sight raised some

eyebrows. Fred felt great being chosen by someone, and before witnesses. It wasn't Del, but it was someone. Dick was a graphic designer
who'd gone to a four-year school back East. Fred thought him terribly
sophisticated.

Staggering out the back at the flip of the house lights, Dick whispered that his place was just over on Pine. He made some firm open-
palmed circles over Fred's ass as though giving it a good polish. Fred
ran a hand over Dick's crotch. Dick grabbed his wrist; "Careful or
you'll set the house afire." Fred closed his eyes and raised his chin to
the breeze. It felt so damn good, every bit of it. He was drunk and
smiling and content as a hound in the sun. Dick's touch took him to
the brink of moaning. They swayed a few yards down the block before
Dick grabbed Fred's hand and swung him around. They deep kissed
against the bumper of an Impala. Fred felt Dick's tongue and heard a
honk at the same time. Joshua, the head mechanic, and his common-
law wife Rose drove by. Tires screeched down the street. Fred stared
bleary-eyed at the tail end of their passing car. Even drunk, he recognized the Rancid 2 plates.

Blood rushed to his face. Each hair on his head seemed to separate
as if making room for the gravity of what had just happened. It was
an instant of worlds colliding—the moment of Fred meets Ed. Dick
asked what was wrong, but Fred just shook his head and said he was
drunk. He still felt committed to going home with Dick and didn't
want to disappoint. His passion was gone, but not his sense of duty.
They walked in silence to Dick's home. The decor was gold and avo-
cado. The curtains had tassels. It was a real nice place. Dick assumed
Fred's silence was on account of his being a virgin, which he was and
remained despite Dick's pointed efforts. Fred was too nervous to relax.

Afterwards, and during actually, Fred lay awake worrying. He imagined Joshua and Rose phoning Mac from their deluxe waterbed and
teasing him about his relationship with a fag. "You two been corn
holing? Is that what you've been up to? Shit man, you having yourself
a grand old time with that dick smoker?"

On Sunday, Fred was worried but too hungover to focus. Mostly he
just lay semi-conscious before the TV and wished everything could
return to two dimensions, safe and flat and black and white with resolution soon at hand. He wanted to go to that place of happy endings.
Thoughts of work the next day gave him the shivers. The shaking
compounded his nausea. Discretion didn't seem a quality to hope for
in Joshua.

In a feeble attempt to clear his head, he walked to work on Monday. When he arrived, there was no mistaking that word had gotten
around. Upon entering the garage, he was met with a heavy silence
that seemed heightened by the ringing telephone. There were some

snickers and whispers, but most just ignored him. Their disgust was clear and hidden all at once.

Fred didn't feel bad about what he'd done, but he felt like the village idiot for trying to be anything else. It was a moment of realization more than pride. Ed would never French kiss another guy, not for a million bucks—but Fred would. He would do it for free and might even do it sober. Mostly it didn't matter. He didn't need to fit in. He'd found another place where he belonged.

The biggest guffaws came when Mac sang the refrain from "Dancing Queen" while doing a wheel alignment. It was made even worse by slow Emmet adding, "Jesus Mac, what the hell are you singing that song for?" It turned the previous snickers into belly laughs.

Mac's betrayal hit Fred hard. Mac had to publicly air his scorn. Kicking Fred when he was down was Mac's way of salvaging his reputation, and that meant an awful lot to Mac. He wasn't Fred's buddy, he was Ed's buddy—and Fred would wager Mac liked Ed mostly because he was based on himself.

Fred eyed Mac's legs stretched out from the bumper and wished the canary yellow Pinto he was working on would fall directly on his face, and explode.

Fred pulled off his Ed smock, balled it up, and tossed it onto the service desk. He wouldn't be needing it. His named wasn't Ed. It was hard to believe Fred was taking a stand, but it was easier to understand since taking a stand meant fleeing the situation. The phone started ringing. He didn't say a word, just walked out the door. There was a big smock less world out there and liberation was only a dance beat away.

He followed the tracks downtown like he did that first day, only this time he didn't dawdle or stop to skip rocks. There was nothing more to think about. That night at the Sand Bar, he had a few beers, mustered his courage, and asked Del to dance. Del looked to his pal Slags and grinned. "Why the fuck not?" Del was already staggering when they moved to the dance floor. Looking at his liquor-limbered partner, Fred couldn't recall being happier. He spun and caught his reflection in the dance floor mirror. In that instant, he knew he was looking at another brand-new Fred.

The Devil's Mouth

The drive could still take his breath away. Five miles south of Devil's Point State Park, the mostly flat blacktop took a sharp incline. Autumn crops parted. Limestone bluffs rose on one side and fell to the river along the other. Fall colors burst in bright puffs on down the slope and blended with the tree line of the flood plain along the opposite side.

Where the blacktop leveled off a road sign read, "The Highest Point in Schuyler County." The gravel entrance to the park was just round the bend. Devil's Point State Park was made up of a shelter house, picnic tables, stationary grills, a ball diamond with bleachers, a swing set, a metal slide, and labyrinth bars. When Ricardo pulled in, there were three cars parked haphazardly across the weed-spotted lot.

Ricardo cursed the company rule of no smoking in the work truck. It was an asinine restriction to be placed on a traveling man, especially since eighty-five percent of the salesmen who worked for the firm smoked. They were serious, too. Those guys at the home office came by and sniffed the interior after he turned in the keys. He hadn't been with the company long and figured most of their policies were ridiculous.

Ricardo popped the glove compartment and fumbled for his smokes. The filter was moist by the time he hefted his stiff ass on out of the truck. Leaning against the driver's door he inhaled. *Shit, that was welcome.* He tilted his head back and let the afternoon sun warm his face. It was near-about pure contentment.

Ricardo crossed the lot to the MEN side of the shelter house. Vines climbed the red brick, crept into the rusted rain gutter, and clung to the window grating. The squat building looked to have settled into the land and seemed a perfect refuge in any storm.

Seeing the vehicle arrangement and the lack of outdoor activity, Ricardo wasn't surprised to hear sounds coming from the men's room. It was just what he was hoping for. The moans were given timbre by the tiled walls. Edging across the cement, Ricardo's heart began to beat a little faster and his cock was already rousing in anticipation.

One sink wept continuously alongside the pair of porcelain urinals. On the far end, two sets of feet were visible beneath the stall partition. From the foot position, one appeared to be squatting on the stool giving head to the other one standing in front of it. Dull-toned work pants bunched at their calves and hooded the scuffling shoes.

"Shit Leo, that's good." A fat hand with a wedding band clamped over the partition lip. The metal whined with each thrust, blending with the rhythm of shifting shoes, slurps, and heavy breathing.

Without hint or warning the standing man arched back from the stall with a vaudeville-sized look of surprise. Ricardo grinned and shook his head to indicate he wasn't a cop. The man motioned him over and held eyes on Ricardo's crotch. Ricardo shrugged and took a step back. He wasn't intending to be rude, but no thanks. The stall fellow looked in his mid-fifties, husky with a gray bristled crewcut and ears so large Ricardo suspected he could hear a cricket pee on a cotton ball. A lump the size of a goose egg sat in the middle of his back halfways above a deflated ass. Ricardo shook his head "No" again. Plenty of times he might've figured, "What the hell?"

Now wasn't one of those times.

Kevin caught sight of Ricardo on his way back to the shelter. He'd decided to go for a walk when the two trolls showed up about fifteen minutes earlier. He'd wanted them to get it on and get out but wasn't real optimistic. That guy from the Sand Bar could be there for hours. This newcomer was an interesting development. Devil's Point was good for fresh flesh, but sometimes getting new meat required a considerable wait.

He light-footed up behind Ricardo and leaned forward. "You don't even want to see the other guy."

Ricardo leapt and turned, startled but ready. He knew how to take care of himself. His arms relaxed a bit at the sight of the amiable redheaded kid. Kevin's hair was center-parted with bangs like gathered curtains over a boxer nose and full lips. He gave Ricardo a gap-toothed grin. Ricardo smiled back. The kid was easy on the eyes. It was clear he had a nice build beneath his sweatshirt and corduroys. This was more what he had in mind.

Kevin cupped his crotch and eyed Ricardo's basket. "I know a place with an incredible view. You won't believe all you can see there." Kevin traced the tube steak swelling in his pants. He lifted his eyes and gave Ricardo a look that said it all and then some.

The feelings that took over Kevin when he was man-flirting came from a different place than those with Stacie. With men it felt aggressive and wild, primal. Nothing he knew rivaled the predatory thrill of it. That all-consuming nature freed him. There was no denying it, but that's what he spent a good amount of time trying to do. The more same-sex encounters he had, the harder it was to fake the other. A patchwork of his favored tricks came to mind whenever he made love to Stacie. At first, he'd fought to block that train of thought, but now it was impossible. Another stiff prick was all he thought of whenever his own dick got hard. Stacie was suspicious, but she still thought he was boning Connie.

The man getting head turned so red that even his pockmarks seemed to flush. "Join in or get out, this ain't a show!"

"That's for sure," shouted Kevin back at him. The rush he felt in predatory mode made him ballsier than usual.

The other pair of feet lifted from the cement to the stool. A greased crown rose like a periscope over the stall top. Bleary eyes emerged, focusing and staring in curiosity. "Hey, how's it going?"

"Oh hey Leo. How you doing?"

"Never better." An inviting grin wormed its way across Leo's mouth, stretching his mustache ear to ear. He licked his lips. That mouth looked born to please, but Ricardo had other plans. He turned to Kevin, "Let's check out that view."

At the threshold Ricardo turned back to Leo. "Take care of yourself."

"I can take care of more than that."

"I've heard."

"Then you heard right."

Ricardo gave a good-natured shake of his head before giving a nod, "So long."

Walking across the lot Kevin introduced himself as Sid. Ricardo said he was John and tried to recall if Leo had called him by his real name. If he had, Sid didn't seem to notice or care.

They shook hands. Ricardo's hand was firm and moist. Fat fingers made Kevin hopeful. He liked big juicy dicks. Kevin felt a fluttering in his gut as though something wild and restless was pressing for release. Knowing and yet not knowing what was coming excited him as much as the sex itself.

"How do you know that Leo guy?"

"I don't really."

"Yeah, I don't really either."

Ricardo looked back to the shelter house. "Though I think he'd like it otherwise."

"Maybe in one of his better dreams!"

Both laughed. Kevin wondered why sometimes it was so easy relaxing with strangers. Maybe because there were no expectations. He could be whatever they wanted or whatever he wanted and being a fantasy was almost as good as having one. It was easy to lie when it was a one-time deal. There was no need to remember his deceptions. That's what made it so tough with Stacie. The lies overran everything and become as interconnected as prison bars or a spider web. It was a constant strain to keep it all straight and be the someone he used to be or maybe the someone he never was.

Crossing the lot, Kevin called, "Come on," over his shoulder. Ricardo loped a few steps to catch up. He'd been dawdling with his eyes steadfast on Kevin's behind. The full high curve and defined thigh line looked to be supreme. Kevin caught him looking and laughed. Tricks didn't give a shit about anything but packaging and performance. It was all so simple.

On the far side of the blacktop they crossed the ditch and tromped through some underbrush to a sloping wood. Roots curled and erupted underfoot as they moved through bars of sunlight. Kevin paused while navigating the steep path. He said Indian scouts used to keep watch from this very rise. "I've even found a few arrowheads. If the cops ever question you around these parts, tell them you're hunting for arrowheads." Kevin liked how saying that made him sound so seasoned. He was still new enough to all this to see experience as a plus.

Kevin paused at a level clearing just ahead. Ricardo tacked down towards him by throwing his weight from tree to tree. Hard bark marked his hands. When he reached the bald patch of earth, Kevin was standing with his back to a wide cave that rose from the leaves and branches. The entrance was three feet by eight and mottled with moss and lichen. Wind howled around the opening, sounding like the laments of some unseen beast.

"It's called Devil's Mouth," said Kevin. A couple moldering Pabst cans were scattered about the entrance. Ricardo looked down the steep embankment to the river. The view was even more stunning than from the road. Taking a deep breath he closed his eyes and felt like an eagle set to soar.

"If you think that's incredible, take a look at this."

Turning around he saw Kevin's pants were undone and his pecker was hanging out. A vein squirmed its length. The shaft began to float and then arch from his body. Ricardo's smile and slow approach encouraged Kevin to free his balls as well. A crow blinked the sun and roosted with a caw atop a nearby oak.

Kevin nodded at Ricardo's crotch. "Join me?"

Ricardo tossed down his windbreaker and unzipped his jeans. The wind rolled up the bluff, rustling the trees and howling around the Devil's Mouth. Maybe that beast in the cave wasn't howling—but moaning with pleasure. Each gust sent a shower of leaves spiraling down onto the ankle deep piling underfoot.

Kevin slipped off his sweatshirt. Red hair formed a fanned pattern over the freckled plates of his chest. His nipples were sharp from the chill. The wind had turned his hide to goose skin, but Kevin didn't notice. The pressing issue was in his fist and it was far from cold. He licked his lips and kept on stroking.

Ricardo took off his t-shirt and turned towards him. Framed by the view and the season, he looked to be the finest man alive. Living art. Kevin swallowed heavy and shuffled over. With his pants around his ankles he gathered quite a pile of leaves in his shorts along the way.

He kissed the nape of Ricardo's neck, nuzzled up his hairline, and licked a trail to his earlobes. He sucked one and then the other before wiggling his tongue inside each canal. Ricardo hunched forward with a shudder and tugged Kevin's nipples. Kevin felt his head roll and a moan rise from his chest.

"Tittie boy, eh?" Ricardo kept tweaking his nubs before reaching down to stroke himself.

Kevin dropped to his knees and took Ricardo in his mouth. His belt buckle clicked on the limestone. Gusts rearranged Ricardo's hair. The wind licked as Kevin lapped. He looked up doe eyed and innocent and stroked Ricardo with extra spit. That look always did it to them. He caught Ricardo's balls with his free hand and tugged them to the brink of pain before licking the taunt sac. A string of saliva swung from his chin before dripping onto the dried leaves.

Kevin felt the underbrush cutting into his knees. It made everything more real. Tricking was such a fevered and isolated thing that when it ended there was usually nothing to keep the memory fresh. He'd remember the cool October breeze, the pain of his knees, and the thick satisfaction filling his mouth. There was so much about that moment worth remembering.

He buried his nose in Ricardo's crotch. Heavy man musk always got him right down to his toes. It smelled like nothing else. Still nuzzling and licking, Kevin began stroking himself. His mouth surrounded Ricardo once more. Kevin could have sucked the whole day through. That fat dick felt perfect there. With a groan he shifted from kneel to squat. Cool wind made him aware of his naked ass and puckered hole just above the leaves.

Ricardo whispered something in Spanish. His eyes were closed tight beneath twitching lashes. Kevin's tongue lapped from eggs to sausage in lingering loops.

Ricardo's low whisper rose until it rivaled the gusting wind and howling cave. His hips began to thrust. In a second his eyes opened quickly. "Better stop or I'll pop."

Kevin's knees cracked as he rose. They deep kissed. Ricardo's tongue tightened and Kevin's mouth commenced to sucking it like a tiny erection. His rough hands roamed Ricardo's chest in narrowing circles with the nipples as the epicenters. Kevin tugged roughly down, then lifted. Ricardo said something else Kevin didn't understand as they stroked and kept on kissing. Saliva framed their mouths. Tongues, not cocks, were controlling the action.

Breaking apart, they looked into each other's eyes. In the brown and blue they saw the longing they'd created. The speed of their strokes increased. Their eyes met again, and the moment seemed to hold and hold and hold—suspended until both felt a tingle rise from their balls. Amidst shudders and groans and howls from the Devil's Mouth they found the highest point in Schuyler County. The moment froze and then quickly melted.

Kevin smiled and shook some jism from his hand. "Shit that was fun."

Ricardo grinned in agreement.

Cum freckled the colored leaves and still hung in thick drops from the heavy sag of their sex. Tugging a red kerchief from his pocket Kevin wiped himself and offered it to Ricardo. They laughed to fill the silence and cover any seriousness the moment might hold. Kevin picked leaves and some twigs from his under shorts. The afternoon was waning and it was getting cooler. The cave howled and leaves swirled in a funnel to the edge of the limestone ledge before settling into a rustle.

Though the chill made it a mite uncomfortable, they sat on a couple limestone chunks and shared a smoke. The Pabst cans made convenient ashtrays. They commented on the scenery, but mostly they sat quiet and watched the river. When the sun hit the surface just right it became a tin ribbon halving the land clean as a plow. It was nearing twilight. Kevin turned back. He'd have good reason to remember today. The cigarettes sizzled when they dropped them in the cans.

"So, you live around here or vacationing?" Kevin wouldn't mind seeing Ricardo again but situation was just too complicated. Stacie and a whole separate life waited for him the minute he stepped off this mountain. He couldn't give all that up just to please this sliver of himself.

"Neither," Ricardo smiled. "I'm on the road. Nothing glamorous, I sell faucet knobs and drain catchers for a company out of Omaha."

Kevin was quiet but his mind was anything but still.

"I've got friends here, so I pass through now and again. Used to live here. About a year or so ago I lived over on Grove Street for a few months." They were quiet again. Ricardo slipped on his windbreaker. "I should be getting back on the road, but I'll be around again on Wednesday—got a big account over in Hadley."

"Oh." Kevin didn't care about his business accounts but couldn't think of anything else to say.

They scaled the trail and crossed to the lot with lumbering satisfied steps. Only Kevin's Dodge and Ricardo's pick-up remained. Kevin was half surprised Leo hadn't found a couple bloodhounds to come hunting for a three-way. He was that kind. They tossed the Pabst cans in the garbage drum and paused aside Ricardo's truck.

Kevin smiled, "Well, good meeting you John."

Ricardo reached around and squeezed Kevin's ass. That backside was one glorious stretch of unexplored territory. "My name is really Ricardo." He handed Kevin his business card. Accents for the Kitchen and Bath just like he'd said. "I'd like to pair up with you again sometime."

Ricardo was fishing for a phone number but Kevin swore that so long as he was living with Stacie that was taboo. No outside callers, no connections, no names, just sex. He hadn't faltered once, but those rules were starting to strangle him. There was so much he wanted to do but couldn't.

Kevin had an urge to blurt that he wasn't Sid, but kept quiet. The moment passed.

He wanted more than a trick. He wanted sex lying down and sex off a mountaintop and sex with his real name. He beat those thoughts down yet again, but they were getting stronger. This was no time to be breaking rules. He'd already lost enough control. Any future meetings would have to be by chance. It was all he could do to slip Ricardo's card in his wallet. He wasn't going to keep it. "If you travel through often enough maybe we'll see each other again. A lot of times I go to the Sand Bar."

Ricardo grinned. "Hey, a guy named Cody still working there?"

The question caught Kevin off guard. "Yeah, he's bartending most nights."

"Hmmm—thought he might've moved on by now." Ricardo rubbed his chin and picked a bit of something there. "I ought to drop in and give him a shock."

"You know him?" Kevin tried to act nonchalant, but he had eyes for Cody.

"Shit yeah!" Ricardo laughed and leaned against his truck. "We hung out quite a bit in Minneapolis. Sad, sad story."

Kevin offered Ricardo a cigarette and tried to act matter-of-fact when he asked what was so sad about Minneapolis.

Ricardo leaned against his truck. He said Cody was a bona fide country bumpkin when he moved up there, "all starry-eyed and crazy in love with some stuck-up queen. Frank was bitchy to the core. He made Cody's life hell following their break-up. It took Cody months to see that no account for what he was. Once it sank in, it was clear there was nothing left." That was when he and Cody started getting tight. They worked together at Starz and shared a common desire to leave town. They weren't lovers, though Ricardo would have liked that. They were pals with a common purpose. They came to Bayetteville because Cody was sure he could find work. Ricardo came because of Cody. He told Kevin he worked the door at Onyx the couple months he lived in town.

"That closed up."

"So I heard. Bayetteville was just too small for me." Ricardo put his smoke out on the gravel. "Haven't seen Cody since I got this job. When I pass through I'm usually on a tight schedule. He would shit to see me doing sales. Next time you see him tell him Ricardo says Hi. Better yet, give him my card."

"Sure."

"Well..." Ricardo laughed.

"Yeah, well."

"Hope to see you again." Ricardo hopped in his truck and started the engine. He cruised to the exit and rolled down the window. "Hey Sid, your sweatshirt is on backwards." With a toothy grin he pulled from the lot in a spray of gravel and dust.

Damn, what a cutie! Kevin took the card from his wallet and looked it over before tearing it to bits. He let the pieces scatter in the wind and imagined all temptation of a repeat performance with Ricardo scattering along with it.

Kevin slipped his arms from the sweatshirt sleeves and righted it. He had to piss like a racehorse. Crossing to the men's room he hoped the memories of today would tide him over for a good long time, but he knew enough to know better.

The john was empty. It was getting awful late for any action. He dropped his britches, pissed a steady stream, and stared at the rusty partition. In the center was the ballpoint rendering of a spurting cock carved into the metal. The Dick guy who signed it was a genuine artist in Kevin's eyes. That pecker was beautiful and exact. It seemed so real that Kevin reached out to touch it more times than he'd care to admit. Like with most icons, it kept his faith strong during the darkest hours.

Kevin felt himself begin to stir. He wasn't ready to head back to town, not just yet. He sat on the stool and began stroking. He stared at the drawing and closed his eyes. He imagined it rising from the metal in all its raging perfection. He imagined going down on it, having the girth of it up his ass, and seeing it swell and explode. In seconds he shot onto the drawing. He watched his juice dribble down the metal. Another example of life imitating art.

Now he was ready for home. The click of overhead lights made him aware of dusk. He was never comfortable with the notion of lights programmed to sense the darkness. He worried someone was controlling them from behind the walls and taking notes on all his perverted doings. He worried it was someone spying for the cops, or for God. Maybe there was a hidden camera. The county might do something like that once the budget got straightened out. Hiking up his corduroys, he was relieved Stacie had class on Tuesdays. He could use a stiff drink and a nap. Guilt and worry needled him when he considered what he'd done. It left him feeling gutted as a catfish. The regret always seemed near-about as strong as the urge, near-about—but not quite.

Kevin hurried across the lot to the Dodge. The stars were just starting to appear. It was a clear sky, a big sparkling ceiling on the world. Looking up, he wished he knew the names of more constellations than just the Dippers and Orion. Astronomy was something he'd always meant to learn. There were a lot of things like that, but he always seemed to keep on doing more of the same without learning a thing.

He got in the car and turned the key. There was nothing but a quick repeated click. He tried again. Same results. He hit the steering wheel. Damn! He gave it a minute and tried again. No response. The fucking piece of shit had finally up and died.

His mother gave him her Dodge when he graduated. That was six years ago. It was old even then. He remembered that damn car from back when he was a kid. It'd been on its death tread all summer, sputtering non-stop and in need of coaxing more often than not, but it never sounded *this* dead.

Mac tried fixing it last summer, but said it was beyond repair. He told Kevin the whole thing needed an overhaul and to just spend his cash on something else instead of sinking another dime into that piece of scrap metal. Kevin should have listened, but Mac's need to always be right made him resist. Those same power games used to cause a lot of friction in the band. Acid Rain eventually fell apart over it.

Kevin hit the dash. It figured the car of his born-again Mother would strand him outside a tearoom. The light from the shelter house, the stars, and a silver sliver of moon were the only bits of illumination. There was no phone there. The park district saw phone installation as courting vandalism and opted for the labyrinth bars instead.

The park was built around a landmark in the middle of nowhere. It was the peak of Schuyler County and not much more. There was nothing around but sloping land in every direction.

Walking back to Bayetteville seemed about his only option. There was nothing much between here and town, only the tumbledown shacks of a few river rats. Car parts were scattered across their overgrown yards and colored bottles tinkled from every tree. He wasn't about to ask one of them for help. You never knew what to expect from those folks. The river folk dabbled in the occult.

Things weren't safe on the river road after dark. He'd heard stories, but this was no time for hauling out his paranoia or even sound-minded fears. He kicked open the door and back-kicked it closed. *Motherfucking piece of shit!*

The night was thickening. There wasn't much at all to be heard over the howling river wind. Kevin looked beyond the thrashing treetops to the stars. The Dodge was dead but almost every constellation seemed to be shining down on him. "Thank the Lord it's only a couple of miles," he thought, jogging out the gravel entrance and down the blacktop towards town.

Dream to Stone

The moon hung like a communion wafer on a fish hook the October night Fred and Del first got together. Along a block of stilted homes, Del paused and cupped his hand to light a smoke. "So lover boy, you all set for your big night?"

Fred nodded. The teasing didn't bother him. He'd been ready for years.

He never figured that Del was doing it for money until the night before last, when Bruschetta broke her chitchat with Anna and scooted over a stool. She decided it was time to switch on the fans and clear that boy's fog a bit. She told him flat out about Del. Fred didn't know whether or not to believe her. Gullibility had embarrassed him before, but Bruschetta wasn't one for spreading misinformation—usually her word could be taken straight to the courthouse. Once the shock of hearing the news passed, Fred realized this hustler business was the answer to his prayers.

The next day, Fred closed his bank account and headed to the mall. He got a salon haircut, fashionable jeans, and a pair of skimpy European underpants. That evening, he spent upwards of an hour getting ready until even Rog and Lila noticed—though neither said a thing. When they caught themselves sharing a look, they quick turned back to the TV. The same question was running through both their heads. *Did Fred have a date?* After a last glance into the full-length mirror, Fred was out the door.

At the bar, Del was straddling a stool, chatting with Slags and Cody, and beating a rhythm on the vinyl between his thighs. Fred walked up and coughed once and then again, before pulling him aside. The entire thing was particularly bold for Fred, but his courage was fortified by the cash tucked in the pocket of his designer jeans. That cash was all the courage he needed. For once, money could buy him something he really wanted. He loved capitalism.

Del grinned when he figured what all Fred's stammering and mumbling was about. He'd been expecting something like this, but he wasn't sure Romeo would have the nuggets to act on it. "For twenty more, you got yourself a deal." Fred pulled two more tens from his wallet and handed them over. Del could've kicked himself for not asking for more.

When they sat back down you could've heard a pin drop—that is if the jukebox wasn't blaring and the ceiling fan wasn't creaking and Sister wasn't coughing himself blue.

Bruschetta nearly sprang hairpins. The whole thing had her quite dismayed. Setting Fred straight about Del hadn't turned out the way she'd planned. His eyes had been opened but he was still blind in love. Bruschetta drew her lips as tight as their inflated shape would allow. Usually she was good at second-guessing folks.

Del raised a beer and slipped the bills in his back pocket while lifting a brow in Leo's direction. That skinny old poof wouldn't see a penny of this money. Not one cent! That fifty was entirely his doing and Del wasn't sharing. He didn't plan to do Fred upstairs anyway.

Fred shifted his weight. Everyone knew outright or had a good idea what was going on. That made it even harder than usual for him to look anyone in the eye.

The Blob said he liked his haircut and that it brought out his features.

Fred nodded thanks but he knew it was just something to fill the silence. Truth was the haircut was an improvement.

Fred knew he was doing the right thing. No question about it. Tonight they'd finally be together. He always knew it would happen. Destiny had taken its sweet time, but in the end making his dream come true couldn't have been easier. It was a simple transaction.

Del winked and said he wanted to do a shot with Slags and a couple other blokes before they left. Fred shrugged. What was a few more minutes? He'd already been waiting for years.

Fred hoped Del would drop the Brit thing soon. It only rose sporadically, but the all of it was still working more than a few last nerves at the bar. Bruschetta said it was a thorn in her arse and Sister called it Main-talk since it was common knowledge Del grew up just over on Main Street. Slagger said Del had been talking that way on account of his moving to London someday. "London, England!" he'd added, which made the Blob, Hester, and Sister laugh, eventually to the brink of tears. Sister exhaled. He didn't have the patience for self-styled someday dreamers.

Del ended up doing a couple shots with Slagger and another with Cody. Fred finally grabbed their jackets and practically yanked him off the barstool. After a quick piss they were out the sticker coated back door. When the door swung closed, there was a brief pause and then the tongues commenced to wagging. Earlier, there'd been nothing to talk about except the Blob's shin splints and Lulu's job hunt.

Cody lowered on his elbows, looked both ways, and flashed an easy smile. "What do you make of that?"

Leo lifted the brim of his ball cap. "I don't make a cent out of that!"

Sister laughed.

"Personally I don't give a good goddamn what Del does, only I told him to get himself back here by nine. I got a date set for then."

The Blob craned his neck either direction. "With who?"

"Pig Shit Bill."

Sister groaned. "Good Lord, get out the Glade."

The Blob shook at the quip and parts of him kept quivering even after he'd stopped laughing. "I don't know—Bill seems like an okay guy."

"Except he stinks to high heaven," laughed Sister.

Lulu shook her head. "I just don't understand you pack of horn dogs, it's always just sex sex sex."

"Sorry, Mother Superior."

"Oh eat fudge, Sister."

Bruschetta took a sip of her margarita. "I thought Bill only came out on Saturdays."

"Then Sunday must be bath day."

"Yeah, and it's a mite too late for him too."

Leo gave a slack-shouldered shrug. "There's a first time for everything I suppose."

Bruschetta nodded. "Seems the theme of the evening." She swiveled back towards the bar and lit a cigarette. Looking up at the slow rotation of the paint-speckled fan she took a thoughtful drag. "I sure hope this is what that kid wants and how he wants to get it. Sometimes all that stuff is better left in your head, and Del can be such a shit."

"*Is* such a shit!" corrected Sister.

"All I got to say on the subject is Del had better treat him right."

Leo cupped a hand to his ear. "Is that the mothering instinct I hear?"

Bruschetta tapped her nails along the side of her glass. Smoke curled up from her cigarette. "I just don't want to see him hurt."

"Yep, that's the mothering instinct," laughed Sister, hopping off his stool and heading for the can.

Bruschetta yelled after him. "It's just concern, you old tramp."

"Who you calling old?"

Cody turned to Slags. "Wonder where he's taking him?" He figured Del might've hinted or said something, but Slagger just gave a blank look and said he didn't know squat. Most of the time, Slags was too pickle-brained to do much more than laugh like a fool or call for another drink.

Del elbowed Fred as they turned from

Elm onto Front. The streets were empty and silent. "So, you afraid?"

Fred said "No" without the slightest hesitation. He was being honest. He wasn't afraid of this. Not in the least. Truth was he was afraid of almost everything else.

"You are so. I can tell by the look on your face." Del wanted Fred to admit feeling something he didn't, so Fred said he was nervous. He wasn't about to botch things now. It was all too close to ruin with a prideful stand. Speaking his mind hadn't been a priority in the past and neither had pride. It seemed foolish to make it important now. Besides, it was all part of the game. Fred knew how things were. Del needed to feel in control and he needed to be with Del. Those were sort of the underlying terms. As Fred saw it, it was all a matter of getting from here to there by whatever means necessary.

They passed the burnt shell of a Greek revival home. The blackened husk had stood that way for twenty years. It was still a popular partying and make out spot for teenagers. Not a year passed that some highschooler didn't get pregnant among those blackened pillars and crumbling ruins.

Del lifted his shoulders and turned a circle against the chill. He gave Fred a push. "I'm onto you! You've been shagged before, don't be giving me none of that virgin crap."

He told Del he'd waited until tonight, until he could be with him.

"What about Dick?"

"Nothing happened, at least not that." His liquored-up frolic with Dick made Fred certain that no one but Del would do. Fred looked up to the moon. The sexual joining was only a fraction of it. There was no way of really explaining the rest. It was beyond Fred's vocabulary and bigger than the both of them.

Fred raised his collar to the chill. He could smell the Frear. The riverbank was just over the road.

Del pushed open the rusted gate of Bartholomew Cemetery. It yawned wide with a sinister whine. The ground was dry. Gusts of wind blew dust and leaves about the stones. It looked like an abandoned chessboard. Fred heard rustling. Filthy shreds of plastic flapped in branches overhead. It was all moonlight and shadow. Fred turned to Del.

Del smirked. The walk and the brisk October night had sobered him considerably. "Tonight I thought up something special. I knew you'd come sniffing around sooner or later." He motioned for Fred to move forward. "Go on—there in the back where the graves aren't so fresh. I'm not entirely lacking in respect."

Fred supposed that was precisely what Del lacked. If he had one ounce of respect they wouldn't be here, and he wouldn't be Del. He lived to uproot and topple things most folks saw as right and proper. His life was about that sort of rebellion. Fred's was mostly one of conformity. That's why they were so right together and so wrong apart.

One couldn't be without the other. They were the poles that held the world together.

The headstones were set in side rows like crops. Weaving through the dead was like going against the grain. Del bounced his hand along the tops of the upright stones as they went. Fred navigated the tilting markers but stumbled once or twice over an exposed root or mound of unseen ground.

He hoped Del *had* really planned something special. That meant Del saw this as a big deal, too. The setting hinted at something unique. Set out along river road near the outskirts of town, Bartholomew Cemetery was certainly out of the way—and Del was taking him to the very edge of it. Maybe he just wanted privacy. Maybe there was less chance of getting caught near the end plots. Or maybe Fred was being set up for some master prank. Fred didn't think Del would do something that low, especially beings that he was paying—but Del was tough to second guess. What he would or wouldn't do had mostly to do with what he'd taken or drank.

When they reached the back row of stones, Del was winded. He cupped his hand and lit a smoke. It was a beautiful night. He gestured to the meadow beyond the iron fence. "They're expanding. They're going to start planting them over there. The cemetery proper is full."

"But that's a flood plain."

Del shrugged. His face was in shadow and his jaw line shone a dark blue. When he moved, his earring flashed a sliver of moonlight. "It's not consecrated ground yet but..."

Fred turned back to Del. "That's why they bury the suicides over there. I heard they bury them face down."

"...With both eyes turned towards hell. That's what they say and it's all hogwash. It's going to be blessed and all soon enough. And even if it does flood now and then, folks can't stop dying just because the Frear acts up."

"I suppose the church can consecrate it and make it okay."

"For a damn buck, the church will do whatever it fucking pleases. Besides, I can't see it mattering much to the poor bastards getting dumped there." Del took a deep drag. "Jack-O told me they always bury paupers closest the river basin."

The moment hung over them until Fred finally spoke. "You expect to die a pauper?"

The wind died down as night sounds rose from the riverbank. Del's voice was suddenly loud or maybe he was just speaking clearly. "Prince or pauper, some bloody extreme. I'm too much a gambler for any in between. Not bad for a lyric. Remind me to remember that."

Fred nodded and looked out over the field. "Sometimes I don't think I've got what it takes to be anything but a pauper." Fred swallowed. "I quit working at the garage almost two months ago and I haven't found anything yet. I tried going back to the Vienna Beef but Mr. Nadir said he didn't need me."

Del shook his head and laughed. Fred was one sorry case. "See, that's a difference between you and me. I never go back and I don't grovel—not for nobody and not ever! I burn those bloody bridges because I got goals and a dream. I'm not content being one of the crowd.'"

Fred looked Del in the eye and then down at his busy hands. He had a dream too. "I spent the last of my savings on tonight, on you."

Del flicked his cigarette in an arc and said not to worry; he'd get his money's worth. Del had taken offense. Fred wanted to say he didn't mean it like that, but Del wouldn't have listened. Del wasn't too good at listening. Besides, he'd already been acting decent for too long. Now he was all business. He told Fred to pull down his pants and bend over the broad tombstone behind him. Fred wanted some tenderness or foreplay or at least a kiss, but didn't know how to ask. Everything he'd planned vanished from his mind.

He unbuckled and shimmied out of his fancy jeans and underpants. He'd slimmed down during his illness, but his clothes were getting tight again. Beer was bloating him. He was planning to do more exercise sometime soon.

He leaned forward and braced his arms on either side of the marble stone. Fred was afraid Del was planning on doing something mean—like stick a branch up his butt, or tickle him with poison oak, or take a Polaroid. He'd been branded a fool too often in the past. That sort of thing never got easier. He couldn't endure being made a laughingstock at the bar. Not in front of those people.

He heard a zipper and glanced over his shoulder. There was no trick. He never should've doubted him. Del's pants were around his knees, his coat draped a grave, and his t-shirt was hooked behind his neck. He was a hollow-chested ghost glowing blue in the moonlight. Standing on a grave he flipped his thing around trying to get hard. Del spit on his fingers and worked it that way. Fred watched with a blank curiosity. Finally Del looked up. "Stop eye-balling me or I'll never throw a bone."

Fred turned and looked beyond the fence to the green rolling down to the riverbank. The grass and wildflowers rustled in the breeze. The wind made a rushing silver path through it all. Beyond the slope he saw the moonlight glissade over the black advance of the Frear. The river seemed to be watching, passing with a slow holding stare.

He felt Del's coarse hands on his hips and his calloused fingers poking around. Fred felt one wiggle and circle about and then there was a sudden surge of pain. It hurt too much to yell. His lungs felt like the shredded plastic bags flapping in the trees above. In a moment he cried out. He wasn't sure what it was or what he said or if it was all in just his head. His arm slipped and Fred's face fell on the rough contrast cut of the gravestone. The raised N of the SPENCE top carving scraped his cheek.

Then...*Oh, God!*

Oh, God, it was terrible!

The stabbing pain of every thrust was too much to absorb. There was a violence to it. It felt like he was being split and he suddenly understood what it meant to get plowed. He wanted Del to slow down or ease up. He didn't want it this way. He didn't want frenzied pig backing. And the moment he opened his mouth to say so it all changed. Suddenly he wanted it that way. He wanted it however it was. Resistance was what had made it awful. He turned his eyes to the Frear and gathered the will to relax. He began to savor the pain, wade through it, and feel everything lying beyond and within it. Each thrust was Del sharing his misery and the violence of his life. Forcing it! Fred winced to absorb his demons and feel them lanced and released. It was the birth of something new and an exorcism as well. With each thrust they were becoming one. In his mind Fred saw lava winding to the sea and heard the hiss as one turned to steam—the other to stone. The pain warmed to an ache, then a throb. It was how things were meant to be.

Del slapped Fred's chubby butt and grunted. "Fuck, maybe you are a virgin? That ass of yours sure has a death grip."

Fred imagined destiny converging and consuming them like a river fog. Destiny was them. Destiny was this. Fred closed his eyes. The red and purple phosphenes behind his lids became stained glass. This joining was the house of God and every thrust lifted him higher. It carried him out the cathedral windows. He rolled over the spired roof, clung weightless to the bell, and then let go to drift nearer the stars and heaven. He and Del could be together forever.

He opened his eyes to the nighttime sky. With a groan, Fred ejaculated on the face of the gravestone. It happened so unexpectedly that he only realized he'd been shouting when he stopped. There'd been words. Del groaned and his thighs began to quiver. His body tensed. Fred turned towards a concrete angel. Its lifted chin and outstretched wings were silhouetted against the sky. Fred knew he was seeing his dream poised for flight.

Del pulled out and took a couple steps backwards. In a stroke, his load fell upon the flat grave at his feet. With a final shake he stepped back and looked down. After a silent moment he blew a glob of snot and said it was his father's grave.

Fred knew Del was telling the truth, but the all of it was too overwhelming for comment. He ached. His insides felt outside and the world pulsed to the beat of his heart. Blood tickled his asshole. Sweat stung the scratches on his face and forehead. The pain was more real than anything he'd known. He'd been awakened from the dead yet again.

Del crouched on his heels and ran a hand across the gravestone. "Every now and then Slags and me come up here with a bottle of red. We make toasts and cut up and all sorts of shit. Before we leave I always pour a glassful in the dirt around his stone. Daddy always loved his wine."

Fred fingered the scrape on his face and stared at the concrete angel. He was a different person now. He could feel it. He'd absorbed some of Del's spunk. He looked at Del and wanted to ask if his daddy liked sperm as well. Instead he asked Del why he'd brought him there.

Del shook his head. Fred saw his cheeks were silver trailed from tears. Del was lost somewhere in liquor and sorrow. Fred had seen the same thing often enough from his own father. Emotions tended to make Fred uncomfortable. With Del, it was different. Consolation came natural. Fred reached out and put a hand on Del's shoulder.

Del froze and stopped his crying. He wiped the snot from his nose and slapped Fred's hand away. Rising from his crouch, it was clear the silver of his tears had dried to stone. That door was closed. Now Del was hard as ever. "So now you're a lady. Was that the fuck you were waiting for?"

It was. None of Del's rudeness could hurt him now. He'd seen the truth of things. He'd felt it. He knew the way things were. He looked up to the moon. "Yeah, that was the fuck I was waiting for."

Del smirked at Fred's sincerity. "Well, you know where to find me when the mood strikes." He zipped up his jeans and checked the cash in his rear pocket. "For both our sakes I hope you find yourself another job real soon. Better get a piece of this while you can. I don't plan on sticking round this backwater forever." Del leapt the iron fence. "See you around, lover boy," he called before heading across the field through a parting path of wind.

Fred watched him go. Tonight had been all he'd hoped for. It was past the scope of his hopes. That fifty bucks was the wisest sum he'd ever spent. It was only money, and he had the feeling he'd find another job real quick. Now he had good reason.

Fred ached with bliss as he walked to the graveyard entrance. At the gates, he saw someone jogging down the road towards town. It was that guy from Acid Rain. Fred was near-about certain his name was Kevin. Last week, Fred had seen him twice at the bar. Plenty of talk was going round about that one. Fred stood stock still as he ran past.

Fred fingered his rabbit's foot key chain. Tonight was a night he'd remember. Those details were a part of him. He looked back but couldn't see the concrete angel. Maybe she'd taken flight.

Under Glass

Amidst the clank of jewelry and clomp
of footwear, Del and Slags climbed the stairs to Fred's top floor apartment. Every few steps they uttered a groan, but since complaining was second nature with them Fred paid it no never mind. They were excited to hear the Sex Pistols tape Fred had bought Del. It wasn't the first pricey import he'd purchased for Del with his stock boy earnings.

Last November, Nadine convinced her boss at the Piggly Wiggly to hire Fred. The job wasn't too interesting, but that didn't matter. Fred was comfortable with the smallness of it. His sole responsibility, aside from showing up and not having his hair touch his collar, was keeping the shelves stocked and tidy. The mundane nature of it appealed to him. He was a good stock boy. Even the crotchety night-manager said so. He'd received two twenty-five cent raises already and had hit the stock boy pay ceiling already. If he wanted to earn more, he'd have to take on added responsibility. Fred wasn't much for that.

The job paid enough for him to rent a small third floor flat on the corner of Tyler and Elm. He chose the first apartment he saw. His parents thought it rash to pick so quick, but didn't raise a fuss. That wasn't their way. They just sighed. Deep down they were pleased he was making his own decision, even if it was likely wrong. Fred knew it was a wise choice. The place was affordable, furnished, and two blocks from the bar. The decor was a hodge-podge of discontinued stock from the discount furniture store on the ground floor.

What sold Fred was the bay window in the living room. It capped a semi-bustling corner and overlooked the slope of Elm down to the river. Even at night, the Frear was visible. Fred could see it, moving black and silent just above the curve of the swan neck streetlights. The river had the power to hypnotize if he stared long enough, as did the rotating time and temperature sign outside the bank.

The night before Del and Slags came over, Fred positioned his pastel-patterned couch for an optimal appreciation of the view. He'd been living there just shy of a month, but other than his parents and a ponytailed meter reader with bad sinuses, he hadn't had any guests.

Fumbling for a moment, Fred found the key and opened the door. The flat was no palace, but it was his. He was proud of it—even if it did smell sort of funny. The odor came with the place. After a quick spritz of lavender air freshener, he gave Del and Slagger a brief tour. Actually it was too awkward moving about with others in the narrow hallway, so he just lifted his arms and called out the names of the four rooms. Nothing about the place was too confusing.

Fred was eager to get their opinion, or rather approval. It was better than what either of them had, but that was likely to sharpen their words. Fred knew how they could be. It was all about tearing folks down. That took some getting used to, but by winter's end Fred had hardened a bit to their teasing.

Del and Slagger didn't say a word about the apartment, though they did mutter a couple asides about the furniture. Fred explained that it wasn't his choice. He wished he had some food to offer. He'd been working at Piggly Wiggly almost four months, but had still avoided grocery shopping—even with that generous employee discount. At the end of his shift, he was always eager to undo his apron and leave. When he got hungry, Fred ate out. He went to the same places and ordered the same thing. He liked knowing what to expect but hated being predictable, so once the waitresses could second-guess his order, he found a new place. It was an expensive habit, but with no food around he was losing weight again.

His folks would be pleased. They figured his balloon butt and double chin were why he had so few friends. He'd trimmed down to merely hefty during his stay at St. Xavier's, but Rog and Lila didn't notice. Seeing him any differently seemed impossible for them. He hoped they'd notice when he visited for the holidays.

Three months ago the phone company

offered Rog a position overseeing public relations provided he up and relocate to Virginia. The promotion came with a hefty pay increase and a relocation bonus. It was the first bone he'd been tossed in years. It was the sort of chance he'd been waiting for. He'd rather dig his own grave with a worn spoon than let this opportunity pass.

The next night at dinner, Fred told his parents he planned on staying in Bayetteville. It was all he knew and all he wanted to know. Thanks to the Sand Bar, for the first time in his life he didn't feel like he was some sort of act in a carnival freak show. Leaving now was impossible. He and Del were getting closer and he could feel it changing both of them. The dream was coming true.

Fred never mentioned Del or the Sand Bar in his explanation on wanting to stay. It wasn't necessary. His parents were well aware of the appeal of the familiar. Lila and Rog had no grounds for disagreement and they were not ones for being contrary. Legally, Fred was old enough to stay in Bayetteville and he had a steady job. His parents muzzled their doubts. Everything would be fine.

Fred seemed happy and Rog and Lila didn't want to go tampering with that. Having his own place would teach him some life lessons and do the boy good. He wasn't being cast out on his own or abandoned. If there was an emergency, he knew people in town. He wasn't the one pulling up stakes and moving to Virginia. That would have been another matter entirely. Things would be fine. It was the Lord's will, or at least Fred's.

"We're still only a phone call away." A confused look crossed Rog's face until he realized he'd just used the slogan from the telephone company's new ad campaign. Lila and Fred shared a look before laughing. Rog joined in soon after. Genuine laughter in the Walsh household was most unusual. All three felt lighter than they had in ages.

The day she hired the movers, Lila cooked a lasagna dinner from scratch with garlic bread and a lettuce salad. She was giddy. She used the good dishes and wore a dress. Another side of her was coming to light. It buoyed her voice and brightened her eyes. All talk of disease and symptoms and discomforts vanished. She was too busy being alive to go worrying about suffering, decay, and lingering death. His father had changed as well. Fred couldn't recall Rog ever being as animated as the Saturday of the garage sale. He was jolly old Rog and everyone thought the world of him. Those Manhattans he'd been nursing didn't hit until the end of the day when he rose from his recliner to remove the balloons and magic-markered Yard Sale sign from aside the mailbox. Near the end of the driveway he hit a patch of ice, slipped, caught himself, and staggered off the sidewalk edge before falling face first into a hedge. He wound up with some nasty scratches.

The sale itself was a success and just a bit remained. The masking-tape prices showed a longing to be unburdened more than any serious moneymaking plans. Every sale was a bit of the past gone. They were starting over and this time they were doing it with some comforts guaranteed. Rog and Lila were eager for a clean slate. Though both would deny it, that slate was much cleaner with Fred staying in Bayetteville.

One drizzly Saturday, they loaded up the Ford and transported Fred's things to his new place. He inherited most of what didn't go at the garage sale. Rog and Lila agreed that the apartment was nicer than they remembered. "Real homey, though I could do without that chair."

When Lila turned to pull some pots and pans from an old hatbox Fred whined for her to stop. It was his place. He didn't mean to be disagreeable, but he wanted to do it himself. Rog picked at the scab on his forehead and agreed. Once she gave some thought to it, Lila did too. She looked almost healthy in the gray rainy glow of the kitchen.

Fred had never seen her that way before. He took several photos that day, but none captured her the way he'd seen her.

"Now get yourself unpacked." Rog slipped him forty dollars in a handshake with the slightest of nods. Two minutes later, his folks were out the door. The abrupt departure made Fred wonder if they were going to have sex! The thought gave him shivers.

Over the next week, he went home for dinner a couple of times.

That Saturday there was a big farewell for his folks attended by a blend of friends, neighbors, and co-workers. Things went smooth until Wayne Tucker barreled into the kitchen with his beer belly bouncing beneath his polo shirt. He staggered up to Melvin from the dry cleaners and began cussing and spitting accusations about him making time with his wife. Everyone was uncomfortable. It was common knowledge Melvin was actually making time with Dottie Nadir. Suddenly, Wayne unbuckled his belt and started swinging it around his head. Lila pushed her way into the kitchen and nearly got clobbered by the weighty Busch belt buckle. Wayne ended up breaking three glasses and the cookie jar. When the police took him away, they told Rog and Lila it might be wise to wrap up the party. No need getting tough with the Walshes. They promptly complied.

The following Monday they left, driving east towards the turnpike with their lives bubble-wrapped, packed, roped, and padded inside a moving van. As he waved goodbye, Fred surprised himself by crying more than a customary tear or two. He'd planned on showing some sadness so as not to appear rude. He wasn't sure his tears were a sign of love, abandonment, gratitude, or what. Maybe shock. He never imagined them not being around.

PlOPPing doWn in the Chair, Del COUghed

into his fist and pulled a jug of wine from the paper bag aside him.

Fred went into the kitchen for glasses.

"Jesus, that thing is the size of a mailbox!" Slags rolled his head along the back of the couch and scratched his magenta buzz cut. His scalp was scabbing again, but the color and his skin tone concealed it fairly well. He called after Fred, "Hey, lover boy, bring a fourth glass, nothing plastic."

Fred prickled at the sound of his nickname. He hated the way it made him sound asinine for feeling something that to his mind was wonderful and true. It began the night he first got with Del. He had hoped it'd pass by now.

Del slipped the cassette in the jaw of the tapeplayer and turned the volume knob beyond the markings. The speakers crackled and vacillated betwixt silence and blasts of static. Del cussed and kicked it with his boot. He fiddled with the frayed speaker wire and roughly turned every knob. "What is this, some sort of fucking audio torture device? Your stereo sucks!"

"My folks bought it for me a couple of Christmases ago."

"Who picked it out for them, your grandma?"

"My grandma is dead."

"That's what I mean." Del moved to the window. He had to admit Fred's bargain barn did have a decent view. It almost made that shit hole of a town look tolerable.

Beyond the double-arrowed drive of the bank, Del saw Bruschetta strutting across the street in all white. Del never understood the whole he-she thing and that was one he-she he had no desire to figure out or know any better. They hadn't liked one another from the get go. They mostly kept a civil distance. "Bruschetta's out." Watching the reactions as she passed people on the sidewalk was hilarious. "That one was a triple-take." He called Slagger over. "You'd think folks would be used to her by now."

Slags shook his head and elbowed his way to the window. "Oh honey, white so early in the season."

"Always too early in the season for that."

"But you got to admit, that chick's got balls." Slagger laughed at his own comment and simultaneously snapped his suspenders. The slap of elastic on his nipples gave him a jolt that made him yelp. Del just shook his head.

Slagger dyed his hair magenta the day after Del bleached his white. That had pissed Slags off. He didn't want folks thinking he and Del were that close. There was too much confusion about what they were already. Lately Slags had been wanting to maybe find someone. Settling down sounded nice. To do that, he needed to make the message that he was unattached clear.

Del liked his blond crewcut from the start. The punters seemed partial to it. A dangerous edge doubled the thrills. Last week he'd pawned his granddaddy's war medallion for a chain link necklace. The look was coming together. Every time someone shied from him on the sidewalk, a rush went right to his crotch. "You *should* be afraid," he'd snicker. To him, intimidation was near-about the same as respect.

Del was planning to scam on Fred to pay for his next tattoo. He wanted a skull with roses sprouting from the eye sockets. A torn rendering of it was tucked in his wallet. It wouldn't be cheap. The price Mac quoted him was steep, and since Mac was just starting out in the body art business his cost was comparatively low. Del needed his working cash for everything else and even then he was hard pressed. Most went for recreational materials, and drugs weren't heading for a price decline anytime soon. Fred had to get him this. This tattoo would make punk a real commitment. He didn't want people thinking this was a rebel phase. He'd sooner stay and rot in Bayetteville than go to London looking like a fake.

Fred set four glasses on the table.

"Abracadabra." Slags slapped his pockets and gave a wide smile when he found what he was looking for. He lifted the foil cube to the ceiling.

"I want to reach out and grab ya." Del ran a hand over his razor-sliced t-shirt. That lopsided smile made him look wasted already. Anticipation had that power sometimes. "Where did you get it?"

"Some dyke across the river sold it to Lulu. Then when her and Anna's dog got hit they needed cash for the vet."

"Excellent, I haven't smoked hash in a long time."

Fred took a seat at the far end of the couch. "How's Sparky?"

"Okay, except for that one leg."

"They'll just have to call that damn mutt Peggy now." Del unscrewed the wine cap and poured three glasses. Slags pulled the empty fourth towards him, unhooked the Fringe button on his shirt, and raised the pin into a stake. He speared a flaky moon of hash and lit it before covering it with the overturned glass. The flame sputtered. The glowing cherry heaved a heavy fog that fell, pillowed, and filled the glass. With an eye on Del, Slagger bent forward, lifted the rim, and sucked in a big old cloud. He sat back up. A smile came quickly. "Yum," he managed around the hit. The glass made a grating sound as he slid it across the table to Del.

Fred watched, amazed by how quickly the glass went from white to clear and back again. He liked this new way of getting stoned, though he liked most ways of doing it just fine. He'd come to enjoy a bit of enhanced reality. Drugs were an exciting part of the new life he was living. It made him feel more decadent than he ever imagined.

Del bent and took in a lungful. He held his hit and looked over. Fred was giving him that typical smitten-to-the-point-of-shittin' look. Del smiled. He'd diddled with him most all winter. Fred had been a minor score, certainly a boom for his tape collection. Fred wasn't rich, but he gave what he could, sometimes more. It'd be worth it for Del to keep stringing him along at least until his birthday. He'd learned that trick from Ben.

Fred saw everything going on between them as dating. He talked on and on about their relationship, their future, and their destiny. Fred was forever gushing devotion despite the crap Del tossed his way, and Del could toss a heap. Del mocked all his sentimental goo, but appreciated that Fred never tried limiting him. Del wouldn't stand for that. His freedom outweighed all else. As Del saw it, the thing they had in common was his love of taking and Fred's willingness to be took.

Del shook himself from the loop of his hash haze and began eyeing Fred's apartment. Not bad really. Serious money could be saved if Fred let him bring tricks there. That'd be pushing it, and Del didn't want to push Fred that far, at least not yet. It was all in the timing. If he played Fred right almost anything was a sure thing and Del didn't have much he could be sure of.

Del watched Fred suck in the cloud. Once he grew out of the zits and flab he didn't turn out bad. He looked to be a different person altogether. Del still didn't find him attractive or sexy. He was too nice for that. Del liked defiance. Guts and balls were what he admired and Fred was lacking both. He could make Del laugh. It wasn't always intentional, but oftentimes that only made things funnier.

The speakers broke into another spate of pops and crackles. "What were you doing, blasting the Bay City Rollers in this thing? I can't listen to Rotten and company on this piece of shit. I don't want to ruin it." He popped the cassette free and slipped it in his jacket.

Fred offered to turn on the radio.

"Nothing worthwhile is being done stateside. The only music with guts..."

Slags rolled his red-rimmed eyes and exhaled a cylinder of smoke. "Not this. Del, don't smother my buzz with a goddamn music lecture." He speared another hunk of hash with the pin. "Let's discuss something worth discussing, like who is the most fuckable man in town."

Slags gave Del a shove, sloshing some wine onto the couch before turning to Fred. "Lover boy, you first."

Fred stared into the dark mirror of his Merlot. "There's just Del."

"Oh Jesus, turn her off!" Slags tossed a tasseled pillow his way. "We know that's your choice. Anyone with eyes or ears has that figured. You probably stink of it too. Then who is the most fuckable man *not* in this room?"

Fred bent and took another hit. Drugs always unhinged him and made him less self-conscious. He was usually scared to expose himself, but drugs ate away at his borders. He said what was and didn't obsess so much over consequences. If anything drugs brought others to his level. Shy paranoia was his usual state.

Del gave him a nudge. "Tell Slags about Mac."

Fred took a sip of wine and blushed.

"Go on."

After a look in Del's direction Fred began to relate the particulars and the highlights of last summer's crush. The words came easily and the telling felt good. In the end, he said, Mac had been nothing but a substitute. He took another sip of wine and rolled the remainder around in his glass. "I was real young then. It was a confusing time. It's always been Del."

Del's eyes were two bloody slits. He took a smoke from his shirt pocket. "Yeah, and I got the bills to prove it." He took a drag. "That greaser Mac has done all right for himself. His new tattoo place down on Magnolia looks to be doing solid business. Maybe you should be the one getting tattooed. How about a big arrow on your big ass?"

"...that says 'Enter Here,'" added Slags.

Fred took a gulp of wine. "What do you mean, maybe I should be the one? You thinking about getting a tattoo?"

Del let loose a laugh that sank to his toes. He stretched out his legs, and knitted his fingers across his crotch. "I'm working on it." Fred was so goddamn simple to manipulate. Del would get that tattoo. No question and no problem. "Maybe Mac would even give you a discount."

Fred shook his head. The thought of seeing Mac brought him back to that awful final day. "I doubt that. I think he hates me for being queer."

Slagger shook his head. "Mac ain't like that. His older brother's gay and he's cool with it."

"See, there's hope for bargaining yet." With the final word Del flicked the wine cap. Fred reached out and caught it in midair. Usually he was so fumble-fingered that the blindly proficient move gave him a rush of pride. Maybe he could do anything. He tossed the cap back.

"Let's try...you." Del flicked the cap a second time, hitting Slags squarely on the forehead.

"You dick!" Slagger was off the sofa and on Del in a second, cussing his fool head off in Spanish. They wrestled and reddened and fell to the floor laughing.

Fred watched them and shook his head. He'd never had male friends before. His only other real friend had been Nadine. Since he'd been on his own and she'd found Walter, their friendship had become little more than the living out of a memory. A few times a week they went on break together, but that was about the extent of their relationship. Mostly they talked about work and Walter. Fred kept his life with Del a secret from her, and once he started keeping secrets there wasn't much to tell. Nadine didn't notice. Having her dream come true had changed her. She squealed to say they were getting engaged as soon as his divorce was finalized.

Fred was happy for her and for himself because he had Del. He'd never had a steady beau. Del would say they were something less but Fred knew better. Fred saw all that was there. He saw them old and even beyond. He saw their graves and entwined roots running deep and wide through the both of them, like a canopy atop the underside with branches breaking through to reach yet another sky.

Slags waved his hands and bounced in his seat. "That red-headed lifeguard at Midtown Pool is hot."

"Oh Kevin, the gap-toothed straight one who's been sniffing around the bar for months on end?"

Slagger nodded. "One and the same."

Del tapped the tobacco down and lit another Camel. "He's not a curious straight boy, I'll tell you that much. He cruises Devil's Point john and even did Everly a couple of times. Maybe he's partial to dark meat, though I hear he takes what he can get. Everly said it wasn't so good, he claimed getting down with him was like two farm boys messing around behind the barn. He did say Kevin had a nice piece."

"Bullshit."

Fred turned to Slagger. "No, I heard that about Kevin too."

"Slags, I can't believe you don't know this. It's been going on for months! You must've been blasted to Mars the first time I heard this because you were sitting right there. If you don't fucking believe me ask Leo. He's seen him up at the Devil's Point shitter. That's where you should hang out if you want to get him."

Slags gave a thoughtful scratch to his chin. The idea was clearly crossing his mind, though clear sight of the crossing was a mite fogged up by the hash. "No shit? What about Stacie?" Slags knew Stacie from junior high. They'd been thick for a couple years.

"That's all smoke screen."

"And old habits."

Slagger leaned back and crossed his arms over his chest. A smile rolled up the corners of his mouth, a little bit fantasy but mostly wasted. "Well, I like the part about a nice cock."

Del sucked in a hit and spoke around the smoke. "Too bloody confused for me."

Slags took a gulp of wine. "I'll show him the light. He probably just hasn't met the right man. Wait 'til he gets a load of this enchilada."

Fred coughed out a hit. His eyes were burning and dry. "Bruschetta says Kevin's been getting more social at the bar."

"Well la-de-dah."

"She says he's ready to take the plunge."

"What's she got, her fucking arm up your butt? Bruschetta this, Bruschetta that, Jesus!"

Fred grew silent. It wasn't him. Del was just being disagreeable.

Slags sighed. "He can take the plunge here anytime."

"Oh brother."

Fred topped off his wine. "Kevin and Mac used to both play guitar in Acid Rain. Remember when I told you about going to hear them rehearse?"

Del flicked an ash on the gold and glass coffee table. "Yeah, I heard them too. I fucking vibrated to that shit." Del stared at the ember of his smoke and felt his ire build just recalling it. Acid Rain had practiced two garages up the alley from his grandma. Sometimes he saw old Mrs. Waverhoffen sitting on the back stoop listening to their shit even though she was stone deaf. By the end of their sessions, Del wished *he* was deaf. Trying to relax with that going on up the alley used to get him so riled that once he hauled off and smashed a row of ball jars lining a shelf.

Slags raised the blackened glass from the pin and ash, pressed the button back into shape, and reattached it to his shirt. "Don't you think that Kevin would be a wild thing once you got him all bare assed and primed?"

"Not according to Everly."

"That dark queen is a lying sack of horseshit. You've said so yourself. Remember when he was going around telling everyone he was born a Siamese Twin but the twin came out dead on account of an exposed heart and Jack-O looked into it and found out it was all lies? Or when Everly claimed he used to be a model in Ebony magazine and dated Bobby Sherman? He'll say about anything so long as he thinks someone's listening. It's all crazy talk!"

Del rested an arm on his knee. He liked messing with Slagger. "Well that's what he told me and I've got no reason to doubt him."

"Doubt him? It's easy to tell when Everly is lying, because his lips are moving!"

Fred put down his glass. "How about you Del? Who's your fantasy man?"

"This game don't work for me. To me, it's all work." He smirked to see a glint of pain in Fred's eyes. He needed to show who was in control. No fawning pansy was going to make him feel beholden. Del straightened up in the chair. "True ecstasy will only come with Johnny Rotten."

Slags snatched a Camel from Del's pack. "Yeah, and I bet Mr. Rotten is just waiting for the likes of you."

Del paid him no never mind. "One day I'll be where he is. You just wait and see. I'm fixing to go to London come November."

Slagger started laughing. "You've been crowing about this how long now? And where are you?"

"Nothing is stopping me but money."

"Oh, that."

"Maybe I'll work one of them steamers to pay my way? You can do that, you know."

"You haven't worked for jack your entire life."

Sweat was beading along Del's lip. "Fuck you Santa's Taco! I know myself and where I'm headed. You'll be laughing out the other end when I take off. I've just got to save some money."

"London is a lot of blow jobs."

"Listen, I'm going. I'm not going to rot in this shit town like the two of you."

His diatribe was nothing new. It upset Fred to hear Del so dead set on leaving, but he knew he'd never go. Everyone knew that. Besides, his destiny was here. He could try and fight it, but it didn't matter.

London was just a necessary paradise. He used it the same way some folks look to heaven. Here was where they were meant to be. This was paradise, if Del would only open his eyes.

Over the past several months he and Del had been keeping company. The night after their graveyard tryst Fred met up with him at the bar and gave Del a handsomely printed copy of his "Prince or pauper, some bloody extreme, too much a gambler for anything in between" lyric. Del looked it over before shoving it in his pocket. He took Fred out in the alley. They split a joint and hopped the bus out to the mini mall. At Wentworth's, Del stuffed candy bars in Fred's pockets and then slipped a hamster inside. The candy wrappers crinkled with its burrowing and clawed up Fred's coat lining. Fred batted it down as they neared the front of the store. He tried to relax. Del's approval was more important than his fear. Del told him to be cool; the old lady clerks never caught a soul. He was right.

When they got back to the bar Fred caused a distraction and Del slipped the rodent in Kitra's purse. She about shattered every glass in the place when she reached for her billfold not a moment later. Del got to pissing himself he was laughing so hard. Fred went blue with apologies, but Kitra wasn't accepting any of it. She left in a huff soon after.

That Saturday, Fred and Del got together again. This time Slags tagged along. The three of them shared a jug of wine beneath Kavanaugh Bridge and launched bottle rockets from the empty. Del lit the fuses with his cigarette and aimed all six at the pigeons roosting in the metal hollows. He missed every time. It was so cold out, they decided to head to a bargain matinee, but got kicked out when Del refused to keep his feet down off the seat in front of him. Though it was still in the first fifteen minutes, Del claimed the movie was boring anyways.

Slagger slammed the glass on the table

and grimaced. "This is the worst fucking wine I have ever tasted."

"That's why it's two ninety-eight a gallon."

"You paid for this?" Slags made a face. "You've got much better taste as a thief."

Del gave him the finger but didn't say diddly. He began drumming his palms on the tabletop. "There's no music here! No action here! No nothing here! Nice tomb you got here, lover boy." He snubbed his butt in the ashtray and hopped from the chair. "Let's fucking do something." He was already slipping on his coat. Del never could relax with a buzz.

Slags nodded in stoned assent. "I could go for some pool and a couple Coronas to wash away the taste of this shit."

"Then we're off."

Fred wasn't feeling terribly social. He was too inside his head. Sometimes drugs hit him that way. "I think I'm going to stay here."

Del screwed on the cap and hefted the merlot to Fred. "Good, then stash this in your fridge."

"Pour it down the drain," hollered Slags over the sound of his pissing. Slags checked his look in the bathroom mirror. He liked the magenta but was giving serious thought to lime for spring.

Del followed Fred to the kitchen. "How about I come back later for a nightcap?"

A rush of heat colored Fred's face and it wasn't due to the hash or the wine. "That'd be great." He could tell Del liked his place. That pleased him. Maybe Del would be comfortable coming over now and again. It was close to everything and Del often needed a place to crash. It was another thing Fred had been waiting for. Making a home with Del was all a part of it. Things were coming to pass like the seasons or the phases of the moon. Fred knew he'd be footing the bills, but it didn't matter. Being used was better than being useless.

Fred smiled as he rinsed the glasses. "You know if you ever..." He stopped midsentence when he heard Del banging on the bathroom door and shouting for Slagger to quit douching and get the hell out of there.

Which Nobody Can Deny

On the night of his forty-third birthday
Jack-O sat slouched on the center barstool. He was pleased to be celebrating, but was unsure another birthday was something worth getting excited over. Forty-three. It was impossible to see his forties as a fluke any longer. Middle age was here to stay.

Though his recall was a mite flawed, when looking back over his life, Jack-O was brought down hard by the redundant nature of the show. What had happened? He'd once thought he was set to do great things and have a life of adventure. Sometimes he still caught glimpses of those dreams, but they'd become the lingering fantasies of his twelve- or twenty-year-old self. So far, most all he'd managed to do with his life was push paper for the coroner and drink.

Liquor had tricked him as surely as a vicious lover. At first it had been a friend, a companion and social lubricant that made smiling so much easier. It had made his isolation crumble and kept his disappointment at bay. It was a wonderful tonic for contentment, but it had deceived. It had gone from being something he *did* to being something he *was*. He lifted his eyes to his framed dollar above the bar. That used to fill him with pride and a sense of belonging. Tonight, it was a reminder of his paychecks all but going direct deposit to the bar.

He twirled the glass between his thumbs and stared into and beyond the amber reflection. Beer foamed over onto the paint-speckled bar, but he didn't bother blotting it. His mind was someplace dark and heavy. Over the past several years, he'd become as much a piece of barroom scenery as the chip rack or pickle jar. He belonged, all right. It was hard for Jack-O to face who or what he'd become, so he drank and became more of what he was. That helped numb the despair. He thought about changing. He swore he would at least once a week. But this was the hell he knew. He downed the rest of his beer and willed the swill to deaden him. All he needed was to reach and cross that border, then he'd be fine for a while.

Cody wiped Jack-O's spill and topped him a refill with a fresh coaster. With a self-conscious swipe across his thinning hair, Cody asked Jack-O if he had any big plans for the coming year.

Jack-O forced a smile, "Not really." Conversation dead-ended there. He hated the way it must have sounded. Maybe the next beer would scatter his blue devils. If only he could've truthfully answered Cody. There was so much he wanted to do and dreams he wanted to resurrect. He'd made those promises plenty of times before, many times from that very barstool. He'd looked in his own eyes and made oaths in the barroom mirror. He'd sworn in his heart and made his resolutions public. He didn't want to fail again. Failing too many times was what made a fellow a failure, but failing properly at least required trying.

Jack-O wiped the oily moons from his glasses, balled up the bar napkin, and tossed it into the trash. Time to realign. This was no way to behave. Not on his birthday! He could feel it coming on. The right attitude was one cocktail or maybe a shot away. He ordered another and apologized to Cody, "There's just too much blood in my alcohol system." The line always got a laugh.

He took a swig of his draft and caught sight of himself in the mirror. So ruddy. That drape of wrinkles had become a part of his face. It wasn't a trick of lighting or a bad angle. It was life. Time would only weigh and widen and deepen them. Fuck gravity. Fuck this life and this world and the future. Fuck it all to hell. He turned from his reflection. He felt like crying. He didn't want that and he didn't want this. It all had to be some mistake or dream. He closed his eyes, finished his beer, and did the shot.

He turned to Bruschetta and tried making light. "Aging is giving me worry lines."

She laughed and straightened the hem of her skirt before looking up and leveling her eyes. Bruschetta was about to talk serious. "Now Jack-O, hear me out and don't say a word. Plastic surgery will take ten years off your face and upwards of twenty off your attitude." She swore his confidence would increase and that he'd be a new, or at least fresher, man by the holidays.

Jack-O wasn't sure how to respond. Being a new man sounded good, but he didn't think becoming a new man was as easy as shrink-wrapping the old one.

Bruschetta said he was more than welcome to tag along when she went to St. Louis in June. "Shhh. Don't say a word yet, but Kitra is going too. We can all take the white convertible down. We'll drive along the river and make a real outing of it. The trip alone will do you good." She assured him that once he saw the clinic his hesitation would go like that, and gave a snap. "I have the feeling it's the solution you've been praying for..."

Jack-O wondered if his aging woe was that obvious.

Bruschetta continued, "Time marches on, but that doesn't mean you necessarily have to stay in formation. All you've got to lose is a little money, and just think what there is to gain."

Jack-O gave her a liquored up grin and thanked her for her advice. A public service announcement was what he wanted to call it. He had to wonder if she got some sort of discount as a finder's fee.

The thought was tempting, but more than his face had sagged. Any remnants of the man he'd been moved to Memphis along with Ben, though most would argue he was broken well before then. That was his last chance. It was when he went from being a drinker to being a drunk though once again many would argue otherwise.

He wasn't sure why he'd left, but Ben clearly wanted to be free of him. Freedom was always an issue with Ben. He claimed that when he misbehaved as a toddler his mother had locked him in a kennel cage out back. "Right in the dirt, out next to Tippy." She couldn't cut hair with him underfoot and causing mischief every other minute. Her kitchen-based Cut N' Snip salon put food on the table. *Better caged than starved,* was her way of thinking. Ben claimed that childhood confinement gave him a need to be free.

Jack-O remembered every one of Ben's excuses. The truth was he'd needed Ben too much and that need drove him away. Jack-O was sure it was all because of him. When Ben left, he swore he'd keep in touch. He'd even held Jack-O's eyes when saying so. In truth he was saying what he needed to escape. Even at the time, Jack-O had doubted him. He wanted to believe Ben, but knew his promises were worth even less than the stack of his IOUs Jack-O kept in his sock drawer.

Ben did send a postcard. A postcard! In three brief sentences of careless scrawl, he made it clear that their time together had been fun but meaningless. He said they'd never actually been a couple. Not in the real sense. Jack-O's lips had trembled. That was news to him.

The Holiday Inn postcard issued odd toned flames when Jack-O ignited it in the ashtray longside his recliner. He would've cried but it was pointless. Crying hadn't made Ben stay and crying wouldn't bring him back. He'd considered their relationship more than a flirting bartender and a big tipping drunk who paired off periodically. It meant something. Maybe it was doomed, but at least for a while he hadn't felt so alone. Doomed at least meant you weren't there yet.

With Ben gone, life was just tying one on night after night until the inevitable, and working for the coroner never let him forget the period at the end of that life sentence.

He watched the orange edge of the paper curl beneath a green flame and wondered why Ben felt compelled to send that note and rob him of his memories. The postcard had made even the memory an embarrassment. When Jack-O reached to save it from the fire, what remained crumbled at his touch.

One night a few weeks back, Jack-O had gotten exceptionally inebriated, even for him. He was slipping from his barstool and sharing
slurred confidences with everyone by eight o'clock. By closing, he'd
practically become a liquid. He couldn't feel parts of his body and
didn't seem much connected to his brain either. Sister and Leo shook
their heads at the thought of what to do with him. Leo fingered his
mustache. "I don't want to lug him upstairs. He tends to get all romantic after a certain point and I am in no mind to deal with that." There
was no arguing that it was downright depressing to fend off the sexual
advances of a drunk and lonely friend.

Sister lit a smoke. Since it was Lent, he was in an exceptionally
merciful state. He'd be a Good Samaritan and drive Jack-O's sorry ass
home. Despite his thoughts to the contrary, Sister's kindness wasn't
purely a Christian act. He and Jack-O only lived a block apart and
Sister didn't fancy trudging home in the March drizzle, not with a
cold anyway.

He and Leo steadied Jack-O out to his car and dropped him into the
front seat. Leo wiped his hands both literally and figuratively and told
Sister to drive careful. "Under no circumstances get pulled over."

Sister nodded. Leo was obvious but right. Over the years he'd had
several encounters with Bayetteville's finest and didn't crave a night in
jail wearing striped pajamas and platinum bracelets. Sister blew into
his hand and grimaced. Good God! His breath was near-about sixty
proof! Figuring a seasoned lush like Jack-O had to have some gum in
the car, Sister reached over and popped the glove compartment. Instead of pulling out some mints or gum, Sister pulled out a crusty pair
of underpants wrapped around a shot glass.

"Ben," sighed Jack-O, wavering from his stupor to grab the briefs and
take a sniff. His eyes rolled back as he groped the front of his trousers. It was hard to decode his slurred words, but the crusty condition
of those bikini underpants told most of the story. Jack-O pulled the
briefs to his crotch. He lolled his head back on the seat and started
moaning. When Sister got over his shock he slapped him. He didn't
want to see another thing.

Jack-O put the underwear away and held up the shot glass. "Ben had
it the night of the farewell party," he slurred. His eyes closed as he
reached over and gave Sister's crotch a squeeze.

Sister pushed his hand away. "I'm not the one you want, I'm not
Ben."

"Yes, it's you."

"No honey, I'm your friend. I am *nice*, Ben is a shithead."

Jack-O leaned back with a defeated sigh and faced the drizzle trickling down the side window. "Ben is gone...it's all gone. It was here and
good and you don't see what's going on and then it's gone."

The entirety of it took Sister aback and he didn't find himself in that state often. It was all so downright disturbing, Sister had thought it was mostly the liquor talking when Jack-O went on about Ben. All drunks had a particular topic; he assumed Ben was Jack-O's loop of the decade.

Sister shifted the car into drive and didn't mention the episode until the following afternoon when he sighed, "I really shouldn't be telling you all this..." and leaning close proceeded to whisper the particulars to Leo and Bruschetta. The three rose from the tight huddle to reach for cigarettes and consider solutions.

They thought about setting him up with someone, but there was a serious dearth of eligible men in town. "Besides," Sister pointed out, "Jack-O isn't what you would call an easy sell."

Leo and Bruschetta nodded.

"Can't get much truer."

Leo sighed. "It'd be easier finding a pair that beat a full house."

With simultaneous shrugs and a sense of futility all three agreed to keep their eyes peeled. They sealed the pact with a shot.

"Happy birthday, you old buzzard!"

squealed Anna.

Jack-O grinned as she bussed him on the cheek and tucked the elastic strap of a birthday hat under his chin. Lulu gave him a crushing hug. Lulu and Anna were a great pair. The way they carried on and meshed tended to make most folks around them eager for romance. They were planning a sacred union in August. It was scheduled to take place at Riverfront Park with a reception afterwards at the bar.

Lulu looked around and asked where the lei was. The comment brought an onslaught of predictable jokes. Saying *lei* at the Sand Bar a body just expected that sort of thing. Anna and Lulu exchanged looks and said they'd be right back. They left something in the car.

The minute they were out of sight, Jack-O took off the hat and put it on the bar. It was a nice thought, but it was too early to be looking like a fool. Half the time he felt like he didn't need a special hat to accomplish that.

Sister spun on his stool and hollered, "Smile". The flash of his instamatic blinded half the patrons. Jack-O had no idea if he was smiling or frowning, eyes open or closed. He never knew with pictures. Sometimes he looked a fright and sometimes not.

The photo with Sister and the Blob from last year's Super Bowl party turned out great. He looked younger than his years and sexier than logic could explain. For a week it was tucked in a corner of the bar mirror with a couple other snapshots. Jack-O planned on asking for it, but by the time he did, the photo was gone. No one knew what had happened to it. He suspected Sister, who looked like a drunken crypt keeper in that picture. Jack-O rightfully assumed Sister took it and tore the damn thing to shreds. He couldn't blame him. He knew how that felt.

Lately Sister had been looking worn as a bald tire with rheumy eyes and a cough that could go on and on and never quite clear. Leo had been trying to persuade, cajole, and connive him to go to a doctor since early February, but when Sister didn't care to do something there wasn't much to be done.

Jack-O did another shot and called Cody a demonic angel. He was that, all right. Jack-O wished he was Cody, with a face like a plate of mortal sins and a body to match. Cody always looked good in pictures. He knew it, too. Jack-O eyed him a minute before tightening his jaw and looking back down into his beer. What he'd do if he were him. Everything would be different. Everything would be possible.

Jack-O's bad photos were more common. The Valentine's Day Polaroids were like a punch in the gut. Seeing that image come to light as the film developed was a horror. That sickly looking juicer with an arm slung over Finn's shoulder couldn't be him. The flash caught him neon-eyed, slack-faced, and jelly-jowled—a grim phantom of the man he carried in his mind's eye. The photo showed why Jack-O was single. In that instant, he realized what he'd become. One day, he'd look like that all the time. Jack-O dreaded the acceptance of that almost more than death. Right after Valentine's, he began using a night paste to draw out wrinkles. So far it'd done nothing but stain the pillowcase.

Jack-O smiled for another picture and tried shaking away those unsettling thoughts. This was a celebration, a night for fun. He turned to Bruschetta and asked where Kitra had been lately.

With an extravagant roll of her eyes Bruschetta said Kitra was back with her ex. "Merlin is ready to give himself an aneurysm over her coming down here. I don't know what she sees in that maniac."

Leo laughed and raised his caterpillar brows. "Must have a big dick."

"That's a fact."

Bruschetta snubbed out her smoke. Each jab betrayed her annoyance. "He is a big dick! He had the nerve, the absolute nerve, to read me two ways to Sunday over the phone and said if I ever had a mind to call his wife again I'd better think twice or I'd be sorry."

Jack-O swallowed and pushed his eyeglasses back up the slope of his nose. He struggled to imagine anyone speaking to Bruschetta that way. "So what did you do?"

"Called her at work. We'd already made plans for going down to St. Louis and I wasn't about to let that no account happenstance of inbreeding put a scare in me. I've dealt with his kind before."

Jack-O figured Kitra's going along must not be a secret anymore.

With a loud laugh, Del slapped Jack-O on the back and smeared a sloppy kiss across his cheek. Another set of hands covered his eyes. Bracelets clanked beside his ears. "Guess."

"Ummmm, Slagger."

"Right every time." Slags draped his spindly arms around Jack-O's neck and gave him another kiss.

Fred walked over and said hello to Bruschetta.

Bruschetta made a point of giving Del a look before getting up and leaving. To say she never cared for Del was phrasing it mildly; Del making a public show of his using Fred took her disdain to a new level.

Jack-O turned. "What's that all about?"

Del gave a shrug, "Nothing but bitchcraft".

Fred said Happy Birthday and tried buying Jack-O a shot, unaware that all his cocktails that night were complimentary. Once he was informed of the fact he bought Alabama Slammers for Del and Slags instead.

Del slammed his shot glass to the bar and grabbed the party hat. "Put this damn thing on or I'll nail it to your skull."

Slagger rubbed a hand over his lime buzz cut. "It's a Taurus thing."

"Hey, Happy Birthday!" Everly offered a chip-toothed grin and extended a fine boned cocoa colored hand. Everly was just being cordial. He was no stranger to southern hospitality. How he felt about someone and how he behaved towards them were oftentimes miles apart. He and Jack-O had never openly exchanged words, but it was no secret that Everly still held a considerable grudge over Jack-O's disproving of his Siamese twin tale. Even if he was prone to telling tales, Jack-O calling him on it with evidence and all was nothing he appreciated.

When Bruschetta thought Jack-O was distracted she snuck a cake on into the back room, but Bruschetta wasn't one to slip by unnoticed. Jack-O caught a flash of sequins in the mirror but pretended to be engaged putting on the birthday hat and listening to Everly's foul breathed prattling. Jack-O looked around and smiled, not for appearances sake, but because he was suddenly happy. He smiled to consider this array of Sand Bar misfits somehow fitting together. Whatever else could be said about them, they were family. Lots of folks didn't have that.

He swung his empty glass to signal Cody for another. His buzz was full on! Cody smiled and blew upwards to clear the bangs from his face. The gesture had lost its purpose with his receding hairline, but none of its charm.

Cody looked around. "Where's the Blob?"

Jack-O took a sizeable swig of his beer. "Bob gave his regrets. His Dad was driving into town today so he has to act like a good little heterosexual for a week. He took me out to Staley's last night."

"Hey Leo, cover for me." Cody was already flipping up the bar gate and heading to the can for his evening pick me up. He was due. He'd been getting jittery the past half hour.

Slags came from the dance floor wiping his sweaty face with the tail of his shirt. Dancing made him look half crazed and drugs typically picked up the other half. He slapped Jack-O on the back. "They're going to be hauling your ass out the back in a wheelbarrow tonight." He leaned on his elbows at the bar and yelled for Leo not to let Jack-O leave standing.

"We want that arse in the gutter!" shouted Del, stomping each word on the stool rung with his boots. His jaw was set and the tendons in his neck were cabled. He was cranked to the brink of explosion.

Leo poured a round of shots. "Least then you two will have some company."

Slags and Del were practically bouncing off the mirror-tiled walls. One whispered to the other and soon both were in convulsions of laughter and struggling to catch a breath. Watching Del and Slagger carry on reminded Jack-O of Ben. If Ben were there he'd certainly be a part of that. He'd be right there between them and on the same drug.

Anna and Lulu rushed in short of breath and tossed a kelly-green lei over Jack-O's head. Lulu set a paper bag down beside her stool. Anna put an arm on Jack-O's shoulder and asked him the precise time he was born before scribbling it on a bar napkin. Next week she promised to do his chart. She'd been studying astrology on the side and was looking to get into that line of work. She'd heard it was lucrative. Doing his chart would be good practice. Jack-O hoped the stars would predict a change or some new direction or turn for his life. He'd been living the same year for an eternity.

"How's Sparky doing?"

Lulu shrugged. "Little better, but it would like to break your heart seeing him hobble around."

Cody returned rubbing his hands and smiling big.

Sister shot Leo a look.

Now was not the time.

The jukebox went abruptly silent. In the mirror Jack-O saw Bruschetta coming towards him with a pink tray cake held out in her arms. A circle of candles lit her chin from below and made her face a mask of shaded planes and angles. Everybody commenced to singing Happy Birthday.

Halfway through the first verse all harmony dissolved and it became an all out contest to see who could out sing the others. Jack-O laughed and plugged his ears. He looked down at the pink waves of cake and felt himself tearing up. He quickly cleared his mind. Too much emotion might spoil the night. If he started crying he worried he might be unable to stop.

Everly cleared his throat. "I used to sing on the second stage back when they were still having the county fair over in Hadley." He did possess a decent voice, but most everyone recognized it as another story. Everly was always trying so hard to be what he wasn't. Most Sand Bar folks could relate to the feeling.

"If he were half as tall as his tales he could find work as a lightning rod," whispered Sister to Lulu.

In a single swooping breath Jack-O blew out the candles to hearty applause and whoops of approval. There was so much to be wishing for that his mind went blank. Instead of a wish he settled on being grateful. This moment was enough. These people were enough. Despite it all he was happy. Contrary to the way he felt, most times he belonged in this body and in this life. Smoke curled from the extinguished candles. The heavy scent of wax hung in the air. He called for Cody to line up a round of shots and rubbed his hands together. "There's no stopping me now!"

"Not so fast." Cody lifted a wrapped gift from aside the ice chest.

Bruschetta gave him a kiss. "It's from all of us babe, Happy Birthday."

Jack-O unwrapped the package and raised the lid. Inside was a blue button down shirt and a pair of dress jeans. It was a nice outfit and the thought was sweet, but it could have been for anyone. He held each up and confirmed the sizes.

Lulu pulled plastic cutlery and paper plates from the bag at her feet.

Jack-O smiled for a couple photos with the cake before he commenced to cutting. Strawberry was his absolute favorite.

"I made that cake myself," said Everly.

Jack-O laughed.

Bruschetta nodded. "He really did,"

Jack-O coughed to cover the awkwardness and told Cody to pass him a second shooter with a beer chaser. Even though he'd had plenty of practice, cutting another birthday cake was apt to require some liquid reinforcement.

Roof Jumping

Fred popped the last of Jack-o's birth-day cake into his mouth as he stood before the bay window in his living room. He took a sip of cola. The weather had been wonderful all day and he was pleased to be able to open the windows wide again.

Spring had arrived a few weeks ago on a strong breeze from the west. Almost overnight the birds returned, the trees dappled with buds and the flowers began to blossom. The Frear swelled with the northern flow and leapt its banks. It was a broad yellow froth churning with fallen trees and branches and debris. The sand bars were all submerged.

Fred flipped off the overhead light, settled on the couch, and watched the river pass in the distance. He hoped spring would carry some of Del's demons downstream as well. Despite everything they were still together. It was an ongoing struggle. Fred had faith that most of their problems would be resolved, but was resigned to the fact that things with them would never be easy.

Since early winter Del had taken to oftentimes spending the night. He'd been coming around even more now that his grandma's garage was no longer an option. That'd all changed last month not one week after Del had taken steps to make the place a bit more comfortable. He'd added an old mattress and a foam-ruptured chair from the alley along with a couple blankets he'd nicked from Fred. The garage was becoming almost cozy, at least compared to the car mat days.

Then last month Del cut down the alley on his way to the bar and saw a pile of planks aside the garage. The door was padlocked. A No Trespassing sign was nailed to the side door. He figured his grandma must have either died or gone into a home. Her house had been sold. Renovation was underway and no one in his family had the financial resources for something like that. On the far side of the garage, beside the trashcans, were his mattress, the chair, and the bundle of blankets. Everything was wet from a morning downpour. The cheesing London map was a gobbet of mush at his feet.

A workman chomping a cigar pushed open the gate with a threatening glare.

Del met his look and pulled a cigarette from his pocket. He didn't cower to intimidation and the thought of someone trying caused a fury in his belly. Oftentimes he'd have started something but it didn't seem worth the bother. There was nothing to gain. It was all gone. "Shit," was all he could think. He lit his smoke and walked down the alley kicking a soda can and cussing beneath his breath.

The garage wasn't much, but it was convenient and Del could claim it as his own if need be. The same could've been said of Fred. Del knew he could always bed with him. That was a given. But he didn't plan on fueling that single sided romance any more than necessary. Fred would never be rich enough to suit him. Turning it into something personal was nothing Del had a mind to do. It was convenient and that was all.

There was no money involved with his staying at Fred's, but it was still a deal. Fred wanted his company and he got it. It was just another sort of transaction. He had no leverage on Del and Del told him so. Del was free to leave whenever he wanted. It was that simple and there was nothing more to it, yet it still managed to confuse Fred. He was always seeing things different than what they were.

Del tried staying at the Roosevelt when he could afford it, but funds had been sparse. Leo hadn't been coming through on connections. He'd gotten a bug up his ass over Del missing a couple dates. Leo would get over it. He had before, only this time he was making a real show of it. As a result over the past few months Del had crashed at Fred's and sometimes with Slags.

Fred remembered the February night Del got drunk and tried to trim his grown-out buzz cut in the tub. He ended up cutting his scalp and one ear and getting blood all over. The next day he had to have it properly done at the barbers across the street. When he came in the bar afterwards snowflakes were glistening on the bristle of his head and on the shoulders of his fog coat. The cut gave him the tragic look. With his emaciated frame, pasty skin, and raccoon eyes he looked more sick than menacing.

Del imagined he looked like a warrior of the apocalypse. "This ought to get 'em." He rifled a hand over his hair and gave Sister a black slap that caused him to slosh his drink.

"Jesus!" Sister rarely took the Lord's name in vain and never sought out Del's company. He started to add something and instead coughed into his fist. The hacking mounted until his eyes grew teary. He spit into a hankie and shoved it in a pocket.

Del laughed. "Shit, call a medic."

Sister's irritation was evident. He'd never cared for Del. He hadn't liked him since he started coming around wet behind the ears and hungry in the eyes. Lately he'd become near-about unbearable. Sister saw Del as a walking vexation. Sister was always harping on Leo to do something about him, but Leo's tolerance was as wide as his wallet and despite the shaky foundation of their business relationship in recent months, he still allowed Del in the bar.

Sister reached into his coat pocket and popped another cough drop. The past few weeks his tongue was as green as the governor's lawn. Del ribbed him that every pecker he sucked would come out the color of collards.

Sister twisted on his stool. Though it was the sort of quip Sister himself may have made, his offense was obvious. He put a hand on his hip. "Honey, I bruise easily, so don't be touching me again. And as for cocksucking, I've never had any complaints."

Fred tried soothing Sister's anger by forcing a smile and making it clear that was Del just being Del. Sister looked Fred in the eye. "Enough already." He wasn't hearing a word of it. Del just being Del was what irked him in the first place. He liked Fred, but Sister couldn't see him as anything but pathetic for pairing up with that no-account.

Sister got up and moved to the end of the bar. He asked Cody to hand him the pictures from Jack-O's birthday. He'd already seen them, but it would pass some time until Leo showed. He eyed Cody's ass when he bent for the packet. It wasn't a new thrill, but it was a reliable one.

After thumbing though the shots Sister realized he enjoyed the pictures more the first time. Handing them back to Cody he turned and asked Jack-O how things were going. The question was social suicide. Jack-O cleaned his glasses on his shirttail. The gesture was ironic, Jack-O hadn't been seeing things clearly in years. He rubbed the rut betwixt his brows. He said he was depressed about processing death certificates and about being alone. It was the basic Jack-O sampler. As he droned on Sister nodded in agreement every so often. He'd heard it all so many times that Jack-O's dirge was as soothing and constant as ocean waves.

Fred looked at Sister and Jack-O hunched by the chip rack near the end of the bar. He hated when Del offended people. Del enjoyed seeing people and things squirm and suffer. That was his way so he made it their way as well. He attributed the brunt of Del's bad behavior to drinking and drugging. Del always claimed a potent combination of drink and drugs was needed to bolster his creative energy. All that was a façade. His creative energy didn't seem to be creating too much. Life outside his haze was just a scramble for the next buzz.

The good times for Fred and Del were becoming rare, but when all the elements aligned the result was magic. Fred lived for those moments. They were worth every ounce of aggravation. Del could engender something in him that no one and nothing else could. Del could open his lungs and bring him to life.

The Sand Bar

Their most recent day together started out wonderful. They each had a lumberjack lunch plate at the Pancake House before returning to Fred's for a nap. Fred was pleased to see Del down a good meal. He lived mostly on booze, pretzels, beers nuts, and an occasional cheeseburger. Being thin as a sick dog was supposedly part of his punk package. Del saw every exposed rib and rising pimple as proof of inner angst fighting to bust through his skin.

Fred didn't doze off that afternoon. He lay staring at the plaster cracks fanning out upon the ceiling, and then at Del. Once Del's breathing evened Fred ran a finger up and down the ridges of his backbone for upwards of two hours. He would've continued but when the mill siren sounded Del sputtered into the pillow and raised his head. With a grunt he stretched his bony arms and flipped onto his back. Fred loved watching Del when he awoke, when he was who he was and not who he tried to be. It usually took him a couple minutes to remember his role. That afternoon Fred wanted to have sex but Del turned away when Fred reached to stroke him.

They ordered pizza and a six-pack, stretched out on opposing ends of Fred's couch, and watched a sleazy made-for-TV thriller. The show was nothing special, but it managed to lightly hold their attention. Del patted the flat of his stomach and said he'd eaten more that day than he had all last week.

When the credits began and a voice-over announced upcoming news highlights Del took Fred by the hand and led him to the bedroom. Fred thought Del had changed his mind about sex, but instead Del led him out the window. The sill was only a foot or so above the tar and pebble roof. They stretched out with arms folded behind their heads. The bumpy roof felt fine to Fred. It wasn't about physical comfort, but about sharing the moment. It was quiet out there, mostly just the soft flap of bats swooping overhead.

Slags had told Del he heard on the news that meteor showers were predicted. They scanned the sky but saw nothing. No hurling star parts were visible above Bayetteville, just the gauzy collared moon set against an inky sky. Del laughed a bit to himself. "Slags never could keep a date straight."

Fred held Del's hand. "Light from those stars has traveled for hundreds of years to shine down on us tonight." It was such a dewy-rose Fred comment that Del had to laugh. Though he'd loathe to admit it, Del was a bit awed by the concept. But his self-image didn't include a sense of awe and Del lived almost entirely within the prison of his image. Their breathing synchronized. Fred curled slightly into Del and watched him stare up into the sky. His spiked hair was growing back and he looked awful cute. Fred put a hand on his chest and inhaled the pleasure of the moment.

Fred wasn't sure if he dozed, but he was suddenly aware of Del's sneakers shifting on the pebbled tar. The beat of his feet increased. Fred assumed he'd taken something after the movie and whatever it was had started to take effect.

When Del turned towards Fred his eyes were dancing. He looked about set to fly out of his skin. A quick smile split his face and he leapt into a crouch. "We can go roof jumping from here."

"That's a dumb idea Del. You're not thinking practical." Fred was rarely so bold about challenging Del, even on issues of common sense. Usually it was easier to let him be and that meant saying nothing. Telling Del "No" only made him do it twice or do it bigger. This looked to be no exception in that regard.

"...But dumb is fun." Del said there was just something about being on top of everything that made his blood quicken. He ran his hands over his sweatshirt and dashed across the roof, leaping the narrow gap between buildings, and landing with a roll onto the neighboring rooftop half a story below. He called for Fred to follow.

Fred looked around at the shadowed steeples and smokestacks and treetops before backing up and running for the rounded tile rim of the roof. It was his destiny to follow. He closed his eyes during the jump. At that instant he could have been leaping onto anywhere or into anything. The fall felt freer than any dream or drug. Falling felt like flying. Del was right, dumb was fun. Landing jolted him, but Fred quickly scrambled to his feet and brushed off his jeans.

Del slapped him on the back and offered a quick smile before running across the rolling tar and leaping the dual gutters to the roof of the next storefront. Without pause he sprinted its narrow width, hurdled a two-foot firewall, and moved to the rear of the next building. Springing from the gutter lip he jumped onto the beamed backside of a muffler billboard.

Fred was close behind, staring at Del's back as he ran. He would follow Del anywhere—off a roof, out of town, to the ends of the earth, or into the grave if necessary. With an excited yelp he leapt onto the plank and fell into Del's arms. Fred could see Del was pleased. He often feared Del was bored with him. He locked arms around Del's neck and they slop-kissed on the scaffold before jumping to the ground.

Lying on the grass beside the billboard base poles they kissed and laughed some more. Del held Fred's face for a moment as though studying it and gave him one last kiss. Then without a word he rose and wove down the sidewalk. Fred got to his knees and watched Del walk away. He didn't understand. Del turned and walked backwards. "I have an eleven-thirty date, I'll be over later."

Fred watched him cross Elm against the light, staggering between the crossing lines. Fred turned and stared up at the muffler billboard and the wall behind it. "Shit!" In the excitement of roof running he'd effectively locked himself out of his apartment. He wondered if Del had planned that. It was something he'd do. Fred felt the night chill more acutely. There was nothing to do except wake Mr. Sawyer. He wasn't looking forward to that.

Fred lightly knocked on his landlord's door. Hearing nothing he knocked louder and nearly rapped Mr. Sawyer on the forehead when he yanked open the door with a grunt. His fleshy face was creased by bedding. He wore a flowery silken robe and glared from behind smudged glasses. Fred shifted his weight and explained the situation best he could. Sawyer exhaled and tightened the sash around his ample waist. Reaching back in the door he grabbed the key before stomping up the three flights of stairs, unlocking Fred's door with a shaking head, and stomping back down. The robe billowed with his descent, greatly softening his display of annoyance. He slammed his door and slid a security chain roughly into place to punctuate the end of the disturbance. In a moment Fred heard Polynesian music coming from inside.

Del never returned that night. Fred stayed awake long as he could, but eventually fell asleep curled on the couch. He awoke a few hours later to the crackle and glow of television snow. Switching off the set he stumbled down the hall to the bedroom.

When his phone rang at eight, Fred leapt to answer it. It was Lila in Virginia. Over two weeks had passed since he'd spoken with his folks. He meant to call more often. He'd even vowed. It was always something he was meaning to do, but forgot more often than not. His parents had become more a part of his history than part of his life.

Lila always began conversation by asking what time it was there as though it might suddenly be tomorrow or six hours ago. It was always an hour behind in Bayetteville. That irked Fred. It irritated him even more when they asked how he was. "How are you?" It wasn't the asking as much as how they asked, quick as though in a rush to show they weren't worried, but at the same time were concerned. "We care but don't want to know" was how Fred heard it. He figured what they were really asking was, "Are you still sane?"

He always said "Fine." It didn't matter what he was. That was what they wanted to hear.

Lila had called twice over the past month and said with a bravely stifled sob that she was certain she had cancer or a mass as she called it. The doctor had said it was nothing but she was sure he just wasn't telling her. Her demons had followed her. She'd gone strange again. In her mind disease was curled at her doorstep and death was parked down the block.

Unless Rog was drinking his phone talk was comprised of "Yes" and "No" and generic questions. After a few cocktails he tended to get decidedly more personal and anecdotal, sometimes even florid. All the change and excitement the move had promised for them appeared to have been smothered by the routine of being themselves. Much of their old life had relocated along with them.

Awkward silences reminded all three of how little they shared. Everything seemed unfit for discussion or too apparent for comment. They were most comfortable keeping secrets and maintaining illusions. Silence was just the easiest way of doing that. Fred was off the phone in three minutes. Both parties usually cited the cost of long distance calling as reason to get going.

At work Fred tried to keep his mind on stacking cereal boxes and arranging a spaghetti sauce display, but he couldn't stop fretting about Del. He assumed the worst—that fate had finally caught up with him and he'd tricked with a madman. The notion stole his breath. He tried to put the risks and reality of Del's work out of his mind, but if he followed that train of thought he worried himself sick over it. Fred imagined the police at his apartment that very minute. Knocking. Having Mr. Sawyer use the pass-key. In no time Fred had concocted a ghastly scenario.

Fred left work during the afternoon break, complaining of stomach cramps and trying to look as nauseous as possible. He told his boss he thought his tuna salad sandwich may have been tainted. The lie wasn't as clever as he supposed. Mr. Manacous was suspicious, but let him leave anyway. Fred was an exceptional worker. He just hoped this sort of thing didn't become a habit.

Fred crossed the lot and caught the downtown bus. He went straight to the bar and rushed inside with a silent prayer on his lips. All he wanted was to see Del hunched on a stool or sweating at the pinball machine. When his eyes adjusted he saw Slags at the bar. He was up on his stool telling Cody about some campground in Indiana. Both were very animated and too enthusiastic for the time or topic. They were hyped up, probably on those Purple Heart things again.

Bruschetta sashayed back from the ladies room. Fred had smelled her perfume when he got there. If she used the talc lilacs all but bloomed beneath her high heels. She smoothed the bottom of her yellow skirt, slipped onto a stool, and turned to Fred. "Where were you party pooper?"

"Yeah," Cody was already pouring Bruschetta another daiquiri.

"Lulu's going to be giving you some attitude."

"Shit!" Anna's birthday party had completely slipped his mind.

"There was an after hours to do and everything, a real blow-out."

With moving into a bigger place they had no mind as to how they left the old one. Lulu told Slags that the cheap son-of-a-bitch they rented from wasn't about to return the security deposit anyways. She said he'd only rented to them because the idea of two lezzies living there got him excited. Once he realized his three-way fantasy was never going to happen he became the vile prick they'd heard he was.

Slags sipped his beer and started peeling an orange. His hands were trembling. When he looked up at Fred he could see hearing the details of last night wasn't the reason he was there. Only Del could give Fred that look of panic. Slags told him Del met a lawyer from Little Rock, "a corporate lawyer, not one dealing with divorces and shit." He sucked out a seed.

Bruschetta added, "The lawyer and Del talked up until closing at that table by the jukebox." Both turned that direction.

Slags continued, "At Anna and Lulu's Del said he was going to spend a few days in Little Rock. Del told me the lawyer guy had money up the ass and packing that ass could be his ticket out of town."

"So what's this lawyer like?"

Slags paused. "Rich, quiet, rich...and stone faced. His look never changed one bit so you had to listen to find out how he felt on things. Maybe it had something to do with his being a lawyer."

Cody tossed Slags' orange rind into the trash and asked Fred if he wanted another beer. Fred nodded. He asked Slagger if Del had said to tell him the details if he asked.

Slags shook his head "No" and wiped his sticky fingers on a napkin. "You didn't come up at all." His feet were tapping maniacally on the stool rungs.

"Del won't leave. He must've been wasted or pulling your leg." Fred's voice cracked a mite. Seeing him raw and flustered made everyone uncomfortable. It was unsettling to see someone outside the shell. Fred hated being pitied and knew that was happening. He tried to react some other way but it was impossible. He knew Del was fed up but never imagined he'd leave, especially not now. "Del wouldn't go and leave all his stuff."

Slags lifted a brow. "If there was the promise of more he sure as hell would."

Bruschetta scooted a stool closer.

"He wouldn't go without saying goodbye..."

Bruschetta tapped a nail on the bar. "Don't go giving yourself an ulcer. So far you haven't got the grounds for a cup of coffee. Del said he was only going for a few days."

Cody grinned. "I don't imagine the guy could tolerate Del much longer." He lifted a boot onto the beer cooler and began toweling a mug. "Del told me it was about time he landed himself a rich beau, but I didn't put much stock in it."

Slags nodded.

Cody continued. "He was always trying to shine by spouting that sort of thing. Del told me they were driving to Little Rock after the party."

The thought of someone giving Del more made the muscles in Fred's jaw twitch. It didn't make sense. He'd given him everything. He chugged his beer and ordered another. Maybe tonight he'd be the one to get sloppy. Maybe he'd just freefall into tomorrow or the day after or until whenever and hope somebody would be there to catch him. He was tired of tending to others and mending fences and being good. I'll give it right back, every bit of it.

Fred worried the dark side of himself was resurfacing. He feared it gaining power and lying in wait to drag him down with hooks. He was still scarred from the barbs that had pulled him under and still torn from yanking free. It took everything he had to come up for air again. He couldn't let himself slip below. If he went down again he might just give himself to the undertow.

Bruschetta leaned over and signaled Cody to freshen her drink. She crossed her legs, causing the black mini to ride high on her thighs. Her cleavage was a freckled chasm. Fred looked up and lit her cigarette.

"Thanks darling." She smiled and called for Cody to line up a couple shots of truth serum. She raised her shooter with a pinkie extended. "Here's to all those stinkers."

Fred thought about how utterly pathetic all this must seem. Maybe his self-respect was lying on the bottom of the Frear as well. Sometimes the things he tolerated shamed him. He may be a doormat, that was one thing, but Del loved making it known to the world. Del wouldn't permit him even the pretense of pride. Only it wasn't Del who'd made this scene. Del had only prompted it.

Bruschetta felt for the kid, but also thought it was about time he developed some survival instincts. Del wasn't going to change. He enjoyed torturing Fred. Del had a heart like a peach pit. The biggest thing Del and Fred shared was an obsession with Del. When you've got no belief in yourself adoration is addictive. There was no future with Del and Bruschetta said so. She looked Fred dead in the eye. "He'll take you through the wringer and not leave enough to hang out to dry." She knew the advice fell on deaf ears. Convincing the lovelorn was never as simple as offering sound advice.

Fred thanked her for the shot and complimented her earrings. She said they were from a current fling and proceeded to share the sordid details of their most recent date. Bruschetta had never discussed things like that with him before. He blushed several times before Bruschetta figured it best to give his nerves a rest. No use exciting the children. She preferred to save her nerve wrecking for the uppity. Bruschetta added that she once dated a man in Little Rock and could say first hand there was nothing in that town for Del. Without taking a breath, she asked Fred if he thought she needed to have her butt lifted.

Fred stammered that it looked okay to him.

Bruschetta waved his comment aside. "Honey, okay is not what I aspire to, my aim is perfection and nothing less. Never you mind, I've already decided. I'm getting freshened up in June and my butt lifted come fall."

Looking into his eyes Bruschetta smiled. She'd discovered Fred's secret years ago when visiting a physician beau at St. Xavier's. She liked surprising Dr. Rudy in the middle of his night shift. Sashaying through the psychiatric ward she imagined herself to be one of the patient's finer hallucinations. It was there that she saw Fred. He was heavily sedated and strapped to a stretcher with big rubber bands holding him like an unruly bundle. When Bruschetta saw Rudy aside the coffee machine she asked Fred's story. His jump from the bridge was common knowledge, but she wanted to know more. Rudy didn't usually break patient confidence, but Bruschetta was awful persuasive. She got her way and got the details but kept it under her wig.

Bruschetta tucked a platinum curl behind one ear, smiled, and put a cigarette between her lips. Fred struck a match and smiled. She steadied his hand as her lit her smoke.

Bruschetta shifted and pulled down the line of her skirt. She didn't want him getting any wrong ideas. Maybe she could fix Fred up with someone who'd treat him right. It couldn't be as tough as pairing off Jack-O. She considered the available men. Too bad Dick had settled down. He thought Fred was cute even if their initial pairing didn't ignite fireworks. Dick understood virgins and was willing to be tolerant, but when he met Winston and got sober that was that. Presently Dick and Winston seemed content going to their meetings and living like married folks over on Maple. Anymore they only stopped by the Sand Bar on occasion to say "Hi" and sip a soda.

Bruschetta snubbed out her cigarette. It was tough playing Cupid, but something had to be done. Fred was desperately in love with a man who would do him in without thinking twice. Bruschetta sighed and wondered if a part of Fred sought out the whole thing as a form of punishment. After all, that's what his hospital stay had been all about.

Punks, Sparklers, and Fireworks

Kevin finally left Stacie during a Fourth of July barbecue at Mac's. The party had been great up until then—everybody was just eating, hanging out, laughing, and getting toasty. About ten guests were sitting in the backyard when Kevin and Stacie arrived. The crowd swelled to thirty at one point. It was typical Independence Day festivities with a horseshoe tourney, a keg, speakers out the back window, and southern rock on the stereo. The party also featured an Acid Rain reunion jam. They were bad as ever, but were none the worse without any practice or rehearsal. That said something. Kevin was thankful the concert was only a song and a half long.

Around sunset Kevin got up from the busted backyard couch to grab another beer. He was already tipsy. He'd only had four beers. The real buzz culprits were the hot July sun and splitting that thick-as-your-finger doob with Elf. Pulling aside the confederate flag that hung across Mac's back porch, Kevin saw Stacie and Mac grinding and slop-kissing against an old refrigerator. They broke apart looking dazed and hormone drunk. Mac turned red and ducked round the drape mumbling about having to check on something in the backyard.

"Yeah, like maybe your fucking loyalty pal." Kevin leaned forward to emphasize his comment. He didn't enjoy being duped. Kevin was genuinely pissed off, but he still realized that it was beyond hypocritical for him to get up on a high horse over things.

Soon as the curtain whooshed back into place Kevin turned to Stacie. They had to face facts. "This isn't working for either of us," he said quietly. Stacie leaned her head back against the fridge. Kevin explained that it was more than just this. People change, life changes. "We're just too young for something like this right now." The speech had occupied his thoughts for so long that once he opened his mouth everything he had to say just came together. Stacie didn't offer an argument. Not one word. Kevin always knew this day would come. He expected it would bring relief or liberation, but all he felt was heaviness. He'd assumed that if only he were a little straighter everything would be fine.

Stacie started to cry. Her face was immobile, but her eyes began to tear and overrun. All their time together came down to those two rivers of sadness running down her cheeks. Kevin wanted to say something soothing but nothing was there. His head felt empty.

Elf and Connie rolled in on a wave of frisky laughter, looked around, and asked to hand them the bottle of vino in the fridge. They were wrapped tight around each other. Without looking their direction Kevin reached inside, grabbed the bottleneck through the bag, and handed it over.

Connie knew they'd walked into the center of something major. The air crackled with it. Kevin looked dazed. Stacie was crying. Scrunching her shoulders Connie quickly passed between them and continued on to the bathroom.

"Fill up a pitcher when you come out," said Elf, slipping around the flag. He was too gone to notice anything deeper than an empty beer cup.

Kevin reached over and squeezed Stacie's arm. When she looked up he sort of smiled to let her know there were no hard feelings, that it wasn't her, it was things. He put a hand on her shoulder. She turned away. Silence. It didn't take words to make a conversation. After a minute Kevin said, "We'll talk later" and went on through the kitchen and out the front.

He walked down the street beneath the maple greenery listening to his footsteps and the pop, whiz, and echo of firecrackers. His mind was mostly blank. The southern wind seemed to carry him along. Five minutes later he arrived at the Sand Bar. Festivities were in progress. Streamers and balloons hung from the speckled ceiling. To the side was a folding table with a steamer of hot dogs surrounded by bowls of chips, potato salad, macaroni salad, coleslaw, a couple pies—the works. Condiments were spread and spilled across the plastic red, white, and blue table cover. There was evening a fanning tissue Liberty Bell as a centerpiece.

Kevin straddled a stool and ordered a beer. Tomorrow he'd begin his apartment search. Maybe he'd move by the weekend. He didn't have much and there was no need to hesitate now. He'd already waited too long. Then it struck him—it was all real. Everything had happened. It had all come to pass. He pressed his fingers to his eyes. He was suddenly on the verge of tears. He didn't understand feeling this way. It was best for the both of them. Maybe he was just worried about being alone. He'd never been on his own before.

Cody put a draft in front of him. Kevin paid with a twenty. Setting down his change their eyes connected. Cody could see Kevin was upset and interested at the same time. "You look like you been rode hard and put away wet."

Kevin smiled and twirled his beer. The distraction was welcome. "Oh, I'm fine, just a little too much celebrating." He wasn't about to say a word. He didn't like people knowing his business. That wasn't the way he was raised. "Keep your cards close," they'd always said.

Kevin and Cody had been eyeing one another for months. Kevin always considered Cody hotter than asphalt in July, but had clung to his canon of sex only with strangers and no entanglements. He took a swig of beer. All those rules of what he would and wouldn't do were moot now. Those weren't his rules any longer.

Kevin and Cody started chitchatting, laughing, and making eyes. Kevin had no idea how serious the flirting was or how far it would go, but he was willing to take it wherever it led—especially beings that it led away from what he was feeling. He ordered another beer with a shooter. After another round the incident with Stacie seemed twenty miles and two lifetimes ago.

Sister and Leo got a charge out of watching the sparks fly. "His Devil's Point antics look to be finally coming down from the mountaintop." Sister picked at his teeth with a book of matches. Leo elbowed him in the ribs and said to hush. His hearing being not what it once was.

Kevin asked Cody if he'd care for a hot dog. They exchanged slow smiles.

Cody gave a grin and said, "Sure."

Leo shook his head. "Good Lord, I bet it gets downright nasty when he asks about condiments." His eyes tracked Kevin's butt over to the food spread. Following the exceptional view he saw Bruschetta sitting at a back table attempting to keep a low profile. She wore a black halter dress and had a gauzy scarf tied around her hair. It was something Lana Turner might wear to meet a married lover for afternoon cocktails and just as inconspicuous.

Sister followed Leo's eyes. "I'm surprised she's not wearing sunglasses too."

Leo had chatted briefly with Bruschetta on the phone but didn't expect to see her in the flesh so soon. Usually Bruschetta was a mite reclusive the first few days after a treatment. In the past she hadn't surfaced until every bit of post-op swelling disappeared. That way the impact was greater.

Since she and Kitra had returned to town only three days ago, Leo and Sister agreed something serious must be afoot. "She ain't here to celebrate the Fourth, I'll tell you that much," said Sister with a signal for Bruschetta to join them. Bruschetta just raised a hand to pass.

At ten minutes to seven, Kitra came clomping in the back and made a beeline for Bruschetta's table. Usually she was such a snappy dresser that Sister and Leo exchanged looks when they saw her baggy stretch pants and car dealership t-shirt. "Disheveled," mouthed Sister. Kitra's hair even looked to be needing a good comb through. It was clear she'd been crying.

Cody leaned over and whispered something in Kevin's ear. Kevin blushed and looked down before slowly smiling and giving a nod.

Sister and Leo pivoted one way and then the other like two weather vanes along a squall line. They couldn't decide which way to turn. Hot damn and Uncle Sam, it sure was a day for fireworks! In the end, drama took precedence over love.

Kitra said Merlin was furious about her eye tightening and breast lift even though every penny to pay for it had come from her own savings. He'd gotten so riled that he threw a full carton of milk against the kitchen wall. She tried explaining that the swelling would go down and reluctantly admitted the scars can take longer to fade. He was having none of it.

"But the scars will fade if you use that cream like I said," said Bruschetta.

Kitra teared up and said Merlin had told her that with those marks on her chest, he couldn't abide making love with her.

Bruschetta said flat out that it was nothing but a big fat excuse. "It leaves him free to continue with his philandering."

Kitra nodded, pulled a hanky from her bag, and balled it up in her fist. "He doesn't want me because he has me. He married me in the first place because he was jealous. I didn't see it then. It's like all those magazines say, the chase is everything to a man. It's no wonder he started showing renewed interest after our divorce." Kitra went on to say he piled most of his things in the car and squealed on out the driveway headed Lord knows where. She said that wasn't the end of it and that he wouldn't leave her alone.

Bruschetta asked what she meant.

Kitra leaned forward and started enumerating the ways he was tormenting her on her fingers. He'd tried having her utilities turned off. He'd tucked offensive notes beneath the wipers on her car. He'd spread rumors, harassed her with hang up calls at all hours. "This is all in the past three days."

"He's doing his best to scare you."

"Well, he's doing a fine job. Look at me! I'm nearly out of my skin. I know that man. He's stubborn and mean and single minded."

"So are a lot of barnyard animals."

"He's not going to stop."

Bruschetta tried to offer some consolation. "It's just a whole lot of big talk."

"No, I know him..." was all Kitra managed before her voice cracked and fell into silence.

Bruschetta reached over to pat her arm. "Honey, you're still exhausted from the operation. This thing with Merlin is not as bad as it seems."

"Yes, it is. It's every bit as bad. He's making threats in that wordless way of his.

Bruschetta shook her head. Merlin was one sorry excuse for a man. She called for a couple of ginger ales. "If this has been going on for three days, why didn't you call me?"

"Well, that's not all, he's jealous of you too."

Bruschetta leaned back and looked as surprised as possible so soon after radical skin tightening surgery. "Of me! Good Lord, you'd think our torrid affair was the talk of the tri-states." She shook her head. "That man is treating you like you're his personal property. I'm not criticizing you sweetie, but didn't that divorce teach you a thing? Merlin is too low for comment. Why are you even worried about him leaving? Consider it a blessing, like passing a kidney stone."

Kitra began a renewed cycle of shaking and sobbing.

Everly turned around in his chair. "I was stalked once."

Bruschetta snapped her head around. "By who, a shit tracker? Turn yourself around and mind your own damn business. And don't go telling tales out of school."

Everly's eyes narrowed and his lips set to trembling. In a tight voice he said, "One day that mouth of yours is going to land you in some big trouble. Don't think for one minute I enjoy being made fun of!"

"Then quit courting ridicule by behaving like such a damn fool!"

"Don't think I don't know what you're all saying about me."

Bruschetta crossed her arms over her chest. "Everly, we'll discuss it later, okay? Right now emotions are a mite high. And this is a private conversation."

Her censure made Leo and Sister uneasy over eavesdropping, but not so uneasy as to make them stop. Everly pivoted on his heel and took a stool longside Finn and Jack-O. Leo and Sister didn't really think of it as eavesdropping. It was more like monitoring the clientele. Any good host would do the same. It went along with being in charge.

Kitra let out a protracted sigh that sounded like it rose all the way from her toes. "I just don't know what I'm going to do. Doesn't he have better things to do with his time?"

"Apparently not! Life is too short to pay assholes like Merlin much mind. You need to wash yourself clean of him. Chalk it up to experience and move on! If he keeps up—save all the notes, write down every particular of what he's doing, and get a restraining order. That's what I'd do."

Kitra nodded in weary agreement and sniffled into a hanky. She seemed somewhat calmer. "I suppose the ways things are, there's really no alternative." She looked to the ceiling and laughed. "Some Independence Day this turned out being."

Bruschetta gave her a wink and a grin. "It ain't over yet!"

"Damn," cursed Sister beneath his breath when he saw Finn sauntering over to the jukebox.

"There goes tonight's episode, shot to hell." Leo lifted himself in his seat and raised his voice over the intro to "What a Feeling." Irene Cara was Finn's new favorite.

Sister turned back to Leo and patted his knee. "At least we got the gist of things."

Kitra and Bruschetta's private talk continued another hour, but all they drank was ginger ale and iced tea. At a quarter of nine, they finally collected their purses and moved over to the bar. No more girl talk. While Bruschetta was using the facilities, Sister asked Kitra what was up. She avoided mentioning any particulars. She just said that she was going to spend the night at Bruschetta's.

Leo and Sister exchanged looks. No one they knew had ever put foot or heel inside Bruschetta's place, much less spent the night. Her living quarters had been a source of speculation for years. It was part of Bruschetta's mystique. They'd need to have a serious talk with Kitra sometime soon, which meant plying her with drinks and interrogating her.

Seeing Kitra distraught pained Bruschetta. Feeling somewhat responsible, she figured a girl party might be just the thing to lift Kitra's spirits. She'd convince Kitra to call in sick tomorrow so they could spend the day shopping or go to a matinee. Over the past several months their friendship had grown, but had remained contained. Maybe now that would change.

Two minutes after they strolled out the back Slagger rolled in bellowing holas and stinking of firecracker smoke and whiskey. He wiped a mascara smudge from beneath his eye and called to Cody for a shot and a beer. Slags lifted his nose in the air as if on the scent of something. Seeing the free eats, he smiled and piled all he could on a paper plate. In a couple minutes, he went back for a smaller second helping. A big meal and a few cocktails had him all but dozing on his stool when Cody announced last call. While Cody locked the back door at closing, Kevin sat on the stoop smoking a cigarette.

The following afternoon Sister, Leo, Bob, and Jack-O were all sitting bar side when Cody arrived. A moment of heavy silence followed. They watched him closely and were eager to hear all the details. Cody was humming, so they figured he'd gotten laid.

"So?" Sister said after about a half minute. If anyone was going to get right to the point, it was him.

At first Cody blushed and tried playing dumb before confessing that they'd been going at it for hours. He acted goofy and said it was "a whole lot of fun." From the way he was behaving, that was a major understatement. He was still riding a post-pleasure wave.

Cody was saved from further prying and embarrassment when the back door opened with a spate of sunlight. It was Fred. Bob swung halfway around on his squeaky stool and asked Fred how things were at work. He could never bring himself to say Piggly Wiggly. Fred said they were okay and asked Bob how things were on his end.

Fred never knew how exactly to refer to Bob's work either. In addition to preparing taxes and his duties as a notary public, Bob skinned animals and stretched the hides over mechanical moving parts. Animating the dead was what he did. Bob was commissioned for every job he did and had a thriving business through the trade magazines and whatnot. Plenty of wealthy folk were willing to pay a good amount to keep Spot's tail wagging and Fluffy purring.

It began near-about a decade ago with Bob's tabby, Buster. He loved that cat. When Buster eventually succumbed, Bob couldn't let go. He stuffed him himself, but didn't add moving parts. That came later. He never felt closer to Buster than when he was gutting him. The past few years, Buster had been collecting dust in Bob's work shed beside a box of nails. The mere mention of his house or his work gave most folks chills.

More than once, Jack-O said he wanted to be Bob's first human subject.

That particular afternoon, Bob grinned. "What makes you think you'd be the first? Like I said, there's a lot of weird rich folks out there."

Jack-O's glasses rode up his spider-veined nose. Leaning forward to demonstrate his sincerity only made him appear more inebriated. It was another long lunch for him. "...And prop me up right here on this stool... No, *that* one. I want to be set on that stool." He poked his finger in the general direction.

Sister coughed. "You are all going to be giving me nightmares."

The telephone rang and Cody grabbed it. "For you, Leo."

Leo reached over the bar for the receiver. He was on the line just long enough for a couple "Uh huhs" before hanging up. As soon as the hand piece hit the cradle he started bitching about Del. "I'm so mad I can't piss straight. I gave him another chance and now this!" His hand shook when he lit a smoke. "That boy is getting mighty close to his sell-by date. He's not exactly fresh goods as it is. I wonder just what he aims to do then?"

"The bloke is getting 'imself to London!" joked Sister in his best Brit accent, which wasn't very good at all but everyone got a good laugh out of it, except for Fred of course.

Fred wished he could set things right, but he'd stopped trying a few weeks ago. Mending fences for Del was a full-time job. Del had been going through a difficult period of late and it was hard to take. Mostly because those times were always toughest on those around him.

After two days in Little Rock that lawyer got so annoyed by him he shoved Del in the car and headed for Bayetteville. Del started working his nerves to such a degree that outside St. Louis, the guy pulled to the shoulder and told him to get out, and left him outside some roadside diner. He said he didn't care give two shits how or even if he got home. The lawyer called the Sand Bar the next afternoon to be sure Del made it back all right.

The door opened again.

Sister coughed into his fist. "Well, as I live and breathe, look who's here! Hey, stranger."

It was Hester. Everyone gave her either a hug or a hello. Hester was a sturdy black girl with dimples and a sandpaper voice. She used to be in almost every weekend for cocktails and the pool tourney but hadn't been around since winter. People were worried but didn't know much about her or her situation so they had no idea what to do about it.

Bob signaled Cody for a round. "We thought you moved to Siberia."

"No, just up home for a few months, to that place where the bullshit never ends."

Leo rolled his eyes, "Don't I know it." He said he knew how crazy family could make a person.

Sister put a hand to his hip. "And just how would you know that?"

Leo shushed him.

Bob chuckled. "Nothing like blood relations to cramp your style. My daddy was in for a visit not too long back."

Hester shook her head. "Yeah, and my people are Baptist so it's bad, real bad."

Leo asked Hester if she was back to stay.

She flashed those dimples. "Yes I am. This is the home I'm talking about."

"I expected to see you under every sheet," laughed Jack-O, "...at work I mean."

There were a couple polite chuckles to rush along the awkward comment.

Leo tapped his ring on the bar and called to Cody. "Hey Romeo, the next round is on the house."

Hester caught Cody's eye, "What's that? You got something going on?"

Cody blushed and tried downplaying it all.

Hester saw through it immediately. Unless things had changed over the past couple months, Cody being interested in someone was news indeed. He'd been relatively chaste since coming back to Bayetteville.

For him to be fooling around and blushing about it was definitely something. "Well, congratulations. The round after that is on me."

"Then I'll go," laughed Jack-O. Everybody got a kick out of that and just with the knowledge that it looked like it was going to be one of those afternoons...and evenings probably.

When Sister went to the bathroom Hester took hold of Leo's sleeve and lowered her voice. "Leo, don't lie now. What the hell is the matter with Sister? He looks like I don't know what. When I hugged him, he felt like nothing but skin and bone."

Leo smoothed his mustache. "I don't rightly know. Sister won't see a doctor. I have a mind to just throw him in a draw sack and take him to one, but I've got to respect his wishes."

Hester nodded.

Bruschetta arrived. The moment she saw Hester, she almost broke every bit of glass in one square block with her squeals. The post-op swelling was gone and Bruschetta's spirits were soaring. She and Hester gushed back and forth. Once Bruschetta settled down she announced that Kitra followed through and filed the restraining order on her ex.

The court order quieted Merlin for a few days but then he got caught filling out a change of address card on Kitra. Bruschetta explained, "Postal tampering is a federal offense so his entire corps of drinking buddies on the force can't do him much good." She added that she hoped they locked him up and threw away the key.

Jack-O said he hoped they melted down the key and threw it in the river.

Hester laughed "Or tie it to a helium balloon and just let it go sailing away."

For the better part of an hour folks were thinking of crazier and more outlandish ways to do away with that damn key. It became quite a drinking game.

In just under a week cody and kevin

exchanged keys. Their blossoming affair couldn't be ignored. They mooned across the bar most every night and were full of secret looks and whispers and touchy-feely stuff. Sister and Leo sighed at the sight. It made both wistful.

Leo cupped his chin in his hand. "You think we'll ever find true love?"

"Problem is I think we find it all the time," snickered Sister.

Cody and Kevin did it at Cody's place, at Kevin's new studio apartment, in the bar basement atop stacked beer cases, on the picnic tables out at the campgrounds. They caused a scandal in public and a ruckus in private and everyone at the bar got ringside seats. Soon Cody was coming to work with strings of hickeys, bags beneath his eyes, sheet lines across his face, and a smile that about wrapped clear around his head. Exhaustion never looked so good.

"Another quiet night at home?" Sister teased, whenever he came in looking like he'd spent the night and morning getting happily ravaged.

When Stacie found out about Kevin, she didn't know what to think. She hated that he'd lied to her and that he was doing another guy. "I can't believe he turned fag!" It puzzled her more than pissed her off. It didn't feel like out and out rejection. The anger came from being deceived. She knew something was going on, but never figured it for this. By then, she had Mac to help soothe her bruised ego.

Mac was a good man and Stacie saw no reason why she wouldn't grow to love him. They moved in together at the start of August. She couldn't afford a decent sized apartment on her own. The night she moved in, Mac gave her a dove tattoo on her ankle. Stacie thought she'd like it more, but with the redness and the swelling it was hard telling. That night, when she and Mac made love, thoughts of Kevin kept creeping into her mind.

She couldn't make sense of it. How could he be doing that? People were spotting him and his fag boyfriend all over town, and they didn't seem to give a good goddamn who saw them.

She felt Mac starting to climax. It was easy telling with him. She wrapped her thighs more tightly about him. Raking her nails across his back, she tried to forget about Kevin and just think how nice it was to have a real man inside her.

Another Showing

Kevin pulled into the alley behind the bar and idled the engine. He'd bought a secondhand Dodge Dart through the classifieds going on a month ago. The car was one of a good number of changes he'd made in his life since then. Checking his look in the rearview mirror, he smiled. He was fit and tan and his red hair had turned spun gold with summer and the chlorine at Midtown Pool. He looked good for other reasons too. The double-life anxiety that had been eating up his insides was gone, replaced by the pleasures of this new thing with Cody. He wasn't sure what to call it, so *thing* was as good a word as any. Love? He wasn't sure what love was, but it was hard to imagine anything better than this goofy bit of bliss he was in. His every waking breath seemed a pant, a moan, or a sigh.

Everyone commented on his being in love. Apparently it was obvious and it got him to thinking that maybe love was easier to see than to know. There was no disguising things. It rose up and bubbled over whenever Cody was near. He and Cody had been an item now for a few weeks and the fire was only blazing all the hotter. Tonight was sure to be another wonderful evening. Kevin had already seen to that.

Just then, Cody emerged from the back door. He was talking with Del about something. Kevin straightened up. He wasn't necessarily jealous, but he wasn't dumb either. Del was an inconsiderate no account who wanted what he wanted and he definitely wanted Cody. Del wouldn't think twice about stealing him away. The shithead didn't even have the decency to do his flirting behind Kevin's back.

Kevin beeped the horn.

Soon as Cody saw the car, he slapped Del on the shoulder and waved his paycheck over his head. Hopping the steps, he loped over to the car. Kevin grinned. The only thing that thrilled him more than seeing Cody was seeing Cody thrilled to see him. Brushing aside his bangs, Cody popped the door handle.

"Hey." He leaned over and kissed Kevin.

"Hey."

"What was Del yammering about?"

"What does he ever go on about—himself."

Kevin laughed. The comment was all he needed to brush away his worries over Del.

"All I've got to say is thank God that Finn is desperate for money. Your place or mine?"

"Neither."

Cody looked over quick and smiled. His brows rose like a draw-bridge.

"I've got a surprise in store." Kevin leaned over and gave Cody another kiss that evolved into an even sloppier one. He cupped the basket of his button flies and broke away. Cody felt primed for the surprise already.

Pulling onto the street, Kevin maintained the crotch massage with one hand while driving with the other draped over the wheel. It was set to be an exceptional night all right. They grinned at one another or kissed at every stoplight and stop sign until they reached the outskirts of town. Kevin squirmed on the seat. "We're going to have us lots of fun. I'll be turning you every which way but loose." With a sidelong glance from the road Kevin gave Cody another flash of his gap-toothed grin.

"I bet you are. Not gonna divulge any of the details huh?"

"Nope." Kevin poked his tongue in his cheek. He looked about fifteen when he did that. He moved his hold from Cody's crotch to his hand. Their fingers laced. It all felt special. This moment and this bond was the real world. It was magical and yet the opposite of magic. It was pure. Together they felt more themselves, and yet more than when they were alone.

Near the overpass, Kevin turned down a patched stretch of nameless blacktop. After a quarter mile he veered off onto a mud-rutted clay road.

Cody squinted up at the setting sun and pulled down the visor. "Where the hell you taking me?"

"You'll see." Kevin smiled. Keeping a happy secret was a welcome change after all the twisted lies and deceptions he'd maintained with Stacie.

Low branches scraped the hood as they rounded a bend. The late summer grass was faded gold and the wind whistled through its dryness. Vine shafts coiled up and around the elm trunks. Along one side of the road a slatted snow fence rolled and buckled. After a few yards the trees parted and the road widened. Cody saw they were bouncing in the age-worn exit of a dilapidated drive-in.

The lot was eroding into the undergrowth. Dry gravel runoff bled from the borders like the edges of a hide stretched to dry. A smattering of weeds poked through the chalky yellow stones. Bracing one hand on the roof, Cody commented that the rutted lot was a sure test for the shocks. Gravel popped and bounced along the Dodge's underbelly. A cloud of dust rose in their wake. With some two-handed maneuvering, Kevin brought the Dart to a stop on a viewing mound facing the screen. He cut the engine and turned to Cody. A gravel cloud overtook them and passed. It was silent save for the hum of crickets and the rolling wind.

Cody shook his head. "Where did you find this place?"

Kevin shrugged. He looked around. It was different than he remembered, but still impressive. With all the overgrowth and the trees and weeds moving with the breeze, it looked like the bottom of the sea, like a world created by currents. "I used to come here."

"With Stacie?"

"Sometimes, but mostly with buddies from school."

"Oh?"

"No, not that way! People do get together for other reasons, you know." Kevin smiled and reached into the visor sleeve for a joint. With a wink he opened his hand, balanced the spliff on his fingertips, hit his wrist, and flipped it between his lips. "Viola!" He turned to Cody with a smug look.

Cody shook his head with a widening grin. "Damn show off."

"You know it."

"Yeah and you show it too." Cody ran a hand up Kevin's thigh. "You are cocky, aren't you?" The heady chemistry they felt from the start was still there. When they were together it sometimes lolled and eddied about, bit it always overtook them eventually.

Kevin took a toke and passed the joint. After it circulated a few times they got silly and did a shotgun. Getting crazy together made them feel saner.

"Tastes good." Cody handed it back.

"Mmm hmm." Kevin shifted his legs. He raised his head from the rest and released his hit. The buzz went straight to his brain. "Let's push this seat back."

At the count of three the seat jerked and Cody dropped the joint. After some groping and giggling he retrieved it from the mat and rubbed the spot where it fell. "Didn't burn."

Kevin gave a half-stoned and full-smitten smile. "It doesn't matter with this beater."

"Thought you liked the Dart?"

"Gets me where I need to be."

"And just where do you need to be?"

"Here." Kevin blushed a bit saying it. Sentiment did that to him. He didn't mean the comment to sound that way—or maybe he did. At any rate, it was the truth.

The caucus of crickets grew louder as they smoked, held hands, and looked towards the tattered screen. All that was missing was the show. Patches of whitewashed plywood still hung in place, but in spots gaping holes exposed the underlying posts and bars. A rusting skeleton was slowly being revealed as the support for all those projected fantasies. In a few years time there'd be nothing left.

Cody turned, suddenly aware of how stoned he was. The sky was slashed red and orange. All he could say was, "Wow," and he ended up just thinking it. To his right was the tar-shingled concession stand, at least the remnants of it. Now it wasn't much more than a lopsided and boarded shell that looked levered by the scrub grass and weeds sprouting thick along the base. Little else stood in the lot. The speakers had been removed, leaving only row after row of corroded pole stumps in cement circles. Poising the joint between his teeth. he listened. Nothing could be heard over the drone of crickets.

A lightning bug flew in the window, flashing and battering the dash. Kevin rolled a magazine lying on the seat and smashed it against the windshield. Bug jelly smudged the glass. He turned to Cody with half-mast eyes. "You've never been here?"

"No."

"Used to be some place."

Cody nodded all glassy-eyed. "What happened?"

"Five or six years back a tornado came through. It tore the crap out of the Sunset so the guy who owned it decided to close it for good. He was going to develop it at one point, but nothing ever came of it." Kevin scooted closer. Pot always made his head go soft and his dick get hard. "But that was then and this is now. Damned if I don't see something showing here again." Kevin reached over and gave Cody's crotch a squeeze. Leaning closer he tongued Cody's neck, licking a path from jaw to chin. Whisker bristle scratched as he shifted to an ear, licking and probing as Cody got to squirming on the seat. That drove him nuts every time. Kevin moved to Cody's lips.

As tongues sucked and mingled, their hands roamed each other's bodies. Both were hungry to touch and to be touched. Kevin popped the buttons of Cody's fly. Their desire generated heat and smelled of sweat. He bent down and began to lick and lap Cody's balls. Kevin knew just how he liked it.

Cody hadn't felt this happy in a long time, at least since last night, and the night before, and the night before that... Prior to meeting Kevin it seemed he was just floating through his days and letting the current take him through life. Being single had suited him, for a while. He pulled Kevin's t-shirt up his back and started teasing his nipples. Kevin continued his sucking as more lightning bugs dipped and flashed in the twilight.

Cody lifted himself off the vinyl and sucked air around his teeth. Crows cawed from the surrounding elms. The holes in the screen went black in the bruised violet of dusk. Gauzy clouds spread pink and purple cross the sky looking like a cotton candy postcard of paradise.

Kevin licked a bit around the crown of Cody's dick. He tongued its length, balls to tip, before tonguing the slit. When he took the full length Cody let out a groan from deep in his belly. Fingers raked Kevin's hair with every bob and Cody's hips commenced to merge with the sucking. Cody leaned forward, pushing Kevin back until their positions reversed. He chewed the worn crotch of Kevin's jeans. His cock tented the thin fabric. Cody gave him a nasty grin. "I think this showing is a double feature."

Kevin let out something between a laugh and a moan. "You're crazy."

Cody unzipped him and smiled when Kevin's dick sprang free and upright. After a few whiffs of crotch musk, Cody swallowed him whole, sucking slow and greedy. Pot made it all the center of the universe. Soon Kevin was twitching with a palsy. Cody ceased his sucking but continued working him with his hand. "Now let's see that ass of yours."

Kevin sucked in a breath, pushed down his dungarees, and flipped over. Red hair fanned across the globes of his ass and feathered up his crack like a thin moss. The sight always took Cody's breath away. He went from one cheek to the other giving licks and pecks before parting that slice of heaven with both hands. Cody bent forward and lapped Kevin's hole a few times before squirming his tongue inside. It was another universe altogether. Kevin was rolling his hips to meet Cody's mouth. "Uh. Yeah. Oh. Man. Shit that feels good."

Cody spit on his palm and ran a finger around the plum-hued hole. "This hot ass needs some cock huh? Needs a fucking cock in it." Kevin liked it when Cody talked dirty. He liked smut whispered low and menacing. Sometimes he liked it shouted. It may have been sex talk but with the right person it was a vow.

The secret to everything was at his fingertips. Cody slipped a digit inside. Kevin winced a second before settling. Cody tongued the muscled ring around his finger and slipped another inside. Kevin was loosening like a sigh. Cody eased his finger free. "Why don't you get out of them jeans?"

Kevin kicked off his boots and shucked his pants from his ankles. Change bounced on the seat and fell to the car mat. Both noticed but neither paid attention. Cody flipped him on his back and knelt on the seat between his legs.

"Grab that towel from the back."

"You were prepared weren't you?" Cody slipped the towel under Kevin's ass and raised Kevin's knees until they pressed against his chest. Another lightning bug flew inside. Kevin watched it batter the roof and farted.

They laughed.

"Ready baby?" Cody returned a finger to the warm hole and rotated it this way and that. "That's it, just relax." Positioning his cock he slowly removed his finger while simultaneously pressing in on the bulls eye.

"God. Shit. Cody."

Cody leaned down and kissed him fully with a hunger that grew into a tenderness and back into a hunger again. "It's okay, nice and slow."

Kevin clenched his teeth and reddened. He winced but kept his eyes open. He never shut them anymore. His imagination had met its match. There was nowhere he'd rather be. The pain went from searing to dull to throbbing before merging with his heartbeat. Calm. Calm. Calm.

They lay still and listened to the crickets until Kevin's breathing evened. Cody bent over him. Kevin's head was pressed against the armrest. Cody kissed him. As his tongue entered Kevin's mouth they gently began to fuck. The joining was sweet as ever and soon their motion began to build. Grinding begat a slow thrusting that grew to a genuine pounding. Cody's neck muscles rose like cables. His pelvis was a rolling wave Kevin rose to meet. Sweat from Cody's hair dripped onto Kevin's face. Wet and sticky. Kevin's business bounced on his abdomen. His face reddened. Yes. Yes. Now. Measured spurts shot onto his belly as Cody continued pounding. A couple seconds later Cody pulled free. In a series of spasms he released across Kevin's chest and his stomach. As his breathing slowed he collapsed, burying his face Kevin's chest.

They lay there panting until Cody plastered his sweaty bangs across his forehead. He sighed and smiled with his eyes. "Damn. That was a good one. This is the best time I've ever had. Not just tonight, but all this—with you." He bent and gave Kevin another kiss.

Kevin caught his eye and turned before looking back. There was no mistaking the enormity of his emotions. He'd been feeling that way for a while, but those voices inside stopped his saying the word. Calling it love took the moment and put it in stone. It made now into forever and that wasn't always the case. To his way of thinking, love was most likely a mood and not a set state. He saw Stacie's name tattooed on his forearm. Love put an obligation on everything.

In a heartbeat, the moment passed.

"I should finagle a free shift more often."

"That would be nice."

With arms and legs entangled, they held each other for another few moments. Kevin was verging on sleep when Cody commenced to scratching his nipple with a thumbnail. "We'd best get going before it gets pitch black or we'll never find our way out of this place."

"Stop it, that tickles." Kevin grabbed Cody's wrist and shook it between his hands.

"That means it's sensitive."

Kevin laughed and finally opened his eyes. "We've been doing this for upwards of a month, by now you ought to know my nipples are sensitive. I know your hot spots."

"Do you now?"

"Damn straight."

A few more moments passed in silence.

"We'd best get going."

"What for?" Kevin sighed and stretched his arms over his head. Arching his back, he let out a grunt before settling back down. "I could stay here all night. The lightning bugs will lead our way."

"Not after you squashed their buddy."

"Oh, hush." Kevin leaned over and gave Cody a kiss. "I'll go on one condition, that we do it all over again when we get to your place."

Cody reached down and gave Kevin's ass a squeeze. "That's no condition, it's a guarantee." He buttoned his jeans and slipped on his t-shirt. This was all so nice. Cody was pleased he could feel this way after getting so soured on men after Frank. That wall had mostly crumbled, but the foundation remained as a reminder. He'd never forget the flip side of all this boyfriend stuff. His jaw clenched. That'd been so humiliating. He'd never get hurt like that again. He sucked snot and spit onto the gravel.

Kevin started the engine and leaned over to give him another kiss. "Good as ever."

"Good as always."

Dead Kennedys

Del had one regular punter named Bill, easy as they come and did he ever. Always easy and always fifty. Every Sunday, sure as preaching, there was Bill. His showing up early in the evening was mighty convenient. That way, Del was done and back at the bar before things got rolling. For him, it was wham bam and cash in the hand. Sundays were becoming one big party for Del, thanks to Bill.

If Del had a mind to put that fifty aside every week, it would've added up to rent. He always thought about doing that, but thinking didn't make it happen. Del was never that way with money. Bill was. Del always figured his whoring money was part of the farm budget, with a labeled jelly jar over the sink between one for gas and another for food. Del knew Bill's type forwards and back two seconds after shaking his hand. Del had seen people like that all his life. The Bayetteville phone directory was full of them.

Despite being pretty scraggly, Bill wasn't bad, as older hicks went. He had a crewcut, a strong body, and a jaw like the maw of a garbage truck. That lazy eye took some getting used to as well, but it was chicken feed compared to the sheer stink of the man. Bill smelled like a barnyard in August. It wasn't just his clothes, but Bill himself. A slaughterhouse, shithouse, muck and manure stink came from his skin and his clothes and was all mixed-up with his breath. Folks at the bar started calling him Pig Shit Bill behind his back. When Leo introduced Del to Bill, his jaw about hit the floor when Del pegged him for a farmer. Bill wondered if he was a mind reader. Del had to laugh. Who'd tell you if you smelled like manure?

Bill wasn't too bright and always seemed two beats behind the band. He was simple in the head and simple in bed. That was Del's experience. There was no shagging or gagging, just Bill, his squat red pecker, and a calloused right hand. He would pound out his pud in five minutes, tops. Most times Del wasn't even on the bed with him when he oozed—and Bill *oozed*, never shot. During the big fireworks moment he was given to fits of squealing, clawing at the spread, and rutting like a half mad hog. First time he pulled that shit Del thought, "Holy Fuck" and almost bolted. He figured it for some mental seizure, but that was just Bill's way. It took him a minute to calm back into being human.

Leaving was awkward. Bill was so lonely he seemed hollow. He was desperate for company but not willing to pay Del more. Most punters seemed to define forever as the time between their cumming and Del's going. If Del had a mind to, he'd stay the full hour. Nothing wrong in that. Bill had paid for it. After he calmed a bit, Bill would get to talking and the things he talked about made his orgasm antics seem tame.

He'd lie there on the bed going on about the Kennedy boys, mainly JFK, but sometimes Bobby. He'd get all moony and say things like, "Boy, I bet them Kennedy boys was hung." He'd be all sticky and panting with that godawful cow stink and then start spouting those things. It was a struggle for Del not to laugh. Bill wouldn't notice anyways. His head was someplace else altogether. Del found it hilarious that Bill was into real dead Kennedys and he was a fan of the band.

Del liked that Bill never acted above him before or after. Lots of guys he was with liked to pull that superior crap. That always set Del off. Degrading him was not part of the deal. Lots of times guys paid him cash dollars to get off but also to say, *I may be doing this but I am not a whore.* They liked putting him in a box along with their desires, and then they quickly hid the all of it beneath the bed until next time. They cursed the contents of their sex box, but only afterwards.

Bill always asked if Del wanted a smoke (yes), a beer (yes—he kept a six in the room), another beer (usually), or a place to crash (no). Del couldn't stomach the stench or hear more than fifteen minutes of all his sick Kennedy shit. After hearing more than that, Del was primed to pull an Oswald himself.

Most times Del just zoned out on whatever he was on. Sometimes he thought about what he was doing later or if he'd left a fag burning at Fred's. Sometimes during Bill's talk, Del tried setting all that wild Kennedy rhapsodizing to music. It was wild enough to lend itself to some crazed song. He got real good at where to put the words and recreating the rapid and excited rhythm of Bill's voice.

Some Sundays, Del thought about the scar on Bill's back. It was a thick purple-pink band that ran from one shoulder to the opposite hip over his backbone ridge. Whatever happened to Bill had almost halved him. The edges looked clean so Del figured it was from a blade. Bill would be lying there going on about Kennedy and Del would picture him caught in a combine, sliced by a barn fan, bent over a silage cutter, and most every sort of rural carnage he could imagine. He never asked outright about it.

One Tuesday afternoon, Cody and Del were at the bar. Hester stopped in for coffee. She brought in some homemade banana bread that they ate in about a minute. She was heading to work at the mall.

She'd gotten a job at Sears but was biding her time until something came along more to her liking. Hester was always either job hunting, juggling jobs, or giving notice. She'd had upwards of ten jobs just since she'd come back to town. She spent more time scanning classifieds than she did collecting a paycheck. That day she was reading the ads at the bar and had circled a couple things, so it was likely she wasn't long for Sears.

After a second cup of coffee she checked her watch, folded her paper, and took off. It was just Cody and Del. It used to be they'd have lots of fun on deserted afternoons drinking and dicking around, but not since Kevin came along. It was just a lazy sort of day with both of them low key. Del was a bit stoned and Cody had been up all night frigging with Kevin. He was all love-dopey and excited about having the night off.

Cody wiped the bar once or twice, let out a sigh, and eventually flipped on the TV and fiddled with the sound. On account of the air conditioning, the TV was real loud. It reminded Del of how loud he and Molly used to play the set at home. That seemed a hundred years ago.

Del had seen Molly not long ago, coming out of Woolworth's. He was a ways away but recognized her immediately. She didn't see him, so he followed her and kept out of sight. She was almost a teenager now. He kicked himself for not calling out, but it panicked him. He was anxious and unsure, and a mite fucked up too. It wasn't the right state for a reunion. He'd just left Slagger's and they'd been sampling inventory. Of all the days to see Molly. Though clearly of his own doing, Del called it his bum luck. He'd been thinking about her on and off ever since.

Cody upped the sound on the TV, which Del took as more his not wanting to chat than out of interest in the movie. The afternoon matinee was *PT 109*, about JFK and what a fine serviceman, hero, citizen, and all around decent fellow he was. It was red, white, and blue even in black and white. Total bullshit. The big message was that JFK was a hero from his head down to his hammertoes and destined for greatness. "Who isn't at one time," was what Del figured. Not everyone was lucky enough to be born into a dynasty. Del figured the greatness that came with a pedigree wasn't all that great. Some grew up on the opposite end of things. Del would've had his own band in a second if he were a Kennedy.

The movie was so corny that Cody and Del bust out laughing a couple times. The battle scenes weren't bad. In the rising black and white cloud of another direct hit, something in Del's head clicked. This all had to be some sort of sign—at least that's what it seemed in his pot haze. Swirling the ice around in his rum and Coke, he decided that when Bill came to town this Sunday he'd give him a session to curl his pubes. The thought made him grin and the more he considered it the funnier it got, until he couldn't stop laughing. Cody turned and gave him a look like he was nuts. People expected that sort of thing from Del, who just pointed to his drink and blamed it on that. Del didn't want Cody thinking crazy Fred was wearing off on him.

When Finn dragged his bony ass through the back door at six, Del left with Cody. Being alone with Finn, and whoever else the town happened to yak-up, was not in Del's plans for the evening. The way Del saw it, aside from the Blob, the sole thing that Finn attracted was flies. He wasn't only a bore, he never gave out free drinks either. There was no reason for sticking around during his shift.

Del asked Cody if he wanted to split a spliff, but when he opened his mouth to answer there was a honk. Kevin's Dart was parked diagonally in the lot. Cody had changed since that romance began. Not that Del gave two shits, but it was like nothing else mattered to Cody. He didn't even give Del an answer, just slapped him on the shoulder and turned right away. Fuck him then. Cody hopped in the car, tickled tonsils with Kevin, and off they went.

Del thought about heading to Fred's but thought better of it. Fred had been acting even weirder lately. He'd been nagging about treating him different and just saying things Del knew wasn't him. Del would lay money it was Bruschetta's doing. As far as he was concerned, she was at the front of the feeding line of folks who could eat shit and die in this town. Del always said she just loved shoving her plastic face where it didn't belong. Del figured Fred for even crazier than he was if he thought he was going to apologize or suddenly respect him.

He headed to Slags' instead. It was business as usual over there. They had a decadent time. When Del told Slags what he had planned for Bill, Slags about coughed up a lung from laughing.

The following Sunday Bill came bustling through the back door of the Sand Bar, red and sweaty as a bulldog's balls and wearing a ball cap and sunglasses. Del overheard Sister whisper to Cody that he always half-expected Bill to be wearing the glasses with attached nose and fake mustache. It was funny, but Del wasn't about to give Sister the satisfaction of a smile, much less a laugh.

Bill was always fretting folks would recognize him. Lord knew how far away he parked or what name he registered under at the motel. His real name wasn't Bill, Del knew that much. Sometimes when Del called him that he'd look confused or even say "Who?" or "Huh?" Once, when Bill was taking a dump, Del rifled through his wallet to check his ID. His given name was Clovis. Seeing that, Del could hardly blame him for wanting to be called Bill.

That Sunday he gave Del a nod and a minute later they were cutting through the lot behind the Golden Calf, down the alley to the Friendship Inn. Bill always got an outer room, less chance being seen Del supposed. All Del knew was Bill's having someplace to go saved him from having to pay Leo.

Leo was still steamed as Eskimo pee over some cancelled dates. Not setting Del up was his way of letting his feelings be known. Del had better things to do than please that pockmarked pervert and he wasn't about to give him the satisfaction of begging. Leo set Bill and Del up the first time After that, Bill always rented a room. He may have smelled like pig shit, but Bill still thought Leo's flat was disgusting.

It was a typical Bill Sunday with typical Bill doings. Five minutes after stepping inside Room 115 he was grunting and baring his big yellow teeth with a load trickling into his belly button. His knees were bent out and his heels together like a bullfrog. A crow's foot vein throbbed on his forehead. Del was a little drunk. The all of it was nauseating, so he just closed his eyes and listened to the hum of the VACANCY sign outside.

Del plopped into a beige side chair and stared at a painting of prairie flowers in a vase. He gave Bill a couple minutes to settle down. When he looked calmer, Del propped his feet on a side table and said he'd met a salesman from Dubuque last Tuesday who said he was in the navy with JFK. Bill cocked his head and began to chew on his lip where he already had a waxy callus. Del said this guy told him JFK was hung like a stallion. Bill's ears perked up and his pecker was close behind. His lazy eye started vibrating and his tongue flicked a time or two. Del said the salesman claimed they got simultaneous blow-jobs from a Polynesian party girl.

Bill's revived stiffy was well in hand by the time Del finished. In a dreamy monotone he asked to hear it again, and not to leave out a single detail. The next time, more lurid particulars came to Del's mind. He wasn't sure if Bill swallowed the story. It didn't matter, though Del doubted it. Bill might've been slow, but believing all that would've put him beyond backward. Mostly, he was grateful for the custom-made sex story.

Feeling such power over Bill really got Del going. The rush he felt making it up went straight to his crank. Del got hard as stone and that hadn't happened with a punter in a long while. He never expected it with Pig Shit Bill. Slipping the elastic of his skivvies below his nuts Del beat off retelling the story. When Bill came a second time, Del blasted a load all over Bill's socks. Bill creased his forehead and didn't seem to care much for that. Maybe those were his Sunday socks.

They always settled money matters straight off. To Del's way of thinking it was the only way to do it. But that Sunday before Del left the room Bill handed him some more rolled up bills. The bundle felt nice and Del was pleased that blasting on his socks didn't cost him the extra. That night Bill paid him triple.

Two weeks later there was talk round town about some farmer out on Highway K who stumbled into a silo and got swallowed up in the harvest. The more the poor sucker struggled, the deeper he sank, until he drowned in that sea of grain. It was said that when they drained the silo he was open-eyed and blue as an Easter egg. The story gave Del chills in an excited way.

Late that week Hester came in with the *The Tristate Journal* tucked under her arm. She was still at Sears and still checking the classifieds during her morning coffee. After she left, Del was thumbing through the pages of the paper she'd left behind. He found an article about the silo-swallowed farmer. There was a picture longside the story. It wasn't Bill. In Del's eyes, it might as well have been. He never saw Pig Shit Bill again. Maybe Bill figured that nothing Del did could top that fantasy. Or maybe Bill was irked over Del spooging on his socks. There was no way of knowing for sure.

Platinum Angel

BRUSChetta's spirits were high that
warm October evening. She'd returned from getting collagen injections in her cheeks and lips just a few days before. Those trips made her purr like a contented puss, and that night she sounded like an idling semi. Something was on her mind. She looked gorgeous but swollen. Fred told her the shots made her look like Maud Adams.

She put a hand on her hip and arched a brow when he called her Octopussy. "Honey, you don't know the half of it."

Fred leaned over to light her smoke and got a whiff of powdered skin. She let out a satisfied sigh, sucked in her cheeks, and eyed herself in a mirrored tile. Brushing back a platinum ringlet she smiled, "I'm damn near perfect now." She said it had been a long journey of lyposculpture, lifts, dermabrasions, defoliation treatments, hair removal, follicle regeneration, and hormone shots. She was the hybrid of science, plastics, and aesthetics. The mysterious funding of Bruschetta's procedures was a great source of bar speculation.

"It's a health care scam."

"She's a thief."

"An heiress."

"Got herself a sugar daddy."

"She's a witness and I'd lay odds it's hush money."

The rumors rotated like a pig on a spit and that was fine with her. Bruschetta enjoyed the speculation. Being the source of so much conjecture pleasured her. She'd merely laugh and keep mum on the subject. If she had told the truth, no one would've believed her.

Cody handed her the pictures from Anna and Lulu's union. "Take a look, Bob just got them back yesterday." Bruschetta flipped through them once quickly and then slower a second time. She offered a running commentary of sighs, gasps, and laughter. The bar had looked so festive that night—white balloons, vanilla scented candles, tissue bells, and Congrats snow-sprayed letter by letter across the mirrors. Anna had been a lovely and elegant sight, with live daisies woven in her hair. That was Kitra's idea. Lulu filled out the tux nicely. Her pride and happiness was clear as the October sky. The last photo showed the entire bar family clowning around and mugging. The enhanced color pictures made reality seem drag longside it. A perfect red nail tapped the photo. "Ooo, I want a copy of this one too, only I wish I would have had my injections...you can see a line there."

Bruschetta handed the envelope back to Cody and asked how things were going with Kevin. She was fishing about Kevin's reaction to the news that Mac and Stacie were engaged. She came upon the item in *The Tristate Journal* the day before last. Word was Stacie had a baby on the way.

Cody shrugged. "Kevin seems fine with it. He hasn't said a word to me, but I imagine it's a relief. It shows she's moved on. That's all a closed chapter in his life now."

Bruschetta nodded. Sometimes things aren't that simple. Kevin and Stacie had been together a good long time. Bruschetta didn't want to stir things up. It was easier just to agree. She finally said, "That's a healthy way of seeing it, I suppose."

"That's what I figure, anyways." Cody rushed off to get Jack-O's re-fill.

Bruschetta turned to Fred. "I tell you Junior, there's nothing like a trip to a spa to renew a gal." The puffiness caused her to slightly slur which made Fred think of a Novocained gun moll. By the way she was smoking, Fred was sure the moment had become a role for her. Fred knew movies better than life itself, but still found it a challenge to disentangle who Bruschetta was being from who she was most times. It was an ongoing game. Over the years he'd gotten keen on catching a glimpse of the real her between scenes. Sometimes, when their eyes connected, he was pretty sure she knew it, too.

To Bruschetta, life was a searchlight and sequins premiere, and the roving spotlight mostly gravitated her direction. To Fred, she was the light itself. She was the source. She was radiance. Glamour meant so much to him and she was the most glamorous person in all of Bayette-ville and Schuyler County. There were no contenders.

It was hard to say how much of the attention Bruschetta received was due to star power and how much was shock value. People didn't expect to see someone of her magnitude walking Main Street in broad daylight. She'd be strutting around in high heels and high fashion hair, swinging her purse and wiggling her butt with that sci-fi body squeezed in a hot pink pantsuit or orange sherbet Capri pants or some out-landish outfit. The townsfolk mostly shifted eyes. Some stared. Some tsked. That sort of thing just wasn't done around these parts. Maybe in Paris or New York, but not in Bayetteville. Bruschetta didn't care, she did it anyways. She'd been in town almost ten years and was still stopping traffic. That was how she liked it.

Margaritas were the drink special that Wednesday. Fred bought them a round and toasted Bruschetta and her dress, a lime green number inspired by Marilyn's dress in *The Seven Year Itch*. It looked like a cardinal sin on her, a low-cut first class ticket to the lusty layers of hell. That dress was the envy of every tri-state drag artiste of taste and breeding.

Fred sat back. He felt heavy and loose from drinking too fast. It was still early. He cradled his glass and figured it wise to nurse this one.

"What?" she said, giving him a look before turning on her stool. Bruschetta laughed at one of Hester's sly asides and nearly spilled out of her dress. Her boobs were gravitational wonders and hard as steel-belted radial tires. Fred had slow-danced with her several times, so he knew. Folks speculated on the subject. It was whispered that at the time of her implants she didn't have the funds for silicone, so she found a doctor willing to insert floor wax instead. The savings was considerable, especially for the size she wanted. Bruschetta had to have the biggest blouse meats in town, no two ways about it. Larger than life was who and what she was. Anything less didn't amount to a hill of beans. Anything less wouldn't have been Bruschetta. Jack-O swore the floor wax tale was true on all he held sacred. The particulars of what Jack-O might hold sacred was another topic to consider, but nobody asked for fear that he'd explain.

Del obsessed over Bruschetta's breasts one night stretched out on Fred's living room floor. He was tripping on mescaline and rolling his head side to side through repeated plays of a Butthole Surfers cassette. Del practically talked himself blue and rocked his head bald theorizing and constructing gruesome scenarios of the wax catching fire or melting or slowly leaking into her bloodstream. He was shooting questions left and right. Did they change shape when they got soft? Would they melt in a hot tub or on a hot August afternoon? Did they resist scuff marks?

The composition and potential consequences of Bruschetta's boobs didn't matter to Fred. The size was proportionate to her personality. Fred wondered if her personality grew with her appearance, or if the enhancements were done so her body could keep pace with her charisma. The quandary led his mind in looping spirals on several occasions.

Bruschetta sipped her margarita and asked Hester about things at the Bargain Barn. Hester had just started a couple weeks ago after leaving Sears. "I can't complain, but I can't rightly recommend it either," she said. "I like that I can use the phone since they have two lines."

Bruschetta turned quick and caught Fred eyeing her breasts. She gave him a naughty smile and reached to tap his hand. "Fred, sweetie, we both know I'm the last thing you want."

She was right. To Fred it would be like sleeping with his mother, his mentoress, or a goddess—but that's not what she meant. It was a butch/femme, top/bottom, and pitcher/catcher brand of comment and the blunt truth of it stung. Fred was sensitive on the subject. He grew up in a house and in a place where one was favored over the other and he always wanted so much to be everything that he wasn't. Her remark was a knee in the nuts of what he saw as his masculinity. Fred looked at her, then Hester, and rose in a huff. He was drunk all right.

Bruschetta shot him a look. "Don't go popping pearls. Plant your butt back down."

Fred ignored her and rushed onto the dance floor. The comment had put him in a foul temper. For her of all people to say that. Her opinion mattered to him. That was why it hurt. Fred swore if he were more of a man things would be different. If he were rugged, he'd have the respect of everybody and wouldn't care what people thought. When he talked, people would listen. If he only was what he wasn't. He swore to himself to become more of a real man, before dancing with Finn to a couple of Irene Cara songs.

Returning to his stool a half hour later, Fred was dewy with sweat. Thoughts of being more a man and all that would entail were still on his mind. He was curious about who did what in Kevin and Cody's relationship. They were both manly. He asked Bruschetta, but she was uninterested. She waved his speculations aside with a call for another cocktail. Looking bored and gorgeous, she strummed her nails along the bar and circled a lime slice around the rim of her glass.

Cody poured Fred another. Looking at the glass all Fred could think was, "Here we go." This would take him back to where he was before dancing, and then some. This was a threshold drink—or rather, an over-the-threshold drink.

Bruschetta turned and Fred lit her cigarette. He couldn't stay mad. He loved her. "Wonder where Kitra has gotten herself off to? She was supposed to meet me here an hour ago. Hope nothing's going on with that no-account Merlin."

Hester plucked a bit of ash from her drink. She had friends out at the jail and wasn't sure about saying anything, but figured it was only a matter of time until she found out. "Well, you know he got out on bail."

"So I heard," she said with a drifting nod. Bruschetta swung her crossed leg in an arc and smiled at Fred. Her look made it clear something was brewing beneath that triple scoop vanilla wig. She was itching for someone to feed her a lead. When he asked what that look was about, she began talking about a gorgeous doctor at the clinic. "He looks like Mark Harmon and he's a plastic surgeon! It's a match made in heaven. When he put that stethoscope to my chest I suspect he heard doves cooing. All I know is that he was showing an interest." Bruschetta reached over and put her hand on Fred's thigh. Her touch excited him. Fred got a little flustered and wondered if Bruschetta knew what was happening.

"When I go in for liposculpture in November, I'll be knocking boots with Dr. Paul come hell or high water. He was interested, but married. The nurse said he and his wife were separated." Bruschetta laughed. "Separated? That's just jumping out the plane without hitting ground yet. No matter, any wedding band is fool's gold when Bruschetta wants a man. Lordy, all this Dr. Paul talk is causing me to perspire." She fanned her bosom and batted her eyes, no simple task with two sets of fake lashes on each lid.

"Hey gorgeous."

"Hello yourself, pull up a chair and drop that tired ass of yours."

"His tired ass dropped years ago," laughed Hester with a smack of gum.

Leo made a face her way and straddled a stool. He asked Bruschetta what she thought about remodeling the place. Everyone within earshot gave a start. Leo wasn't one to go spending money that way. It made more sense when he said he set aside three hundred dollars for the remodeling. That wasn't even enough for a full coat of paint.

Bruschetta looked around and then up at the speckled ceiling fan. "I'm kind of attached to it this way, but for that amount of money I doubt you'll be going hog wild."

"I'll leave that to Pig Shit Bill."

Hester just laughed, "You are all crazy!"

"My my my" was all Bruschetta said. One Sunday after Bill had left, Del had given a bar-side rendition of all the barnyard specifics of Bill's cumming fits.

Slags came in a minute later. He'd returned to his Idol look. All the chains and medals made him a clunky dancer. He and Fred cavorted to the Thompson Twins and talked throughout the song. When Slags was flying, talking with him was the easiest way to find out what was going on with Del. Fred knew something was. Slagger prattled on about most everything else. He was having too good a time to be focused. Fred could about hear the thoughts ricochet around in Slags' head. Two songs later, Del sauntered over with a cocktail and started sloshing alongside them. They swayed in pretty much the same spot for the rest of the night, moving to the music more than really dancing.

At last call, Fred saw Bruschetta collect her bag and get ready to leave as he headed out the back. Slags and Del were just ahead of him. Bruschetta cocked a brow at Fred, or at least the ridge on her forehead where a brow had once been. She thought Fred had gotten wise to that jerk. "Del doesn't give a good goddamn about anyone but himself. He's a son-of-a-bitch any way you cut it." Lately she thought he'd actually been listening.

Swaying forward, Fred picked a housefly from her lacquered wig and asked if she wanted a ride. She made a face when she saw the bug, then smiled and adjusted an ankle strap. "I believe I'll stroll tonight." It didn't take a fortuneteller to see the plans she had for her immediate future. The question was who. No man was safe. Bruschetta was on the prowl.

Slags laughed and threw his emaciated body back against the mirror-tiled wall. Leo told him he was going to break one of them someday, "...and when you do you'll be paying for it." With Slags it was always hard telling if he was as wasted as he behaved. Some thought it mostly an act and some thought he'd been wasted so much that behaving that was was just his natural state.

Del didn't need theatrics to seem tragic. He stood there with his hands buried in his pockets and his chin tucked in his collar. He was as chalky and flat as a grave marker.

A moment later, they rounded the corner in the used Buick that Slags had bought for seventy-five bucks. Bruschetta was strutting down the moon-splashed sidewalk whistling "At Last." Fred hollered to her at the stoplight. She yelled something back, but they couldn't hear a word over the cough of the Buick's engine. When the light changed, they were gone. Slagger was driving like a maniac, and a drunken one at that. It was a huge relief when he screeched to a stop in front of Fred's place.

When Fred's phone rang at ten the
next morning he and Del were in the middle of a nasty argument. It was their worst one yet. Del had clipped the phone bill money and bought a pair of boots. Fred said he deserved better. He was starting to see the flip side of destiny was a life sentence. He told Del he was losing patience. That was a leap for him. He'd never acknowledged, much less confronted, Del's thieving before, so Del didn't expect it.

When the phone rang, Del said he was out of there and slammed the door so hard he cracked the frosted glass pane. Fred called after him, but he could hear Del's bootsteps go right on down the stairs and out the front. Fred heard Mr. Sawyer crack his door to see what the commotion was about.

Cody was on the line. He'd never called Fred before. He asked Fred if he'd heard anything about Bruschetta. Fred could hear Kevin whispering in the background. He thought again about who did what to who. When Cody came back on the line, he relayed to Fred what he'd heard from Leo and Sister. The details were so vague they didn't make much sense.

Fred figured it must be mostly hearsay. He couldn't imagine Bruschetta being anyone's victim. She was too intimidating. She could stare down a Cyclops. One mere point of her pump and all attackers would scatter. To Fred she was invincible and beyond harm. That was the myth she lived and the myth he believed.

Cody said that when he phoned her place there was no answer.

"Did you try the hospital?"

"I didn't think of that."

Not thinking to do something like that was more than just a matter of being upset or not being a morning person. Sometimes things didn't connect with Cody. Fred suspected too much speed for too many years. Fred and Cody said they'd call each other soon as they heard a word. Fred hung up and dialed the hospital.

His gut commenced to turning as he sat on hold.

"St. Xavier's, how may I direct your call?" The name of the place sent a tingle running up him from toes to earlobes. Was it the same voice his parents had heard? He wondered if that gut shame would ever disappear or if it's taken root and become the foundation and underside of everything since.

The tension in his stomach clustered. The knot tightened as the nurse explained that a woman by that description had been admitted earlier and was in intensive care. It didn't strike Fred as odd until later that they hadn't discovered Bruschetta was a biologically a man. St. Xavier's wasn't renown for attentive or even competent medical care. Their concern was more aligned to keeping a sure grip on souls.

The receptionist was pleasant enough, but bound by rules and regulations. Fred imagined her fiddling with chain-dangling glasses as she explained that no additional information could be given unless he was a member of the immediate family. Before hanging up she asked him to spell B-R-U-S-C-H-E-T-T-A. There was a pause and a slight intake of air before she asked him to repeat it. "Like the cheese," he offered. If they needed identification, Bruschetta must be unconscious. After hanging up, Fred called Cody.

Fred imagined the bandages wound around her Kim Novak face— dark glasses, a dangling cigarette, squared nails chipped. He imagined Bruschetta cussing a blue streak over the fact that she'd only had a manicure the day before. But with each breath that fantasy faded and the brutality of the attack burned through. This was beyond broken nails and a mussed wig. The movie had stopped. The film broke and jittered off a harsh naked square of projector light. There was no glamour, just a black and white newspaper item.

That afternoon Fred sat on his couch and tucked his feet beneath him. He looked out the window. The view could still soothe him. The river was there, as always. The black expanse of the Frear hadn't lost its magic, but Bruschetta had. His heart rose to his throat as he poured a glass of wine.

She told Fred she left home at sixteen to pursue a life of drag after her daddy backhanded her across the face and said what she was doing was against God's plan. Slamming the front door on her family killed the person she'd been and was expected to become. She was a baby born dead and slapped to life. The day he hit her, she started to be what she always knew she was. The trick was making the outsides match the insides. The birth of Bruschetta wasn't immediate. A masterpiece is rarely an artist's first work. She went through several incarnations that included Claudette Deneuve, Andrea Trulove, and Vicki St. James. Changing identity was just another way Fred related to her.

Life on her own was difficult at times, but it got easier somewhere between getting her boobs done and her nose bobbed. One New Year's Eve she traded Vicki St. James' chestnut mane for platinum, and Bruschetta was born. A week later she packed her make-up, zipped her garment bag, and boarded a westbound train for Bayetteville. Trains were more glamorous than buses, and Bruschetta always went the route of glamour. After settling in town, she went and bought herself a convertible. It was as much a part of her as anything, even if she only took it out of Sister's garage rarely.

Bruschetta didn't like being called an impersonator or any sort of drag. "I am not a drag queen and I am not an impersonator. I am real." She was an independent spirit, living without apology and hell bent on having it all. To her that was absolute beauty, true love, mass adoration, and sexual gratification. For anyone else it would seem an awful lot to expect. Fort Bruschetta, it was a requirement.

Her conquests could fill a book with a good-sized spine and tiny print. She regaled Fred, and all within earshot, with an array of torrid and comic tales. She told of seducing hockey players, classical violinists, longshoreman, two crewman from Cousteau's Calypso, four star chefs and short order cooks, a Jehovah's Witness who came knocking, and the ex-governor of a southern state who cried like a baby afterwards. No guy was safe if he registered a blip on her mantenna. She'd even been with three of the eight aldermen in town, two of them more than once. Bruschetta always claimed nothing could happen to her because she knew where all the bodies were buried.

Fred thought about recording her tales in a notebook or on tape, but never got around to it. He could have sat at her heels and listened for hours, and oftentimes he did. He heard about when she was run out of Hadley for performing oral sex in the black maze of the Jaycees Haunted House, and how she worked in the circus hanging from the high wire by her teeth until it caused her to develop an overbite so she had her teeth fixed and capped and worked as a receptionist in the dentist's office for two months afterwards. That was hard to understand until she explained how adorable she looked in her little white get-up. She claimed it was a great way to meet men. The typing was hell on her nails, so she quit after a bit and worked as an exotic dancer in a club outside Evansville. Her slew of fans never discovered her tightly tucked secret. Fellas always told her she was too classy to be working there.

Bruschetta even had celebrity stories. She met Onassis while he was married to Jackie. He groped himself when he saw her, "and we all know what that means," but nothing came of it. Bobby Meso asked her out after a nightclub appearance and stared at her breasts from appetizer until dessert. She claimed he was much more charismatic on stage. A big rock star introduced himself by going tongue spelunking down Bruschetta's throat at Mardi Gras. Despite his brazenness, she claimed he was just a shy little thing beneath it all.

Heaping portions of life experience gave her a well-earned air of knowing. People constantly sought her counsel and Fred couldn't recall a single divulgence, event, or confession that shocked her or prompted a blush. Cruelty for its own sake was about the sole thing she didn't understand.

Just when it seemed she'd uttered the last of her fantastic tales, another event or adventure was brought to light. Del told Fred if he believed her he was even more of a moron than he figured. "You really think someone who did all that is going to be *here*?"

A number of folks thought that she was mostly spinning yarns. Fred had no reason to doubt her. His favorite story was when she was working as a cocktail waitress on a phony visa in Europe as Andrea Trulove. Outside an Austrian bakery, she was kidnapped by two Yugoslavian truckers and was taken hostage for a two-day chase. They never discovered her secret either.

Bruschetta was tough. Those kidnappers must have perked her interest or else she wouldn't have allowed herself to be taken. No one was going to break her or control her or make her live any different than she wanted. She left home because she wouldn't bend to the wishes of another and that willful streak was still as much a part of her as the silicone and the collagen and Lord knew what all else.

Bruschetta tried remaining somewhat detached, but despite her sometimes aloof demeanor, many things and people were very close to her heart. She seemed to put a great deal of effort into covering up her real self, but the person beneath the flip and the arch and the snap was apparent. She wasn't an icy vamp, a selfish sexpot, or a hooker with a heart of gold. She was none of the movie types and none of the things she portrayed. Her warm qualities were part of her but not part of the blueprint. Compassion wasn't high on her list of things to aspire to. That was a quality lesser queens might need, but not her. She pitied the sisters who had to rely on conversation and charm. "It must be so difficult not to be physically devastating."

Bruschetta could also be the queen bee, poised to chastise and sting her third-world sisters when she felt they were shaming the order. Most told her to mind her own affairs and it was rumored she came to

Bayetteville to escape a hostile pack of he-shes. It was plausible. She had as many enemies as admirers. She claimed that meant you stood for something. She fully owned that her biggest flaw was her inconsistency. A lot depended on her mood. Bruschetta claimed it was the hormones.

Fred sat on his pastel couch and wondered which of Bruschetta's enemies would do such a thing. He didn't flip on the light at dusk or go into work when the time came or answer the phone when it rang. He ended up missing two shifts and got fired from Piggly Wiggly. He didn't care. That job was nothing but a habit. Bruschetta always said it was the habits that'll kill you. "A rut is just a few feet shy of a grave."

Later, he learned that Cody had been trying to call that night. Along with Leo and Hester, he'd gone over to St. Xavier's to see Bruschetta. No one was admitted. She had regained consciousness and was out of intensive care, but had barred all visitors. A lesbian nurse who knew Hester told them that much. The grand diva nature of Bruschetta's ban on all guests made Fred grin. All but incapacitated, she was still managing to control the situation.

The following week, she arranged to be transferred to a hospital near Eagleton. Fred sent a bouquet of mums and two Get Well cards, but never got a response. Eventually, he assumed she just wanted to be left alone.

The police didn't ask many questions. That alone caused some people to suspect Merlin's involvement, what with his contacts on the force. The investigation closed real quick with little more than a consternated shaking of heads and a shrug from local authorities. In Bayetteville, justice had its own rules. Some saw her as deserving of it.

Cody made sure some retribution was made. He and Kevin hid outside Merlin's place one night. When they peeked through the bushes and saw him coming, they covered their heads with cut-off pantyhose and beat his ass bloody. He never lodged a formal complaint, so everyone figured that for an outright admission of guilt. Beating him may not have right, but that was just the flip side of small town justice.

Fred didn't see Bruschetta until late December, when she arrived unexpectedly at Sister's Stuff My Stockings bash. The party had been in progress several hours when she came through the door. She only stopped to get her car and pickup a couple boxes of jewelry and mementos she'd stored there. She wasn't expecting the festivities.

By the time she arrived, most everyone was lounging about baked or in the backyard making snow angels. Spiked eggnog, generous shots, and plentiful joints made it one of the great parties everyone wished they could recall a bit more clearly. Fred was in better shape than most since he got there so late. He'd worked until closing at Staley's. Finn had got him a busing job there after he was let go from Piggly Wiggly.

Bruschetta was disguised—or at least as incognito as she could be. She wore a black wig, a white scarf, and tinted sunglasses. In the dim Christmas light, she brought to mind a chipped doll someone had haphazardly puttied together. Fred was excited to see her, but she seemed embarrassed to be less than almost perfect. She recoiled when he bent to kiss her hello and wish her happy holidays. When he asked if she was okay, she said she didn't need any help with the boxes. That wasn't what Fred meant and she knew it. Bruschetta believed her looks were the attraction and never realized that wasn't the reason Fred loved her, or maybe just one part of it. Glamour was sparkle, but it wasn't everything. Unsure what to say, Fred whispered that she was right, Del had proven himself an asshole for the last time. Their final row had been on Thanksgiving Day.

She smiled, opened a cloth-lined silver box, and handed him a blue and green starburst brooch. It was a big vibrant peacock of light, radiant even in the dim light. The perfect thing to remember her by.

She folded Fred's hand over it and turned to the back stairs just as people began to recognize her. Bruschetta waved hello and made a hasty departure. She was no longer living without apology. That divine incarnation was gone forever, bled bone dry by the small minded brutality she'd struggled to rise above. She was no longer Bruschetta. Someone new and nameless had taken her place.

Everything she'd worked for and towards had been shattered. Even if she began all over, she could never approach how close she'd been to perfection. All the cosmetic tinkering had been destroyed. In some spots, the parts appeared to had shifted and recongealed beneath her overly powdered skin. No surgery could restore that degree of damage. Nothing could. The bashing had broken almost every bone in her almost perfect face.

The Fowlest Day

Jack-O took a sip of beer and checked his watch. It seemed a downright ironic gesture to Cody. The only times Jack-O cared about were happy hour and closing time. He gave Cody a grin and did his change-jangling thing. "So what are you doing for turkey day?"

Cody flipped on the TV. "Kevin and me are heading up to Chicago for a long weekend—see the sights, get out of town a spell." It annoyed Cody when Jack-O repeated himself or asked about things he already knew. Booze had effectively burned a path through his brain and what remained seemed as porous as a slab of Swiss cheese, and what was left of that seemed to be going bad. Jack-O knew damn well about those Thanksgiving plans. He'd been sitting right there when they decided to go.

Leo had handed them the envelope with three hundred dollars. "Now I want you boys to take this and do something special. Bruschetta would have wanted it that way." The money was payment for giving Merlin his black and blue comeuppance. Beating him was a pleasure. In fact, once they started working him over it was tough to stop. Cody wasn't prone to fighting, but was thankful his daddy had taught him how to land a punch. The thrashing sent Merlin to the hospital. They broke teeth, cracked ribs, and swelled shut an eye. Every inch of him was bruised or bloody. They heard he looked just like a mummy.

Jack-O spun his beer around on the coaster and raised his head. His glasses were so smudged it looked like he saw the world through two saucers of fish scales. "I used to go up to Chicago quite a bit."

"Is that so?" This conversation had occurred almost verbatim as well. Cody tried being a bit kinder. He ran a hand through his thinning hair and shook his bangs back. He was desperate to get away. Five days free of the Sand Bar was sure to be either a slice of heaven or a reprieve from hell—it basically amounted to the same thing. He and Kevin were packed and eager to head out.

Though his relationship with Kevin was going well, a part of Cody wished he was taking this vacation alone. Feeling that way bothered him. Cody knew they had a great thing, but a side of him hungered for something more or maybe something different or maybe the chance to step outside that great thing and experience something else. It might have been love, but love could be stagnant. His gut told him there was nothing wrong with some exploring, and his gut could be awful insistent.

The day after they played handball with Merlin's sorry ass hide, Kevin and Cody were rehashing the particulars of the encounter with Leo, Jack-O, and Everly when the back door opened. It was Kitra. Her footfalls said she meant business. She looked wild as Medusa and madder than hell. She brought her face close to Cody's. "You didn't have to do it."

Everyone looked at her blankly. "Do what?"

"Don't give me that. I know you did it."

Leo spun around on his stool. He'd had enough! Her behavior was pissing him off something fierce and he wasn't about to listen to another word. Not in his own bar! "Yeah, and we know he done it too."

"He's a good man."

"Good for nothing."

Her self-righteous name calling appalled Leo, seeing as her crazy ex was the cause of all the violence in the first place. She wasn't one of them. This was the sort of thing the straights brought. Merlin got what he had coming and nothing more. She was lucky Leo didn't do worse. He knew people who'd do anything for a price. Kitra was acting like Bruschetta or Cody were the ones at fault.

"Merlin is vile and vindictive. You've sat right here and said so yourself." Leo was gritting his teeth and practically spitting words by that point.

Everly nodded towards the door. "Now, Snow White, don't you have somewhere to be?"

Kitra's lips thinned and a forked vein rose like a river branch along her forehead. "You're all in a heap of trouble. Don't think I don't know what's what!" Shaking with rage, she picked up Leo's gin and tonic and tossed it in his face.

He licked his lips and stroked either side of his mustache. "Thanks for saving me some hand work."

Kitra opened her mouth once and then twice, but was mute with rage. Seeing the futility of her visit she pivoted on a heel and headed out the back, nearly ripping the door from its hinges.

"Good riddance," said Leo with the wave of a hand. "What old Lana Turner movie was that scene from?"

Anna and Lulu were just coming down the hallway. "Good God," Lulu said, removing her sunglasses. "Who put the cockleburs in her brassiere?"

All five shared an extended look before busting into laughter.

"Can't you guess?"

Lulu laughed and shook her head side to side. "That's what I figured. You boys did good. Merlin shouldn't have gotten away with that."

Kevin reached over and took hold of Cody's hand.

"Bet that's the last we see of her," Everly said with a grin.

"She's got no business coming here anyway. What's her reasoning?"

Anna crossed her thin arms and scratched at a patch of eczema on an elbow. She didn't want to get into it with anyone, but she didn't go much for character assassination neither. She was a firm believer in thinking positive thoughts and not speaking ill. That was one of the things Lulu loved about her. "Come on, Kitra's not that bad. She helped me out during our union didn't she? She's just upset."

Leo snubbed out his cigarette. "Well, she's got cause to be. She's the reason her supposed best friend almost got killed. This is the way a lot of the straights are. They come on like it's all okay and they're open minded and such, but in a crisis those true colors come out. She seems of the mind that life in the straight world is somehow more important than the life that any of us might be living."

"I don't think she said that."

"Well, you weren't here."

Lulu put an arm around Anna.

Everly peeled the shell from a hard-boiled egg. He never cared for Kitra or her hoity-toity attitude and treating him like he was nothing more than a gay black guy, like his being around was worth two points in her game of being open-minded. He always figured her for a phony and resented the fact that she probably saw coming to the bar as slumming. Like they were all lowlifes.

Leo couldn't say he was remorseful to see her go either. He wiped his face with some napkins and lit a smoke. "Pour me another one, that bitch has me shaking! " He smiled to himself. "Merlin must have really been a sorry sight to cause her to behave that way."

"You know, that sort of behavior doesn't surprise me at all. I think she was always that way."

"Dora over at the hospital claims that Merlin looks like an eggplant swelled to bursting."

Cody slid down on his elbows in front of Leo. "I wasn't pulling your chain when I said me and Kevin left him broken and bloody alongside that spinning laundry tree out behind his place. He was so loose at that point we could have pinned him on that clothesline and given him a spin or two."

"I didn't doubt it for a minute." Leo said he had an errand to run and would be back in a few. When he sidled onto the same stool a half hour later, he gave Cody and Kevin a rheumy-eyed smile along with a bulging envelope of cash. It contained the three hundred dollars set aside for remodeling. Payment for services rendered. Cash for a bash. That was when they decided on a trip to Chicago.

Kitra's clomping stomping tirade was just the tip of the iceberg. Everyone started behaving a little strangely in the aftermath of the beatings.

A week or so later and without reason

or warning, Fred began dressing in drag. He didn't do it to fulfill a calling—but to fill a void. Maybe by being this he'd find out what he was missing. Buschetta always claimed she started on a lark. Misty Blue was the name he used. He found an old blue party dress at a thrift store along with some navy pumps, a cinch belt, gloves, and a black bubble wig with gardenia combs. It was a haphazard prom tragedy circa 1963. Misty Blue only came to life for two evenings before vanishing. The first night no one knew quite how to behave, so everyone either pretended they had no idea who he was or that everything was the same. Luckily Jack-O was too gone to see straight, much less formulate a sentence.

The first night Misty Blue came through the back door, there was absolute silence. Once the shock wore off, most couldn't believe he had come in off the street looking that way. The second evening, the whispers rivaled a hive of bees, but no one was straight out cruel about it, until Del arrived.

Slags had given Del the lowdown on Misty Blue that afternoon. Del didn't believe him at first. A few hours later, after seeing with his own eyes, Del made sure Fred felt the sting.

Seeing Misty perched on an end barstool, Del shook his head like he couldn't believe his eyes, gathered himself, and walked over. He spun Fred around by the shoulder and eyed him head to toe before stepping backwards and breaking into a wide smile. "You look asinine."

Fred gave him a blank look from his blue eye-shadowed eyes and nervously fiddled with the spit curls of his wig.

"You've gone off the deep end this time, and let me tell you, it's not a pretty sight."

Fred looked around and then down. "Nobody else seems to think so."

"Everybody thinks so, you damn lint head. You think these people don't think you're *loco*? Or is it *loca*? I am the one willing to tell you the truth. I'm the voice of logic you don't seem to have in your own head. Nobody here knows what to say. Look around. You think this is being accepted? They all just pity you."

"I was just..." Nerves began to lift Fred's lips at the corners. He looked up and then around. The new skin had been rejected. Any reason for being Misty vanished. He was suddenly and completely a fool, naked and in costume. He was Crazy Fred, exposed yet again and looking more foolish than ever.

Del wasn't about to let go of the jugular. "Are you *trying* to make an ass of yourself. For the life of me there is no other earthly explanation. How many times you been a fool now? A hundred this year? Let me tell you, this sure tops the list. You've gone and out done yourself and I didn't see that as fucking possible."

Fred looked down the row of folks along the bar. Everybody had their heads bent to the floor as if searching for a hole to crawl in. All those downcast eyes gave Fred his answer. Del was right. It'd happened yet again.

Humiliation was something he never got used to. Embarrassment had him in a panic. He slung the purse strap over his shoulder, rose from the barstool, and fell flat off the navy-blue heels. Everyone tried to stifle their laughter, but once Del started it wasn't long before most everyone joined in. When Fred got up, he felt skinned to the core. He put on his shoe and clomped out the back. He was in tears. *Damn it all to hell!* He'd just thought that if he... Fred shook his head. It didn't matter what he thought.

On his way home, Fred walked a bit out of his way and tossed his wig into the Frear. He stood on the bridge a moment and watched it float downstream. His breath fogged the November air. Even in the autumn chill, the river smelled of dead fish. It wasn't long before the wig sank. "You go live down there now with the others." Fred stared at the place where it disappeared. In some ways it felt as if those black waters had swallowed him as well. No matter what he did or how hard he tried, it just kept swallowing him over and over. It'd been that way long as he could remember. This was the last skin he'd shed. He watched his darkened reflection glissade across the river surface and the speckled reflection of the stars beyond. Never again.

When the bar door slammed Hester

gave an extended whistle through her teeth.

Bob shifted himself about on the stool. He looked around and wiped a string of sweat beads from his forehead. "Well, that was an ugly way to start the night."

Sister shook his head and went into a coughing fit. Those jags were taking him over. Everyone was too concerned to voice their worries. It was just another scary something to ignore. "Yeah," he finally managed.

"Every bit of it makes me feel like hell."

Sister rubbed his forehead. Lately he'd been looking so raw-boned. The folds on his face seemed the only spare skin on his entire body. He didn't enjoy that scene any more than the Blob, but that was life. "You're always paying the price for your doings and sometimes you pay for nothing you've really done." Sister knew that now more than ever.

"I still feel like hell."

"You're always feeling guilty. Let the healing waters of Sister Christian free your mind and soul." Sister bought Bob a shooter and, after matching throwbacks, Sister initiated talk on a deeper level. "This whole damn thing hasn't been easy for any of us. I think the world of Bruschetta too. She was family, but Fred thought she hung the moon and stars."

"And then some," added Everly. For once he wasn't exaggerating, though he was still eavesdropping.

Del laughed. "And now she's hanging by a thread."

Sister shot him a look. It riled him seeing Del's glee at the misfortune of others. He was a predator of the worst kind. He was the sort that killed for sport and laughed all the while. The worst part was watching him gloat over Fred's embarrassment. He was a wicked son-of-a-bitch without a heart, and one wasn't about to sprout from that lump of coal he had in that bony chest of his. Being ugly was one thing. Acting that way was something else entirely.

Sister sighed. "This talk is getting us nowhere but further down in the dumps. I'll give Fred a ring later and make sure he's doing all right." His voice was raw from whiskey and smokes.

Slags laughed and ran a hand over his bleached flattop. "Oh yeah, and how you going to tell with him?"

Del laughed into his drink. "Poor little prom queen."

Bob wondered aloud if it wasn't best for Finn to just ask Fred at work the following day. "That way it won't seem like it was quite as big of a scene."

Hester agreed.

Everybody turned to Finn, who wasn't even aware anything was being asked of him. Once he figured out what was going on, he started to turn a bright shade of pink. He made it a rule not to get involved, but with everyone staring he found it impossible saying no. Usually he'd pretend not to understand but this time he said, "Sure, no problem."

"How's he doing there anyway?"

Finn shrugged. "Okay."

Sister sighed. That response said next to nothing. Sometimes asking Finn anything but the time of day amounted to so much wasted breath.

Truth be told, Fred was doing fairly well at the restaurant. From the first day, he'd been intent on being a good employee. What he lacked in experience he made up for in effort. After two shifts, he was better than Finn, or speedier anyways. The owners seemed pleased. He knew they appreciated his work as well, because a couple weeks later Fred saw on the schedule that he'd been given Thanksgiving Day off. Seeing it posted above the rolled silverware, he decided he was going to make some big plans.

Nadine called that night and invited him to come over and celebrate with her and Walter and the kids. He passed. He didn't want to intrude. Whenever he went to their place everyone was nice enough, but it only made him realize how much he missed having Nadine to himself. Those Saturdays of TV and snacks were some of the finest he could recall, but things had changed an awful lot since then.

His mother called early that week. Lila was teary and sentimental and kept referring to him as her baby. She missed him—least she thought she did. She missed the distraction of him. Fred figured it was more her mood or the medication doing the talking. She was giving her despair an airing and at present her focus was on him. Holidays were always trying for Lila, and even more so for those near and dear to her.

Fred sat with the phone crooked to his ear and thought about everything but his mother's monologue. To somewhat soothe her despondent way of thinking he finally said he'd be there for Christmas. She said Virginia was a lonesome state. A minute later Rog was on the line, all but apologizing for her display. He grew uncomfortable when Lila's emotions got too big. He was sober but Fred heard the ice clinking and his slow sips. Rog asked how work was going. Fred said okay and no more. He hadn't said a word about changing jobs. It would upset them and he didn't have the energy to get into that discussion. He couldn't stand the heavy sighs. When Lila returned to the phone Fred asked a myriad of questions about cooking a turkey dinner for four and scribbled notes on an old school tablet. She seemed pleased to be needed and pleased he wasn't spending the holiday alone.

The next day he bought a turkey and invited Del, Slags, and Finn over for a real Thanksgiving dinner. A nice celebration would be the fine way to usher in the holidays. Asking Finn was risky, but when Fred needed help he'd been there with the job referral. Fred didn't forget that sort of thing. Del had apologized, in a roundabout Del sort of way, the day after the Misty Blue fiasco.

Things went wrong from the start. Everyone was asked to arrive around two. Finn arrived on time, Slagger was about twenty minutes late, and Del didn't show until near-about four. Del arrived loud and energized, bursting through the door shouting "Happy fucking Thanksgiving".

Fred was mostly checking, chopping, and generally fussing in the kitchen. There was a lot to coordinate for a novice cook. Timing was everything. The biscuits and potatoes and salad were ready, but the turkey still had some time to go. He would take a sip of wine, go to the oven, take another drink, have another look... He wondered if the little red knob that was supposed to pop up was defective.

Del came into the kitchen and poured a glass of wine. He gave Fred a peck on the cheek and a solid slap across the behind. Fred smiled.

He liked when Del acted frisky and vaguely possessive. It cancelled out things like the other night.

"When do we eat?"

"It shouldn't be long now."

Del took a seat on the couch longside Slags. When he saw Finn in the chair by the window, he gave a look. He had no use for that bland ghost and found no reason to hide it. Rolling his eyes, he turned to Slags. "How about a party favor to get the things rolling? Here's something to really be thankful for." He fished a spliff from his coat and tossed it to Slags.

"I thought you'd never get here."

The comment caused them both to turn from the joint to Finn. He was sitting stiff as a frozen fish stick with a half smile plastered on his face. Del thought he resembled one of the Blob's taxidermied creations, the kind without moving parts. Maybe that's why Bob was sweet on him. That sort of thing made you wonder.

Fred came into the living room and perched on the arm of the sofa.

Slags lit the joint and sucked in a hit. With a tight smile he proclaimed that it tasted awful fine.

Slagger passed it to Del. After a heavy toke, Del said he had a good reason for being late. He'd run into Molly on the street. And he'd mustered the nerve to talk to her this time.

"Molly your sister?"

"No, Molly fucking Ringwald!"

Finn's eyes lit up. "She's great."

Del looked his way for a minute before shaking his head and continuing, "I ran into her right here on the corner."

"Well, good God."

"She's in high school."

"That's so fucking hard to believe."

Del smiled to recall their meeting. "I nearly didn't recognize her. You should see her, Slags. She's not even the same girl, not by a mile."

"Let's face it, it's been a while. How long has it been since you left home?"

"Four years, five, maybe longer. Something like that." It was hard for Del to calculate. Years didn't mean a thing. Seemed he'd been gone his entire life. "When she recognized me, her squeals nearly busted half the windows on Main. I'm surprised you guys didn't hear it. She said she knew I was still in town, but she was nervous over tracking me down."

His face softened. Fred smiled just looking at him. There was so much there. So much beneath it all. Why couldn't Del let all this surface more often? Most times his false bravado made caring about anything or anyone impossible. It was rare to see him without a protective armor.

"We went and had a Coke at that Korean place. Those people don't celebrate the holiday so it was open."

"Staley's is open today, eleven to five." Everyone turned to stare at Finn.

Del went on. "Seems to have her head on straight. She's anxious to get through high school. Even has some of those same nuns that we had. She's anxious to leave home. I took that as a good sign. A definite sign of sanity."

Slags nodded.

"Mum and Lester got hitched."

Fred looked down and plucked some random fuzzies from his sweater. Nadine told him Del's mother had remarried a few months ago. Fred was torn over breaking the news to Del. There was no telling what he'd do even without drugs or alcohol. Fred didn't care to be bombarded by the waves of rage that news might spark.

Finn looked around the room with a vacuous smile whitewashed across his face. Once Del and Slags noticed they started to laugh.

With a lift of his hand and his eyebrows Slags offered Finn the joint. "Have a toke, it'll make you less weird, maybe even interesting." Del eyed him. He didn't appreciate sharing his drugs to begin with, much less with him. There was no reason for it. Slags shrugged like he didn't know what else to do. After all, it was Thanksgiving. Finn passed so it turned out to be a non-issue.

Fred's wine tippling continued. With a couple hits off the joint on top of it he was decidedly unsteady by the next time he went to check on the turkey. All talking paused during the metal yawn of the oven door and resumed with its slow closing creak. Fred returned to the living room a minute later. Checking the ready button every other minute was adding anxiety to his buzz.

Del sat up. "I'm bored."

Slagger punched him in the arm. "I've been here practically two hours longer than you, so quit your bitching." His comment caused both of them to look over at Finn.

Del leaned back on the couch and turned to Fred. "Why don't you entertain us?"

He recognized the glint in Del's eye. He knew the sort of behavior that was coming. Fred took a deep sip of wine and looked into the glass. He felt himself diving into it. He looked into the dark surface. It would be a good place to hide. He finished the glass

"Come on, aren't you gonna dress up like a girl today? Just one little number. Put something sexy on your shit stereo and give us a drag show. Finn wants you to do Cher." Del started chanting "Dark Lady, Dark Lady."

Finn grew increasingly uncomfortable. Slapping his hands to his knees he rose and said he had to use the bathroom. No one paid him the slightest bit of attention as he quietly sidled over to the facilities and closed the door.

"I'm not doing that, Del."

"Calm down and have a hit."

Fred took a deep drag off the joint and passed it back to Del. His brows met in a scowl above his nose. "Sometimes you can be such a hateful shit."

Del laughed.

The buzz was bringing all that Fred had been feeling to the surface and pushing it out his mouth. "I mean it, sometimes you can just get to be too much to handle."

"That's what all the johns tell me."

Fred got up from the arm of the couch. It was all rising like steam from a kettle—his body, his ire, their history. "Well, judging from the amount of money you bring home that's not too many." He'd never confronted Del on his whoring or freeloading before.

"This ain't my home."

Fred looked from Del to Slags, then back to the kitchen. He didn't want to get into this or have a scene. The argument was futile. It was getting him nowhere and taking the day somewhere he didn't want it to go. "I'd better go check on the turkey."

"Why don't you do that?" Del wasn't backing down. His hands were embedded in an arm of the couch. He wasn't about to let Fred have the last word, especially not in front of Slags. *Who the fuck does he think he's talking to, acting like he's so smart and mouthing off?*

Fred disappeared into the kitchen and braced his arms on either side of the counter. He was breathing heavy. He shook his head. He shouldn't have said a word. If life had taught him anything it was to hold his tongue and just adapt, but that strategy wasn't working so well anymore. He couldn't go on taking what he once took. He couldn't lie still and let it all pass through him. He felt the years of doing that knot and rot in his belly.

The toilet flushed. Finn entered the kitchen still hitching up his pants. "Are you okay?"

Fred nodded. "Thanks, I'm fine. Go back into the living room. I'll be there in a minute."

Finn nodded but lingered a bit longer. He wasn't concerned about Fred as much as he was hesitant to return.

Fred stood at the kitchen window and traced a drop of rain down the pane. He started wishing he'd gone to Nadine's. It made him feel apart but at least it didn't make him feel alone. Damn Del. After so many years and so much sacrifice Del was still behaving this way. Del was the one who ought to be thankful. Fred could give from now to the grave, it wouldn't matter. Nothing would ever be enough. Del didn't want to be lifted up; he wanted to drag others down. That's what this was about. That's what it'd always been about. He was a hook with a name.

After five minutes Del came into the kitchen. Fred heard him before he saw him. "Where's the turkey? You invited me over to eat, I'm starved."

"It's not ready."

Del opened the oven door and poked the bird with a fork. "Yeah, this is done."

"No it isn't, that button has to pop up."

"I know what's what and this thing is cooked." Del grabbed the oven mitts and reached into the stove to grab the pan. His arms buckled under its weight. As if in slow motion the turkey slid to one side of the pan, rolled over the low foil lip, and flipped onto the floor in a greasy heap.

"Goddamn it, Del!"

Del just stood there staring at the mess. He continued to hold the pan sideways as more grease dripped onto the speckled linoleum. For a moment all was silent save for the tick of the kitchen clock, the drip of grease, and the patter of rain. Del picked up his drink. "Probably no good anyways," he laughed into his glass of wine, "It'll be fine if you wash it off."

Fred saw all his hopes for the day crash along with the bird carcass. Anger rose until he shook. "God, I hate you! You hear that? I hate your fucking guts! I hate you even more than you hate yourself! Goddamn you!" Fred grabbed the turkey from beneath and hurled it at Del. It knocked the glass out of his hands and the bottle off the table before thudding against the wall.

Del jumped back. "Shit!"

Hearing the commotion, Finn and Slags ran to the doorway of the kitchen and stood there in disbelief. After a pause, Finn said he had to get going and ducked out the front door.

When the door closed, Fred turned to Del. "You happy now, huh? You goddamn selfish jerk." Fred's face reddened. His mouth was a tight line. He picked up the turkey and rammed it into Del's chest. The blow knocked the wind out of Del, who slipped on the spilled grease, stumbled backwards, and fell to the floor beside the refrigerator.

After catching his breath, Del leapt from the linoleum. "You little fucking shit." He lunged at Fred. The battle they'd been having all along finally crossed a line and became physical. He pounded Fred over the head with the rapidly disintegrating turkey. Grease and stuffing and bits of bird flew everywhere. Fred lifted his arms to block the blows. His face and hair were covered with it. His arms were greasy and lined with scratches. He was bleeding from the nose. "You little fuck, who the hell do you think you are? Who the fucking hell do you think you are?"

Fred was bent to the floor with his arms over his head. There was pounding on the floor from the apartment below. Slags tried stopping the fight, but Del was ranting and in a frenzy. He was beyond listening to reason. Seeing no alternative, Slags ran to the phone and dialed the police. He could barely hear the operator over Del's shouting and Fred's yelps and the awful thudding of the holiday turkey. Returning to the kitchen Slags yelled to Del about what he'd done. The mention of cops en route shook Del from his fury. With a final whack he grabbed his coat and ran out the front.

Slags looked at Fred cowering aside the kitchen table. He wanted to help but had his loyalties. Del was his pal and partying buddy, but Fred didn't rate this sort of treatment. No one did. Slags said he couldn't be around when the cops showed. "I don't want them getting used to seeing this face." When Fred remained silent Slags said, "Thanks" before grabbing the roach from the living room table and heading down the stairs.

When the police arrived Fred was on his knees beneath the kitchen table. He was crying and bloody and trembling as he ate bits of turkey from the filthy floor. He'd done everything he could, but everything wasn't enough. He'd loved Del ever since he rose from the river years ago. He still felt the things he always had, but it was no longer enough. They were destined, but feeling things were destined and going along with it were two different things. He was through. He recalled tossing the Misty wig from the bridge and tossing himself from the bridge. He wasn't going under for anyone ever again, including Del. Maybe that was the lesson life had been trying to show all along. Destiny was a way to walk a path. The route was a lot easier if a body didn't look to the sides or wonder at a fork or sideway. Folks paid a steep price for that brand of comfort. That frame of mind wasn't worth it anymore. It was plain as the veins on the back of Fred's hand. It was time to toss Del into the Frear.

One of the policemen helped him up. Fred said he'd be all right. It was all just a misunderstanding. One that'd dragged on for near-about a decade. Everything was under control. There was nothing left to do but clean up the mess.

The cops left shaking their heads. They saw it all around the holidays. Seemed no one could elicit hatred and violence like a houseful of loved ones. One cop nudged the other. It was sure an awful waste of a fine looking bird.

Not Reborn,
But Unborn.

Fred was despondent the rest of Thanksgiving Day. He couldn't do a thing. He left turkey and grease splattered and splintered across his kitchen. He shrugged at the filth. It wasn't crucial. Who cared? He staggered to the living room and collapsed upon the couch. He drank the rest of the wine right from the bottle and opened a second while staring at the town through a veil of rain. Drops were still tapping against the pane when he crawled into bed and pulled the covers up to his neck. It felt as though he'd drank himself sober. He studied the spider cracks on the ceiling and turned on his side. For so long, loving Del had been everything. It was how he saw the world and his future. Now all that was over. The idea of the future being a choice rather than destined was frightening. Choice made it all wide as the sky.

Awakening the next morning with a desperate thirst and a brutal hangover, Fred hoped yesterday was nothing but a twisted dream. His body told him otherwise. He shuffled to the kitchen. One look was all it took to prove yesterday was all too real. Fred ignored the mess and poured a glass of water. Before taking a sip he followed a wave of nausea into the bathroom. Flipping on the light he gasped to see he looked even worse than he felt. He had a black eye, a split lip, a forehead crusted with blood, bruises and grease up and down his arms, bits of stuffing stuck in his hair... He bent over the toilet and felt the vomit pulse from him. More was coming out than could ever be held in. He felt himself turning inside out, purging everything he'd been. When it was over he sat back on the rug. His head still throbbed but it felt better.

He called in sick to work that day and the day after. All he said was he wasn't feeling well. The management at Staley's didn't give a word of protest. Fred's sorry state was apparent in his voice. He doubted Finn would've uttered word about Thanksgiving. Finn had a habit of never wanting to get involved. Fred was thankful. The thought of having his shame made public would only make things worse. Born into a drinking family, Fred had learned secrecy along with toilet training and his ABCs.

Sidestepping the kitchen fallout, he made a pot of coffee. The turkey was starting to smell and the drippings made the floor both sticky and slick. He turned his back to the chaos. That mess wasn't going anywhere.

Fred draped an afghan over his shoulders and sat looking out the living room window. Putting his head back and his feet up he figured it was high time to get his shambles of a life in order. There was plenty to sort through and it was clear some of those pieces didn't fit. Pulling out his school tablet, he made a list of what he'd done and what he wanted to do. The list wasn't especially long or impressive, but having some goals on paper helped him scribble some more. He'd never given much thought about tomorrow. Del had always been his future and that was a full-time, extra hours, and round the clock job.

Fred rolled the pen between his fingers. Though never a deep thinker, Fred put his pen to paper and began looking for the words to express all he was feeling. He was surprised to be feeling so much beneath the numbness. He was beginning to run out of words when he flipped the page and saw mother's turkey dinner tips. He just shook his head. It was foolish to think that was anything but a recipe for disaster. He ripped the page from the binder and tore it forwards and crossways and let the pieces fall to the worn carpet.

He walked softly into the kitchen, still aching from the bird beating and the cheap wine. He surveyed the mess with a shake of his head and poured another cup of coffee. Leaning against the counter he tried to decide just where to begin cleaning. The wishbone was sticking out from under the stove. He smiled and his scabbed lip split. That looked as good a place to start as any. Picking it up he took each end and figured he'd get his wish no matter how it split. There was so much he had to wish for.

Fred spent the next two hours sponging, wiping, squeezing, and sweeping away every trace of the day before until it looked as though Thanksgiving Day had never happened. When he finished the kitchen was cleaner than the day he moved in. He continued on through the afternoon and into the evening going around his apartment, purging and cleaning. His energy seemed to increase. Grabbing a second trash bag, he tossed all Del's clothes, tapes, and whatnot inside. There'd been more evidence of him around than Fred had thought. Two full bags in the end.

The next morning, Fred slipped on his winter coat, gave the neck of each bag a good spin, and hefted them to the bar. Plopping the bags atop the stools on either side of him, Fred asked Leo to see Del got them. It was odd to be seeing Leo working until Fred remembered Cody was still in Chicago.

Leo fingered his mustache. "I'll see Del gets it, all right." The way he said it, Fred he could tell he'd heard.

Removing all evidence of Del from his place may have taken away some of the reminders, but Del was no dream. Signs of him were still everywhere, even in the mirror. Loving Del had made Fred most everything he was. Those bruises happened long before yesterday, and those bruises wouldn't disappear. Maybe that was for the best. Forgetting would make it a waste and he doubted he could stand learning that lesson a second time.

The video game blipped and called for challengers.

Hester raised her coffee mug to him. "Good for you. Sister had the feeling you'd be showing up."

Fred reddened and caught sight of his battered reflection in the mirror. Jesus! He looked a fright.

"Sister and that gift of his." Leo straightened and tucked his flannel shirttail into his fancy pocket jeans.

"Yeah, him and his gift. I wish he would put that gift of his to use and tell me where a black girl can find a decent job...or a halfway decent girlfriend." Hester gave a husky laugh and Leo joined in as he topped off her coffee.

"But a decent girlfriend wouldn't be near as fun as an indecent one."

"I said halfway decent. She can be as nasty as she wants when the lights are low."

A second round of banter jump-started their laughter. It was fast and a mite forced and Fred wondered if it was because it was morning or because they were working to keep the focus off of him.

He wondered what they'd heard. Something had gotten back to them. They were staring, but tried being matter-of-fact about it. Neither one said a word about his appearance. It made perfect sense when Fred stopped to think that Slags wasn't quite so tight-lipped as Finn. Fred paid it no never mind. It saved him the burden of an explanation. He had no desire to relive the particulars.

Leo offered him a coffee or beer or whatever. Fred said he'd take a raincheck. Leo joked that he'd never made one of those. It was nothing personal. He had things to do, but mostly he didn't want to encounter Del. Fred kept half expecting him to come busting on through the back door. It was easy to say he'd never get drawn back into the drama. He'd said it before. Fred figured the best way to stick to it was to avoid the Sand Bar altogether. There were no guarantees some night Del wouldn't come pounding on his door drunk on dollar wine and full of alibis. Fred figured he'd worry about it then.

Rising from his stool, Fred said he'd see them around. Hester and Leo said so long and exchanged a look. He could only imagine what that was about. He figured their lips would be flapping the minute the door swung shut. He figured right.

Fred cut through the back alley. It was cold enough to see his breath. Bob was rocking out of the driver's seat of his Lincoln and giving the shocks a good workout. Getting to his feet took every damn ounce of the Blob's concentration. Fred pulled his stocking cap down low and was thankful Bob didn't see him.

Fred slipped between the Pharmacy and Shoe Repair and began taking a crooked course of back ways towards the river. The alleys still glistened from last night's rain. Memories of all those Saturdays of dumpsters and catwalks and canopies of wires returned. Memories of the bottle caps returned to him as well. He'd forgotten all that. He hadn't thought of collecting anything in a good long time.

He looked to the asphalt. Most of the splits had been sealed. Patched cracks meant that entry into the underside had been sealed. He used to get to wondering what side of life he'd be on when those doors finally closed. Now he knew. He was here, in the real world and not a world of roots with an ice-floe sky. Walking the alleys brought it back. It was like seeing things in the flash of a nighttime storm, frozen and then gone. It was nothing like he remembered it to be. Emerging onto Front Street, he caught his breath.

Crossing the road and ditch, he continued down to the river. The brown grass crunched beneath his feet as he took a seat on the bank near the rusted metal girders of Kavanaugh Bridge. The Frear looked heavy with the cold and was starting to crust along the bank. Fred stared into the deep blue center. A lot of memories lurked there as well. Those were mostly memories of forgetting. He'd lost and baptized so much of himself in those waters. It could cure or cauterize most anything. He always considered the river as part of the town and standing there he finally realized that it wasn't. It was just passing through on a journey someplace else. Bayetteville was just part of the journey. Fred lay back on the grass. A hawk rode the wind. A few high clouds formed, reformed, resembled, dissembled, and coursed across the sky. Everything was in motion. Maybe that was his problem.

He sat up and raised his collar. Rubbing his hands, he wrapped his arms around his knees. He kept staring at the surface of the water until things cleared. Situations weren't going to change. Del wasn't likely to transform. Bayetteville wouldn't become someplace else. And he wasn't likely to change by sitting around wishing things different. He couldn't become someone new by destroying himself and he couldn't dream a life into being. Dreaming hadn't gotten Del to London, won Lulu the lottery, kept Ben around, gotten Hester a girlfriend, or brought Bob and Finn together. Dreaming hadn't made his mother secure or his father sober. If anything, it had done the opposite.

Walking home, he stopped at church. He hadn't stepped foot inside St. Elizabeth's for years. He used to be able to get a grip on his thoughts there. Prayer seemed better than pretending. He had nothing to lose. Who knew? Maybe God would listen this time.

Fred sat straight in his pew. He eyed the stained glass windows, the arched ceilings, and the cement saints. Sitting there still made him feel perched on a ledge to another world, or maybe it was just a different view on the same one. Here all eyes were intent on a world above and the world below. A mostly new smattering of old folks was still sitting here and there muttering, placing their bets on the hereafter now that their race was nearing the home stretch.

A cough echoed in that grand expanse. Looking across the aisle, Fred saw Sister. He was kneeling a few rows ahead with his nose buried in the triangle of his hands. The hollows beneath his cheekbones seemed deeper in candlelight. His body was shaking but Fred wasn't sure if that was on account of torment, fear, or liquor. Something was going on. Sister usually confined his churchgoing to Sunday services. A half hour later Fred genuflected on his way out. Sister was still bent in prayer.

Fred didn't see Sister or any other Sand Bar folks, except for Finn at work, until the end of December. People were beginning to voice concerns. Finally Anna took charge. Following a few persuasive phone calls, some cajoling, handwringing, and a promise Del wouldn't be present, she convinced him to attend Sister's Christmas party. She swore it would be a festive evening.

Fred went without much expectation and had himself a pleasant time. Staying mostly sober allowed him to see things a little more clearly. It was apparent most of the Sand Bar crowd enjoyed going a little overboard on a regular basis. Fred could do that. He go on drinking himself into a satiated stupor and let the flow of contentment carry him along. Liquor could help him tolerate where and what he was. The appeal was clear. There was real comfort fitting in and being a part of this family The downside was it didn't allow for much change. He was Fred to them and he would always be Fred to them and chances were he'd always be the same old Fred to them. He'd been needy and naïve and a somewhat sorry case. He wasn't that person anymore. That wasn't going to be his niche. He wanted something more. Leaving seemed the best solution. A flutter rose in his stomach at the thought of leaving Bayetteville.

Seeing Bruschetta that night was a surprise. He was happy for the chance to talk with her, but disturbed by the change. Seeing her shy from the light, Fred sighed. He knew Bruschetta would rather be hated than pitied. It was hard believing it was the same person. He wondered if all those bar expectations and perceptions were why she vanished after the bashing. Maybe she saw herself as not filling her role anymore either. The sass and fire seemed extinguished. Now she just seemed fragile. Fred found it ironic his own beating did almost the opposite. After she left the party Fred turned the brooch she'd given him over in his hand. It tossed glints of light about the room. It was a reminder not to hide his light under a basket. It made him aware that he had a light to give.

Two days later, Fred took a bus to St. Louis, before flying to Virginia. When his folks called a couple weeks before, he'd said he wanted cash for the holidays. He joked that it was easy to carry and always the right color. Rog and Lila got a good laugh out of that. "I'm going to use that one," Rog had said. Getting out of town for good was going to take money and determination. He had the latter. It was Del's parting gift.

Lila's perfume was smothering on the ride home from the airport. Her personality was just as overpowering. They weren't even out of the lot when she spun in her seat, wedged her sunglasses into her sausage curls, and divulged having a dream the other night that she was lying in her coffin beneath a spray of lilacs. "I tell you, it made me think about things. I could be dying right now."

Fred was tempted to tell her that she was. They all were. He wanted to tell her she was insane to think any different but knew the truth would only depress her or make her think he was being fresh. He let it pass. The dream was no surprise. Half her life was spent pondering such things. Rog had deafened to it years back. He just groused about traffic and didn't utter a word.

Lila was dying, Rog was drinking, and Fred was shrinking into the confines of his skin. Life at home was near-about the same, but returning to the part he played didn't happen. The part was there and he was there, but now he saw it and didn't become it.

On Christmas Eve he dropped several hints about moving and finally told them outright. Lila lit up like a string of lights and suggested he move there. Rog nodded in agreement and gave his Manhattan a forward thrust. Fred smiled at the offer. It was a comfort to know they wanted him around, but he knew living there would bring nothing but boundaries and bitten nails. He didn't want to hate them again. He said he wasn't yet set on where he was headed. There was another long pause. The comment lay flopping like a suffocating fish in the middle of the living room. Rog and Lila didn't care for vague plans of that nature, but eventually they sighed into silence and changed the subject.

When he returned to Bayetteville two days later, Fred put every cent of his Christmas money into a freedom account. He had a plan and for the first time that plan wasn't about Del or fitting in.

Lit Fuses

The day after Thanksgiving, Del arrived at the Sand Bar for his usual fill of cocktails and trouble. Leo took a long drink. He was ready for him. Hefting the two garbage bags onto and then over the bar he said in a low voice to "Take them and get out, and don't bother coming back." Sister was right. It was something he should've done ages ago.

It was one of those rare occasions that Del was dumbstruck. He stood staring at Leo with his jaw hanging halfway to his elbows. Opening one of the plastic bags, he looked inside. So Fred had gone and told his sad story. He was so motherfucking pathetic. Apparently that victim routine wasn't as stale as Del had thought. Few things were more pathetic than mewling for pity and making a show of weakness. The way Del saw it, Fred did that near as often as he took a breath.

He was about to say something when Leo crossed his arms and told him to get out, louder and more firmly than before. "I mean it Del, you're not welcome in here no more."

Del eyed him square. *Well, fuck him then!* Del was mostly set on not showing his upset. Life made him an expert at that. "Well good, that's about the best news I've had all bloody day." He grabbed a bag in either fist and with a heavy tread headed down the hall. The folks who were there and even a few who weren't said it didn't surprise them one bit when Del yelled, "You'll be sorry for this Leo Dunsten," before slam-kicking the door to the men's room and continuing out the back.

Seconds later Jack-O slowly peeked his head out from the bathroom. With wide eyes he looked either way. Sight of him broke the tension. Hester and Leo got a good laugh at the sight. Once she caught her breath Hester added, "You can come out now" in her best Glinda voice.

Determined to be included in most everything that went on around him, Everly slid a couple stools closer. "Glad you done that, Leo. If you didn't, I was about set to."

Leo turned to him, "And by what goddamned right would you go barring someone from my tavern?"

Everly swallowed so heavy his adam's apple moved up and down like a ripe plum. He spun his draft in either direction.

Leo pushed a pile of quarters across the bar. "Sorry, Everly. Why don't you go play us some music?"

Pointing towards Leo's pack of Marlboros and raising her brows, Hester bummed a cigarette and tilted her head towards the door. "Least that bit of drama is over and done with. Good for you, Leo. Hope he don't go causing you any trouble."

Leo swatted the thought aside. "Whatever he could do can't be more trouble than it is having him around. Del is all talk anyways, and he's about the only one not wise to that fact."

Hester agreed.

Jack-O came back and slid on his stool. He adjusted his glasses and was still looking shaken. He didn't appreciate being startled in the middle of doing his business. It was more than likely he'd be constipated now. He ordered another draft and tried not thinking about it.

While ringing up Jack-O's beer Leo caught sight of himself in the bar mirror. His smile was one of relief. He'd finally gone and done it. Sister had been after him to ban Del for years. The only remorse he had was not doing it sooner. Leo had been more than tolerant, partially due to their business arrangement but also on account of seeing some of his young self in Del. He'd always had a place in his heart for a no-account kid like that, but Del wasn't a kid anymore. He'd graduated from being a nuisance to being an asshole. Leo already had himself one of them.

Sister arrived at the Sand Bar a moment later, resembling something a hound from hell might've hacked up. He admitted being worn to the bone. When Leo told him about what he'd just missed, Sister still mustered the energy to stomp his boots and slap his thighs. He regretted not being there when Del got his comeuppance. Sister wasn't sure why, but the gift hadn't disclosed any of it. He wasn't having his premonitions at all anymore.

Hester agreed that missing it must have been a disappointment, but she was already out of her seat and headed for the pool table. She and Everly were having a vendetta tournament. When she beat him two weeks ago he accused her of having a lucky day. That steamed a prideful pool shark like Hester. "Lucky day nothing." She said she could beat him twenty days straight. The challenge was on. They bet a pork chop dinner. This was day twelve.

The day after Everly bought Hester that pork chop meal, Del snuck back into the Sand Bar to discuss some things with Cody. He rubbed some circulation into his arms and told Cody he was counting on him to reason with Leo. "You gotta help me." Del leaned onto his elbows. He hated begging, but there was nothing else to do. Besides, it wasn't begging so much as asking Cody to get Leo to set things straight.

"Fred and me have nothing to do with him or this place. Leo is taking sides in something that's none of his business."

Cody didn't want to hear a word of it. "And all this has even less to do with me," was what Cody felt like replying. Any closeness they had was mostly a creation of Del's ego, his fantasies, or his addiction. Cody had never been anything more than a captive audience. Del's being there or not being there was inconsequential to him. He didn't tip, anyways.

As a seasoned bartender, Cody nodded to Del and said "uh huh" while reminiscing about his Thanksgiving trip to Chicago. He and Kevin had themselves quite a time indeed. It seemed most everything was legal up there, and with a tax on it to boot. The goings on in the back rooms at some of those places were unbelievable. He didn't do a damn thing, but he liked what he saw. The thought of it still excited him.

He was considering a drive up there in February. Going with Kevin was fun, but this time he wanted to go alone. It was hard telling what might happen then. He began having doubts over being tied down. Things with Kevin were going nowhere even though they were wedged in a mighty pleasant rut. Cody thought the world of him. Kevin had brought a whole side of him back to life, but there was so much out there. Cody hadn't quite sown his full bag of wild oats. His façade of worldly experience was a sham. In truth he could count the men he'd been with on his fingers, if he considered Leo and Sister as one. Eleven wasn't many at all. It was nothing compared to most men he knew.

In a moment he realized Del had stopped his bitching and blaming. Cody said he'd put in a good word for him with Leo. He was blatantly lying, mostly on account of being tired of listening. He ended the conversation by busying himself with odds and ends.

With a wave over his shoulder, Del headed out the back. He lit a smoke alongside the dumpsters and crossed the lot with a lazy jog and flapping arms. "Shit shit shit" was what he thought. It was just as cold and gray as yesterday. He cursed Fred for about the billionth time as he cut over to Oak and headed for Slagger's place. It was his entire damn fault.

Things were strange all right. Not too far back, Slags found himself a beau. He was over the moon about a man named Nash. It started Thanksgiving Day afternoon after Slags left Fred cowering beneath his kitchen table. When he came down the stairs Fred's landlord was standing outside his apartment and gave him a holding stare, as though one day he may be asked to pick Slags out of a police line-up. That look gave him chills even before he got out into the cool rain. He headed for the bar. What else was he going to do? Besides, he had quite a tale to tell.

Coming in from the drizzle he ordered a draft. After a long swig, he leaned against the bar, and began relating every detail of the day to Leo, Bob, Anna, Lulu, and Hester. He didn't embellish much. With a story like that, there wasn't a need. When he finished, there wasn't a closed mouth within earshot. He turned to the stool on his right. There was Nash. He was at the Sand Bar for only the second time in his twenty-nine years. It wasn't that he considered the first time unpleasant, it just wasn't his sort of place. Nash was there to avoid any more Thanksgiving day clashes between his sister and his aunt. They'd battle over anything and everything. The particulars of cooking a turkey dinner were cause for an all out war. He told them he'd be back later. That was two hours ago.

Slags and Nash met eyes a couple of times before Nash commented that it sounded like they'd both had themselves quite a day. Conversation didn't necessarily flow, but the juices did. There was no denying their attraction on a chemical level. By their second beer they'd swiveled towards each other and by their fourth they'd laced legs and were full of meaningful looks.

Nash wore Calvin Klein cologne and was the manager of the Cloven Hoof. Slags knew the place. "Good food," was all he could think of to say. He'd never actually eaten there, but he'd heard it was good. That night they went back to Nash's and got naked and sweaty and sated. They were both still heady from their pairing the next morning when they did it again.

Since that night Slags had become a fixture both at Nash's and the Cloven Hoof. He'd go the restaurant, have some drinks, and watch the man he loved. *Loved.* He knew it was love on account of he even sometimes offered to help at the restaurant. That was definitely uncharacteristic behavior. Nash said if he got his hair a natural shade and dressed proper he'd hire him part time. Slags considered it. He couldn't go on being a punk indefinitely. At some point it just got sad. He'd been pressing his luck long enough with the drug business. Nash wouldn't go for that and Slags didn't want to lose him. Nash called him Santiago.

Hanging out at the Cloven Hoof as often as he did, Santiago got friendly with the bartender there. Barry was cool for an old guy. It didn't bother him that Santiago and Nash were boyfriends, causing Santiago to wonder if Barry was that way too. Nash didn't think so. Barry would've said. Nash rightly supposed Barry figured his being with Santiago as just the way things were. Barry wasn't one to judge, especially the person who signed his paycheck.

Santiago rhapsodized about his new beau endlessly. He wanted everyone to meet Nash. One snowy December night, he arranged for them to meet Del for drinks at the Riddle Room. Del was late and loud and raging about getting even with Leo and Fred. When Del was

agitated, everyone had to agree or else. Nash did not agree. He was
uneasy and growing more so all the while.

After a bit Nash said he had to be leaving. Santiago went with him.
"So long Santa's Taco! So long Hash," yelled Del.

Outside in the falling snow Nash turned to Santiago. He was clearly
in a state. Nash said he had a position of respect in this town and
didn't appreciate being associated with that sort of character or that
brand of behavior. Santiago might not have understood a month or a
week ago, but that night Santiago understood. Del's behavior embarrassed him, too. At the next stoplight, Nash added that he didn't want
Del frequenting the restaurant. Santiago told him not to worry.

With Santiago spending most nights with Nash, Del at least had a
free place to crash. Having a place to himself was nice, but Del realized it wouldn't last forever. It was wise for him to start setting plans
for his future. With Santiago being fucked senseless by that snob, Del
couldn't count on anything. He wondered what had gotten into everyone. It was this town.

Nash's disapproval of Santiago's friends went beyond Del. He didn't
care much for the bar folk in general. He claimed they lacked ambi-
tion. Even if he had possessed the verbal skills necessary, it wasn't a
comment Santiago could easily argue.

The sole exception to his condemnation was Hester. For whatever
reason, she and Nash got along famously. Nash ended up hiring her
as a waitress the week before Christmas. It was a difficult time to
break in a new server, but she did fine. Her even nature and common
sense were quite popular with patrons and staff alike, especially Barry
the bartender. In two weeks time those two became frequent drinking buddies. By the end of January, Hester was making good money
and for once seemed halfway satisfied with her job. "Now, if I only
could find a woman," she confided to Barry one night after closing.
He smoothed the creases alongside his mouth and fixed her another
while he finished cleaning up.

Fred and Finn were still busing at Staley's. Most times when Fred
was clearing tables, filling glasses, or rolling silverware, his mind was
elsewhere. He was firming up plans for leaving town. By his calcula-
tions, it was likely he'd have the money by spring. Saving was so much
simpler without going out every night or providing for Del. It was also
a lot easier with a plan.

Fred hadn't decided where he was going yet. Florida sounded nice
and so did Seattle. New Orleans had long held a certain magic. Where
wasn't as important as elsewhere. He liked Bruschetta's method of
just going where the train took her. She still inspired him. He kept
her brooch on his nightstand so it would be the first thing he saw in
the morning and the last thing he saw at night. She'd always be his

bona-fide guardian angel. He'd always held her in such high regard that making her sacred wasn't much of a stretch at all.

The Roach King

Del flipped out the light and onto his stomach. Even as a boy he could always gather his thoughts best in the dark. Lying there he thought about things and listened to the clock. Aside from the hissing radiator, that ticking seemed the only sound in the world.

He lit a smoke and rolled it along the lip of the ashtray. He'd been staying at Slag's place near-about three months. A free apartment was about the only positive thing Del could see in Slags being with Nash. He wasn't Slagger anymore, he was Santiago and Santiago wasn't someone Del particularly cared for. It was all that Nash's doing. Del thought Nash was about the biggest snob in all Schuyler County.

None of it made sense. Slags had given up a lucrative dealing career to become a minimum-wage host at a restaurant. Santiago had adopted this snooty way of holding himself and saying certain words. He was even dressing like a bank teller or something. Plastic! Who did he think he was fooling?

Last week, Slags informed Del that he was giving up his place on April first. He was moving in with Nash. April Fools, indeed! Nash lived in a modern complex near the expressway with built-in air conditioning, an intercom, and a courtyard pool. Slags said it was like nothing he'd known. That was all going to come back and bite him in the ass one day. He'd find out who his real friends were and when that happened Del would be waiting to say he told him so. He'd say he knew all along. Del was counting the minutes.

Del took another drag and tried thinking on other things. This was doing nothing but getting him pissed off. He looked around the room. If he focused on a single space for more than a moment he could see shadows moving across the floor and down the walls. Roaches. It made him think twice about eating or sleeping there, but he didn't have many options. Reaching out, he nabbed one of those filthy bugs as it scurried cross the night table. He killed it by pressing in on its sides before throwing it into the ashtray. He moved the cherry of his cigarette closer until he heard it pop and fizzle. Filthy fucking things. He killed a second one. In a half hour's time he'd singed and exploded four. The room took on an unpleasant stench, but an ashtray of smoldering carcasses cheered him a bit. Adjusting his eyes to the spots around the room, it didn't take a genius to see that those four bodies didn't amount to much. It sure as hell didn't make him in control. There were more pests about than he could ever hope to kill.

Del wished destroying Fred was as simple as bringing a cigarette to his belly and POP! Last evening, he was leaving the drugstore as Del was entering. They came within arm's length of one another before either noticed. Del scowled and Fred's eyes widened as he passed. Both kept their mouths set. Neither spoke. A moment later Del wished he had dragged him into the alley or at least yelled something cutting and painful. It burned him when Fred walked on without even turning to check his back. "Shows what an idiot he is," muttered Del.

Del was planning a payback by giving Fred his just desserts. If being a victim was what he wanted, Del was more than happy to comply. Del was thinking about breaking into Fred's apartment to strip it bare. He knew it came furnished and Fred would be held accountable. He knew how to break in as well as Fred's schedule. The biggest snag would be timing it around the landlord. Sawyer poked his nose out the door every time a stair creaked. But if it all went as he'd planned he'd be richer, Fred would be poorer, and not a soul would be the wiser. Maybe he'd even bring along a tin with a couple dozen roaches to let loose. He smiled to think of it. He could make a life out of payback and Fred deserved every bit of what he had coming.

Del had a score to settle with Leo as well. POP! That'd have to be something else entirely. Del recalled Leo's filthy squat up from the bar. Stripping that place bare would be a service, and doing it would require rubber gloves. More than once Del thought about torching the Sand Bar, but reasoned against it. Leo had insurance anyways. Getting even with him would require some ingenuity. They'd all pay in the end.

For now Del had to keep a focus on the particulars of his living arrangements. He was against the wall over having no place to go. He had no Plan B—no Slags, no garage, no Fred. Money was less than scarce. He'd borrowed more than he should've and owed all the wrong people. His earning potential came from clipping here and there or random tricks. It was too little to live on and nothing dependable.

He had wondered for a bit if Molly would get a place with him, but that didn't work out. One rainy day early in the month he'd waited across the street from St. Elizabeth's. Standing there brought back every rut in that wretched stretch of his past. After what seemed like hours, Molly appeared. She smiled to see him, but that faded soon as he brought up getting a place together. Her response hurt more than he dared to admit. He stood with his skinny arms stiff at his sides as she hemmed and hawed and explained. Ma had been sick and she needed to get home. Del didn't ask anymore about it.

If worst came to worst he could always hide out in one of the burned-out homes or abandoned trailers down along the river past the graveyard. It wasn't a bad idea. They were sturdy and mostly rainproof. It would work until he thought of something better. That collection of husks and shells was ideal for those wishing to disappear. Del sure fell into that category.

The clank and rattle of the radiator roused his mind. Del turned on his side and let his eyes move to his new London map on the wall. Times might be tough, but he still had to credit himself with not losing sight of his goal. Just last week, he'd gone to the library on Pine and headed straight for reference. In two minutes he found what he was looking for and slipped the map into his coat pocket. The librarians didn't notice, or if they did they were too timid to say a word. That gave him as much satisfaction as nicking the map.

Seeing his ideal city spread and pinned to the wall made him feel better, even with a roach moving cross town. On the downside, London was still there and he was still here. He didn't like to dwell on the thought of years passing and nothing changing and his being stuck in Bayetteville muck. There was plenty of it to sink in. It was nothing but a sinkhole and an open grave. The thought of being trapped and buried alive knotted his insides. He awoke anxious and covered in sweat. Between the roaches and those dreams and that goddamn ticking, he was afraid to close his eyes.

Del heard scuffling outside. He went to the window and slit the blinds. He wanted to check that no one was creeping up the alley stairs looking to collect on his debt. He breathed easier to see the metal side steps empty. It took a moment just to tell where the sound was coming from. When he finally did, it was clear those folks had other things in mind. Seeing it was two men down in the shadows, he leaned closer until his head touched the glass. He figured them for male by their size and moans. They were down longside the dumpsters. He couldn't see more than a flash now and again, but the effort took him out of himself. From what he could tell, it was a salt and pepper pairing. What he couldn't see he imagined. The action grew more frantic. He opened the outer door so nothing but the screen and distance was between them.

They were between the bins at the end of the alley. They were screwing. Their moans spiraled louder. Del began fucking his fist. His breath rose in tiny huffs and he ended up cumming onto the mesh of the screen at about the same time they blasted down below. Hearing the door close, they zipped, buckled, and were gone in seconds.

Del opened his eyes. Spilling seed hadn't calmed him. It was but a brief reprieve that ushered him right back to where he was, only more upset and unsettled. He felt a faint tickling. A roach crawled across his toes. Those bugs were like everything else in this town—on him, consuming him, and making him feel like garbage.

"Goddamn it!" He picked up the ashtray and hurled it at a crawling form in a corner. The thick green glass shattered. The remnants scattered across the floor. Two more were crawling over London. He ripped the map from the wall and crushed them inside. Only the pinned corners remained. Reaching onto the dresser he grabbed the clock. He felt the weight in his hand and the tick tick tick on his skin. With gritted teeth he smashed it against the radiator. The pieces flew everywhere. At least the ticking had stopped. All was quiet save for the in-out in-out of his panting. Had that been the tick-tock tick-tock all along?

Alley Cats

CODY rinsed the last of the glasses and shook his hair back. He was thankful the bar had taken on someone new. Leo had been at Sister's almost non-stop since they'd returned from St. Louis with the diagnosis. The doctors didn't offer a sliver of hope. "The horses are already out the gate," was how they phrased it. Cody was planning to stop by Sister's for a visit sometime early next week.

With all that going on, Cody never did make it back to Chicago and here it was Easter already. He still thought about it. He wondered if Kevin could tell. Cody knew Kevin been slipping around on the side. No way something like that was going to stay a secret in a wide-mouthed town. Despite his knowing, Cody found Kevin's stepping out near about impossible to discuss. It was always there, but just below the surface.

Cody swept the entirety of his relationship problems aside and got Hester and Barry another round. The Cloven Hoof was closed for the holiday and they were already beyond tipsy from toasting and celebrating Jesus' rise form the dead.

"He is arisen!"

"Damn straight he is."

Barry laughed. "Resurrection sure sounds good to me."

Two stools down Jack-O shook his head and raised a lecturing finger. Working with cadavers and all, he claimed expertise on the subject. "Trust me, both of you, it is best to let the dead rest. It's silly to want some of those things coming back. Besides, you don't want me losing my job now do you?"

Everyone had a genial laugh over the comment, mostly as a polite means to reclaim conversation. Besides, the common line of thinking was that with his drinking problem, if Jack-O hadn't lost his job already, it didn't seem likely it was going to happen anytime soon.

Hester and Barry said they had to get moving, but they'd said the same thing twenty minutes before. They were already late for a ham dinner with Barry's daughter and her family. Tossing back their cocktails they said, "So long," to Cody and Jack-O. Barry overtipped and gave Cody a wink. He was a firm believer in bartender camaraderie.

Hester hopped off her barstool with a loose-legged stumble. "Whoopsie!"

Jack-O pressed his spectacles back up his nose. "Some drunks go, some stay, and some just don't know any better."

Barry raised a hand goodbye.

As they headed out the back, Jack-O turned to Cody. "I like that Barry. He's a decent sort."

Cody agreed and looked at his watch. Five more minutes until Ray arrived. Ray was a gravel-voiced sweet talker somewhere in his forties and sexy as hell as far as Cody was concerned. He'd started coming around about a month ago and was friendly and companionable with most everyone. When Sister started getting sick, Leo hired him to cover some shifts and Ray happily complied. "Call me the bottom feeder," he joked, "I'll take all the unwanted hours." Ray was on disability from his regular job due to back problems.

A flash of light came with the opening of the back door. Ray was coming down the hall in black jeans and a vintage vest. Dressing like an Old West gambler suited him. It all looked good with his more salt than pepper hair and beard. Ray always looked prepared for anything or anyone, dressy and dirty at the same time. He gave Cody an effortless smile. Cody liked the way that grin came so easy.

"Hey, you old stud," Cody replied.

The mere proximity of Ray sparked something. Cody had a rule about sex with co-workers, but he'd never been tempted before. He gave Ray a sly once over that wasn't half as foxy as he'd intended. Maybe if things were different. Definitely if things were different! He'd heard gay men were most attracted to who they want to be. That narcissistic line of thinking always seemed like so much bull crap to him, until now. He wanted Ray's confidence and sex appeal. Aging into someone like him made getting older seem an entirely different prospect. Ray was vintage wine. Before meeting him, Cody had always thought of aging as losing something.

"Let me pour you a shift shot." Ray raised the bar door, came around, and grabbed the tequila. That was his drink. He got the limes and salt and a couple shot glasses. "Jack-O?" he said, already flipping over a third. Asking Jack-O was mostly a formality.

Cody grinned and moved to the patron side. He rolled his shoulders, rocked his neck, and took a seat aside Jack-O. "I forgot what it was like being off."

Ray nodded and looked to the shooters. "Salut!" he said, licking the salt and raising his glass.

Jack-O slammed down his shot glass and back-wiped his mouth with a sleeve before chomping on the lime wedge. He straightened on his stool. "Ray, I got something to say. I got something to tell you. Did you know that's my dollar up there?" Jack-O pointed to the framed bill above the register. "I was the very first one. The very first." Ray shared a look with Cody. Jack-O told him only yesterday.

Cody dallied for another hour and was feeling no earthly pain by the time he headed to the bathroom at seven. He saw his smile in the dingy mirror and caught himself for being so open in his interest for Ray. He shook his business and tried shaking loose a bit of his buzz before getting his coat. He needed to leave before he really embarrassed himself. He made his goodbyes and wished both a happy holiday. In two minutes he was walking down Elm. Fresh air felt good. Spring was here, nudging the world awake after a winter's nap. Flowers were blooming and the trees were commencing to bud.

Cody thought of Ray, how he looked in those jeans...how he might look out of them. He smiled at the way Ray lifted his brows when he was surprised and how he stroked his beard when listening. Cody was lost in thought when a blaring horn and screeching brakes brought him back. He jumped back on the curb and just missed being run-down by a van. "Damn fool," he hollered more out of surprise than actual anger. He must be drunker than he figured. He was already five blocks beyond where he should've turned.

A couple hundred feet ahead was a bald black man smoking a cigarette and leaning against a light pole. Beneath his denim jacket a white t-shirt was stretched across his chest. His thumbs were hooked in his belt hoops and two fingers grazed the faded bulge in his jeans. The glare caused Cody to visor his eyes. It was no mirage. The man held his gaze. Cody swallowed and smiled. The man's hand moved across his crotch again. One more rub and he'd get his wish.

Cody looked around. Not a soul on the street. As he approached the man broke his stare and swaggered into an adjoining back way. Cody heard the fading scrape of boots. A fluttering in his belly dove to his nuts. His dick had been at half-mast ruminating about Ray.

Cody approached and looked down the alley. Sizeable brick buildings stood on either side, making it seem darker and narrower than it actually was. Aligned catwalks and wires cast a tangle of shadows across the asphalt. Garbage was strewn over the buckled cement. If he listened, he could hear rats. If he looked close he figured he'd see them. Cody looked either way. Still no one. He looked back down the alley. Nothing but a short distance between him and adventure. The man was leaning against a phone pole at the edge of an intersecting alley. His legs were crossed at the ankle, offering a prime view of that tantalizing crotch. When he saw Cody approach he eyed his basket, gave another grin, and moved back between two dumpsters. A cracked and faded beer ad was painted on the red brick behind him.

Cody rounded some rusted metal stairs and came closer. The man set to undoing his jeans.

Looking into Cody's eyes and then back down, the man undid a final button. A thick uncut cock hung heavy from his fly. He bent his head. A glob of spit fell into his palm and he set about pleasuring himself. He was rising fast. The man hung his coat on a phone pole rung and lifted and hooked his t-shirt behind his neck. Balls of deodorant were caked in the curls of his armpits. He spread his legs wide. A gold medal bounced on his chest, catching light from an unknown source.

He had a strong jaw, a boxer's nose, and a generous mouth that promised pleasure. His build was exceptional, both lean and broad with an ass that defined love at first sight. Cody licked his lips, ran a hand through his hair and trailed it down his chest to his crotch. He squeezed himself. "Mmm mmm," he thought, passing a line of over-flowing trashcans. His foot hit a decomposing bit of something but he didn't look down.

The man tugged the silver rings lacing his nipples. Cody had seen that in Chicago and in some XXX magazines. Reaching over he fingered the hoops between a thumb and forefinger. The stranger grabbed him by the wrist and guided his hand, before shutting his eyes and giving a rumbling moan that echoed between the buildings. He'd started a fire and the flames were spreading. Cody trailed a hand down the man's stomach, moving over the muscled grooves, down the stitch of hair that fanned into pubes. He gave the man's business a few strokes. Thick and veiny with a feisty upward angle. "Nice," was what Cody said, "Real nice". He bent and buried his nose there. The smell was a heady concoction. His dick throbbed against Cody's chin. He took firm hold and stroked a couple drops of precum back onto the head with a circling thumb. The stranger buckled his knees to meet the strokes.

Maybe this was what he'd been looking for. Sometimes the world had a way of giving just what a body needs. Cody knelt on a crushed anti-freeze carton and licked the man's scrotum. He sucked each ball into his mouth before drawing both inside. That was only the appe-tizer. In a moment Cody licked up the shaft, savoring every inch and angle of it.

A car honked somewheres. He remembered the rats and the decom-posing lump and thought better of kneeling. Getting to his feet, he bent at the waist and kept taking that wonderful slab of manhood in his mouth. Bobbing on it only made him want it more. Pubes were already tickling his nose. His hands rubbed the stranger's stomach before reaching to tug the tittie rings. The stranger uttered another deep-bellied moan. Cody's hands trailed the arch of his spine to that full behind. His fingers ran the length of the furry crevice before slip-ping between. He turned the man around and licked there a bit. It was musky and manly and soon his tongue had wiggled inside. The stranger began to grind his ass in Cody's face. Cody spit on his fingers and began to massage that inviting hole. He moved his middle digits in pressing circles. A finger slipped inside and paused before slowly starting to move. The man bent slightly for more penetration. Cody continued his manipulations. Soon the stranger was riding two fingers to the knuckle before resting his elbows on the dumpster, arching his back, and presenting his ass for further exploration. He was primed for drilling. Cody reached down and stroked himself before maneuvering into position. He pushed gentle and steady. He heard a door squeak somewhere, but it felt too good to care. The thought of someone watching aroused him even more.

The stranger sucked in a breath and told Cody to "Hold up a bit". He hadn't spoken a word up until then. Cody felt the muscled ring relax and then it all slowly opened like a flower. The man maintained his measured breathing before urging Cody to continue. Using hipbones as handles he began pumping, thrusting deep and retreating to the tip. The tight heat was everything. It was the answer to his prayers. It shut off his head and his heart and moved that heat and energy elsewhere. Wind shuffled papers and trash and whistled around the buildings. When it subsided the alley stink arose again.

Cody's foot slipped and sent a bottle spinning. It frightened a cat perched on a nearby ledge. Cody caught a side glimpse of it slinking through the ruptured chain link fence. The town and the bar and Kevin and Ray all seemed a world away. This was all that mattered. The world was the measured slap of his nuts on a stranger's ass. It mixed with the moans and throb of his heart. Sweat trickled down their legs and behind their knees. Cody reached around to tug the nipple rings. His chest suctioned the stranger's back.

The man's moans grew shorter. His ass clenched. He stiffened and froze. At the moment of primed heat his seed hit the side of the dumpster and then dribbled down onto a smashed milk carton.

The stranger's gasps slowed as Cody's quickened. Feeling a load rise he gave half a dozen shallow thrusts. Now it was Cody's turn to ride over the edge on those currents of pleasure. His legs buckled. He fought to suppress a cry. He clenched and clenched and shook before slumping onto the stranger's back. Curled into one another, they were locked in the moment. The instant pulsed and poised and passed. The door squeaked again as Cody slowly withdrew.

Zipping up, they nodded. Cody slicked his hair back and slapped the stranger's shoulder. He pulled Cody close and kissed him hard on the mouth. Breaking apart, they exchanged smiles. What could be said after something like that? The stranger lowered his t-shirt and grabbed his coat. He struck a match for Cody's smoke. The stranger said he had to get home. Cody nodded. He would've invited the stranger back to his place for more fun, but figured it best to get going. Some things weren't meant to be anything more.

Both said, "See you later," and headed out the alley in separate directions. Cody whistled on his walk home. A fresh lift had returned to his step. Easter had been quite a day. He felt reborn and only the slightest bit guilty.

Carson's Peak

Sister wasn't a bit surprised by the diagnosis. The gift had revealed as much even before the coughing. He knew something was there. At first the lung shadow came in flashes, as a dark flowering that widened to eclipse his insides. He didn't want to believe it and did what he could to ignore it until it was downright impossible to bury any longer.

When he finally went to the clinic, it was a formality. Mostly he went to quiet Leo. The results lifted the cancer from the depths, brought to light, and made it a fact. Cancer. According to the doctors it had spread. In some ways, having it named was a relief. At least the game was over. Sister no longer had to pretend he was fine or his cough was a lingering cold or that he was having allergic reactions.

After the official diagnosis, Sister's health went on a steep decline. In no time the cancer made itself fully known. Overnight, Sister's strength and the desire to go out carousing or even to the bar vanished. Leo hired a new bartender so he'd be able to go to Sister's near-about every night. Mostly they watched old movies and talked and did a whole lot of nothing. After a couple weeks both were getting fidgety.

"Leo, I feel dead already."

Leo laughed. He was grateful the cancer hadn't sapped Sister's spirit. He lowered the volume on *Mrs. Miniver* and asked what Sister had in mind.

"Things are ridiculous like this, we're all but sitting here watching *Dark Victory* or something." Sister pulled the afghan higher about his shoulders. His feet wrestled beneath the covering as he looked up, "I'd like to be a bit of a slut, but I'm not up for it."

"A dog don't have to bark to make it a dog."

Sister smiled. "I was never much for being a bit of a slut anyways." Sister regretted that over the past few weeks his oral gratification didn't go much beyond sucking on cough drops and Popsicles. It was awful humbling. He never thought he'd get too sick for sex. "Tell you the truth, Leo, I'd like to get out in nature some."

Leo stroked the corners of his mustache. "We could take a drive."

After a minute or so, Sister said he wanted to go for a picnic up at Carson's Peak. The idea sounded perfect. Carson's Peak was only seven miles outside of town. There were nothing but good memories associated with it, and as an added incentive—if he felt strong and nasty enough—there was a tearoom right there.

The night before, Leo stopped at Piggly Wiggly. He browsed the deli counter for their picnic and splurged on a decent bottle of wine. Before the clerk rang up his Merlot she asked Leo if he knew this wasn't the one on special. She'd waited on him before.

Leo stored everything in the bar cooler and told Ray to guard it with his gonads. It would probably be safe, but there was no harm making sure. Leo didn't intend on wasting one minute of the day having to go back to the store. He needed to make smooth what he could. Sister's loss of stamina was getting worse. Now the fatigue seemed to bother Sister more than the coughing or the pain.

At ten-thirty the next morning, Leo pulled into the gravel drive outside Sister's and honked the horn of his Impala. In a moment he heard the whine of the screen door and watched Sister's slow advance across the crushed granite. It was horrible seeing him so compromised. Leo vowed he'd make the day something wonderful. It had to be. Looking up to the sky, he smiled to see the weather was cooperating.

Leo leaned over and popped the door handle. It swung wide as Sister backed up, lowered himself into the passenger seat, and swung his feet inside. He caught his breath and faced forward. He was suddenly ancient. Death was in him, on him, about him. Skin hung from his bones like a coat set to shed. He turned to Leo with a weary smile. "Afraid I can't much recommend cancer." He was too drained from that bit of walking to pull the car door closed.

Leo looked down at his fidgeting hands and then up again. "Are you sure you're well enough to go? I mean, don't be pushing yourself on my account."

"On your account! Not likely. I'm looking forward to this more than you know. Now get this beater in gear before I change my mind."

Leo rounded the front and slammed Sister's door. He hoped the April day, some fresh air, and fine scenery would give Sister a rightful boost and a will to keep going. He backed out the drive. "Hope you're hungry. I brought ham and cheese on rye with German potato salad."

"Along with something to wash it down, I hope."

"Who do you think you're picnicking with, Missy?" Leo slapped the paper bag with the wine inside and pointed to two more bottles clanking in the backseat. When it came to liquor, Leo always believed in being prepared.

Sister laughed in the shallow rasp he'd adopted of late. He was still smoking, but in a grave compromise he'd gone from Marlboro Reds to Merits. Dr. Ross had pestered him to quit, but Sister didn't see the point. Ross was the one calling it hopeless. A couple fags here and there weren't going to make it any less terminal. He'd cut down, but that wasn't so much a conscious decision as just not being able. Otherwise he'd be up half the night hacking.

"Well, you look good."

Sister rolled his head across the rest. His eyes were paler than Leo recalled, so faded it seemed the clouds were passing behind them. "Who you trying to bullshit? I look like hell."

"Well, compared to how you did."

"Dammit Leo, quit walking on eggshells. I've told you half a dozen times on that drive back from St. Louis I won't abide with that sort of behavior, not from you. Treat me like normal, that's all I want."

"Okay, but it's hard."

Sister let his butt fly out the window and turned back. "Always was."

Leo looked over from the road and grinned. If Sister wanted things playful, he'd try. He'd damn well try. He owed Sister that much. He owed him all he could give. He owed Sister near-about everything. He could do this. "Garbage mouth."

"Tramp."

"Cocksucker."

"Got that right." Sister's laugh ushered in a coughing jag. Name calling always brought them closer. It was damn ironic that so many of the foul things they tended to call one another were mostly true.

Leo turned the car onto River Road. Conversation was shrouded by an awkward silence as they passed the graveyard. Sister turned to Leo, suddenly needing to say something. He opened his mouth and closed it, and then said something else entirely. "Remember when..."

"I was just going to say..."

"Things change." Sister smiled. "I never thought Fred would give Del the heave-ho."

"He sure took his sweet time serving those walking papers."

"That's the Bayetteville way. But once Fred set his mind to being free of him he stuck to it, at least so far."

It would've been Sister's habit to continue from there, but instead he turned back towards the cemetery. All this talk was nothing but a distraction from everything those tombstones made him feel and see and fear. He kept staring out the window. If he demanded honesty from Leo, he should expect the same from himself. "Leo, those damn Fates are working overtime to give my tapestry its fringe."

Leo smoothed his mustache. He didn't know what to say. Over the last couple weeks Leo had grown slightly more at ease with Sister's illness, but only slightly. He hated that this was happening. It made him feel awkward and powerless. It was impossible to say the right thing. Death seemed hellbent on separating them even before it arrived.

Sister only had a few folks over since his diagnosis—Anna and Lulu, Cody, Hester, Jack-O... Company buoyed his spirits, but even marginal hospitality fatigued him something awful. Leo was the only person he felt comfortable enough to be miserable around. There wasn't much shame or disguise between them, only the vast space of the cancer.

Despite a bit of the chills, Sister was adamant that Leo drive with the windows down. He watched the bright flashes of birds, bushes, and trees. He looked at the cluster of corroding trailers lying in the lowlands. Between the flashes of sunlight, he thought he saw a form moving among the trees. He wondered if it was Del. That boy wasn't fooling anyone with his disappearing act. It was only a matter of time until the cops or the wrong people found him.

Sister closed his eyes and traced the colors across the darkness. He opened them again as they passed a stretch of river shacks with tire gardens in the yard. Spirit trees stood on the property borders. Sister pointed to a tree laden with half a dozen colored bottles. "Are you going to hang a bottle for me someplace?"

"Am I what?"

"Going to hang a spirit bottle for me?"

Leo looked at him.

"One of those tiny glass bottles folks hook on trees that are supposed to catch spirits."

"What the fuck are you going on about, girl?"

Sister was getting peeved at Leo's not understanding. "Those bottles are hung to catch spirits. Are you planning to hang one to catch me?"

Leo looked over. Now he understood. "Sister, if I was going to catch you in a bottle it'd have to be an awful lot bigger than them samplers, and it sure as hell wouldn't be empty. I'd have more luck catching you with a full jug."

"Amen." Sister laughed. He closed his eyes and leaned back against the headrest. Thin hair lapped the angles of his skull. "Nothing in the world feels freer than driving along with river with the windows wide. It's like flying." Sunlight slashed through the trees and over his ashen face. "...Maybe one more thing. The radio needs to be blaring too." Sister leaned forward and stuck his tongue between his lips turning the stereo knob one way and then the other. "Damn it Leo, it wouldn't hurt you to clean the bird shit off that coat hanger every month of so."

Leo gave a half grin.

When they passed out of the trees the lion's share of the static cleared. Sister leaned back with a sigh. "Country is my mood today. I got them doing-the-dishes-and-crying-at-the-sink-with-a-baby-on-my-hip blues."

"I'll be damned if you ain't got more than that. You're in a goofy mood. Is all that pain medicine making you high?"

"Trust me, what's coming out of my mouth is nothing compared to what's rattling around in my head. The pain killers they're feeding me sure as hell ain't baby aspirin."

Leo wanted to rib him on the virtues of sharing, but surprised himself by asking Sister if he was doing much reminiscing with all that was going on.

"What do you mean?"

Leo was embarrassed at having to explain. He narrowed his eyes as if trying to see the words more clearly. "I mean, are you sort of taking stock of your life?"

"It's not flashing before me, if that's what you mean."

"Not that, just remembering."

Sister didn't answer immediately. The only sounds were the wind and the engine and Tammy's wailing over lost love, two kids, and a mortgage due. It took so long for Sister to answer that Leo figured he'd forgot the question. "When I take stock of things I got to say the past few years have been my best, at least what I remember of them." He shot Leo a tight grin. "The part of me that was Christian died so many years ago that I don't think about that too often." Sister paused. "Leo, you've heard all this. My childhood wasn't worth remembering then and time hasn't sweetened the tale. Back then I was mostly daddy's meal ticket and God was just another somebody to please and second guess."

Leo kept his eyes on the road. *Breathe.* The next question seemed natural. "So, with you going to church and all, what's God now?"

Sister thought for a bit, "When I stopped trying to second guess God, it got simpler. Life got so it was nothing more than trying to be decent and not get in God's way. The path to heaven isn't that rules of the road crap that the Church preaches. I think it's just being a good person. God made me this way, if he has problems with that or wants me reformed I would know. Guess I'll know soon enough." Sister kept his eyes out the window. "Strange to think it's all coming to an end."

Leo rode his finger over the top of the steering wheel. "Maybe this will just be something different."

"That's what I'm banking on."

Leo kept looking straight out the bug-splattered windshield at the road. "You got any regrets?"

Sister paused again before reaching down to take hold of his hand. He squeezed it tight. "Nope."

Leo looked over and squeezed back. Sister's hand felt like a soft leather sack of bones. "Take a look at that." Kevin's car was parked alongside with two others by the shelter house on the park side of the road. Tearoom action was a certainty. Leo craned for a better look, but didn't recognize the other cars.

Sister nodded. "That's a tough thing getting out of your blood."

"Don't I know." Leo pulled onto the gravel shoulder a couple hundred yards ahead.

The view was incredible. Carson's Peak was a grassy meadow sloping down and spreading out to the wide sweep of the Frear below. Bright clusters of dandelions and scattered wildflowers rolled in the spring sun.

Leo helped Sister out of the car. They walked out into the field. Spreading a blue sheet out on the ground, Leo put a red blanket on top of it. "Sometimes this grass can be like a bed of nails poking me in the ass."

Sister crossed his spindly arms over his chest. "I could say something, but I won't."

"Well, that'll be a first, you nasty old banshee." Leo laid the basket beside the blanket.

Sister sat down slow, his joints creaked and groaned with the effort. Daylight deepened every crease of his disease. He looked so fragile. When he laughed Leo could see the paleness of his gums. As the wind died down a strange scent settled around him. The same smell scented Sister's bungalow. Leo suspected that Sister smelled death too and his desire to be temporarily rid of it was the reason he wanted to have the car windows rolled down. Maybe it would just blow out the window and away.

Leo uncorked the wine and fished two glasses from the basket.

"I can't believe it. Leo Dunsten sprang for a decent bottle of wine. Never thought I'd live to see the day." The comment made them both feel awkward.

Leo laughed. "You're surprised, you should've seen the salesgirl... Guess I'm just a sentimental fool."

"You're no fool." Sister closed his eyes and tilted his head so the sun shone square upon his face. Sometimes he hoped heaven was nothing more than warmth and the forever feel of the sun upon his skin. Would he have a new skin, his old skin, or no skin at all? Maybe he would just be turned inside out. It was more than he wanted to consider. And what he wondered didn't matter anyways. "It feels so gorgeous here, so peaceful."

Leo eyed Sister. Tears rose to his eyes. He stood abruptly and walked down the slope to the edge of the field. He didn't want Sister to see. Damn this cancer and the rebel cells or phagocytes or whatever the fuck they were. *Fuck them to motherfucking hell!* He hated this. He cursed it from every angle and in every degree. He didn't want to lose his best friend. What they had was a lifetime deal. He didn't want to be left alone. Leo wondered what he'd be without Sister. Lacking. Incomplete. Lonesome. Someone else.

In a moment Leo's tears stopped and in a minute more he'd collected himself enough to return. "The river sure is swelled this spring. The sand bars are all but gone."

"They fished out two drowned sows just two days back."

Grief still gripped Leo's voice, but its hold was loosening. "Yeah, from here Ritter Island looks like a big old shrub smack dab in the middle of the Frear."

"Lordy, Lordy," was all Sister said.

Leo shielded his eyes and pointed south. He looked towards the horizon and took a breath. *Relax.* He took a second and a third until he eventually felt calmer. He had to keep breathing slow and thinking peaceful thoughts. "I didn't realize you could see the lock and dam from here."

Sister kept his face turned towards the sun. "Mmmm hmmm, and what's your interest there? Recalling your tryst with Danny from Dundee?"

Leo fell to his knees. "You know me so well."

Sister took a gulp of wine. "An old pig-backer like you wears his cock on his sleeve."

"Among other places." Leo reclined on the blanket with a deflating sigh. "Donkey-dick Dan was one I might have settled down with if he wasn't already married."

"...Or you weren't so all out cock crazy."

"That too."

Sister laughed. "Remember when we got wind of his wife and family and how he nearly shit a gold brick when we said we were going to crash his son's confirmation?"

"I can't believe he took us serious."

"I can't believe anyone takes us serious."

"I near forgot about the confirmation."

Sister looked at his friend and tossed a daisy onto Leo's chest, then another, and another. "Think you'll forget much after I'm gone?"

Leo kept his eyes closed and his face raised to the sun. He had to be strong, for Sister's sake as well as his own. It was all about breathing. "I wouldn't be surprised if I remember more. There's an awful lot worth recalling." *Oh God!* "Everything in this town reminds me of you—every bar, diner, man..."

Sister laughed. "Yeah, and I reckon I sampled most all of them."

Leo scratched an elbow and grinned. "You sure didn't miss many chances."

"That's a fact. I'm bucking for glory holes in heaven, but I'll settle for a bare ass Jack Wrangler and a pitcher of Cody's margaritas. That'd be living."

Leo refilled his wine. "Save a place for me."

"You can rest assured if it's glory hole heaven and there's a God there'll be no need to elbow for kneeling space."

"Fair enough."

Sister smiled and lit a smoke. He picked a fleck of tobacco from his swollen tongue. "As much as Dr. Ross tried making these things my enemies, I could never see them as anything but pals or accessories. I wouldn't be me without them."

Leo opened his eyes. The river was so blue from there. So blue. "You're just more forgiving than most."

Sister took a sip of wine and nodded in a thoughtful fashion. "I suppose." He liked the sound of that even if it was blatantly untrue. Sister could hold a grudge tighter than a half-starved dog with a bone. He'd been mad at some so long he couldn't recall the particulars of why he was mad.

Both grew silent. Sometimes getting quiet said more than talking ever could. At that moment, it said the bond they felt as friends was stronger than any disease. It felt more powerful than death itself. Sister propped himself on an elbow. "Truth is, I never needed a lover with a friend like you. I saw it in your eyes that first night."

Leo looked over. It was one of Sister's favorite anecdotes.

Sister took another sip. "You were sitting on that bar stool and right then everything was so clear. I felt a warmth in my insides and the gift whispered I'd be closer to you than anyone. It was never more accurate...and that's the God's honest truth." He smiled. "We sure turned it into one hell of a party."

Leo kept staring out at the river. The sun slipped behind a cloud and Sister began to shiver with the sudden chill. Leo had grown accustomed to the nuances of Sister's health. The heightened awareness made it sometimes feel it was happening to him as much as to his friend.

When the clouds passed and the sun returned Sister's shivering subsided. He lit a cigarette. "No visions prepared me for this. Nothing. I knew what it was, but not how it was going to be." He picked at another bit of tobacco. "I'm scared, Leo. I'm scared because I'm not having visions anymore. Nothing. It's stopped altogether and I don't know if that's because I'm tired all the time or because of the drugs or because there's nothing to see. Whenever I try all I get is nothing, and whenever I think too hard about it all I get is upset. This isn't how it should be. I don't want this to be happening."

Leo was unsure how to respond. He didn't want it to be happening either, but it was. Wishes had nothing to do with it. It was happening of its own accord. He shooed a honeybee circling his wine and followed the movement until his arm settled on Sister's back. "You're being so brave."

Sister looked over. For the first time since it had all come to light, Leo could see tears welling in Sister's eyes. "I wish I was brave, but I'm not. I'm not brave, there's just nothing I can do."

Leo reached up and touched Sister's cheek before wrapping both arms about him. Sister was shaking. Leo held him tighter and looked to the sky. Sister's cries were muffled. "I'm not brave, Leo, I'm not."

Leo shushed him. He kissed Sister's forehead. "You don't have to be brave. You don't have to be nothing."

Sister's words emerged half-choked with emotion. "I'm not doing anything different and it's scary because it all seems to matter so much more." Sister paused to catch a breath. "I used to think dying would make it all clear and I'd be full of wisdom, but it's been nothing like that. Peace hasn't been part of the package—not at all." Sister sat up and dried his eyes.

Leo plucked some grass and tossed it to the wind.

Sister looked out over the river. Just watching the white caps along the Frear seemed to quiet him. Eventually he returned to the moment. Another cloud passed. "It's glorious here—the river, the breeze, the sun, the trees, my best friend." He closed his eyes and tried to imagine going blank. He wondered if that glimpse of nothing was death. He breathed too deeply and felt the rattling that would eventually drown him. Death would be a string of gasps until eventually he'd be too spent to gasp any more. Death would be as easy as drowning...then it was only a matter of floating downstream from all he'd known...and giving in to the mystery that was pulling him.

He turned to Leo. "If they rush me to the hospital, don't let them put all those tubes in my arms and up my nose. I get panicked just thinking about being hooked up to some buzzing and beeping life machine."

"You got it." To cover the silence and simply do something Leo handed him a paper plate weighted with a sandwich and a hearty dollop of potato salad. When he refilled the glasses, their eyes met. "Nobody is going to make you do anything you don't have a mind to, not while I'm around."

Sister smiled. It didn't need to be said, but he wanted to. "I love you." Reaching over he held Leo's hand.

"Always baby, always." Leo felt himself begin to tear again but he didn't want to walk away this time. The day had taken them beyond that. This time he wanted Sister to see every tear and know the love that was there...so much and so deep that he couldn't find words to make it understood. He wanted Sister to know how much the past decade had meant. It meant everything. Ten years. He took a full gulp of red. Was that all it had been?

Sister coursed his hand up and then down Leo's back.

Leo lit a smoke. "Promise me something too."

"Anything."

"If you can, come visit me in my dreams. It's going to be so damn lonely here without you." Leo laughed abruptly. At the same time more tears came. All the compressed sentiment seemed to expand and come out bigger. His crying didn't end anytime soon.

They sat mostly in silence for another hour until Sister began shaking. This time it wasn't the result of a cloud and the chill didn't pass. Leo got up and wrapped the red blanket around his friend. Sister smiled through chattering teeth. He said sometimes the chill slipped inside him and there was just no shaking it free.

"We should be getting back anyways. The bottle is empty and the other two ain't half as good. Besides, you look set for a nap."

Sister smiled, a bit dopey from the combination of wine and painkillers. "It was a great day, but a nap sounds like heaven."

Leo lifted him to his feet. "I thought heaven would be napping with Jack Wrangler?"

Sister looked up. His lids were at half-mast. "Honey, if Jack Wrangler was lying longside me I'd be doing everything but napping."

Three weeks later Sister lapsed into a coma. An ambulance rushed him to Infant of Prague. Leo said no when they suggested life support, though the doctor did persuade him into a feeding tube and vitamin drip. Sister wasn't about to be rushed into the hereafter. Once it was at the threshold, death took its sweet time coming. It didn't come that day or the next or the day after that. It came one hazy May afternoon a full week later, without warning or fanfare. Sister passed alone in the room.

Leo had been there more on than off the entire time. He'd gone to get lunch. When he returned the floor nurse looked up from her clipboard, said she was sorry. It was clear she was uncomfortable breaking the news.

Leo asked to see his friend. She looked up and said she'd wait a minute before calling to have them come zip him up.

The door closed slowly behind as Leo neared the bed. He didn't recognize Sister. That skin didn't hold his friend any longer. All that came to mind was a cornhusk. Leo looked up to the ceiling. He'd heard that was where spirits first go after taking leave from a body. He didn't see a shadow or a wiggle. There was no sound or chill. Nothing. He opened his mouth to call Sister back, but stopped. That was nothing but selfish. He walked round the bed and cracked the window. "You're free now. Free, baby. There'll never be another like you. See you in my dreams." There was nothing more to say. Leo stood at the window and wondered what the hell he'd do without him.

He called the bar from the hall phone and gave Cody the sad news. Cody conveyed his regrets and asked Leo how he was doing. He suggested that Leo come down to the bar and be around family, but Leo didn't feel like being there, not yet. He didn't know where he wanted to be, only that he preferred being alone. He left the Impala in the hospital lot and walked round town remembering. There was an awful lot to recall.

Sister left all he had to Leo, including his body. Sister wanted to be cremated and have his ashes scattered. Father O'Neill got flustered. He was of the mind that cremated remains should be interred on holy ground. Leo just stared at the ruddy-faced priest as he expounded on the issue. He didn't care what Father O'Neill or the Catholic Church or God in Heaven himself had to say. Sister was goddamn well getting what he wanted and Leo said so. He didn't give a shit about anything else.

A week after the memorial service Leo drove to Carson's Peak with Sister's remains in the passenger seat and a bottle of red between his legs. He'd bought an even better vintage than he had before. He tuned in the country station and rolled down the windows. He looked over at the urn. Now it was his turn to be sobbing into the dishwater.

Leo parked the car and composed himself before walking across the meadow. The shifting wind cut through the grass and wildflowers. Leo could almost see the phantom of something crossing the field. He watched the wind patterns and wondered if Sister was dancing about him on that hilltop.

It was time to do what he came to do. Leo read a prayer he'd written the night before and scattered some ashes. Some of Sister stuck to his clothing and his hands. He poured himself a glass of wine and raised it in a toast. "Hope heaven is all you wanted—Jack Wrangler, margaritas, the works. You deserve it all." Leo scattered more ashes and made more toasts. Eventually the bottle and most of the urn were empty. Sister was all around and upon him. He was in his hair and in his lungs. Leo lay back upon the grass and looked to the sky. It was so idyllic and warm. He studied the shifting clouds and tried finding one that reminded him of Sister. When his eyes began to strain he closed them for a bit.

He woke a full hour later from a dream about Sister and knew there was one last thing he had to do. Grabbing the urn by the neck he crossed the blacktop towards the park and entered the men's room. It was deserted and smelled of cum and mildew. Closing his eyes he said the prayer again. Taking the final fistful of ashes, he sprinkled them between and around the urinals and stalls. He took a deep breath. It was done. Leo lit a cigarette. The smoke rose to the cement ceiling. He took another drag and heard a car pull into the gravel lot. "You're home baby, home."

Ghosts

Fred began tearing up at Mrs. Miniver.
Courage always got to him. He added another shirt to the pile. He
didn't reckon he owned so many. He was doing his best to purge all
but what he could carry. Finn thought he was being foolish, but Fred
didn't intend on starting a new life in a new place with the same old
things. He had himself plenty of baggage as it was. He tossed another
shirt on the heap. He was but six weeks from leaving.

The day Fred settled on a departure date, Finn arrived late at Staley's. He was usually pretty punctual. At the first opportunity, he pulled
Fred aside and glanced either way before speaking. He explained as
best he could that the cops had been around the Sand Bar asking
questions. Finn didn't know quite how to say it. Del had disappeared.

The words ricocheted about Fred's insides. The news hit him in so
many places in such rapid succession that he felt removed from all he
was being told.

The police had asked Leo about barring Del and the reasons for doing so. Leo told them a mostly truthful, but legalized, version of the
story. He was too focused on Sister's illness to concern himself much
with Del.

That night, Fred had a pack of troublesome dreams. The worst was
when he saw Del floating down the river with his bloated white face
angled to the sky. He was hooking on branches, circling and spinning
in eddies. He was fish food and a bit of rot set to settle to the river's
belly and roll downstream. The image of his tumbling advance awoke
Fred in a sweat.

The following day, the police arrived to question him. Mr. Sawyer
got genuine satisfaction seeing the two officers climb the stairs. Fred
had nothing to tell. He wasn't part of the story anymore. Save for that
one time in passing, he hadn't seen Del in months. The investigation
was short lived. A small time hood leaving town or offing himself was
no real concern to the police. Didn't seem worth the trouble or the
taxpayer dollars. At the end of the day, Del was a missing person who
wasn't terribly missed by much of anyone.

The report intimated suicide though there was no body. A hot car covered with Del's prints was parked below the lock and dam. He'd folded his clothes on the hood and stuck a note in his shoe. The Frear was so distended and swollen with the season that not finding the body wasn't surprising. Whole towns had been known to vanish in the muck.

Finn told Fred talk at the bar was that Del had staged the entire thing on account of the money he owed and who he owed it to. Fred sighed. That didn't surprise him. If he saw the suicide note, Fred figured he could tell if it was genuine. The fact that there was one at all gave him suspicions. Fred found it difficult to imagine Del leaving more than a scrap of lyrics and a burning cigarette. The folded clothes made him wonder too. Why bother being tidy?

There was no doubt of his being in trouble. Nobody weaseled out on repaying those folks. If Del was hiding out, he'd better hope the police found him before those thugs. That bunch would collect in blood if need be.

Thoughts of Del being that desperate brought a pang of sympathy. Fred knew what it was like to feel cornered by life. He straddled an arm of his couch and looked out to the Frear. Borrowing money from those people was crazier than anything Del hounded him for doing, that was for damn sure. It was probably no more than a couple hundred. Fred wondered why Del didn't come to him. He'd have probably given him something. Maybe borrowing from that crowd was a way of offing himself after all. It was putting the gun to his head and waiting for them to squeeze the trigger. One way or another, taking his life was what he'd gone and done. Even if he was alive, he couldn't rightly waltz back into town. Fred doubted he could settle anywhere what with all the reports that had been filed. He'd be living underground from that point on. He'd already been doing that to some degree, but now he'd gone and sealed the sky of his underside. It had become his permanent home. Now Fred and Del were locked in separate worlds.

Slipping on a windbreaker, Fred grabbed a couple cardboard boxes stacked in the hall. Walking boxes to the donation bin in front of the Salvation Army always brought a feel of relief. Fred was already down the stairs and out the door when he decided to stop by the bar afterwards. The Salvation Army was right on the way. It wouldn't hurt to see everyone. Maybe he'd hear something about Del. One thing was for sure, there'd be no danger of running into him.

Opening the sticker-spotted door to the Sand Bar, he felt a rush of the past. It'd been almost five months since stepping foot inside. The air was heavy with stale beer and cigarettes.

"As I live and breathe." Hester caught sight of him in the mirror. She spun around on her stool and was on her feet giving him a hug in five seconds flat. Fred was moved that she squeezed so hard, though that may have been on account of her being drunk or showing her strength just as easily as it could be from missing him so much.

Bob gave a wave.

"Hey." Jack-O looked a mite grayer and puffier. His new glasses were filthy as the old ones, but Fred complimented them nonetheless.

Fred didn't recognize the bartender who offered a grin and asked, "What'll it be?"

The ceiling fan clicked as it turned. Fred slipped onto a stool. It all seemed suspended in time, as though all this thought of leaving was but a moment's fancy between cocktails. Five months could've been five minutes.

"Ray, this is Fred." They shook. "Fred is one of the sweetest fellows you could ever meet." Hester was drunk and leaning on some fellow Fred didn't know. "This is Barry," she shouted over the opening chords of "Thriller." "Barry is a friend from work."

They exchanged hellos. Fred said the Cloven Hoof was a great restaurant. He hadn't eaten there since he was a kid.

Hester continued, "Santiago is working there now too." Fred nodded. He'd heard about Slags and his new beau. "Santiago gave up his place and moved in with Nash last month. They live in that building out by the expressway, the one with the rounded flowerbeds." Hester lifted a chin slightly to show that apartment building had a bit of tone to it.

Fred knew that too.

Hester exhaled. "For not having much of a handle on the language, Finn sure can channel the gossip."

"He manages." Fred said it was a matter of asking Finn the right questions.

Bob opened his mouth to comment but thought better of it.

Bob leaned over and told Fred he looked well rested. He leaned closer and said he had some sad news. "My father passed last month." Bob said he missed having him around. Fred imagined that old man stuffed with sawdust and giving a mechanical wave with a hinge-jawed smile. Stranger things happened every day. Bob interpreted his glazed look for empathy and apologized for burdening him. Fred said not to worry.

Hester turned, took a drag from her cigarette, and said in a loud voice, "Barry here is straight, so you know, keep off him." Barry grinned.

Fred was startled by a punch to his bicep. It was Everly. "Aloha, *mi amigo*." Fred was pleased for the distraction. Everly looked to be straightening his hair and had put on weight. The pounds were flattering and seemed mostly muscle. He said he'd been working with the county road crew and that it was good money.

Ray popped Fred a complimentary longneck and laid a line of tequila shots cross the speckled bar.

"An amber necklace," muttered Jack-O, making a circle with a finger.

Hester laughed and then got quiet. She put a hand on Fred's knee. "You heard about Sister taking sick?" She said it choked her up just thinking about it. "Leo is functioning on automatic these days. That man is aside himself. No question about it." Hester said she'd been over to see Sister twice.

Finn told Fred about it one night at work. Fred had been intending to visit, but hadn't. Those were the easiest sort of visits to postpone. He justified it by telling himself he needed to remain focused on leaving town. Being here, he saw how selfish that way of thinking was.

Bob raised his shooter. "To friends reunited." Everyone replied in scattered echoes before tossing the shots back. Fred felt odd toasting that. Not coming around had been a choice and not one he especially regretted. He didn't hate it here or harbor any brand of ill feelings. This place and these people would always be a considerable part of him; only it wasn't much a part of his life anymore.

Five seconds after the toast, Fred grabbed Everly by the shirttail and pulled him aside to ask about Del. If anyone had his ear to the town's undercurrents it was Everly.

After bumming a smoke, Everly shook his head and exhaled. The people Del left owing didn't buy the whole suicide set-up. Few did. Del didn't have the guts. "Del is going to wish those fish got him when those boys get hold of his bony ass. I don't even want to think about it. I hope he's halfway to Memphis."

Fred nodded.

Jack-O tsked and said it was a shame however it was. "He just threw it all away. Just threw it!" Jack-O looked back down into his drink.

Fred told them all the latest on his plans for moving. Everyone was real excited, or at least pretended to be. Finn had told them everything already. It caused a fluttering when Fred said he hadn't settled on a destination just yet. Finn had said he didn't know, but they figured that was Finn not knowing and not the actual answer. That sort of uncertainty didn't seem like the Fred they knew. Hester said so right to his face. Fred paid little attention. The Fred they knew wasn't the Fred that was.

Barry reached over. "Let me shake your hand young man." He said he envied his youthful optimism and reckoned there were great adventures in store for him. "Take it from an old fart, getting out there and doing is what life is all about." He raised a cocktail to him.

Everyone agreed it was an exciting undertaking. It was difficult hearing Fred's plans, or lack of plans, and not have it trigger at bit of jealousy. Most all had thought about leaving town at one time or another. Some of them had even made plans, but here they all were.

Jack-O wrapped an arm around his waist. "Looks like you're seeing ghosts."

Fred smiled and wriggled free while downing the remainder of his beer. He had no idea what Jack-O meant by that. Fred made his good-byes, but allowed Hester to talk him into another drink. Bob bought the one after that. Fred drank half of it before passing it onto Jack-O and heading for home.

It felt good to see everyone, but it felt better outside. He could breathe out here. Looking down the slope of Elm to the Frear he watched the moonlight on the water and wondered if Del was seeing it too. Was he watching it from the shore or a ship or from the depths of the river? Fred tried not to care. Soon he'd be a ghost to this town, too. He lifted his eyes to the stars. In a few weeks, he'd be seeing the night sky from a different place altogether.

Fond Farewells

one entire wall was lined with photos.
Sister had told Leo he wanted everyone to bring a framed picture to
his memorial service. Almost everyone complied. Santiago didn't. He
claimed not to have any, but he did bring a fancy frame from out at
the Crate and Barrel.

Fred didn't bring a picture or a frame. He'd forgotten.

Bob got noticeably flustered at the idea of having the majority of
the town's gay folk framed and hanging right there for the world to
see. No one else seemed to give it much mind. Leo told him his anxiety was ungrounded. "Bob, the Sand Bar is more a den than some sort
of public thoroughfare."

"Except you're charging for use of the liquor cabinet," laughed Hester, slapping the baggy seat of Leo's pants.

"Not tonight I ain't."

Once Bob calmed down he remarked on how nice the place looked.
Leo said Ray should be the one getting credit for that. The night before, Ray stayed several hours late and cleaned. He swept and mopped
and brought the molded plastic chairs up from the basement. He'd
Windexed the mirrors and cleaned the bathrooms too.

Ray's diligence wasn't on account of knowing Sister well. They'd
only talked twice on the phone. Ray had lost enough friends over the
past couple years to want everything looking proper. It was a matter
of showing respect for the dead. Cleaning made him feel useful. It
gave him purpose in a powerless situation. He also assumed bartending chores for the occasion even though it was rightly his day off. That
way Leo, Cody and Finn could focus on remembering Sister and not
on the level of everyone's cocktail.

Leo posted announcements about the memorial and sent out twen-
ty-four handwritten invitations. Almost everyone showed up at the
bar that Sunday.

Cody was there, as was Kevin, but they weren't a couple anymore.
They'd become something like good friends who stepped back over
the line once and a while. They were still doing it, but with the understanding that it was only for convenience sake. They weren't a couple

so much as a couple horny guys who meshed well between the sheets. It was sad things didn't work out, but a lot of good things didn't. Neither one wanted to end up resenting the other. Forever could get to feeling awful restrictive. Leo wondered how long it would be before Cody and Ray got together. Sister would've bet him on a date. It was only a matter of time.

Jack-O wore a clean shirt and was relatively sober. Most saw both states as temporary. He was shaky and red. It pained him seeing Ben's smile plastered in several of the photos. Nobody had heard a word from Ben in eons.

Anna and Lulu were longside Jack-O with their knees touching and their heads bent together. They were each other's support. That was their priority. Everything else was outside of them. Never *me* and *her*, always *us*—always. Most everyone wanted what they had.

Santiago came in a suit, but without Nash. He looked like the better half of a makeover and was full of smiles. He cornered most everybody and rhapsodized with Nash this and Nash that and how everything was marvelous between them. He claimed they were soul mates and that they could hop on a plane to Hawaii tomorrow if they saw fit. He even spoke of those rounded flower beds and the pool out back of the building.

Leo guffawed when Jack-O sloshed his drink and cautioned Santiago not to try so damned hard to convince everyone he was happy. "You are going to give yourself a hernia trying to pull yourself up," he'd added.

Everly looked dead set on changing his image too. He was shaved and gelled and wearing dress pants. His highway job paid a decent wage and he enjoyed spending. It was all an investment. If he made a conscious effort to refine his appearance, people would start seeing and treating him different. Some did, but most folks assumed the change didn't go much deeper than his shaven face and fashion sense.

Hester and Bob brought two sprays of violets along with a catered lunch from the new Jewel out on 91. Everly, Fred, and Finn helped carry the foiled serving trays inside and arranged them on the long folding tables in back.

Earlier in the day Leo picked up Sister's neighbor Beatrice. Her lemon bundt cake and pecan pie were the only other food plates on the table. Bea was squat and scented. She mostly sat teary and wide-eyed and fiddled nervously with the rosary in her lap.

Finn took a seat longside Fred. He wore a sport jacket and a puzzled look. He craned his neck one way and then the other but claimed not to be he looking for anyone in particular. Fred assumed he was just uncomfortable with grieving and was anxious to play some Irene Cara or Cher.

Fred looked over at Dick and his slope-shouldered lover Winston. Neither one drank a drop of liquor anymore. They were in the program. Sister always had mixed feelings about that. Fred recalled the day Leo told Sister that Dick was getting sober. Sister said, "I don't like what that says about me." Leo looked at him. "That don't say a thing about you." And Sister had quipped, "That's what I don't like about it," before downing his cocktail.

Fred smiled. He wondered if Dick remembered him. Fred recalled their fumbling night of drunken foreplay and how things got out at Frear Park Auto. He shook his head. It was for the best, he supposed. That had been the start of finding this place and these folks. That was when the door opened onto another world. He sighed at how naïve he'd been. He was so innocent. Maybe leaving town he'd regain some of that. He wondered if life put a limit on fresh starts or if people put those limits on themselves.

Maybe Sister was starting all over someplace else, or maybe she was right here taking every bit of this in. The urn was centered on the white spread at the front table. Jack-O brought in one of his mother's hand sewn coverings for the occasion. It was a lovely touch Sister would have appreciated. When the violet sprays were displayed on either side of the urn there was a flash of photographs.

After everyone was settled, Ray dimmed the lights. Leo had prepared a brief speech but stopped when he saw himself in the mirror. Reading something all set and prepared seemed wrong. This had to come straight from the heart. That's where Sister was for him, not on a sheet of paper. He folded it and put it back in his sport coat pocket. He took a breath and welcomed everyone, "Tonight I dug this suit out of storage so I apologize for smelling like mothballs—though some might say that's an improvement." Leo smiled, "Sister would've said something like that and he'd have said it with love because that's how we were together. I don't doubt he's clutching his pearls and watching all this from somewhere..." Leo talked of some of their adventures and ribald good times. He tried to keep it clean, but that wasn't always possible with Sister. Leo said losing Sister was like losing a part of himself. He said nobody could make him laugh harder. "Sometimes he didn't have to even do anything. Just knowing how he'd think about something could make me laugh. That's something you don't find every day, or sometimes ever. I was lucky to have ten years of it. I'm going to miss him more than I can say." Leo's reminiscences set a relaxed tone for the evening. He said they were here tonight to celebrate a life. Sister would have wanted his memorial to be comfortable. He'd want laughs and libations and maybe just a tasteful number of tears.

Lulu and Anna got up with locked hands and announced they were planning to become parents with the aid of a sperm donor.

Jack-O bolted upright in his seat. "Right now?"

Lulu shook her head his direction while Anna explained they were intending to name the infant after Sister. The announcement brought cheers and whistles. It was exciting news, though some thought Anna and Lulu were getting a bit carried away. It seemed lunacy to name a child either Sister or Christian.

Hester got up and told half a dozen Sister stories that had everyone laughing, blushing, and even stomping at points. With Sister, there were so many tales to choose from.

Beatrice blushed behind her hands at several anecdotes before waddling up to the front. She straightened her glasses and cleared her throat. She said she couldn't speak for certain parts of his character, but Christian was always a fine neighbor. "Every Monday and Thursday he carried my trash around back...for the collector. He hung some curtains and also arranged rides for me. A man like that would make any parent proud," she added, clearing her throat and sitting back down.

Several folks exchanged looks, knowing how Sister was estranged from his biological kin.

After wiping his brow with a hankie, Bob said Sister had a talent for connecting with people. The comment brought a lewd giggle from Leo. If Sister were there, he'd have been giggling too.

Bob blushed when he caught the innuendo. Regaining his composure, Bob said the dead tended to stay in the places where they lived and knew love. For him Sister would always be here. "Sitting right there." He raised an arm towards the bar, which caused one and all to turn, including Beatrice who was stiff on that side. The notion of Sister permanently perched on a bar stool sent chills down several spines, but in a good way. That slant on ghosts and death made it all unthreatening, more like a social visit than a haunting.

The longer Leo considered Bob's words, the more he felt it was true. It gave him solace, or at least a good taste of it. There wasn't a lick of hard evidence, but over the years he'd learned to trust his gut. He clasped his hands over his belt buckle and looked up to the ceiling fan. Sister was here as sure as anything.

Fred stammered and was told to speak louder. He cleared his throat and began telling of his plans for leaving next week. It didn't seem possible. He said he'd remember all of them, and that he'd bring fond memories of Sister along with him. "He opened my eyes..."

...And half the town's thighs, thought Leo with a lurid grin.

"...He shocked me a lot and taught me more. He was always one to show concern and you could see the sincerity in his eyes." Fred caught his breath. It felt strange to be looking out at all those faces and not see Del muttering something foul. Fred didn't need that disrespect anymore. Life had changed with Del underground or underwater or wherever he was. The loss of Del and the destiny he came to represent left a void inside. Leaving town was an ideal way to fill that hollow. The thought hadn't occurred to Fred until just then.

After he sat down Leo went to the pile of framed pictures waiting to be hung and grabbed one that Anna and Lulu had brought. Leo told Fred it was fitting for him to have some remembrance of the place. Then he shook Fred's hand. The moment as well as the show of respect caused tears to rise in Fred's eyes. He blinked them away. Fred wondered how he'd be remembered.

The picture was a nice group shot taken at Anna and Lulu's nuptials. Everyone had shown up for that occasion as well. Fred wondered aloud who took the photo and nodded his head when Anna said it was Kitra. He'd forgotten about her. It had been almost a year since she moved to Hadley. Her ex, Merlin, had disappeared altogether.

Fred kept recalling the snippets of his life there. It was like moving through a fog that suddenly lifts to reveal an image here or there. He leaned back in his chair and watched the ghosts and moments appear and vanish.

Thinking on it all made Fred recall Bruschetta. His tribute to her was going to be stepping on that train. Fred wondered where she'd driven that snowy December night he'd last seen her. He wondered who she'd become and if that new beginning was only a reaction to that terrible act of violence.

He looked at the picture in his hands and traced a finger round the pine frame. Lifting his head he saw everyone in the gold-veined mirror behind the dance floor. There appeared to be more people reflected than were in the room. A different world was inside the mirror. For a moment he saw there was an other side as well as an underside. The number of potential sides and places was infinite. When Fred finally stopped considering the possibilities, the picture in his hands was as smudged as Jack-O's glasses.

By the time the eulogies were finished, everyone was eager to eat and have a few cocktails. The food spread was mighty impressive. There were ham and cheese and Sloppy Joes, two cold salads, garlic bread and baked beans, as well as Beatrice's home-baked desserts.

It was a night of laughter and fellowship and the well-lubricated retelling of stories. Everyone was excited for Fred and full of questions, advice, and well wishes. At a quarter past twelve he staggered down the hall and out the back. He took note of hearing the door close as he went down the steps. He kicked a rock up the alley and listened to the rustle of leaves in the wind. He ran a hand over his face. The last longneck had boosted him over the threshold of drunk. It didn't matter. Tomorrow's hangover would be just another souvenir of the Sand Bar. The street was deserted. He was the sole resident of a ghost town. A strong wind pushed him on down the street. He felt the framed photo beneath his arm and wove home with a smile on his face.

Into Gold

Fred awoke that last morning a full
fifteen minutes before the alarm. Though excited, he didn't immediately hop out of bed, but lay playing with his hair and thinking. His furnished place above the furniture store was clean and ready. If need be he could just get on out of bed, grab his suitcase and backpack, and head for the door. A six a.m. train required preparation, especially when you were buying a one-way ticket. He rolled onto his back and reminded himself to slip the key under Mr. Sawyer's door.

He stumbled into the bathroom and flipped on the light. The mirror behind the toilet always startled him. Del had loved it, but he always loved looking at himself. Fred didn't. The whole point of a mirror was lost on him. He never saw what was really reflected there anyways. He was usually curious, but without ever knowing just what to expect.

As he went about getting ready, it seemed he was doing everything either for the first or the last time. There was an awareness in every bit of it. After pouring the last of the coffee, he called for a cab. It would be approximately ten minutes. Fred flipped off the coffee machine. He was leaving it for the next tenant.

He walked from room to room and back again, checking this and that. Everything was done. Stove off. Water off. Phone service was ending at noon. Nothing lying around. He unzipped the front pocket of his backpack. Bruschetta's brooch was pinned there. Inside were cash and ID, along with a toothbrush, toiletries, and the photo Leo had given him. The rest of his pictures were rubber-banded and buried in his suitcase.

Fred brushed his teeth, wet his hair, and slipped on his jacket. He checked everything again, then once more. The second-to-last look got his heart to racing. This place had meant a lot to him. So much of his growing up and becoming who he was had happened within these walls. Life had happened here. Thinking back on the day he moved in and how he was back then gave him pause.

He checked his watch and flipped off the light. Standing at the threshold, he took a last look around. As he closed the door, he watched it all narrow to a sliver and vanish. He descended the stairs and slipped his key under Sawyer's door. He was relieved to hear only silence inside. He looked back up the steps before going down the last flight and out to the street. No sign of the cab. It was misting and still dark. Thunder rumbled in the distance.

When he saw the headlights turn onto Main, the rain began to increase. He was hopping from one foot to the other by the time the taxi pulled to the curb. He was starting this new life wet. Fred tossed his bags inside and ducked into the backseat. The radio played the farm report. The wipers beat a rhythm as the raw-boned driver caught his eye in the rearview. Fred finger combed his hair and said the train station. The driver grumbled, "Got it," around a plug of tobacco big as a golf ball.

At the tail end of livestock prices, they were idling at the red light where Oak merged with River Road. On the shoulder ahead, Fred saw some shoes sticking out of a large section of cement piping. The sight startled him. He wondered if it was Del. Almost immediately he had himself convinced. Seeing him now would make perfect sense. Fred still believed in destiny and tidy conclusions. It all fit, it was just a matter of understanding the whole. It was an oversized jigsaw puzzle coming together piece by piece. He was about to ask the driver to hold on a moment while he roused his pal in the pipe, but the light changed. The headlights flashed inside the tube. There was no one there. It was nothing but a pair of sneakers. Maybe destiny was no more than a trick of light and shadow.

Fred sat back and tried relaxing. The windows had grown too steamed to see. Grain prices were read along with the forecast. Fred picked his fingers and watched between swipes of the wipers.

When the taxicab pulled into the station lot the dashboard meter read $4.20. Fred gave him a five. The rain had let up. "Looks like it was just a clearing shower," said the driver, leaning forward and looking to the sky.

Going through the front doors, Fred turned. The cabbie was still sitting there, staring. Fred didn't think it had anything to do with him, but worried nonetheless. He checked his fly, his bags, and his wallet. The driver must just be waiting for another fare. He sure hoped it was a five that he gave him.

Fred went up to the ticket counter. Putting down his suitcase he swung his backpack around. With the hint of an exhalation, the girl at the desk put down her book. Fred had gone to high school with her. He recalled Maryellen Tucker as reading the same dark-windowed horror novels even then. She had no idea who he was either then or now. At least that was the way both of them played it.

Fred slid several bills across the counter. "One way."

"Where to?"

"Wherever."

She stared.

"How far will it take me?"

She counted it out—twice—and said it would take him as far as Dallas. Fred was indifferent, though he did enjoy the series. Maryellen said his connecting train should be along in about fifteen minutes before returning to her thriller.

Fred bought a Danish from the bakery tray at the end of the counter. Maryellen didn't even look up when she gave him his fifty cents change. He took a bite. It was a little on the stale side and tasted more like the cellophane wrapping than any sort of pastry.

He stepped onto the flat wooden platform. The horizon was brightening by the moment. The light put everything behind him in black shadows and gave the things before him a flat-lit front. It all looked to be nothing but a ruse, a set. Morning birds gave it a soundtrack. He could see their silhouettes in the trees and along the wires. A car came down the street, crossed the side ties and tracks, and continued on down the hill. Inside, Maryellen was bent over her book. Fred tore off bits of his Danish and watched the birds swoop from the trees. He'd drawn quite a few by the time he heard the clanging. They scattered at the sound of a distant whistle. The crossing light flashed and the striped traffic arm commenced to descending.

A moment later the train slid into the station. Fred fell up the steps while boarding. His heart was frantically beating. He hefted his suitcase into the overhead bin and tossed his backpack into the empty aisle seat. There was plenty of room. He sat by the window. Closing his eyes he breathed for what seemed like the first time since stepping on board. A rush ran through him as the train began to move forward. This was it.

The crown of the sun was coming through the trees. The flashes entranced him before the woods parted at the gravel approach to the bridge. Up ahead he could see the treetops reflected in the river. It was where he'd jumped. The memory didn't have the same rush of shame it'd had for so many years. Maybe it was just the fact of seeing it from above. It was a memory and little more. He was headed someplace where the past didn't matter, not his anyways. He could be anything or anyone. The past was nothing but a story.

Fred leaned his head against the glass. If he'd have written anything on it, it would have been the word Yes. Looking out the scratched window was like seeing a strip of paradise. The sun had risen above the tree line and turned the Frear into gold. From the bridge the sand bars looked to be on the same level as the water. The wind rolled over the river's surface and made it shimmer. Fred put a hand to his stomach and imagined his insides rippling with a similar excitement. He closed his eyes and felt the warmth on his face. He felt alive and ripe with potential. Anything might happen and yet for the first time in years he was free of fear. It was a moment he carried with him until the day he died.

Inducted in the Chicago Gay and Lesbian Hall of Fame in 2011, writer and historian OWEN KEEHNEN's fiction, essays, erotica, reviews and interviews have appeared in hundreds of magazines, newspapers and anthologies worldwide including the upcoming University of Wisconsin collection *Windy City Queer*. He co-authored with Tracy Baim, two pivotal historical biographies about Chicago gay icons—*Leatherman: The Legend of Chuck Renslow* as well as *Jim Flint: The Boy From Peoria*. He is also the author of *We're Here, We're Queer*, a collection of over one hundred interviews with LGBTQ writers, artists and activists who helped shape contemporary gay culture and the modern gay movement. Keehnen is the author of the horror novel *Doorway Unto Darkness*, and his humorous gay novel *I May Not Be Much But I'm All I Think About* is available at e-gaymag.com. In addition he co-edited *Nothing Personal: Chronicles of Chicago's LGBTQ Community 1977–1997* and contributed ten essays in the groundbreaking coffee-table book *Out and Proud in Chicago*. He is also the author of the *Starz* series, four books of interviews with the men of the XXX film industry. Keehnen was the former programming director of Gerber Hart Library, and long-time Chicago volunteer to various political, social, and service organizations. He was on the founding committee of The Legacy Project and currently serves as secretary for the LGBT history-education-arts program focused on pride, acceptance, and bringing recognition to the courageous lives and contributions of international LGBTQ historical figures. He lives in Chicago with his tolerant partner Carl and their spoiled dogs Flannery and Fitzgerald.

CPSIA information can be obtained at www.ICGtesting.com
Printed in the USA
LVOW11s2309070314

376511LV00005B/193/P